AMULET

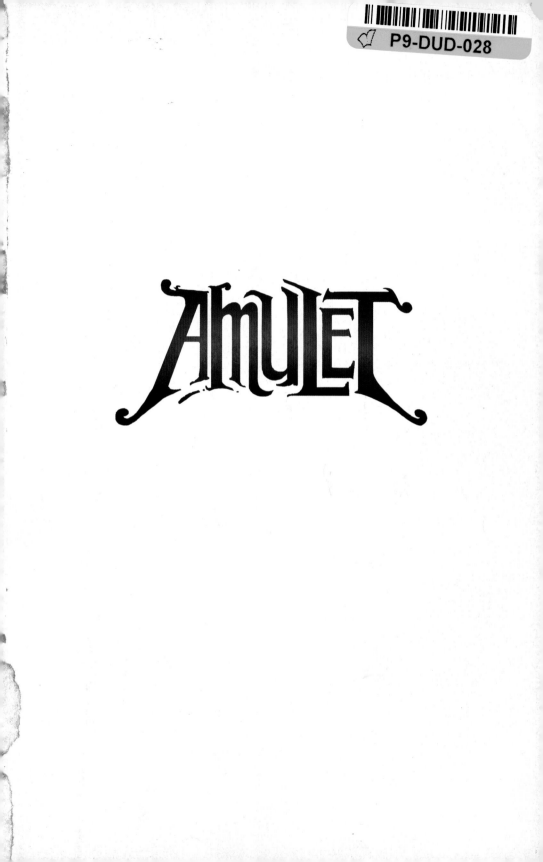

Library of Congress Control Number: 2009942987

ISBN 978-0-545-20884-0 (hardcover)
ISBN 978-0-545-20885-7 (paperback)

10 9 8 7 6 5 17 18 19

Printed in Malaysia 108
First edition, September 2010
Edited by Cassandra Pelham
Book design by Kazu Kibuishi and Phil Falco
Creative Director: David Saylor

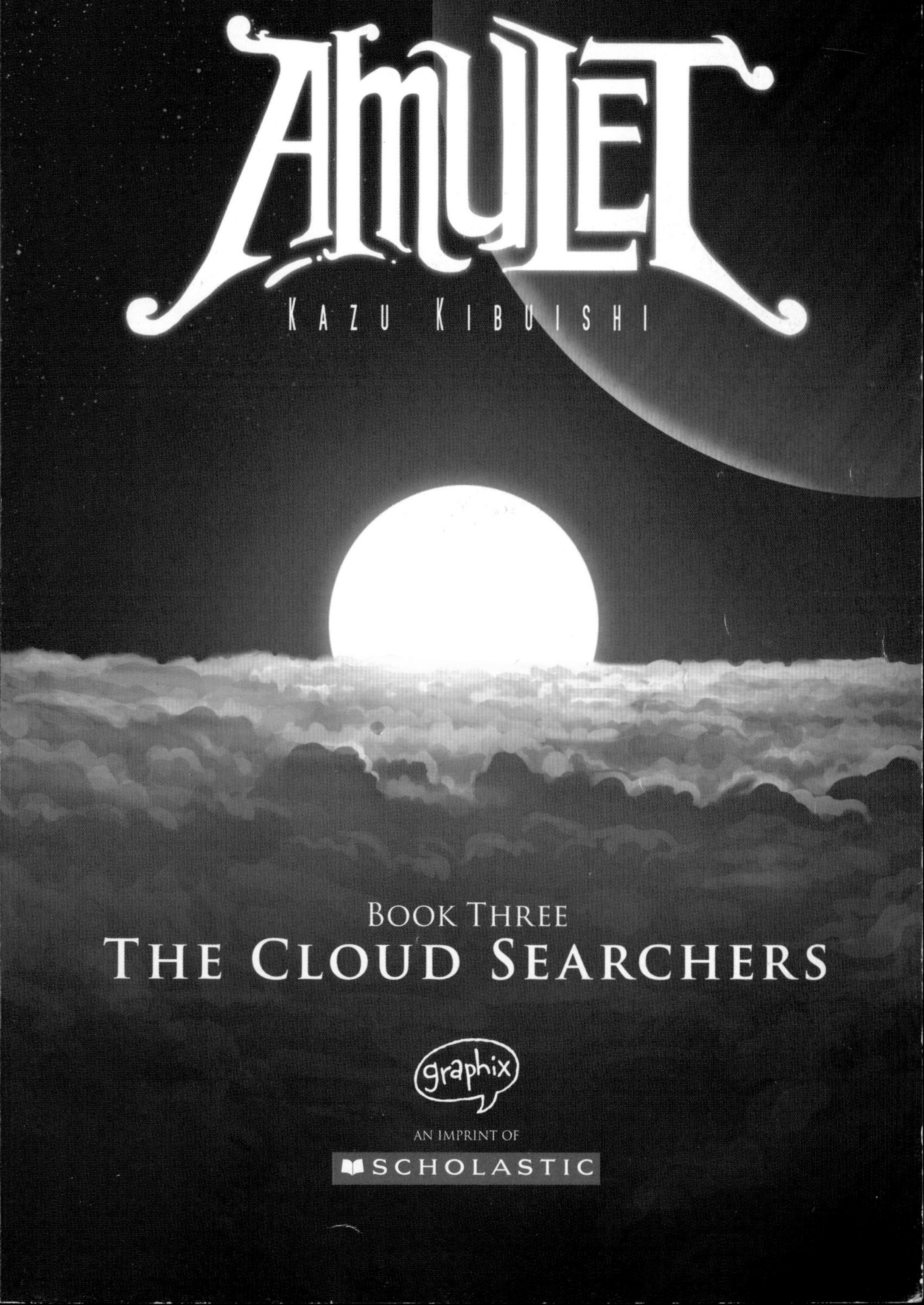

AMULET

KAZU KIBUISHI

BOOK THREE
THE CLOUD SEARCHERS

graphix
AN IMPRINT OF
SCHOLASTIC

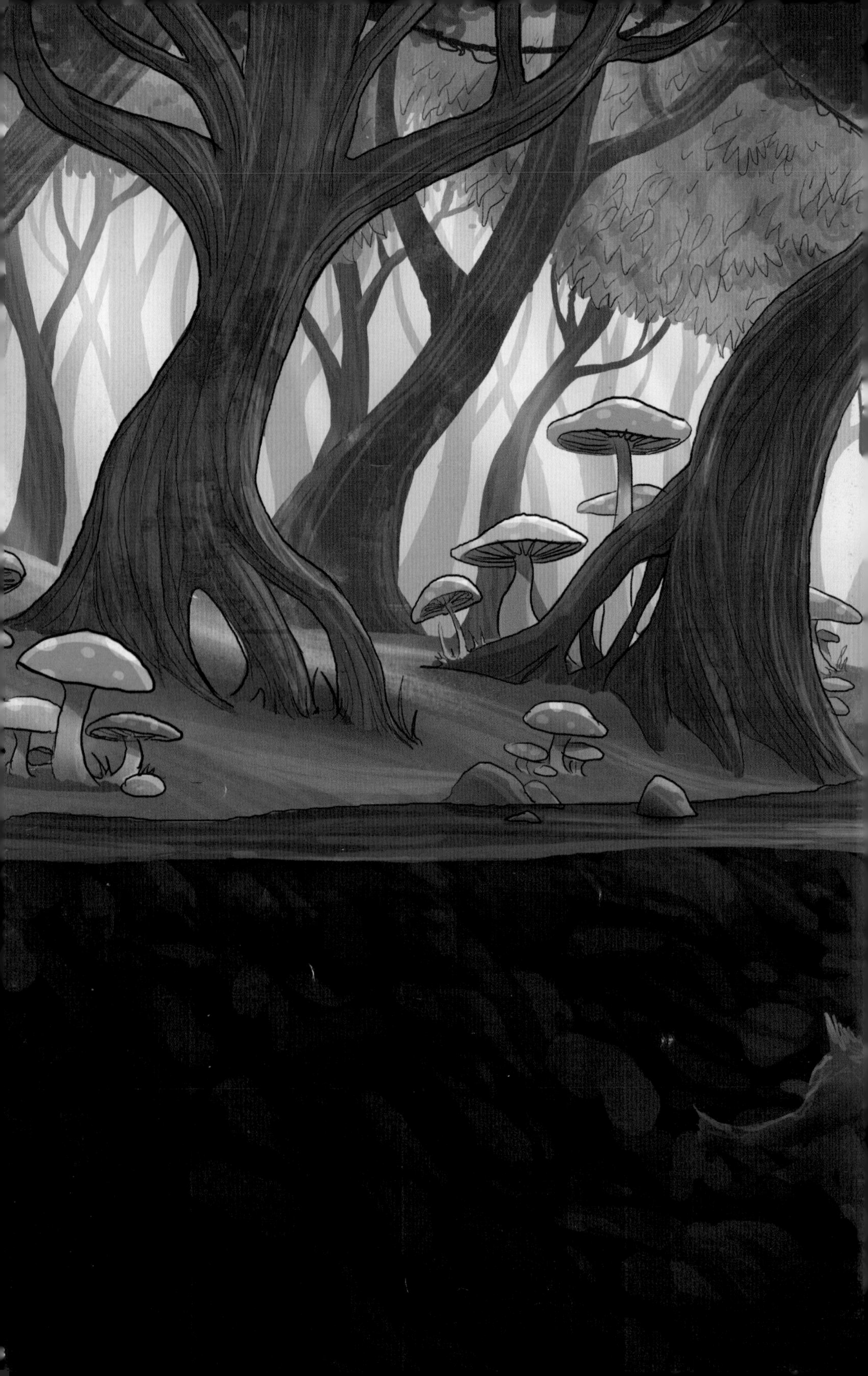

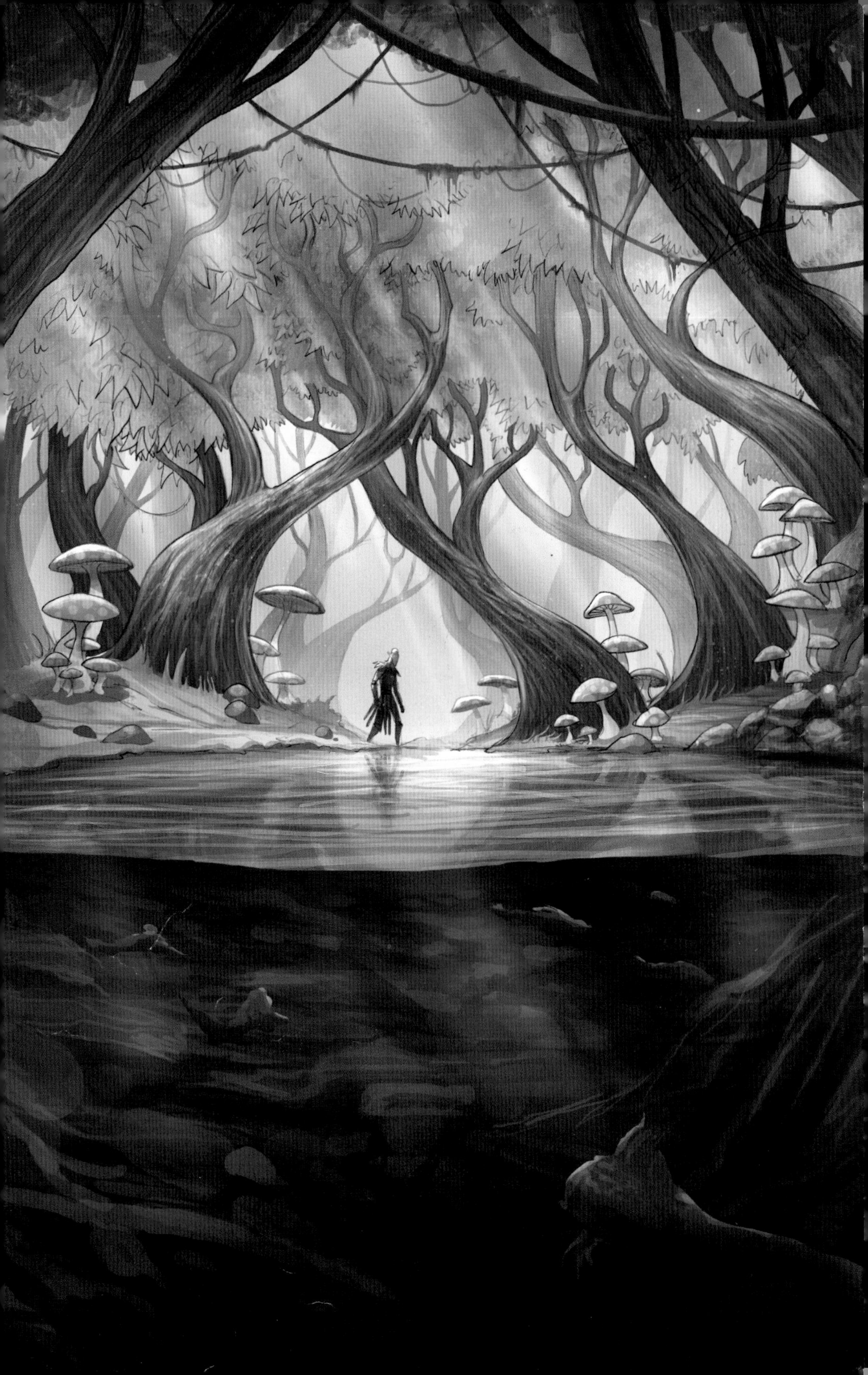

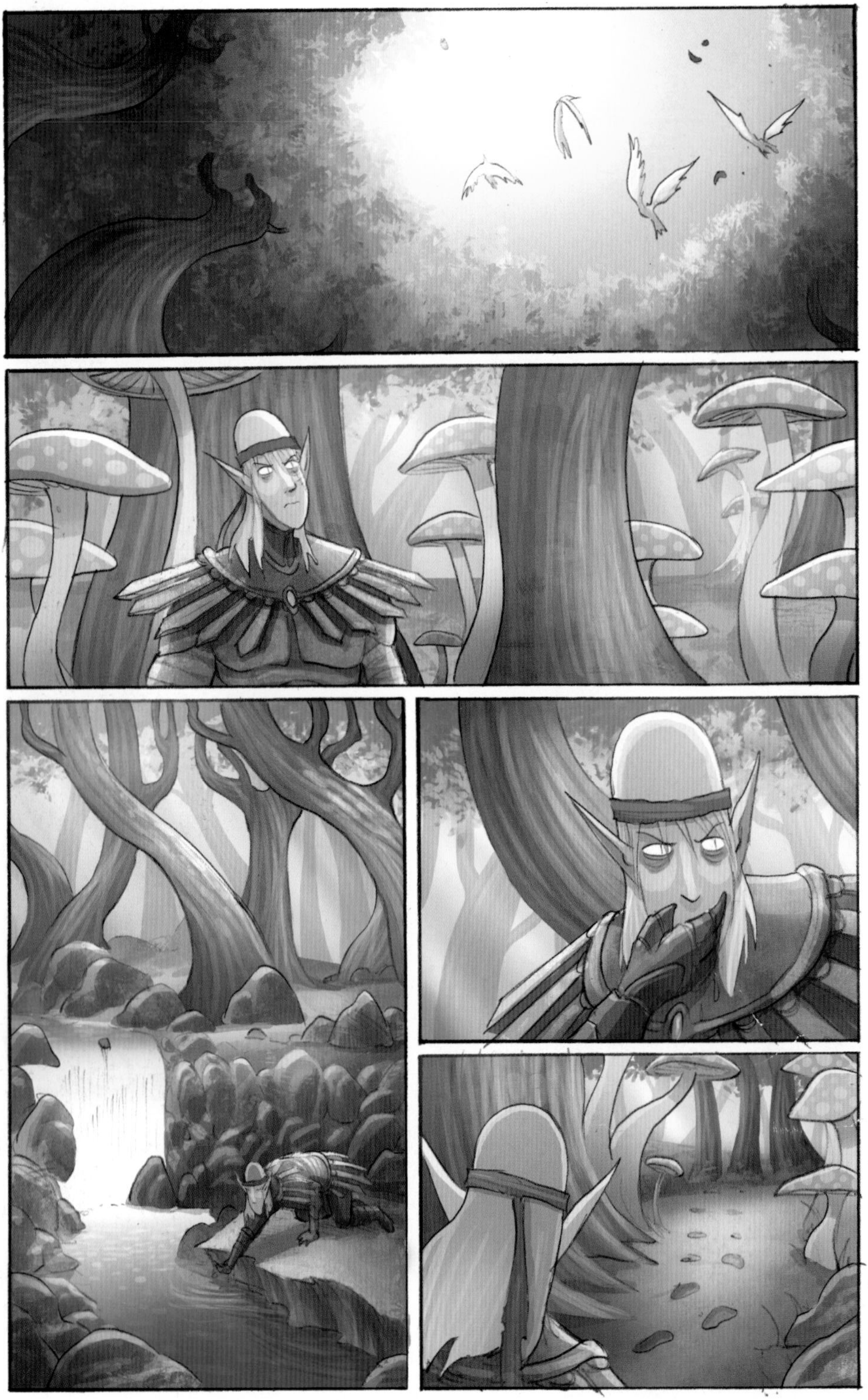

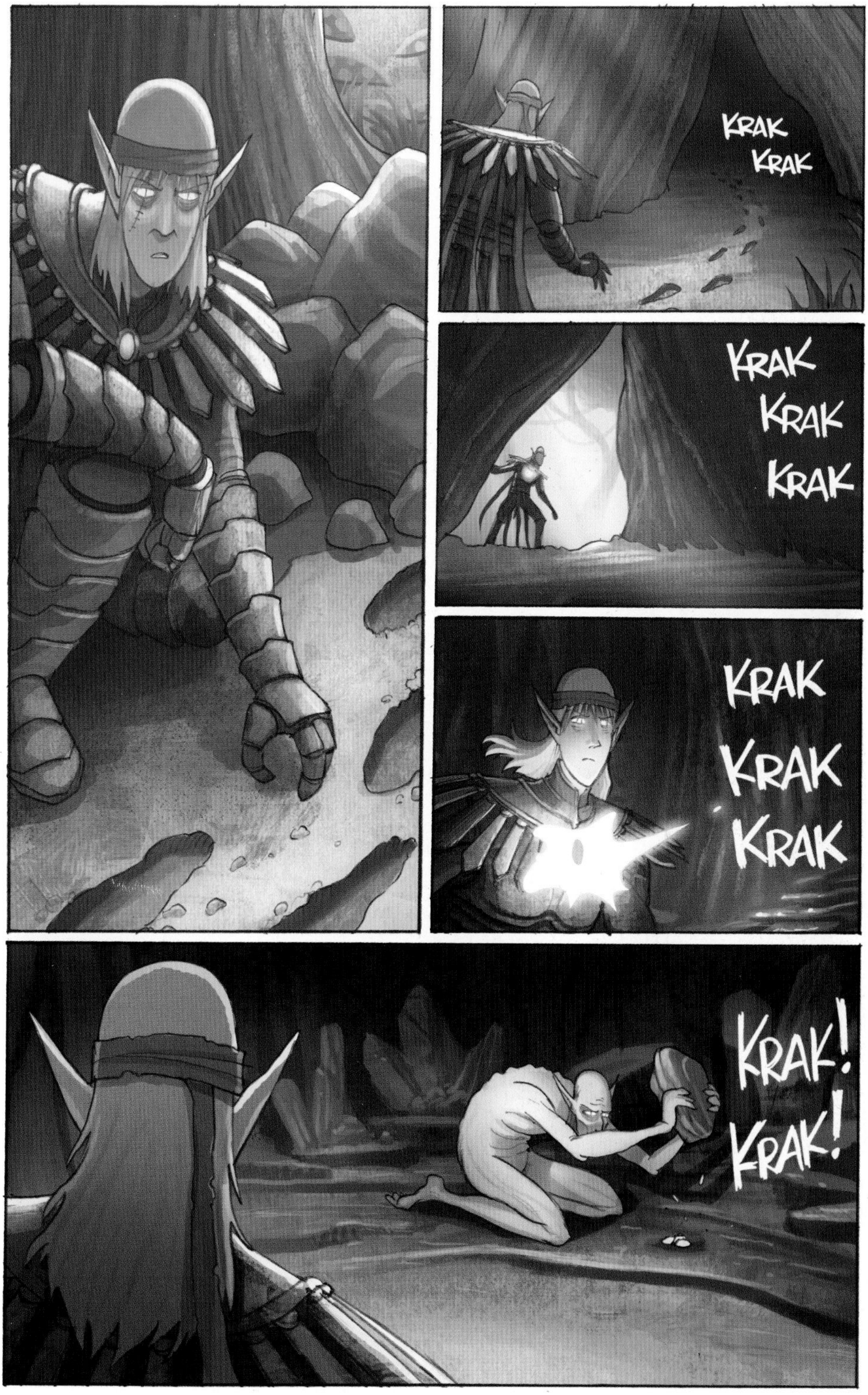
KRAK
KRAK
KRAK
KRAK
KRAK
KRAK
KRAK
KRAK
KRAK!
KRAK!

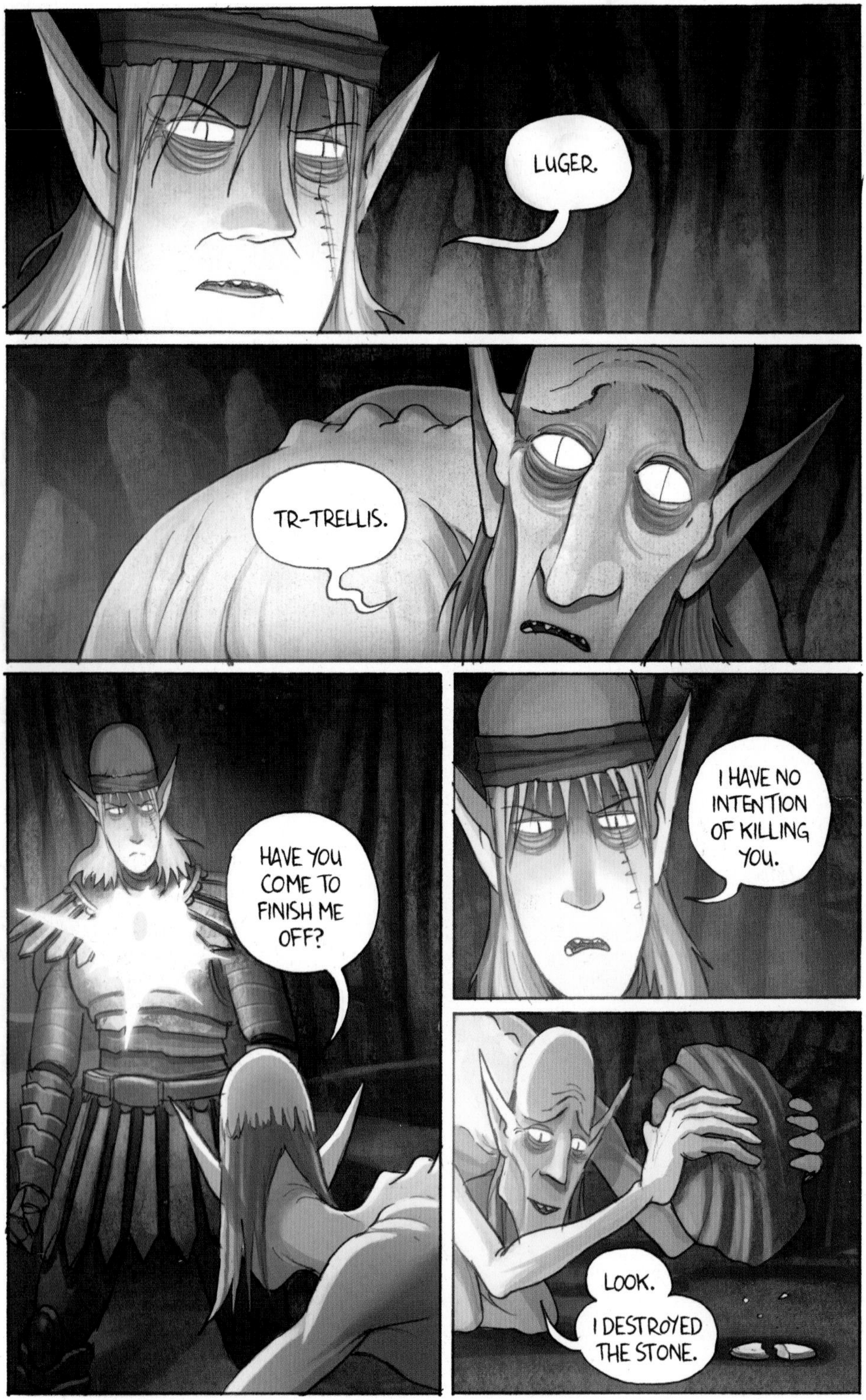
LUGER.
TR-TRELLIS.
HAVE YOU COME TO FINISH ME OFF?
I HAVE NO INTENTION OF KILLING YOU.
LOOK.
I DESTROYED THE STONE.

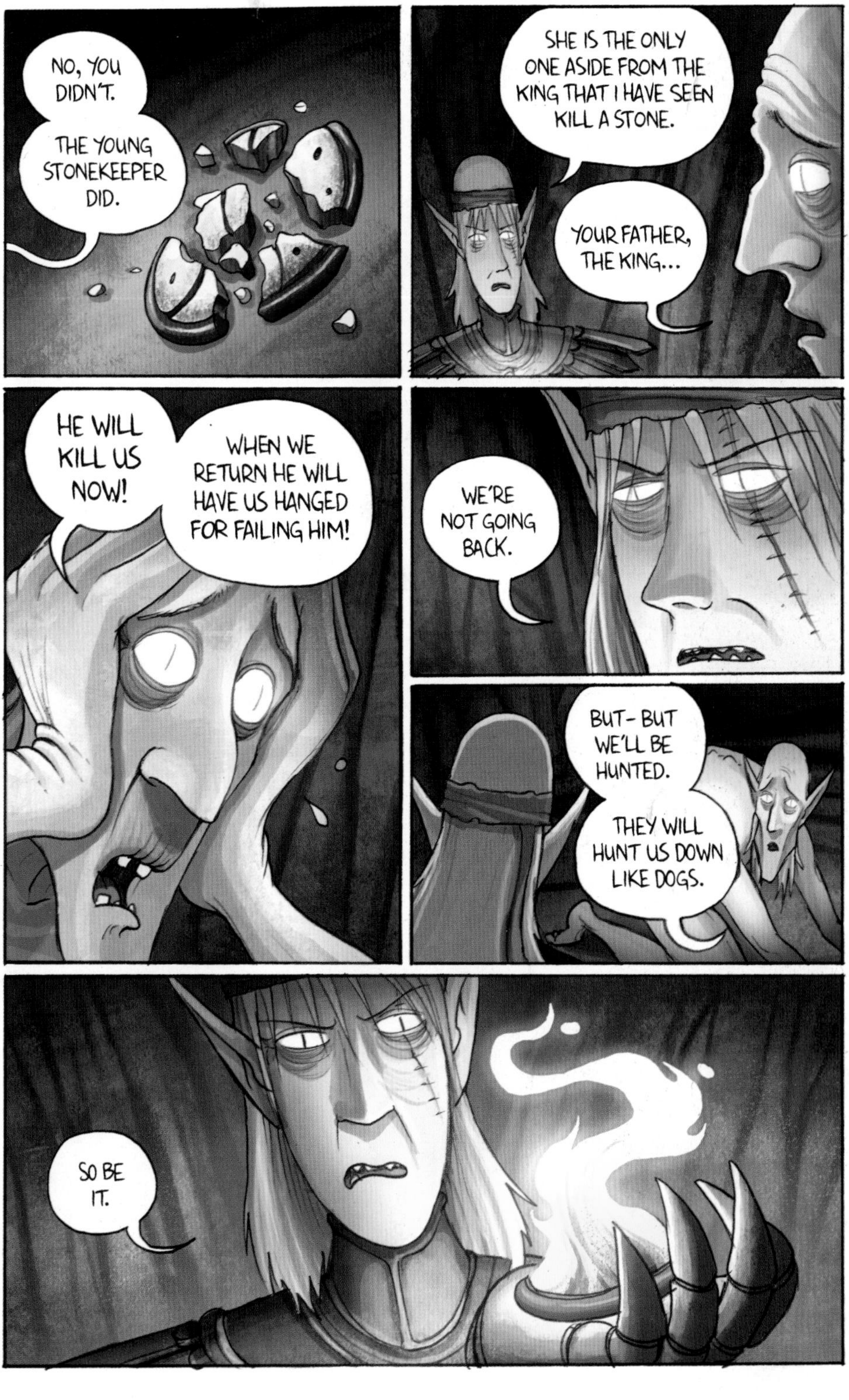
NO, YOU DIDN'T.
THE YOUNG STONEKEEPER DID.
SHE IS THE ONLY ONE ASIDE FROM THE KING THAT I HAVE SEEN KILL A STONE.
YOUR FATHER, THE KING...
HE WILL KILL US NOW!
WHEN WE RETURN HE WILL HAVE US HANGED FOR FAILING HIM!
WE'RE NOT GOING BACK.
BUT- BUT WE'LL BE HUNTED.
THEY WILL HUNT US DOWN LIKE DOGS.
SO BE IT.

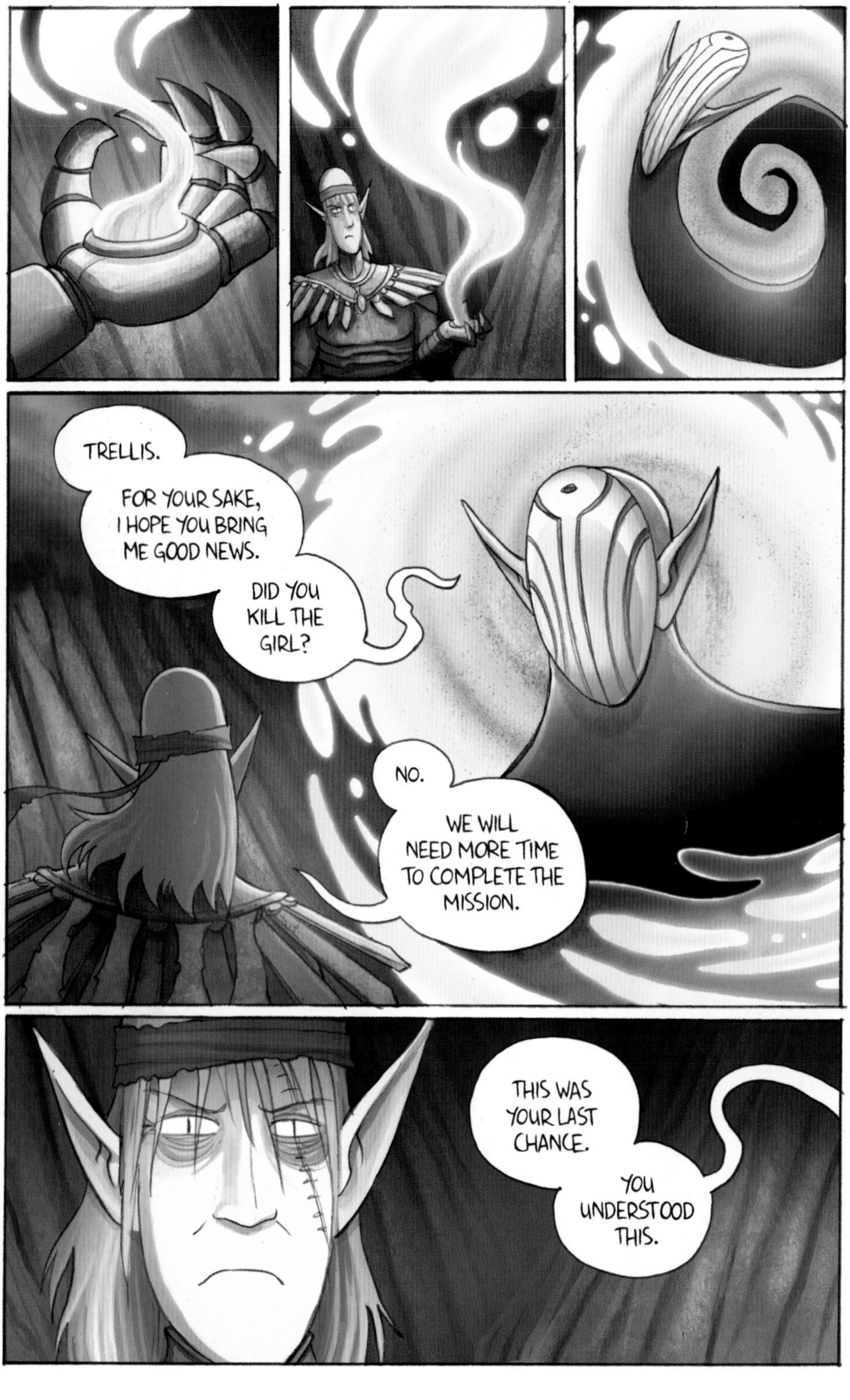
TRELLIS.
FOR YOUR SAKE, I HOPE YOU BRING ME GOOD NEWS.
DID YOU KILL THE GIRL?
NO.
WE WILL NEED MORE TIME TO COMPLETE THE MISSION.
THIS WAS YOUR LAST CHANCE.
YOU UNDERSTOOD THIS.

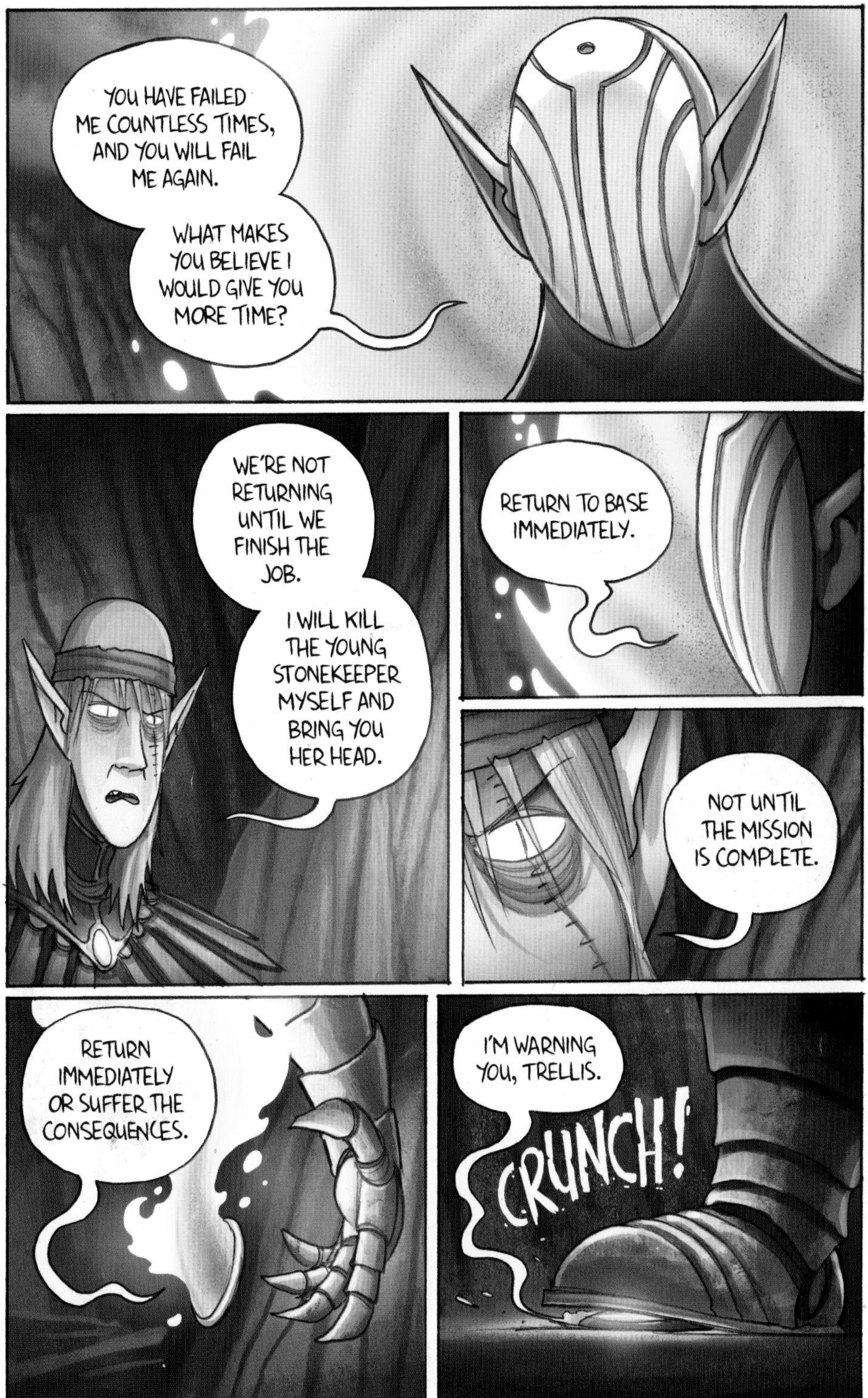
YOU HAVE FAILED ME COUNTLESS TIMES, AND YOU WILL FAIL ME AGAIN.
WHAT MAKES YOU BELIEVE I WOULD GIVE YOU MORE TIME?
WE'RE NOT RETURNING UNTIL WE FINISH THE JOB.
I WILL KILL THE YOUNG STONEKEEPER MYSELF AND BRING YOU HER HEAD.
RETURN TO BASE IMMEDIATELY.
NOT UNTIL THE MISSION IS COMPLETE.
RETURN IMMEDIATELY OR SUFFER THE CONSEQUENCES.
I'M WARNING YOU, TRELLIS.
CRUNCH!

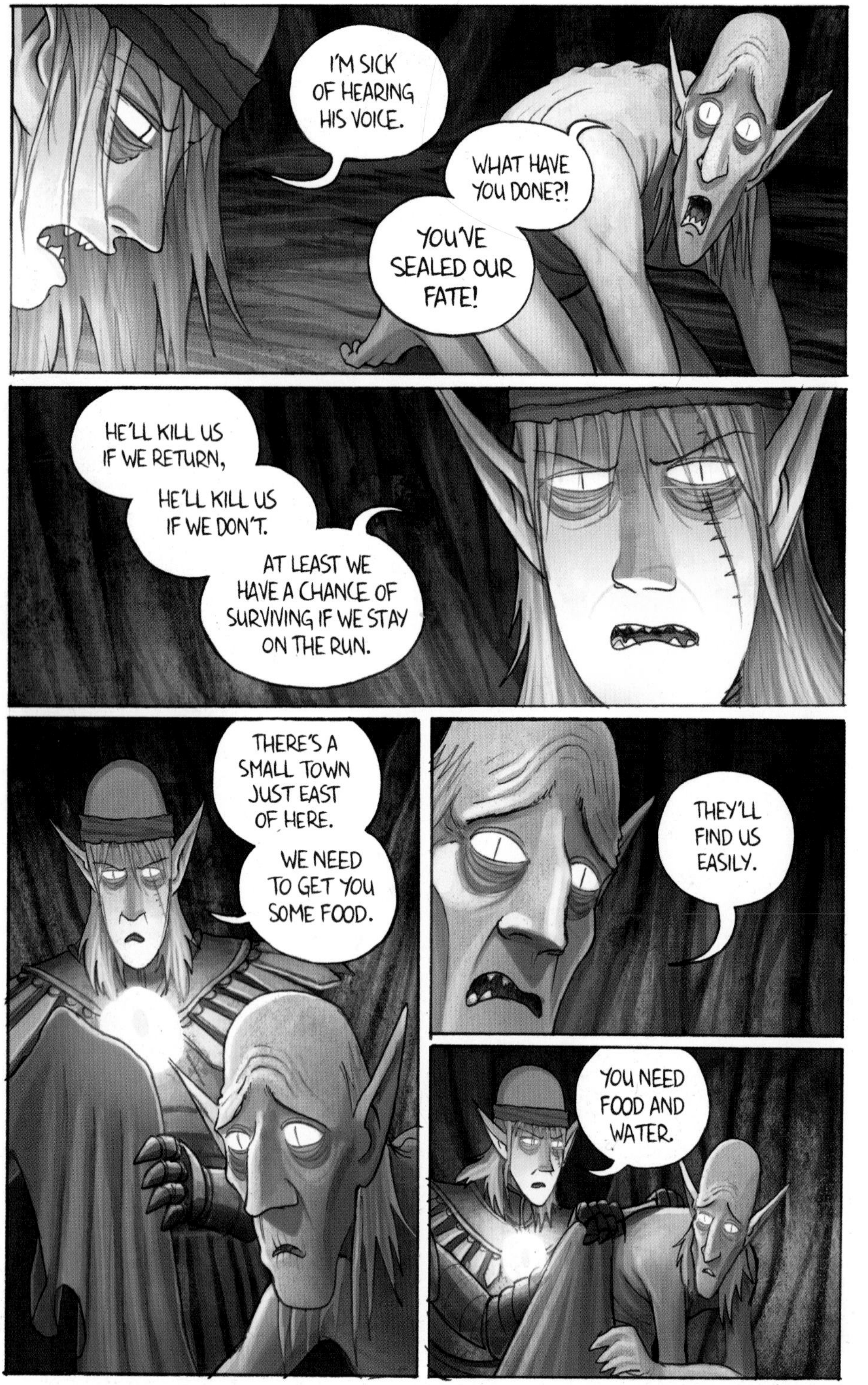
I'M SICK OF HEARING HIS VOICE.
WHAT HAVE YOU DONE?!
YOU'VE SEALED OUR FATE!
HE'LL KILL US IF WE RETURN,
HE'LL KILL US IF WE DON'T.
AT LEAST WE HAVE A CHANCE OF SURVIVING IF WE STAY ON THE RUN.
THERE'S A SMALL TOWN JUST EAST OF HERE.
WE NEED TO GET YOU SOME FOOD.
THEY'LL FIND US EASILY.
YOU NEED FOOD AND WATER.

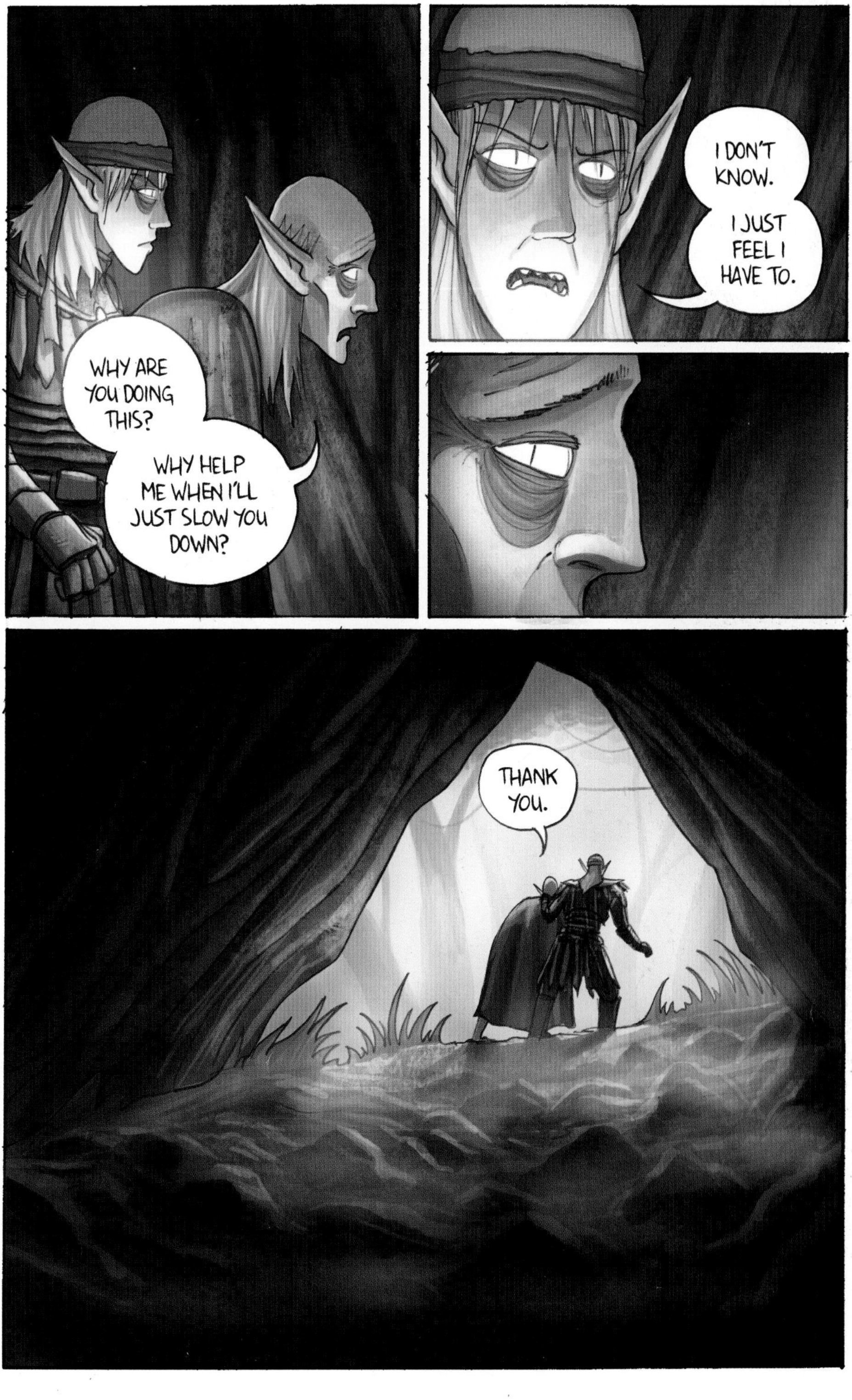
WHY ARE YOU DOING THIS?
WHY HELP ME WHEN I'LL JUST SLOW YOU DOWN?
I DON'T KNOW.
I JUST FEEL I HAVE TO.
THANK YOU.

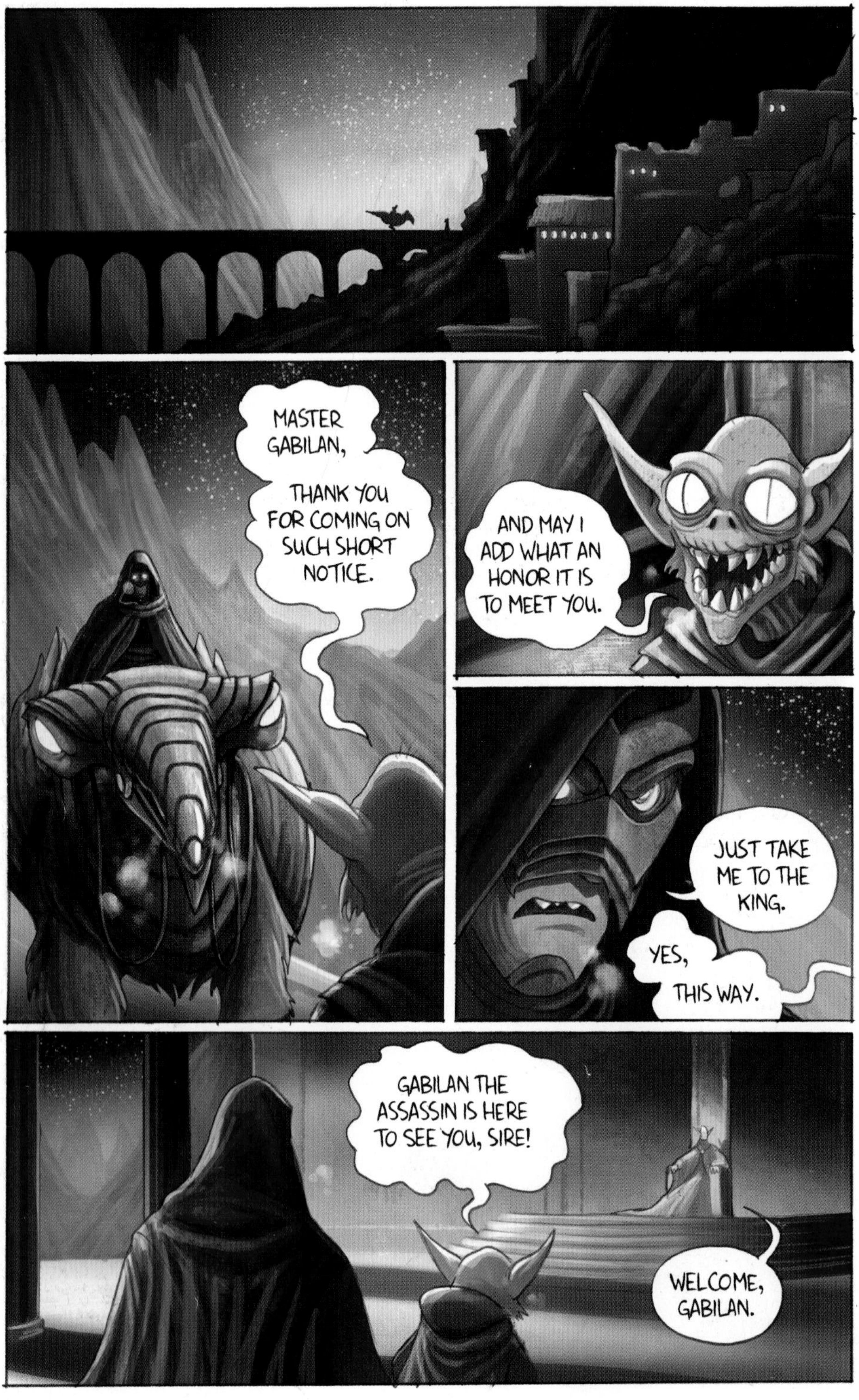
MASTER GABILAN,
THANK YOU FOR COMING ON SUCH SHORT NOTICE.
AND MAY I ADD WHAT AN HONOR IT IS TO MEET YOU.
JUST TAKE ME TO THE KING.
YES,
THIS WAY.
GABILAN THE ASSASSIN IS HERE TO SEE YOU, SIRE!
WELCOME, GABILAN.

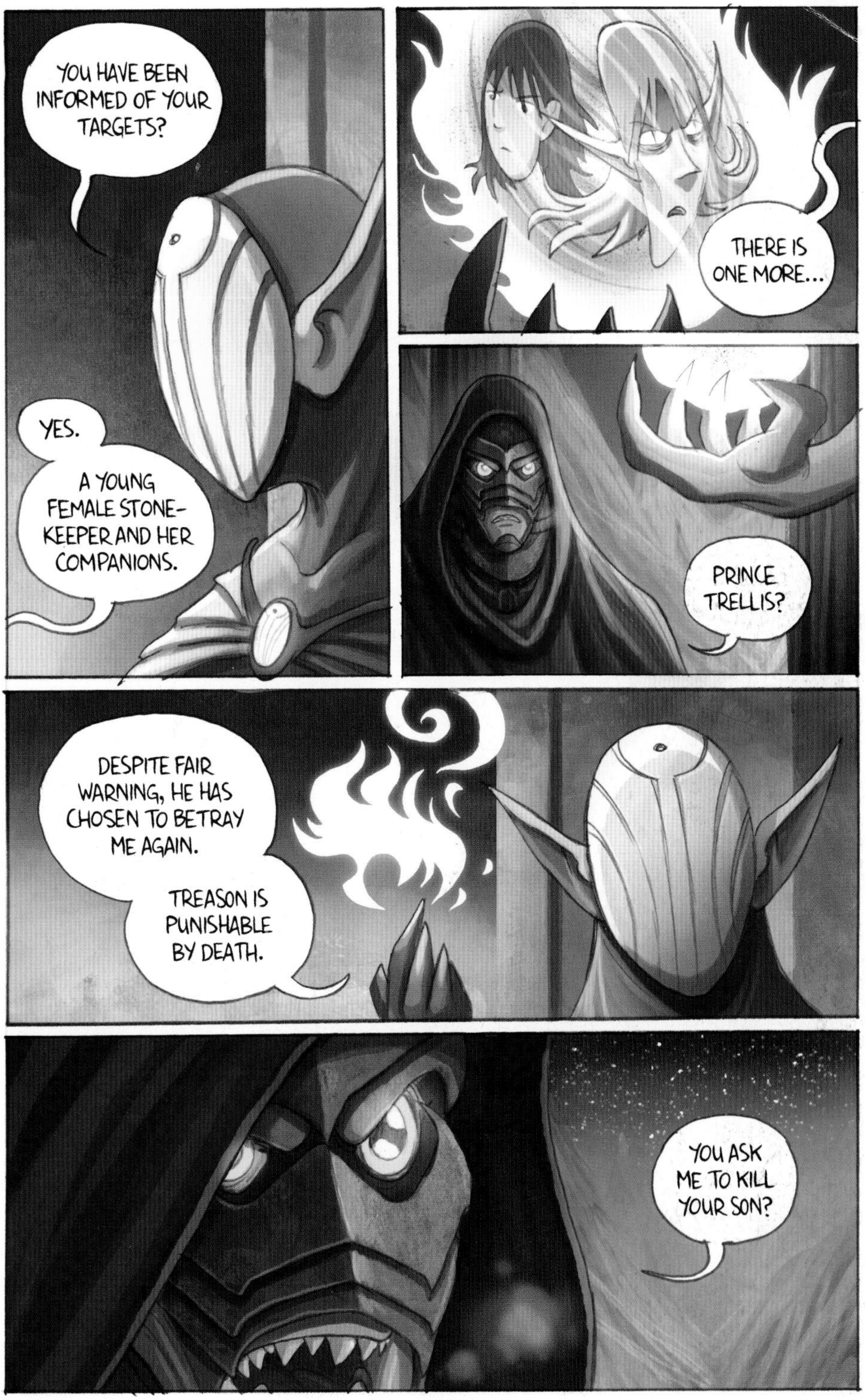
YOU HAVE BEEN INFORMED OF YOUR TARGETS?
YES.
A YOUNG FEMALE STONE-KEEPER AND HER COMPANIONS.
THERE IS ONE MORE...
PRINCE TRELLIS?
DESPITE FAIR WARNING, HE HAS CHOSEN TO BETRAY ME AGAIN.
TREASON IS PUNISHABLE BY DEATH.
YOU ASK ME TO KILL YOUR SON?

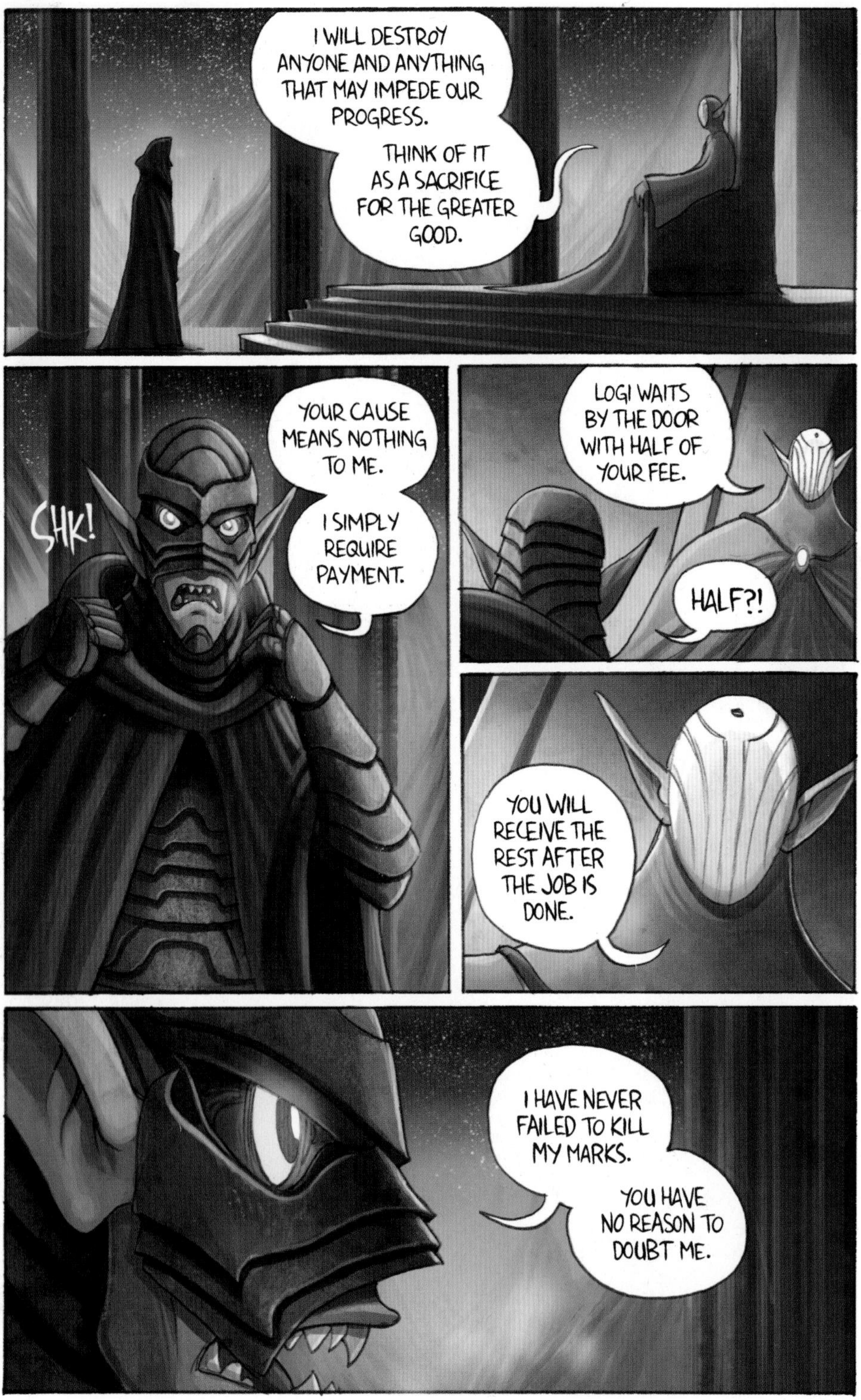
I WILL DESTROY ANYONE AND ANYTHING THAT MAY IMPEDE OUR PROGRESS.
THINK OF IT AS A SACRIFICE FOR THE GREATER GOOD.
SHK!
YOUR CAUSE MEANS NOTHING TO ME.
I SIMPLY REQUIRE PAYMENT.
LOGI WAITS BY THE DOOR WITH HALF OF YOUR FEE.
HALF?!
YOU WILL RECEIVE THE REST AFTER THE JOB IS DONE.
I HAVE NEVER FAILED TO KILL MY MARKS.
YOU HAVE NO REASON TO DOUBT ME.

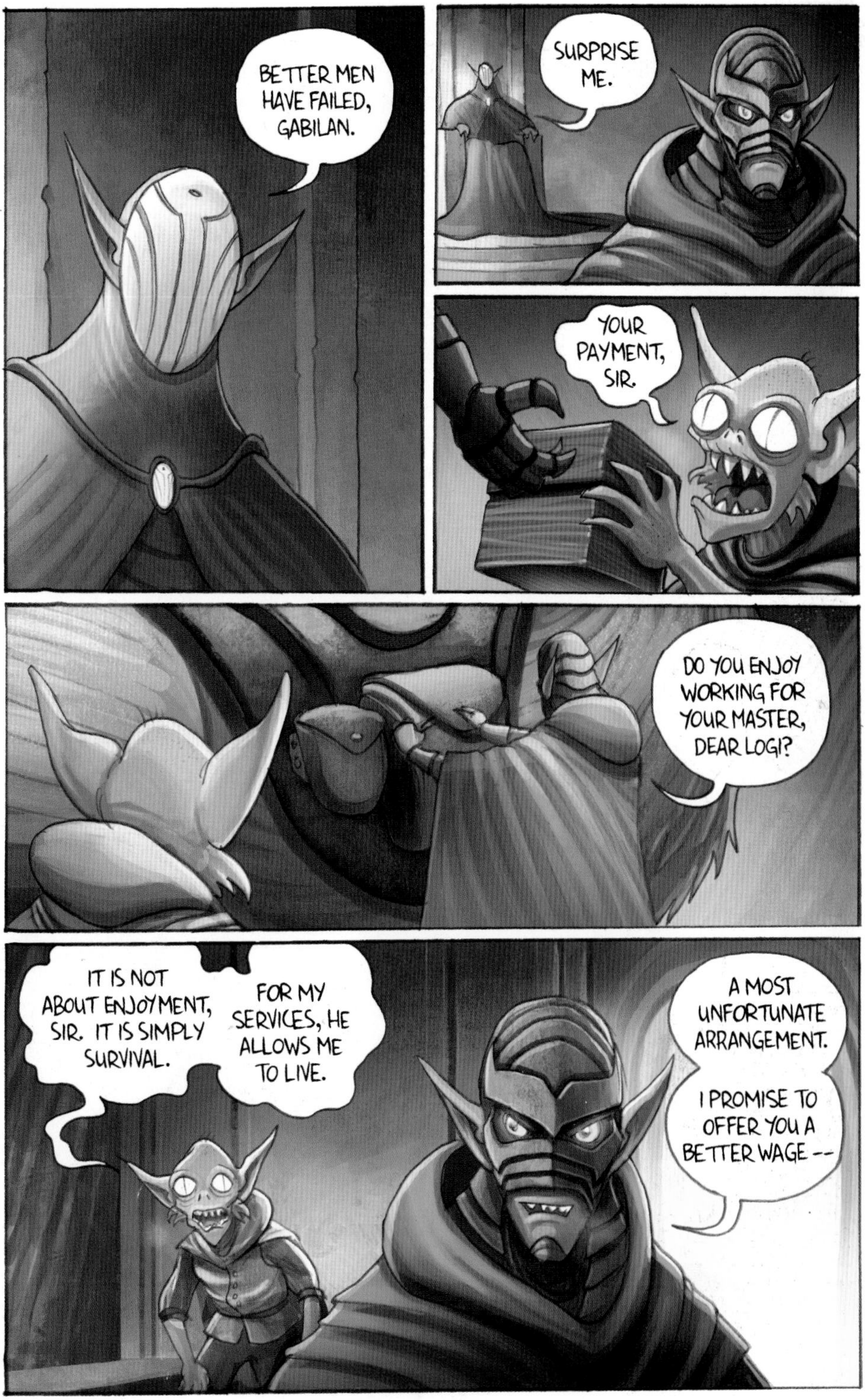
BETTER MEN HAVE FAILED, GABILAN.
SURPRISE ME.
YOUR PAYMENT, SIR.
DO YOU ENJOY WORKING FOR YOUR MASTER, DEAR LOGI?
IT IS NOT ABOUT ENJOYMENT, SIR. IT IS SIMPLY SURVIVAL.
FOR MY SERVICES, HE ALLOWS ME TO LIVE.
A MOST UNFORTUNATE ARRANGEMENT.
I PROMISE TO OFFER YOU A BETTER WAGE --

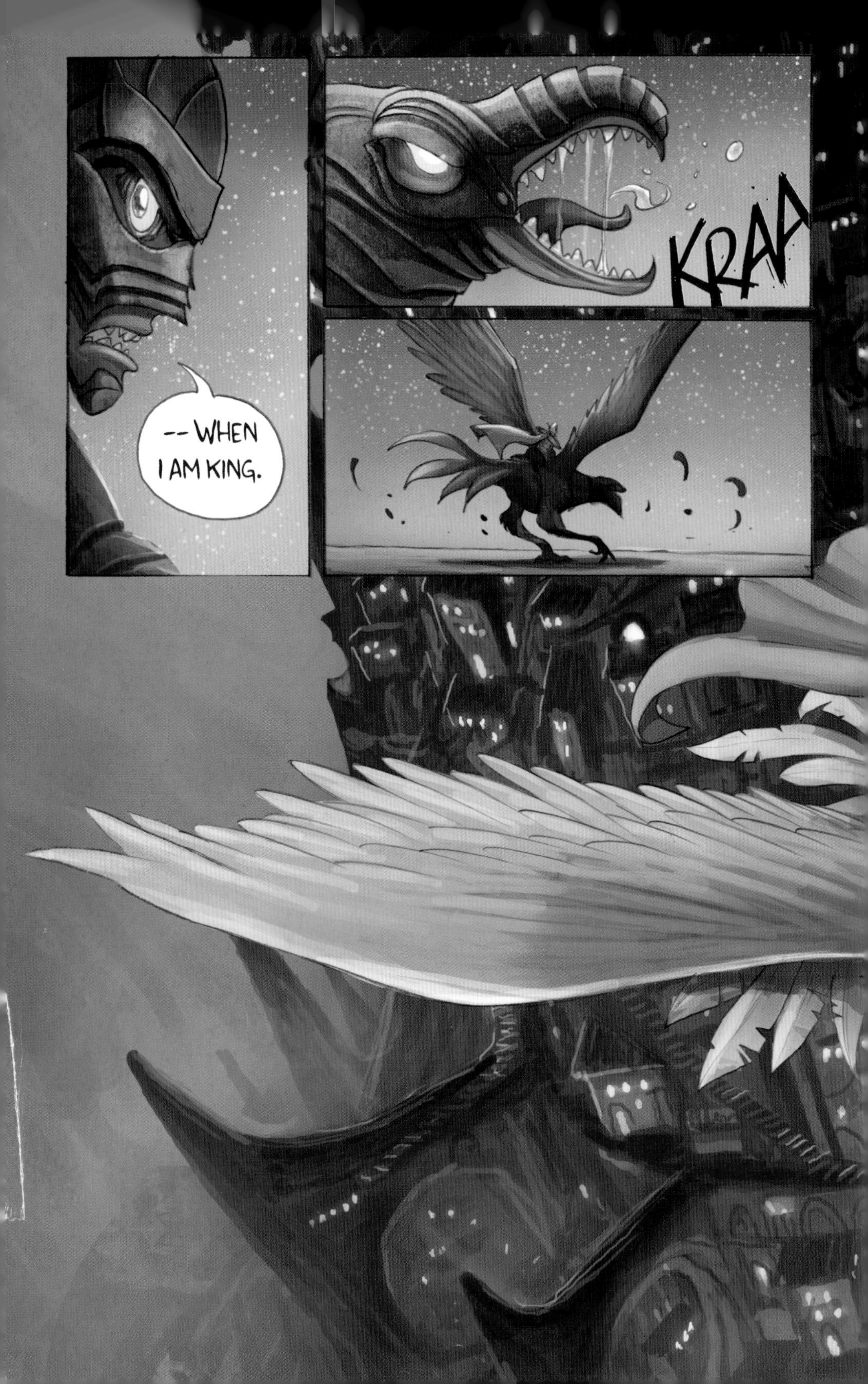
-- WHEN I AM KING.
KRAA

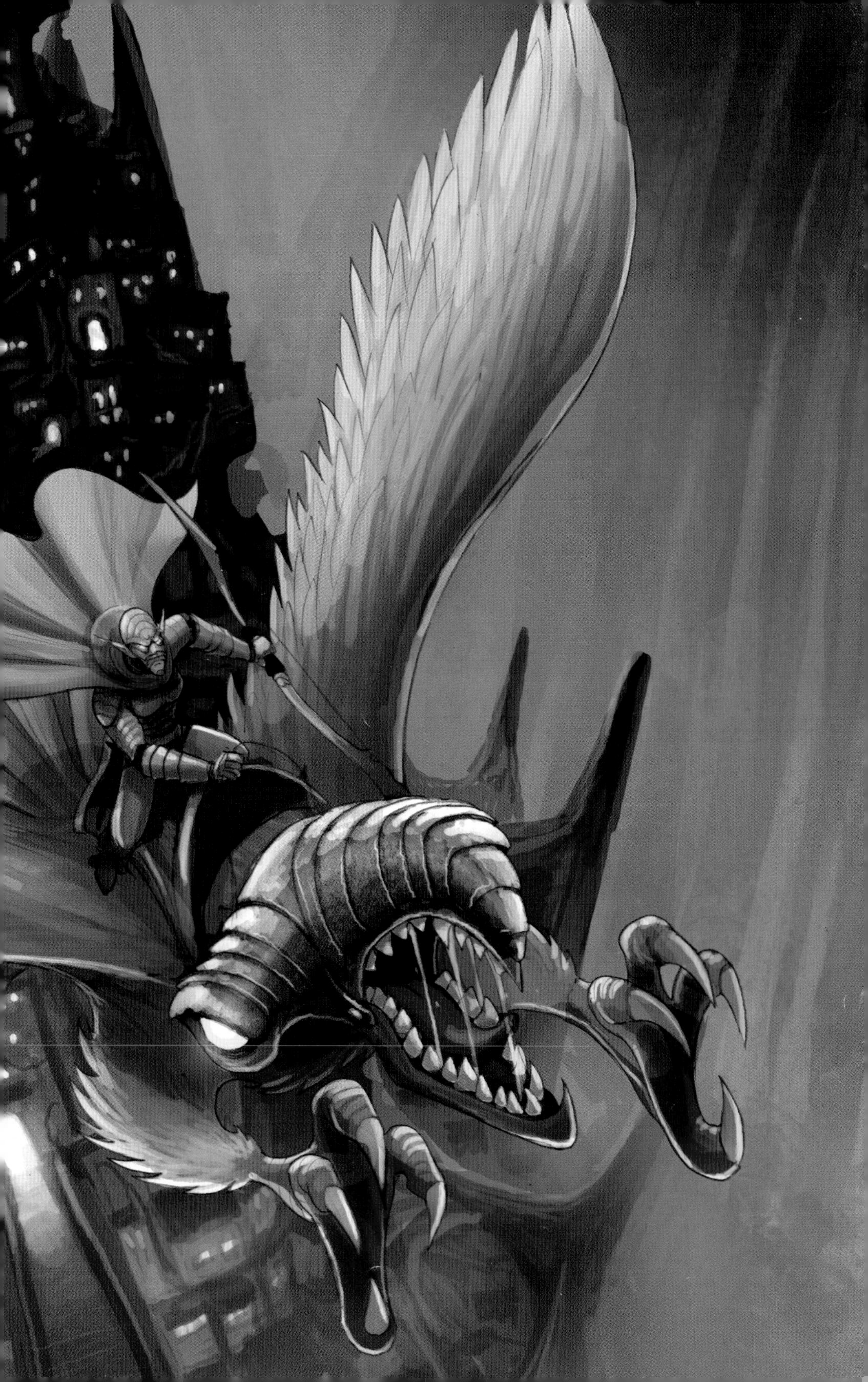

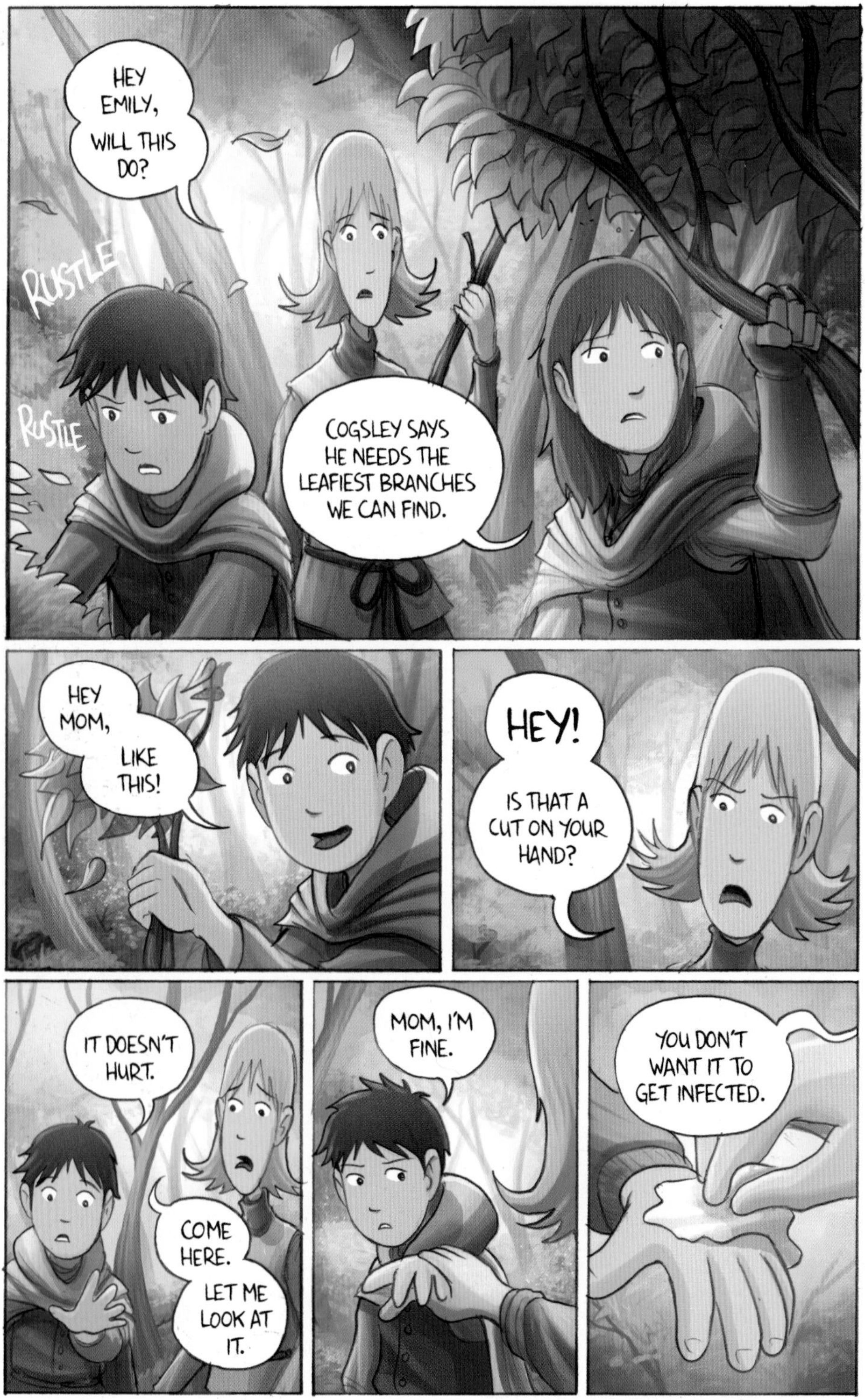
HEY EMILY, WILL THIS DO?
RUSTLE
RUSTLE
COGSLEY SAYS HE NEEDS THE LEAFIEST BRANCHES WE CAN FIND.
HEY MOM, LIKE THIS!
HEY!
IS THAT A CUT ON YOUR HAND?
IT DOESN'T HURT.
COME HERE.
LET ME LOOK AT IT.
MOM, I'M FINE.
YOU DON'T WANT IT TO GET INFECTED.

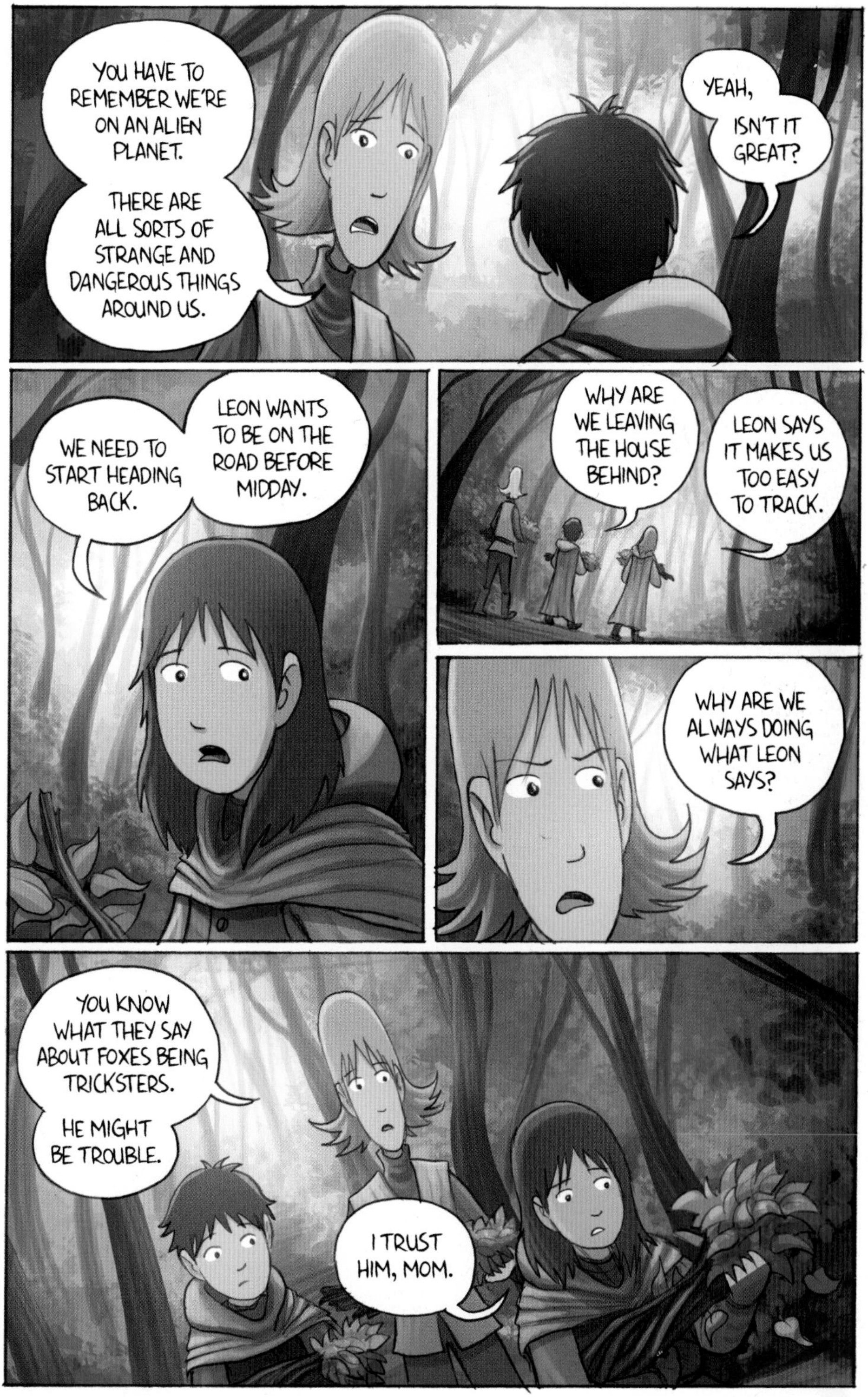
YOU HAVE TO REMEMBER WE'RE ON AN ALIEN PLANET.
THERE ARE ALL SORTS OF STRANGE AND DANGEROUS THINGS AROUND US.
YEAH,
ISN'T IT GREAT?
WE NEED TO START HEADING BACK.
LEON WANTS TO BE ON THE ROAD BEFORE MIDDAY.
WHY ARE WE LEAVING THE HOUSE BEHIND?
LEON SAYS IT MAKES US TOO EASY TO TRACK.
WHY ARE WE ALWAYS DOING WHAT LEON SAYS?
YOU KNOW WHAT THEY SAY ABOUT FOXES BEING TRICKSTERS.
HE MIGHT BE TROUBLE.
I TRUST HIM, MOM.

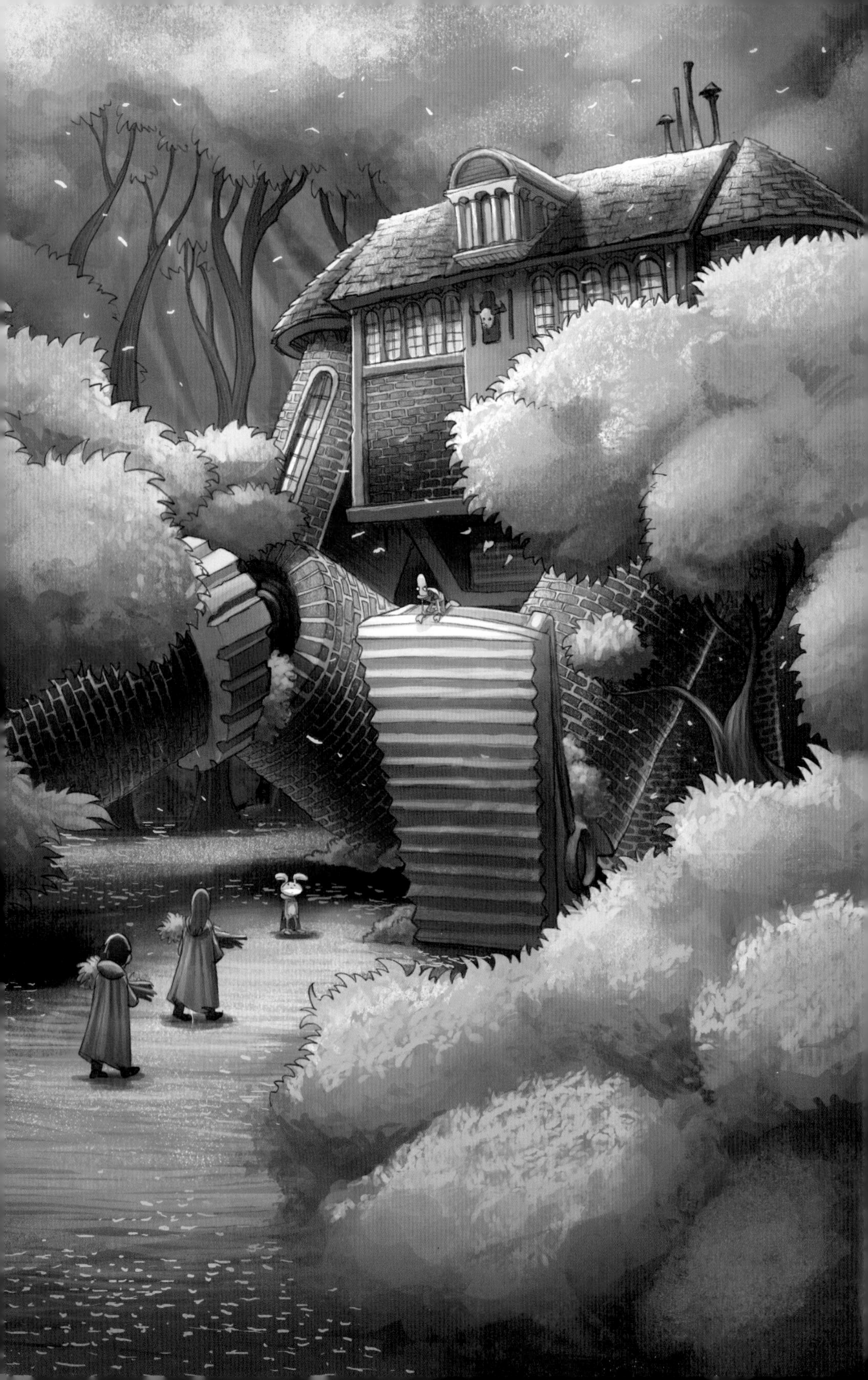

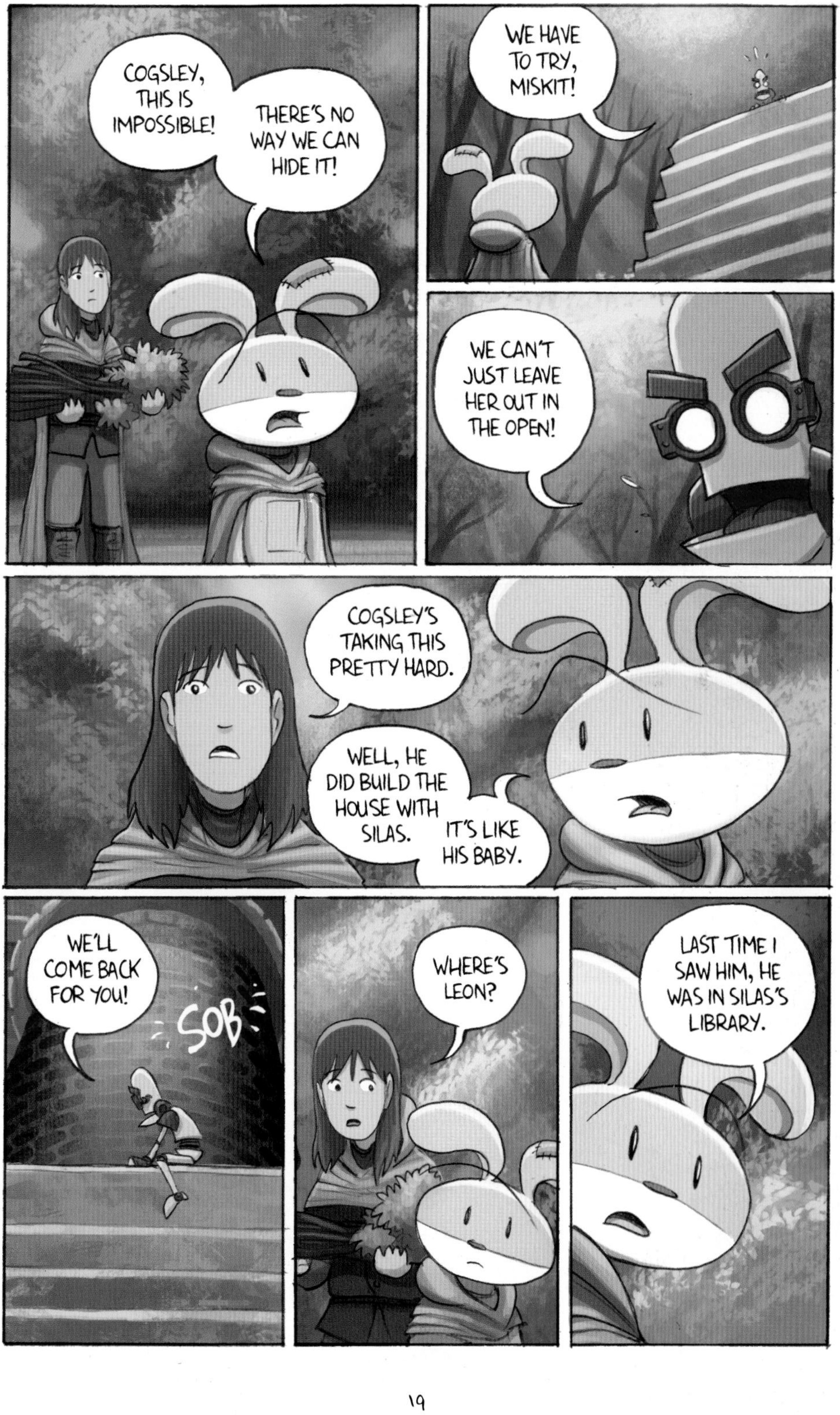
COGSLEY, THIS IS IMPOSSIBLE!
THERE'S NO WAY WE CAN HIDE IT!
WE HAVE TO TRY, MISKIT!
WE CAN'T JUST LEAVE HER OUT IN THE OPEN!
COGSLEY'S TAKING THIS PRETTY HARD.
WELL, HE DID BUILD THE HOUSE WITH SILAS.
IT'S LIKE HIS BABY.
WE'LL COME BACK FOR YOU!
SOB
WHERE'S LEON?
LAST TIME I SAW HIM, HE WAS IN SILAS'S LIBRARY.

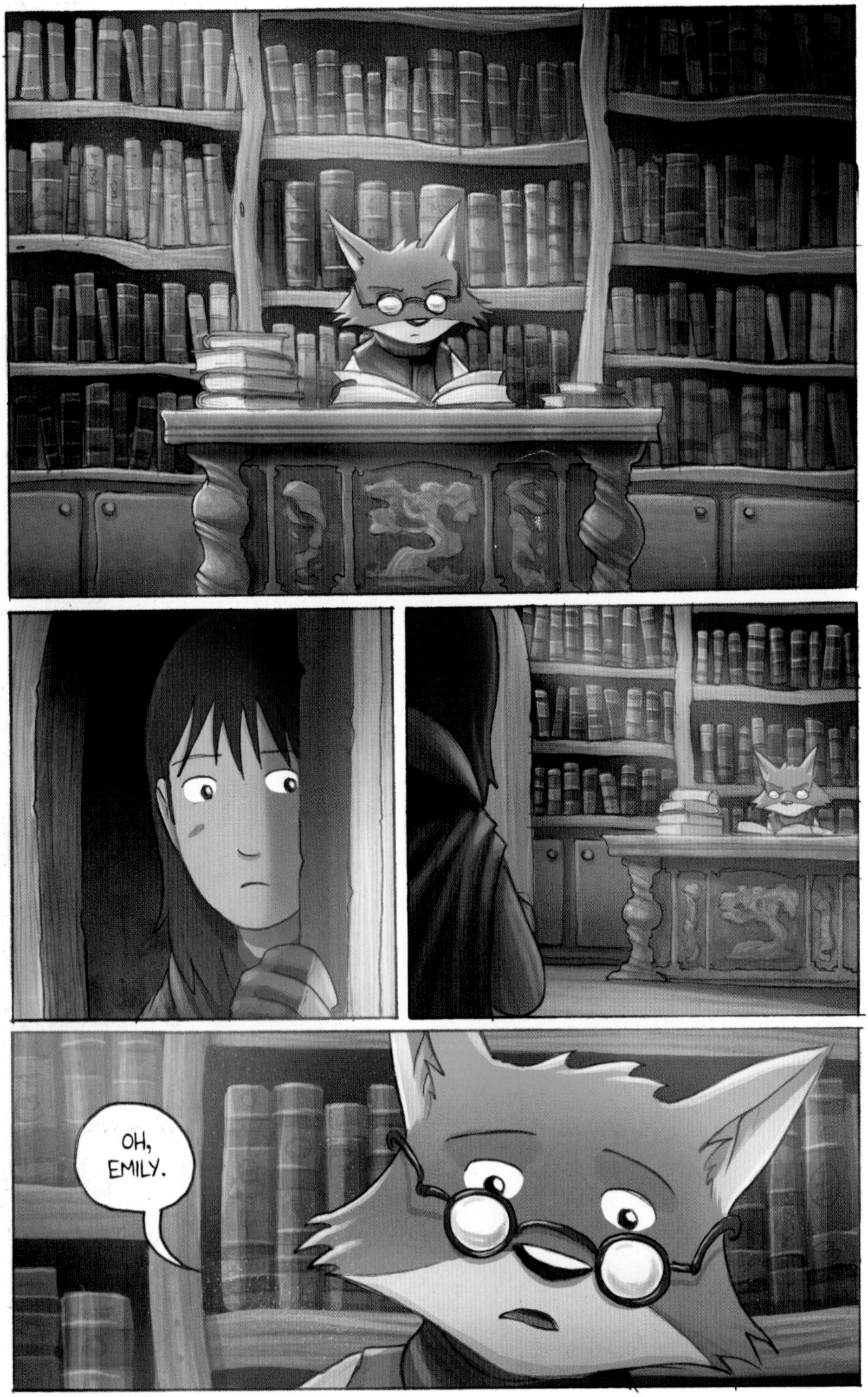
OH, EMILY.

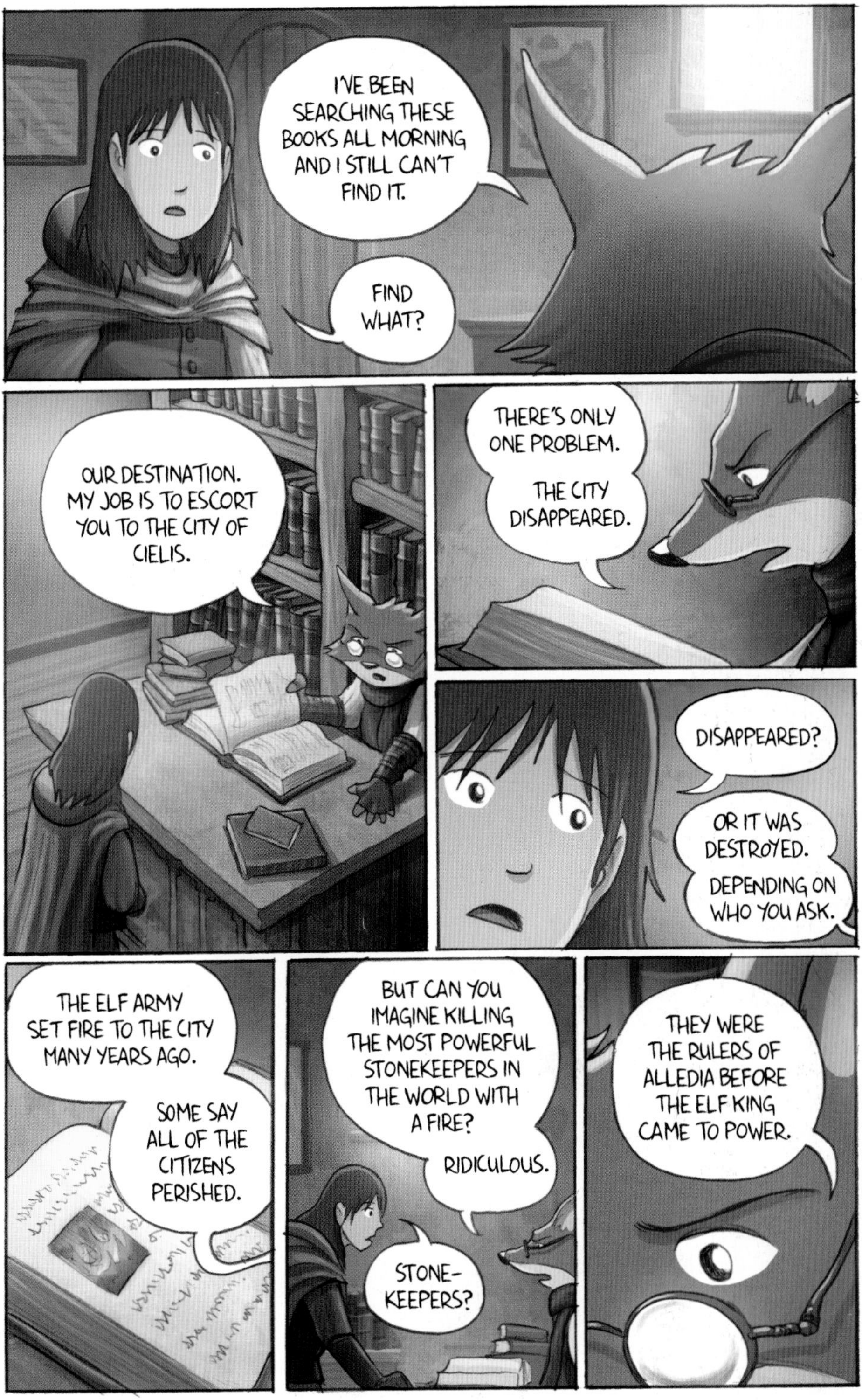

I'VE BEEN SEARCHING THESE BOOKS ALL MORNING AND I STILL CAN'T FIND IT.
FIND WHAT?
OUR DESTINATION. MY JOB IS TO ESCORT YOU TO THE CITY OF CIELIS.
THERE'S ONLY ONE PROBLEM.
THE CITY DISAPPEARED.
DISAPPEARED?
OR IT WAS DESTROYED.
DEPENDING ON WHO YOU ASK.
THE ELF ARMY SET FIRE TO THE CITY MANY YEARS AGO.
SOME SAY ALL OF THE CITIZENS PERISHED.
BUT CAN YOU IMAGINE KILLING THE MOST POWERFUL STONEKEEPERS IN THE WORLD WITH A FIRE?
RIDICULOUS.
STONE-KEEPERS?
THEY WERE THE RULERS OF ALLEDIA BEFORE THE ELF KING CAME TO POWER.

THE LEADERS OF THIS CITY CAME TO BE KNOWN AS THE GUARDIAN COUNCIL.

THE FIVE GREAT STONEKEEPERS WHO COMPRISED THE GUARDIAN COUNCIL WERE CHOSEN TO GOVERN ALLEDIA. FOR MANY YEARS, THINGS WENT ACCORDING TO THEIR PLANS AND ALLEDIA BENEFITED FROM A CENTURY OF PEACE.

SO IT CAME AS A SURPRISE WHEN GULFEN, THE NATION OF ELVES, ROSE UP AND BEGAN INVADING ITS NEIGHBORS WITHOUT WARNING. WHAT WAS ONCE A PEACEFUL NATION HAD BECOME A RUTHLESS AGGRESSOR.

THE GUARDIAN COUNCIL RETALIATED, BUT THEY SEVERELY UNDERESTIMATED THE ELF KING'S POWER.

THE GREAT CITY OF CIELIS SUFFERED THE FIERCEST ATTACK DURING THE WAR. IN A BATTLE FOR THE THRONE OF ALLEDIA, THE ELVES BURNED MOST OF IT TO THE GROUND.

WHEN THE DUST CLEARED, ALL THAT WAS LEFT OF CIELIS WAS A GIANT CRATER.

MOST BELIEVE THAT THE PEOPLE OF CIELIS PERISHED IN THE FLAMES. BUT THERE ARE A FEW, LIKE THE RESISTANCE, WHO BELIEVE THE CITY STILL EXISTS INTACT.

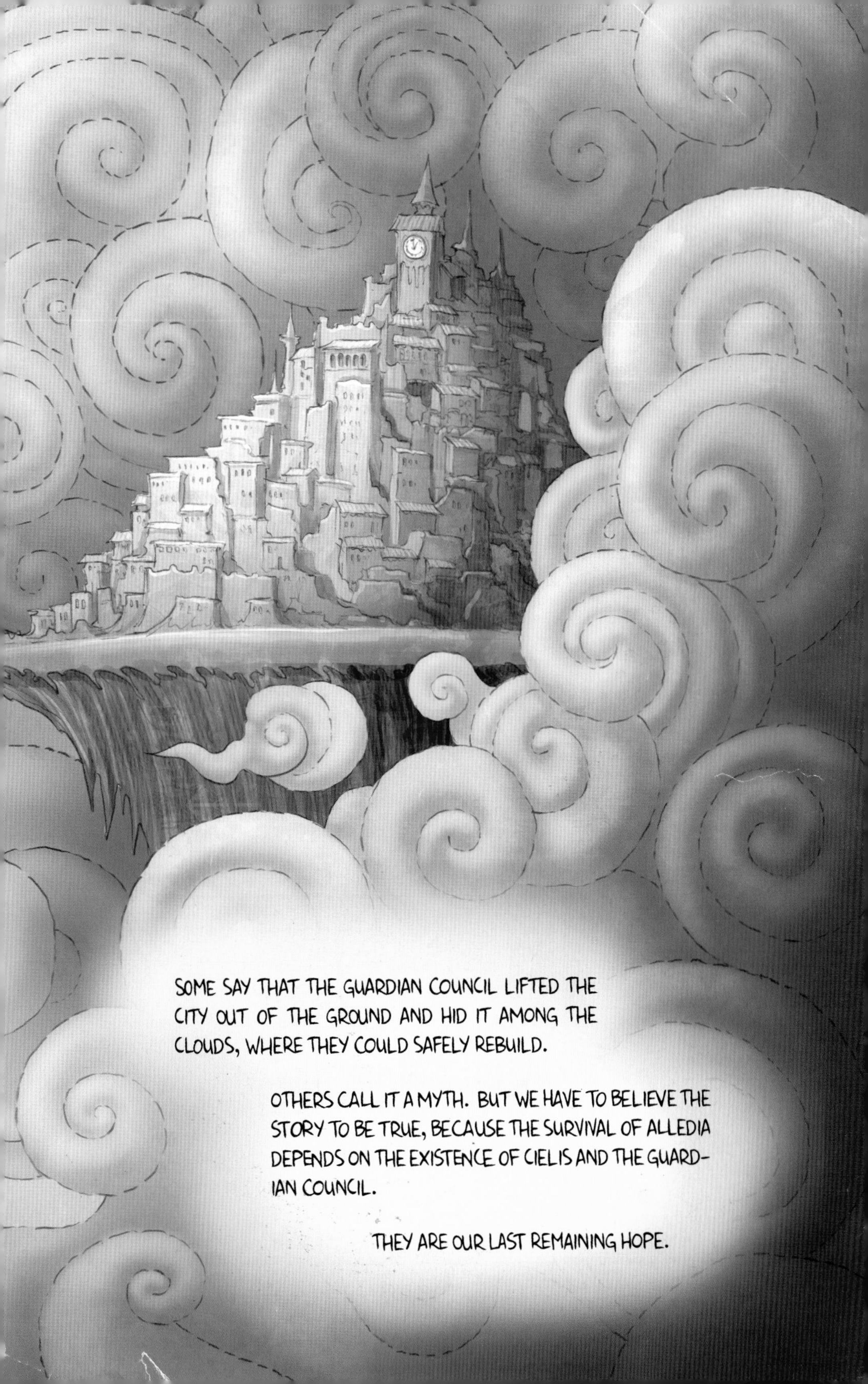
SOME SAY THAT THE GUARDIAN COUNCIL LIFTED THE CITY OUT OF THE GROUND AND HID IT AMONG THE CLOUDS, WHERE THEY COULD SAFELY REBUILD.
OTHERS CALL IT A MYTH. BUT WE HAVE TO BELIEVE THE STORY TO BE TRUE, BECAUSE THE SURVIVAL OF ALLEDIA DEPENDS ON THE EXISTENCE OF CIELIS AND THE GUARDIAN COUNCIL.
THEY ARE OUR LAST REMAINING HOPE.

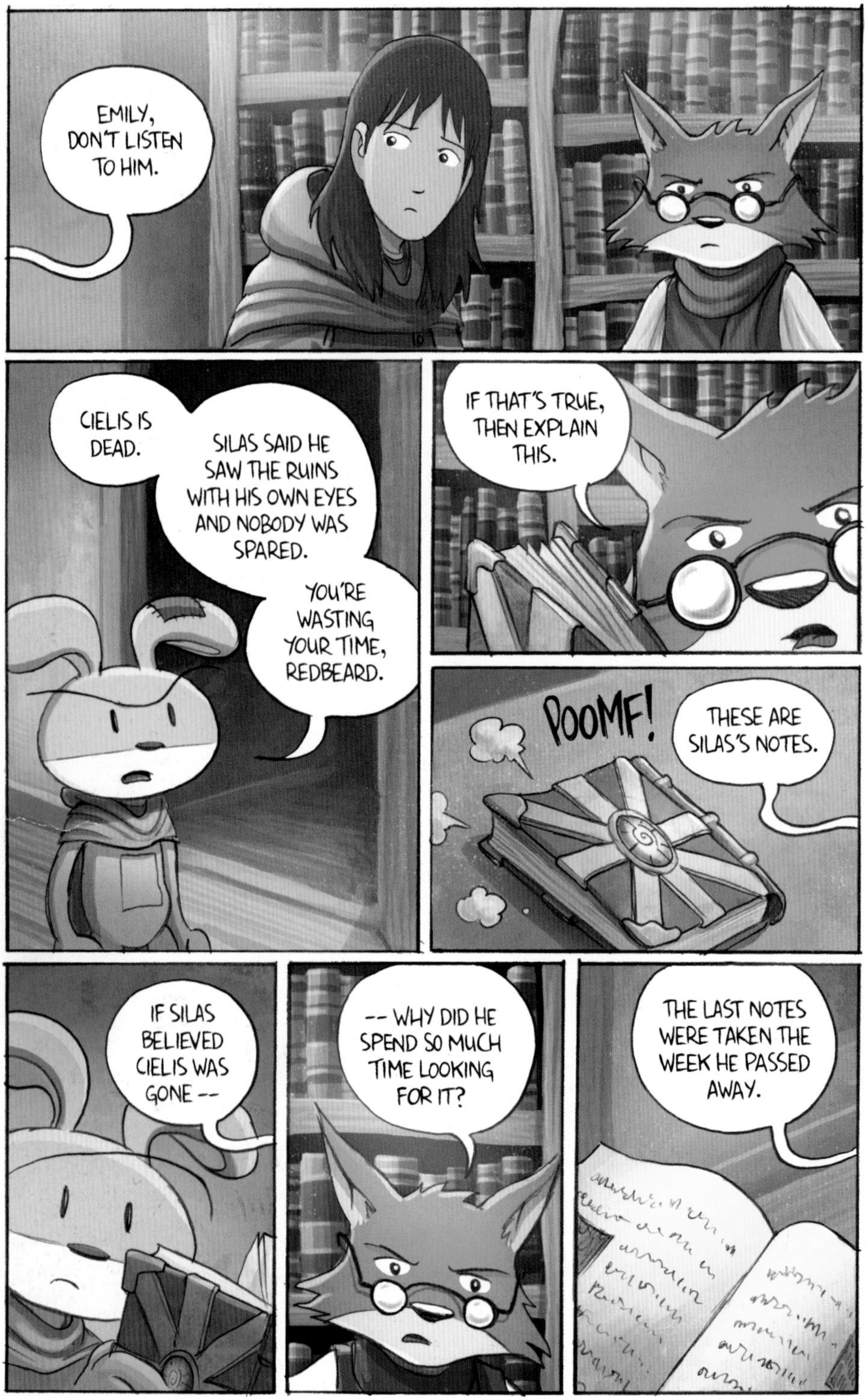
EMILY, DON'T LISTEN TO HIM.
CIELIS IS DEAD.
SILAS SAID HE SAW THE RUINS WITH HIS OWN EYES AND NOBODY WAS SPARED.
YOU'RE WASTING YOUR TIME, REDBEARD.
IF THAT'S TRUE, THEN EXPLAIN THIS.
POOMF!
THESE ARE SILAS'S NOTES.
IF SILAS BELIEVED CIELIS WAS GONE --
-- WHY DID HE SPEND SO MUCH TIME LOOKING FOR IT?
THE LAST NOTES WERE TAKEN THE WEEK HE PASSED AWAY.

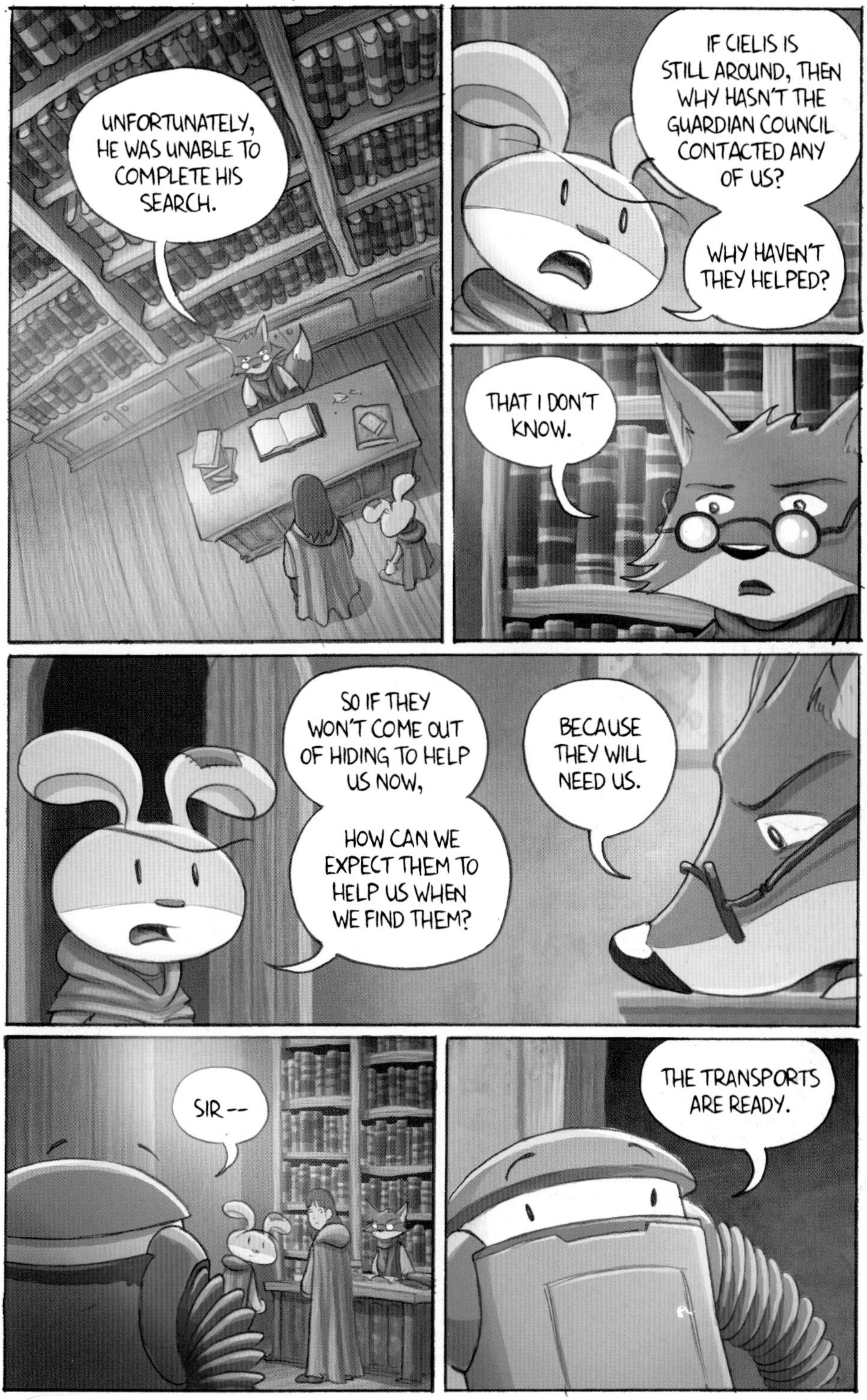
UNFORTUNATELY, HE WAS UNABLE TO COMPLETE HIS SEARCH.
IF CIELIS IS STILL AROUND, THEN WHY HASN'T THE GUARDIAN COUNCIL CONTACTED ANY OF US?
WHY HAVEN'T THEY HELPED?
THAT I DON'T KNOW.
SO IF THEY WON'T COME OUT OF HIDING TO HELP US NOW,
HOW CAN WE EXPECT THEM TO HELP US WHEN WE FIND THEM?
BECAUSE THEY WILL NEED US.
SIR --
THE TRANSPORTS ARE READY.

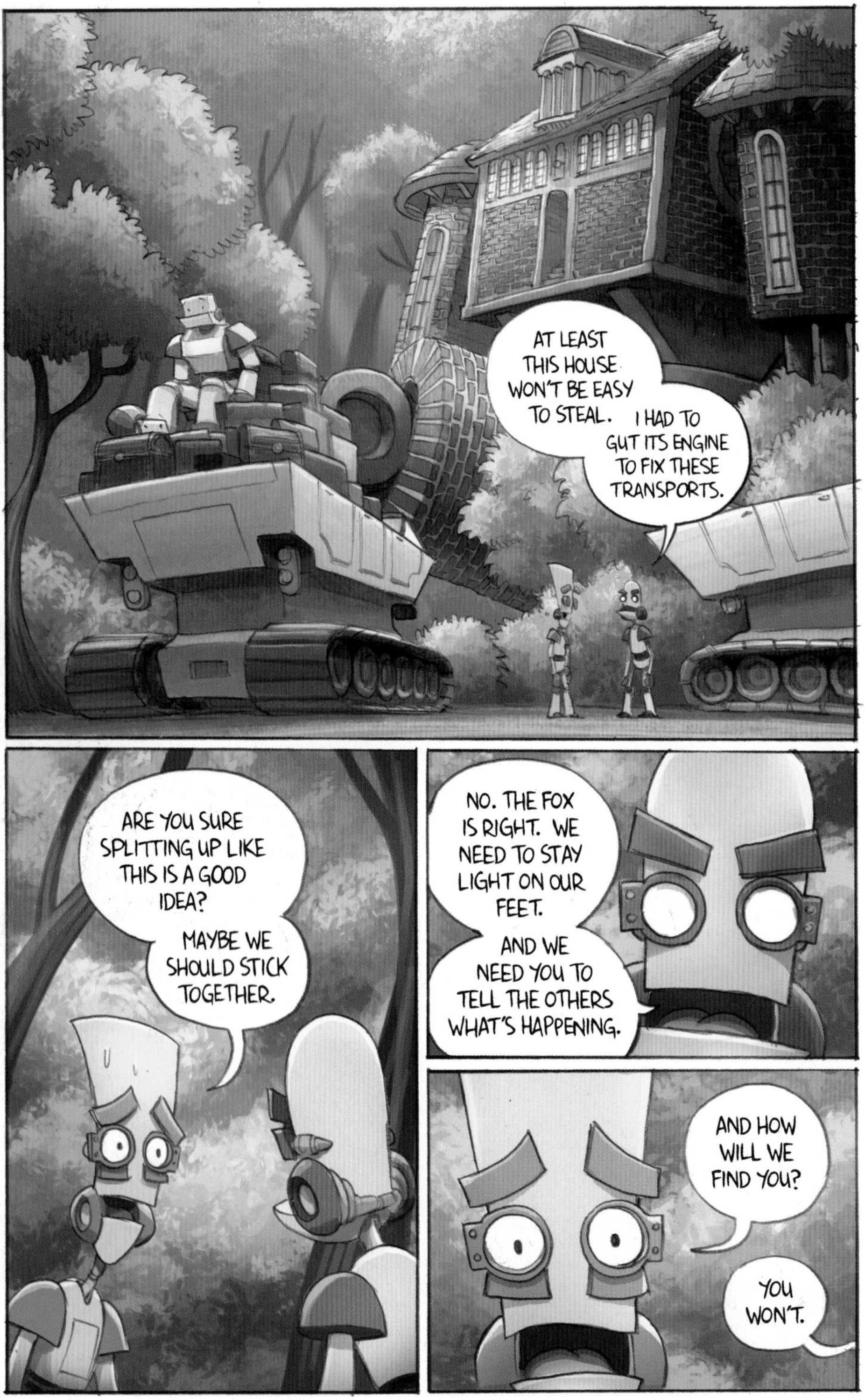

AT LEAST THIS HOUSE WON'T BE EASY TO STEAL.
I HAD TO GUT ITS ENGINE TO FIX THESE TRANSPORTS.
ARE YOU SURE SPLITTING UP LIKE THIS IS A GOOD IDEA?
MAYBE WE SHOULD STICK TOGETHER.
NO. THE FOX IS RIGHT. WE NEED TO STAY LIGHT ON OUR FEET.
AND WE NEED YOU TO TELL THE OTHERS WHAT'S HAPPENING.
AND HOW WILL WE FIND YOU?
YOU WON'T.

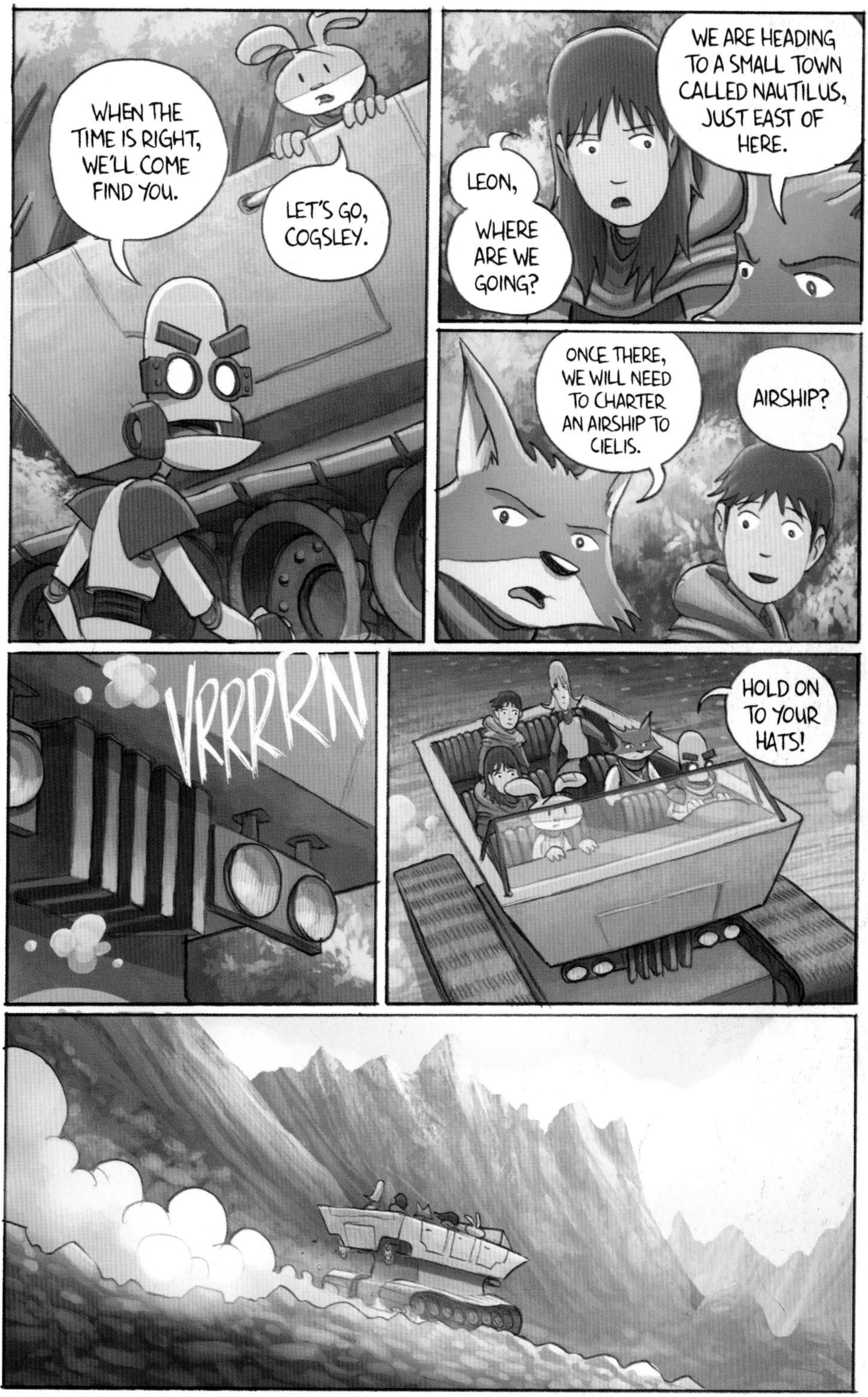
WHEN THE TIME IS RIGHT, WE'LL COME FIND YOU.
LET'S GO, COGSLEY.
LEON,
WHERE ARE WE GOING?
WE ARE HEADING TO A SMALL TOWN CALLED NAUTILUS, JUST EAST OF HERE.
ONCE THERE, WE WILL NEED TO CHARTER AN AIRSHIP TO CIELIS.
AIRSHIP?
VRRRRN
HOLD ON TO YOUR HATS!

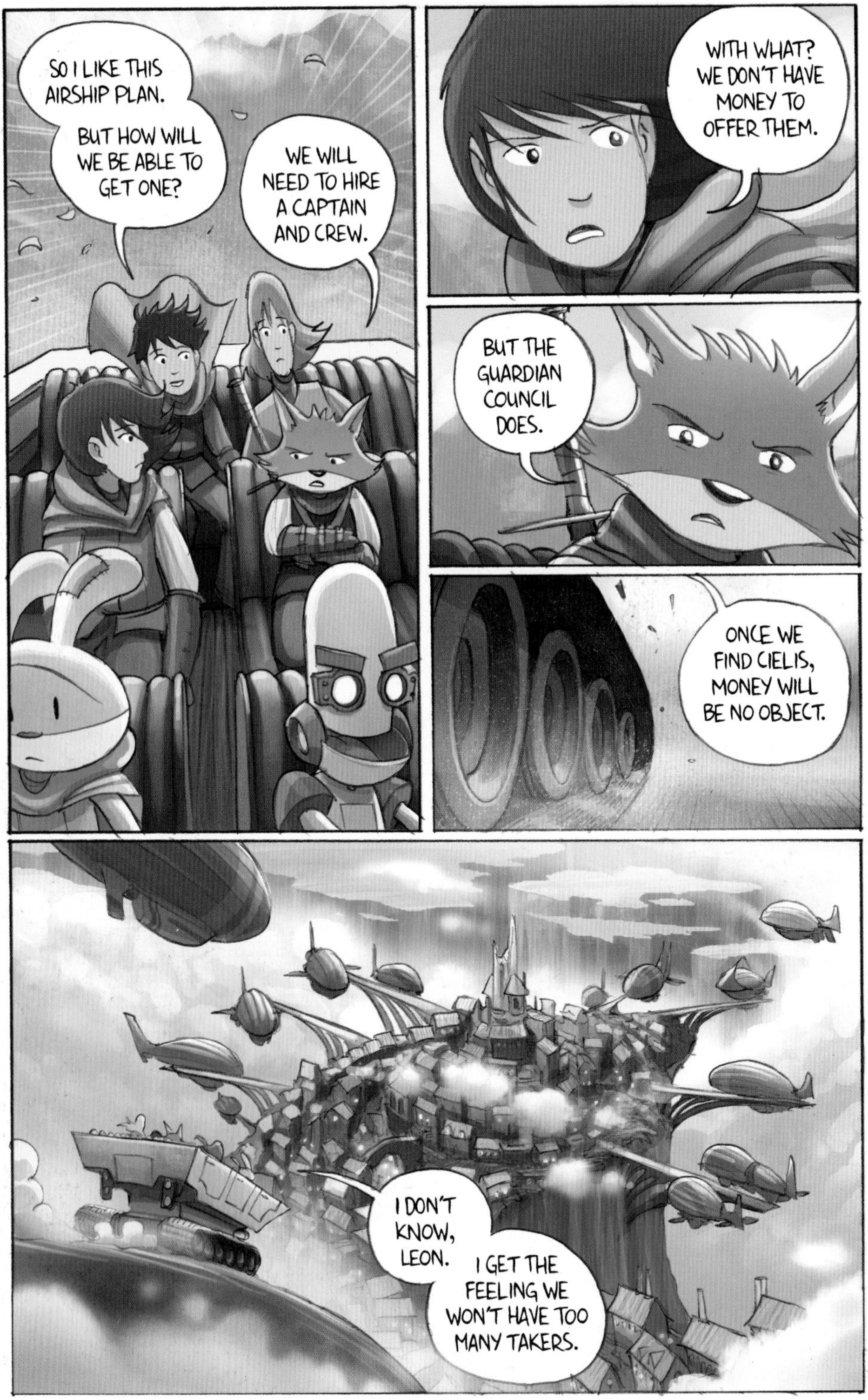
SO I LIKE THIS AIRSHIP PLAN.
BUT HOW WILL WE BE ABLE TO GET ONE?
WE WILL NEED TO HIRE A CAPTAIN AND CREW.
WITH WHAT? WE DON'T HAVE MONEY TO OFFER THEM.
BUT THE GUARDIAN COUNCIL DOES.
ONCE WE FIND CIELIS, MONEY WILL BE NO OBJECT.
I DON'T KNOW, LEON.
I GET THE FEELING WE WON'T HAVE TOO MANY TAKERS.

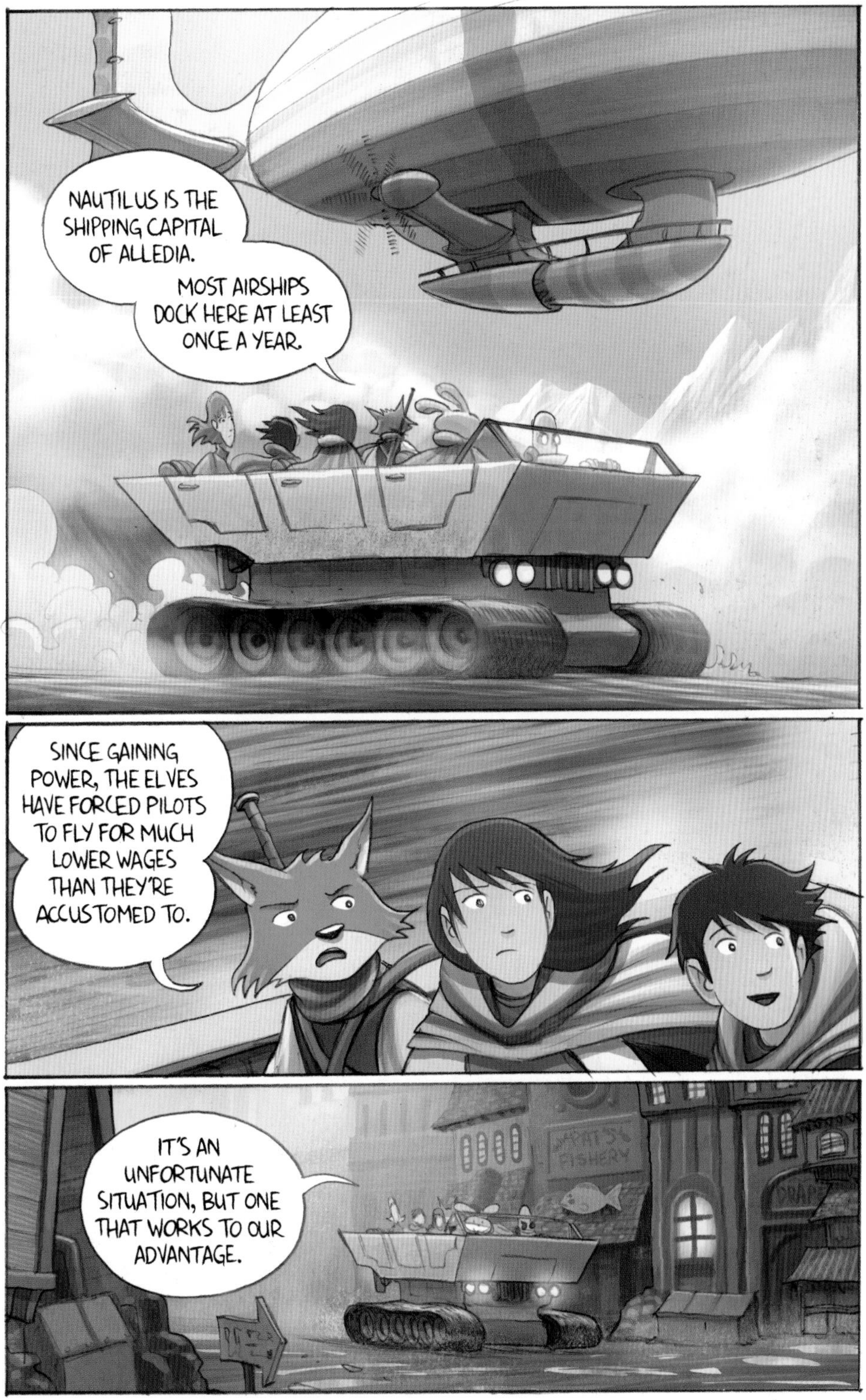
NAUTILUS IS THE SHIPPING CAPITAL OF ALLEDIA.
MOST AIRSHIPS DOCK HERE AT LEAST ONCE A YEAR.
SINCE GAINING POWER, THE ELVES HAVE FORCED PILOTS TO FLY FOR MUCH LOWER WAGES THAN THEY'RE ACCUSTOMED TO.
IT'S AN UNFORTUNATE SITUATION, BUT ONE THAT WORKS TO OUR ADVANTAGE.

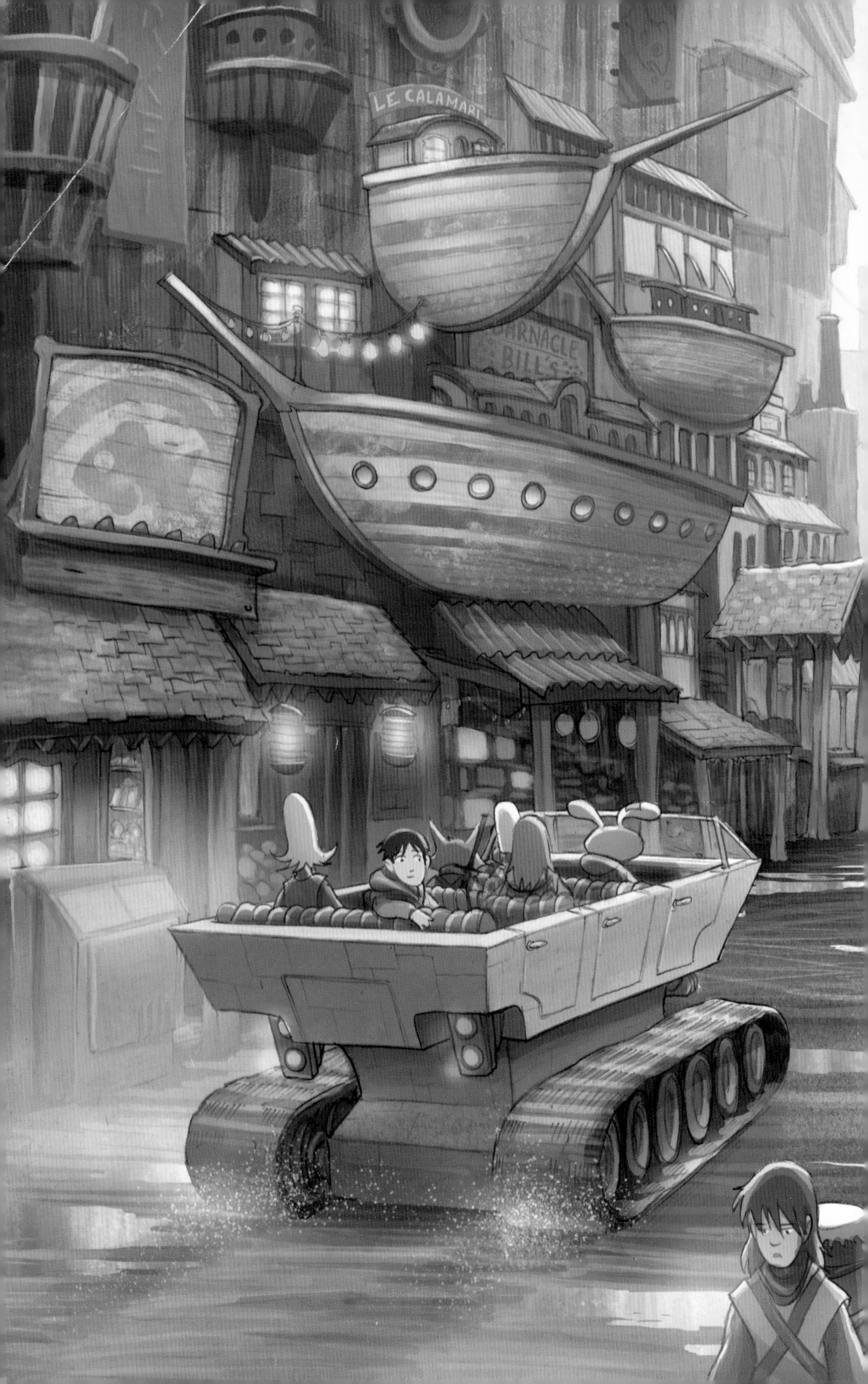
LE CALAMARI
ARNACLE BILL'S

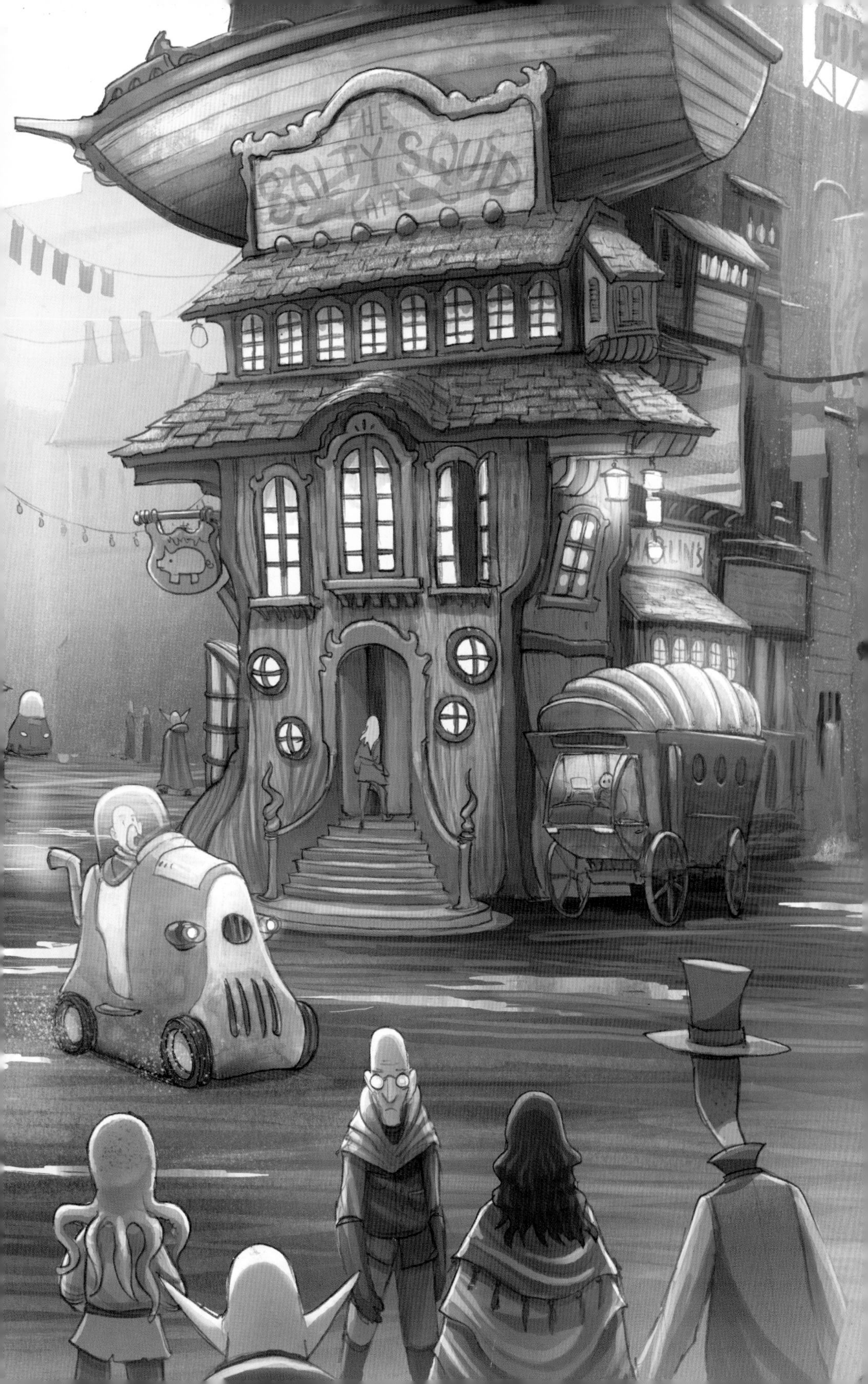
THE
SALTY SQUID
CAFE

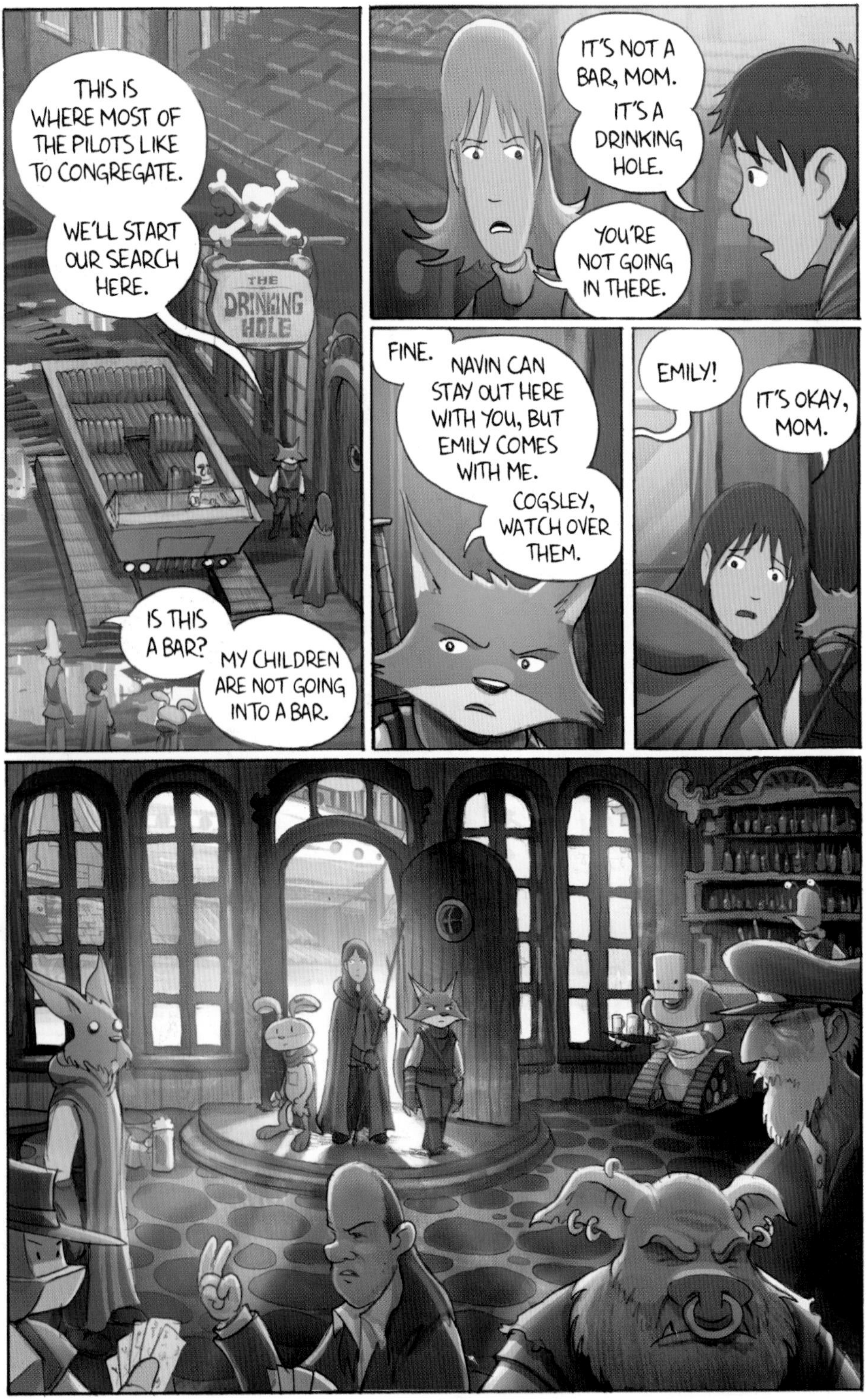
THIS IS WHERE MOST OF THE PILOTS LIKE TO CONGREGATE.
WE'LL START OUR SEARCH HERE.
THE DRINKING HOLE
IS THIS A BAR?
MY CHILDREN ARE NOT GOING INTO A BAR.
IT'S NOT A BAR, MOM.
IT'S A DRINKING HOLE.
YOU'RE NOT GOING IN THERE.
FINE.
NAVIN CAN STAY OUT HERE WITH YOU, BUT EMILY COMES WITH ME.
COGSLEY, WATCH OVER THEM.
EMILY!
IT'S OKAY, MOM.

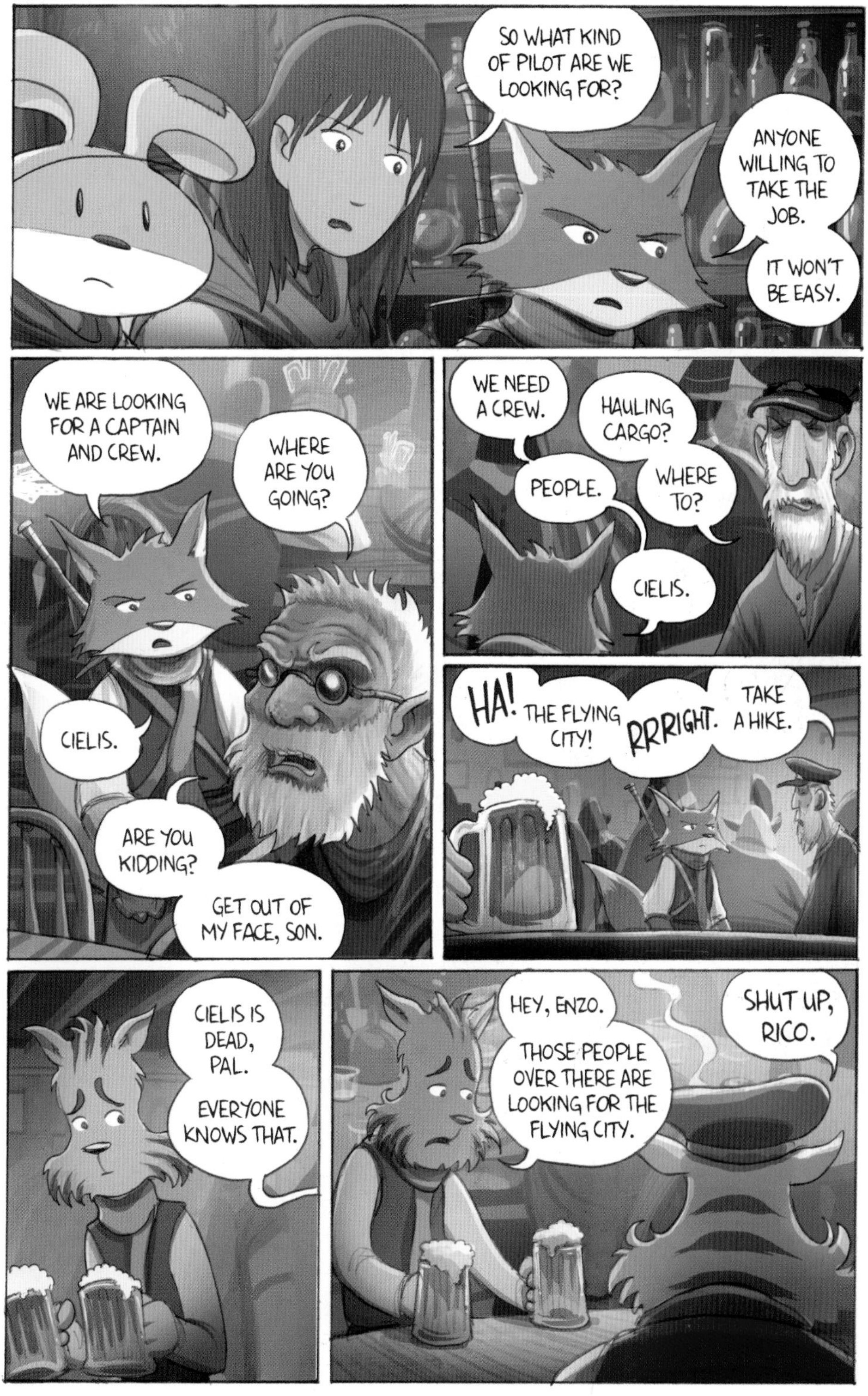
SO WHAT KIND OF PILOT ARE WE LOOKING FOR?
ANYONE WILLING TO TAKE THE JOB.
IT WON'T BE EASY.
WE ARE LOOKING FOR A CAPTAIN AND CREW.
WHERE ARE YOU GOING?
CIELIS.
ARE YOU KIDDING?
GET OUT OF MY FACE, SON.
WE NEED A CREW.
HAULING CARGO?
PEOPLE.
WHERE TO?
CIELIS.
HA!
THE FLYING CITY!
RRRIGHT.
TAKE A HIKE.
CIELIS IS DEAD, PAL.
EVERYONE KNOWS THAT.
HEY, ENZO.
THOSE PEOPLE OVER THERE ARE LOOKING FOR THE FLYING CITY.
SHUT UP, RICO.

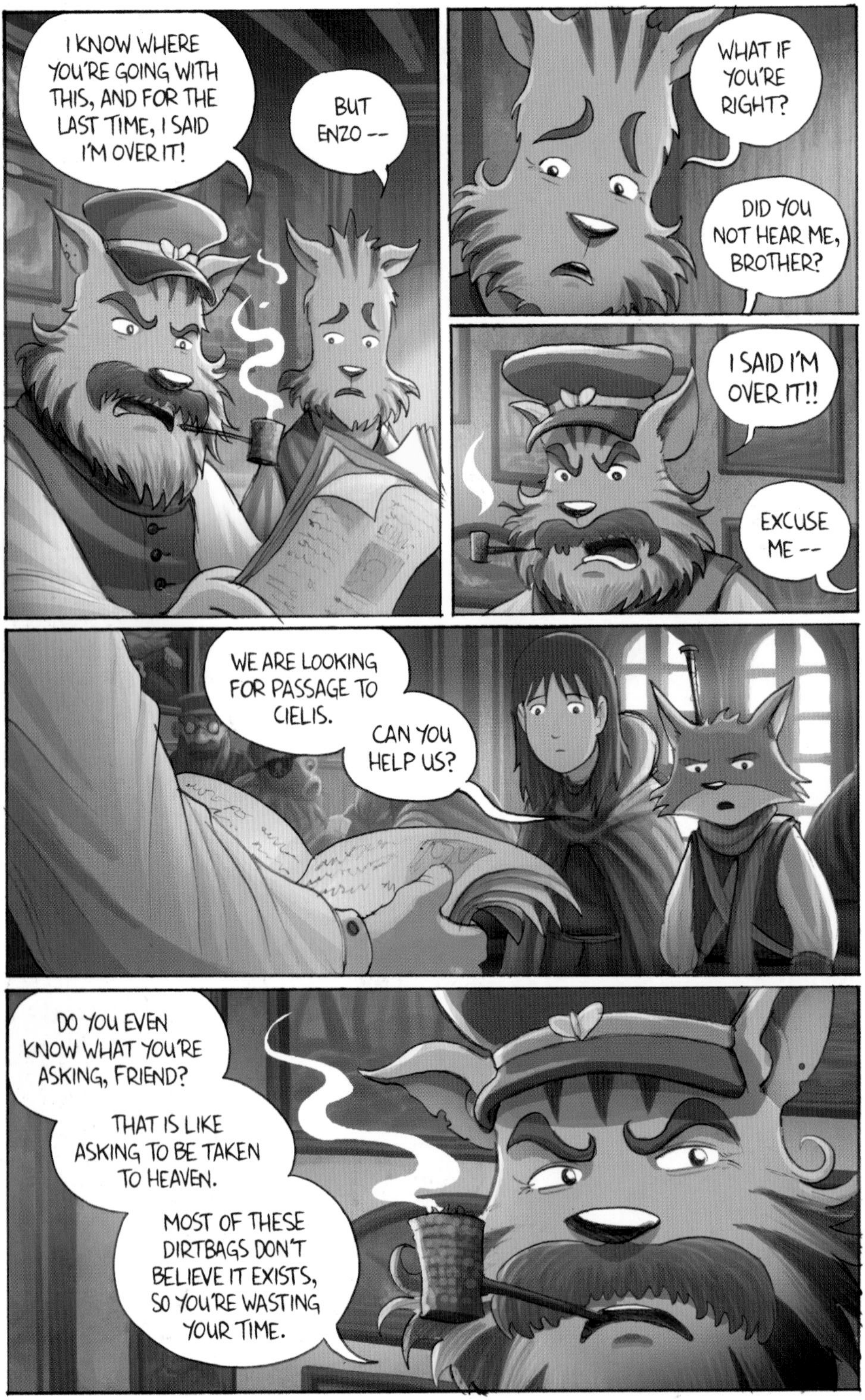
I KNOW WHERE YOU'RE GOING WITH THIS, AND FOR THE LAST TIME, I SAID I'M OVER IT!
BUT ENZO --
WHAT IF YOU'RE RIGHT?
DID YOU NOT HEAR ME, BROTHER?
I SAID I'M OVER IT!!
EXCUSE ME --
WE ARE LOOKING FOR PASSAGE TO CIELIS.
CAN YOU HELP US?
DO YOU EVEN KNOW WHAT YOU'RE ASKING, FRIEND?
THAT IS LIKE ASKING TO BE TAKEN TO HEAVEN.
MOST OF THESE DIRTBAGS DON'T BELIEVE IT EXISTS, SO YOU'RE WASTING YOUR TIME.

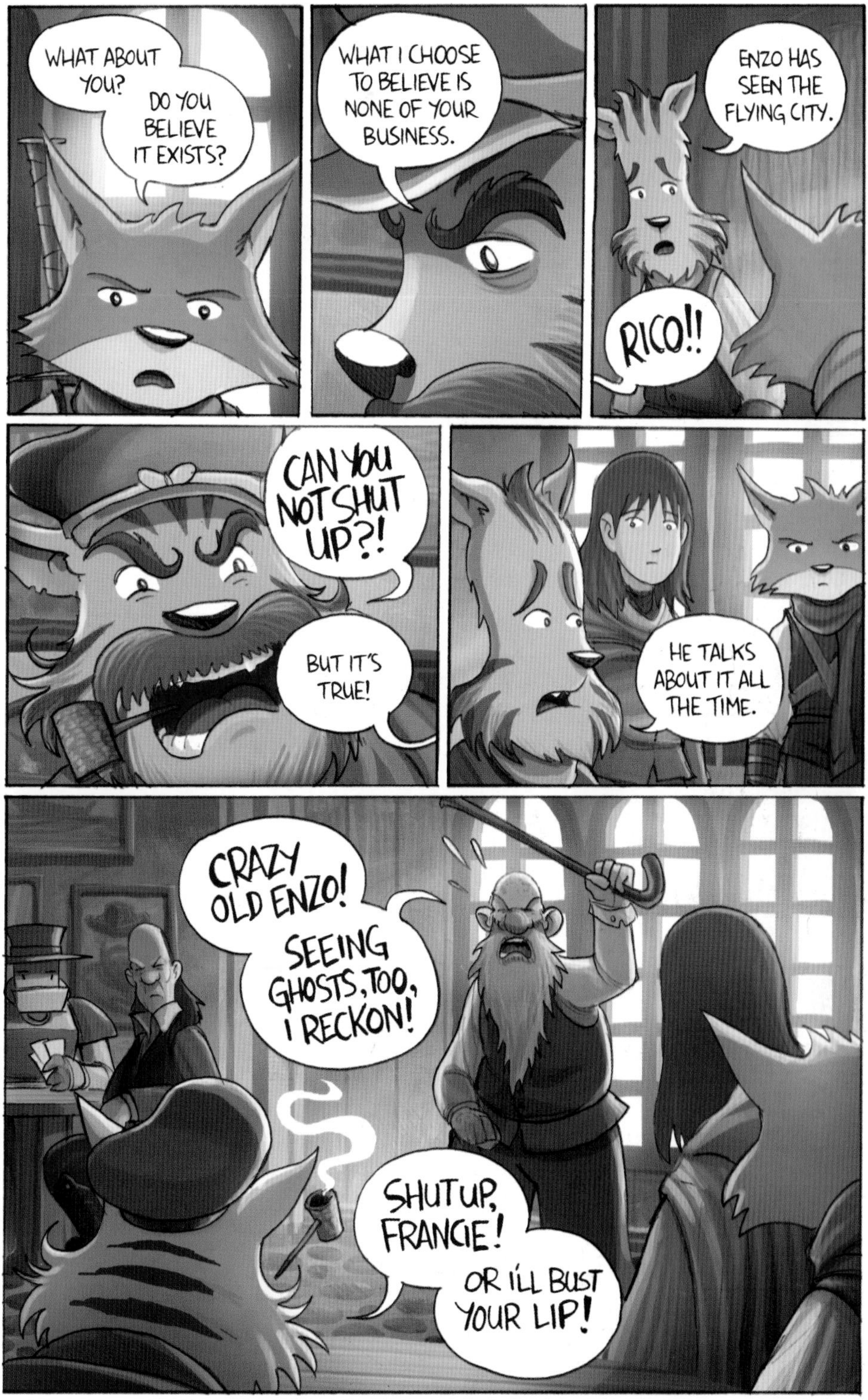
WHAT ABOUT YOU?
DO YOU BELIEVE IT EXISTS?
WHAT I CHOOSE TO BELIEVE IS NONE OF YOUR BUSINESS.
ENZO HAS SEEN THE FLYING CITY.
RICO!!
CAN YOU NOT SHUT UP?!
BUT IT'S TRUE!
HE TALKS ABOUT IT ALL THE TIME.
CRAZY OLD ENZO!
SEEING GHOSTS, TOO, I RECKON!
SHUT UP, FRANCIE!
OR I'LL BUST YOUR LIP!

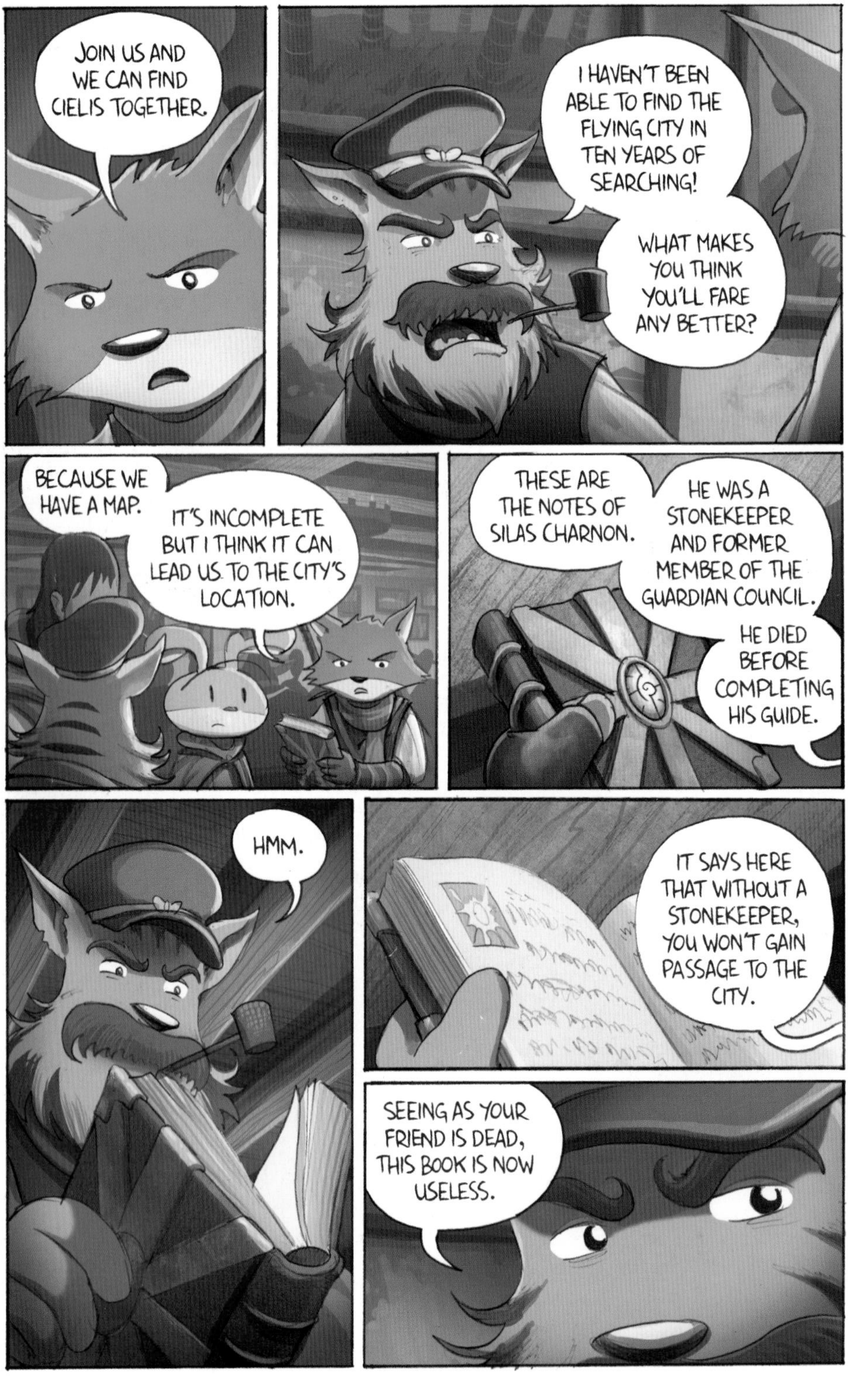
JOIN US AND WE CAN FIND CIELIS TOGETHER.
I HAVEN'T BEEN ABLE TO FIND THE FLYING CITY IN TEN YEARS OF SEARCHING!
WHAT MAKES YOU THINK YOU'LL FARE ANY BETTER?
BECAUSE WE HAVE A MAP.
IT'S INCOMPLETE BUT I THINK IT CAN LEAD US TO THE CITY'S LOCATION.
THESE ARE THE NOTES OF SILAS CHARNON.
HE WAS A STONEKEEPER AND FORMER MEMBER OF THE GUARDIAN COUNCIL.
HE DIED BEFORE COMPLETING HIS GUIDE.
HMM.
IT SAYS HERE THAT WITHOUT A STONEKEEPER, YOU WON'T GAIN PASSAGE TO THE CITY.
SEEING AS YOUR FRIEND IS DEAD, THIS BOOK IS NOW USELESS.

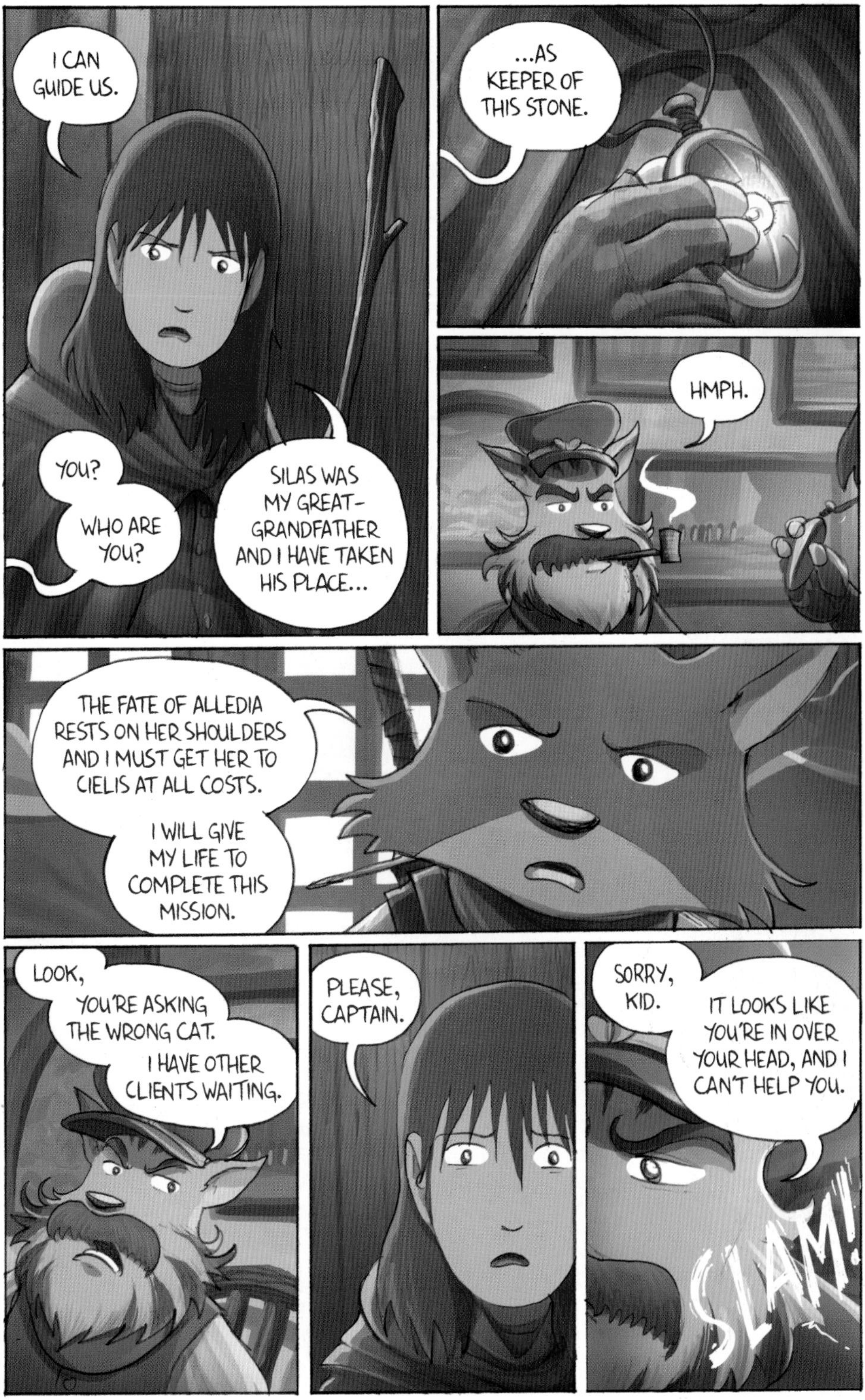
I CAN GUIDE US.
...AS KEEPER OF THIS STONE.
HMPH.
YOU?
WHO ARE YOU?
SILAS WAS MY GREAT-GRANDFATHER AND I HAVE TAKEN HIS PLACE...
THE FATE OF ALLEDIA RESTS ON HER SHOULDERS AND I MUST GET HER TO CIELIS AT ALL COSTS.
I WILL GIVE MY LIFE TO COMPLETE THIS MISSION.
LOOK, YOU'RE ASKING THE WRONG CAT.
I HAVE OTHER CLIENTS WAITING.
PLEASE, CAPTAIN.
SORRY, KID.
IT LOOKS LIKE YOU'RE IN OVER YOUR HEAD, AND I CAN'T HELP YOU.
SLAM!

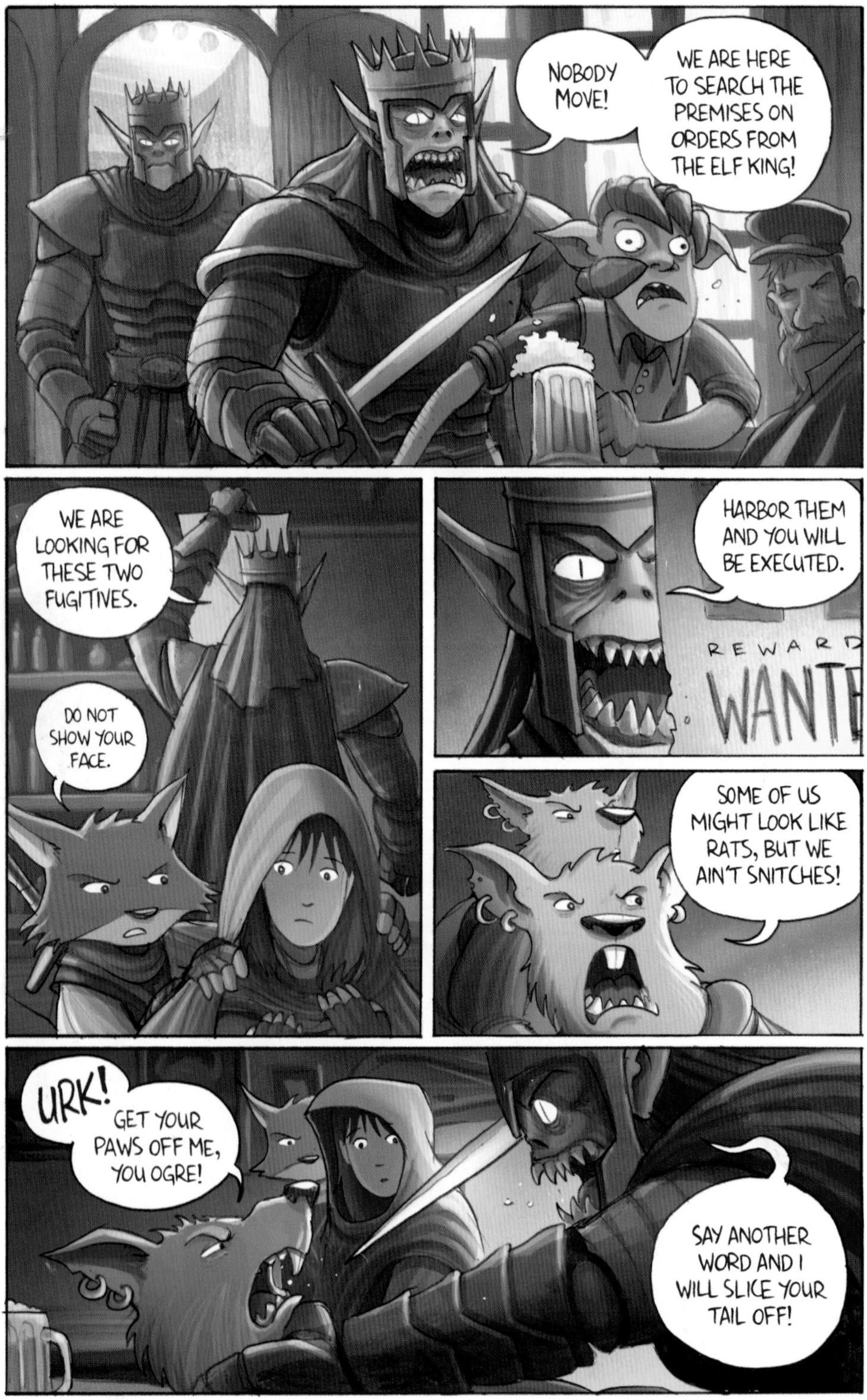
NOBODY MOVE!
WE ARE HERE TO SEARCH THE PREMISES ON ORDERS FROM THE ELF KING!
WE ARE LOOKING FOR THESE TWO FUGITIVES.
HARBOR THEM AND YOU WILL BE EXECUTED.
REWARD
WANTE
DO NOT SHOW YOUR FACE.
SOME OF US MIGHT LOOK LIKE RATS, BUT WE AIN'T SNITCHES!
URK!
GET YOUR PAWS OFF ME, YOU OGRE!
SAY ANOTHER WORD AND I WILL SLICE YOUR TAIL OFF!

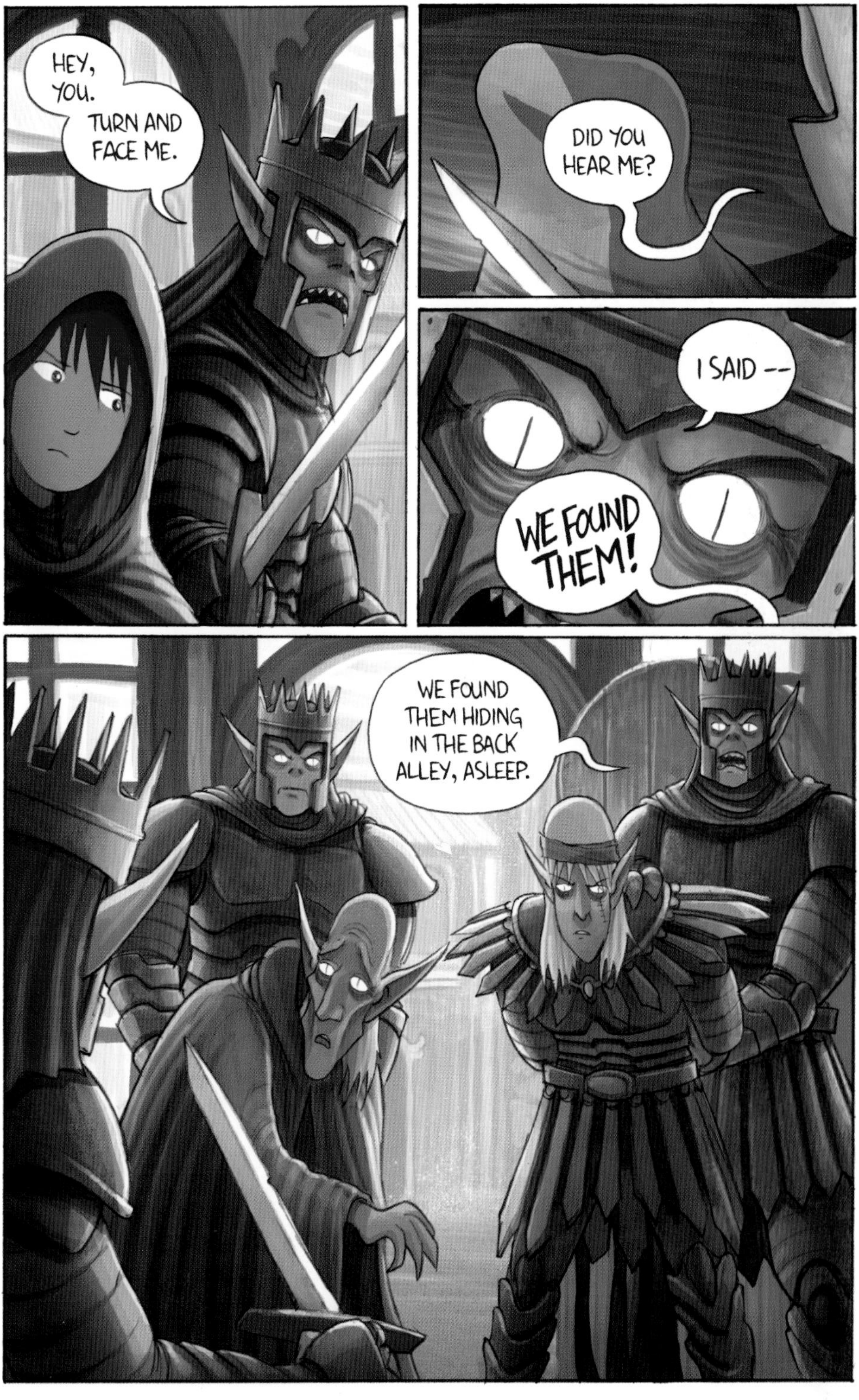
HEY, YOU. TURN AND FACE ME.
DID YOU HEAR ME?
I SAID --
WE FOUND THEM!
WE FOUND THEM HIDING IN THE BACK ALLEY, ASLEEP.

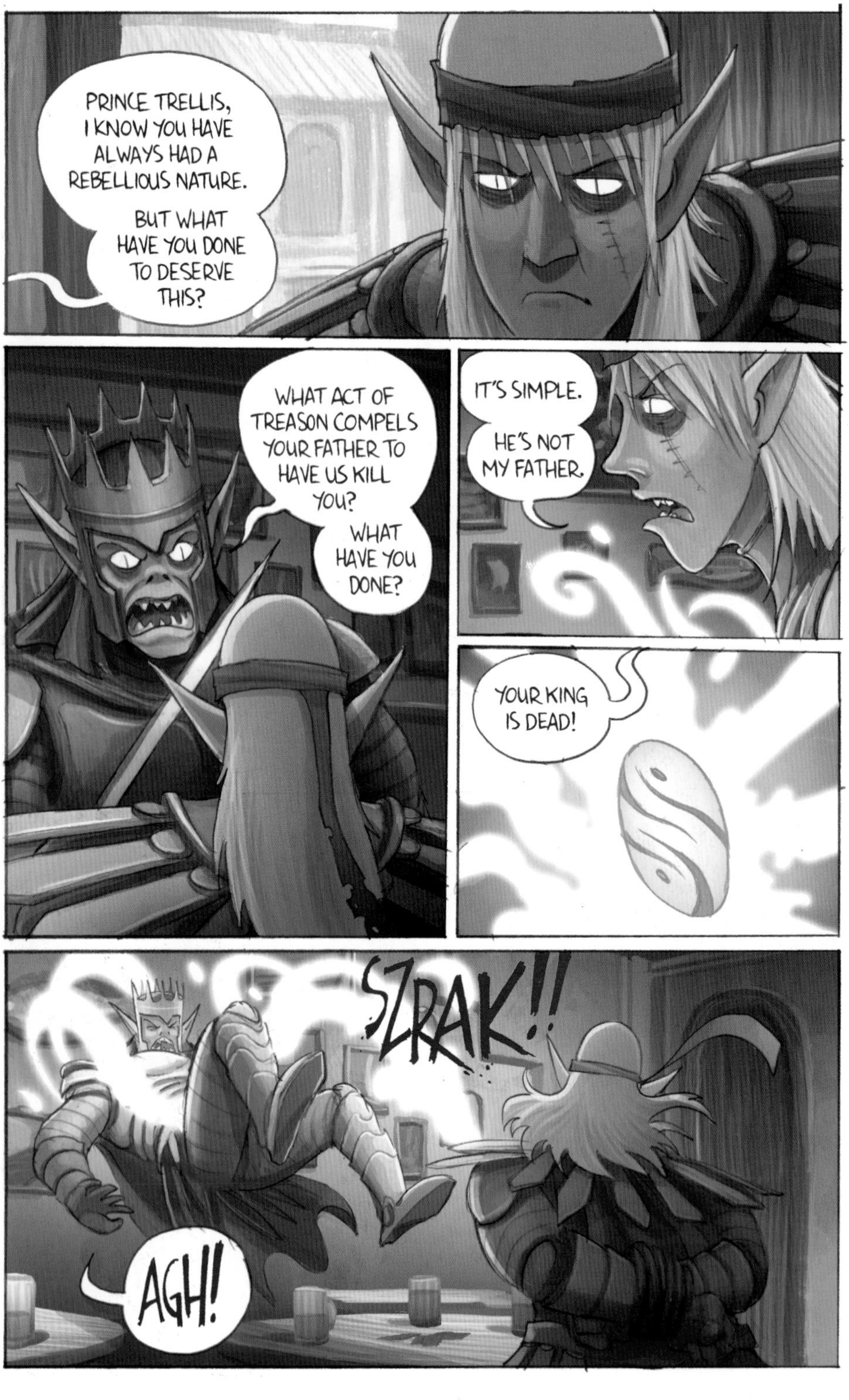
PRINCE TRELLIS, I KNOW YOU HAVE ALWAYS HAD A REBELLIOUS NATURE.
BUT WHAT HAVE YOU DONE TO DESERVE THIS?
WHAT ACT OF TREASON COMPELS YOUR FATHER TO HAVE US KILL YOU?
WHAT HAVE YOU DONE?
IT'S SIMPLE.
HE'S NOT MY FATHER.
YOUR KING IS DEAD!
SZRAK!!
AGH!

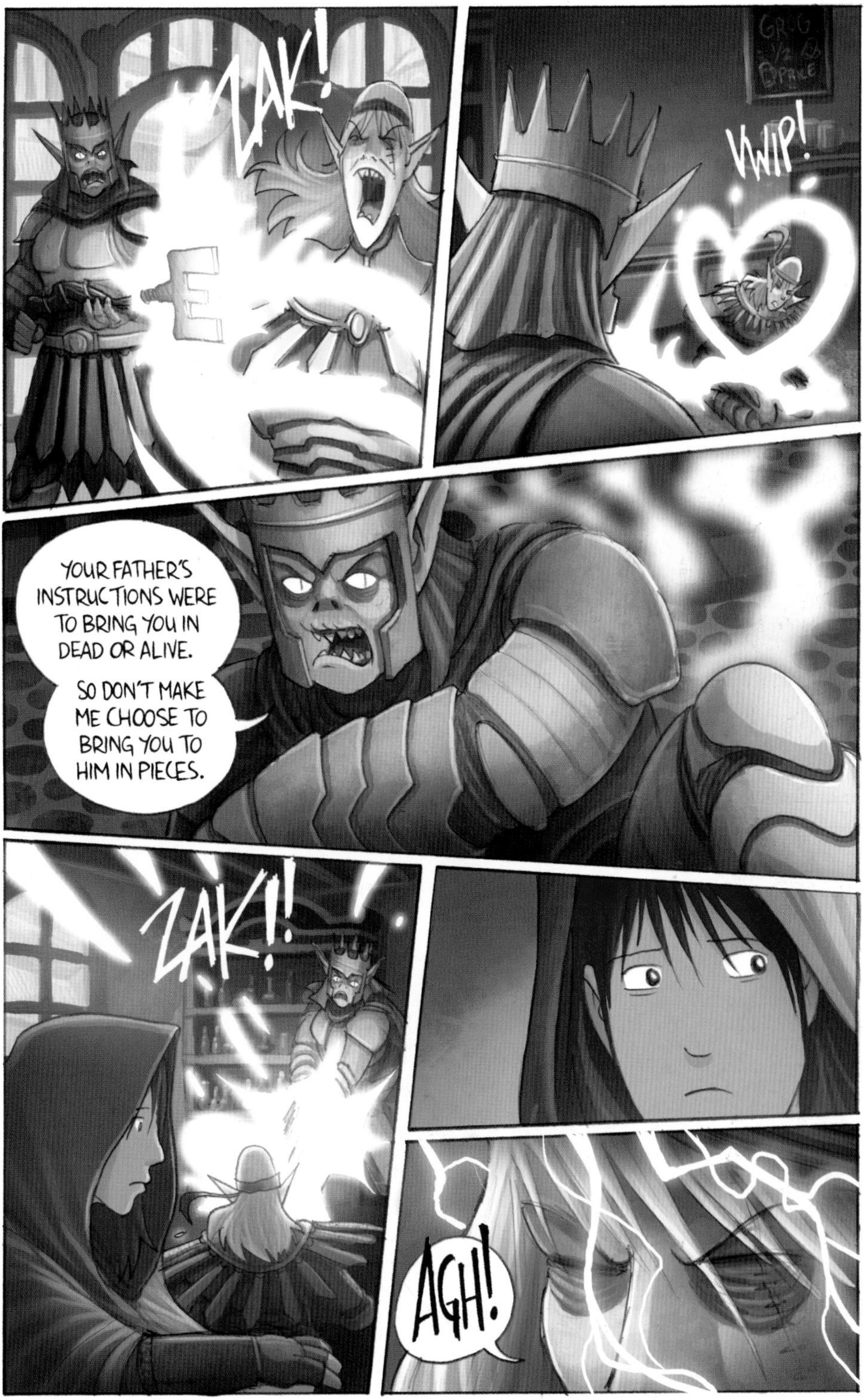
ZAK!
VWIP!
YOUR FATHER'S INSTRUCTIONS WERE TO BRING YOU IN DEAD OR ALIVE.
SO DON'T MAKE ME CHOOSE TO BRING YOU TO HIM IN PIECES.
ZAK!!
AGH!

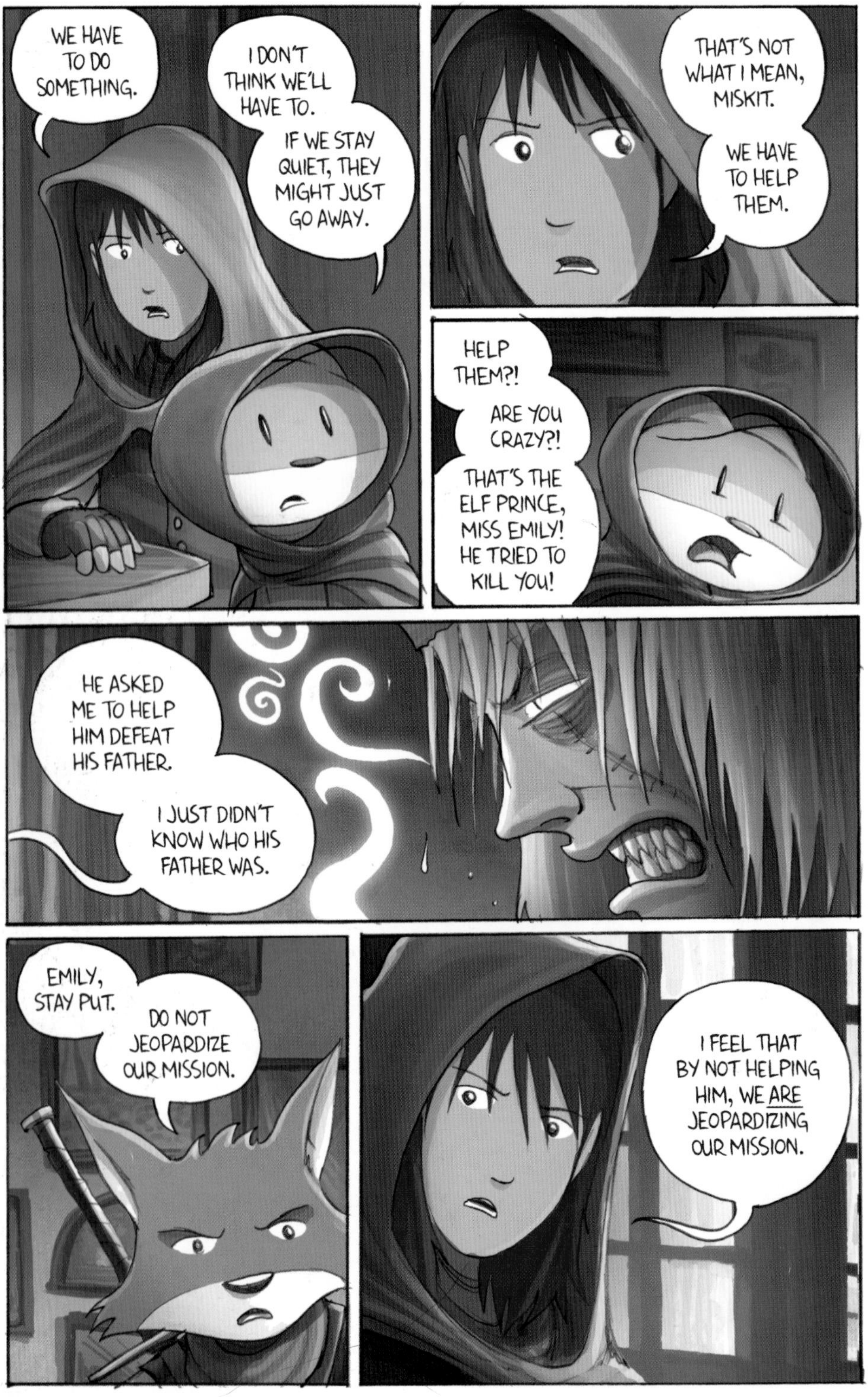
WE HAVE TO DO SOMETHING.
I DON'T THINK WE'LL HAVE TO.
IF WE STAY QUIET, THEY MIGHT JUST GO AWAY.
THAT'S NOT WHAT I MEAN, MISKIT.
WE HAVE TO HELP THEM.
HELP THEM?!
ARE YOU CRAZY?!
THAT'S THE ELF PRINCE, MISS EMILY! HE TRIED TO KILL YOU!
HE ASKED ME TO HELP HIM DEFEAT HIS FATHER.
I JUST DIDN'T KNOW WHO HIS FATHER WAS.
EMILY, STAY PUT.
DO NOT JEOPARDIZE OUR MISSION.
I FEEL THAT BY NOT HELPING HIM, WE ARE JEOPARDIZING OUR MISSION.

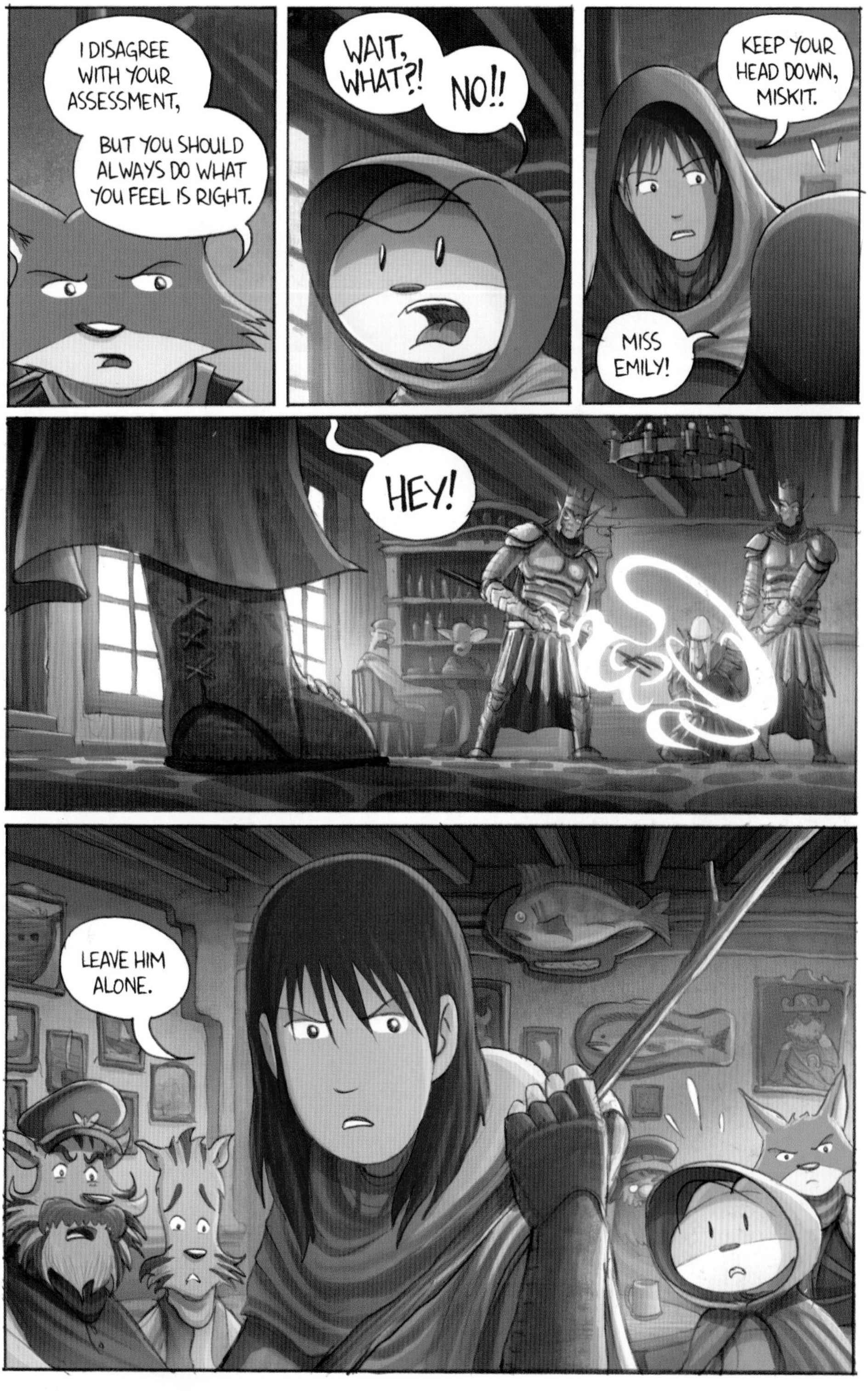
I DISAGREE WITH YOUR ASSESSMENT,
BUT YOU SHOULD ALWAYS DO WHAT YOU FEEL IS RIGHT.
WAIT, WHAT?!
NO!!
KEEP YOUR HEAD DOWN, MISKIT.
MISS EMILY!
HEY!
LEAVE HIM ALONE.

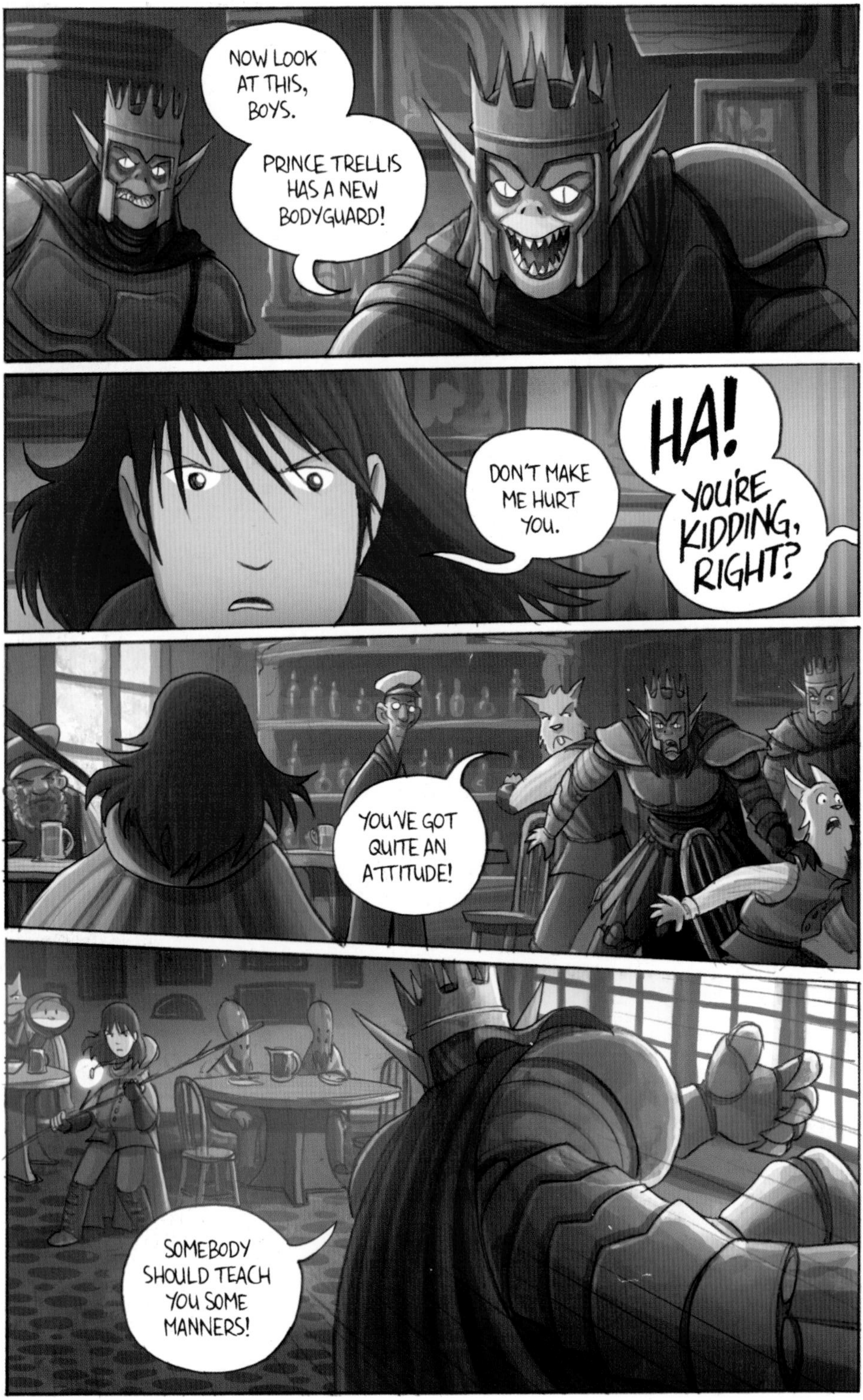
NOW LOOK AT THIS, BOYS.
PRINCE TRELLIS HAS A NEW BODYGUARD!
DON'T MAKE ME HURT YOU.
HA! YOU'RE KIDDING, RIGHT?
YOU'VE GOT QUITE AN ATTITUDE!
SOMEBODY SHOULD TEACH YOU SOME MANNERS!

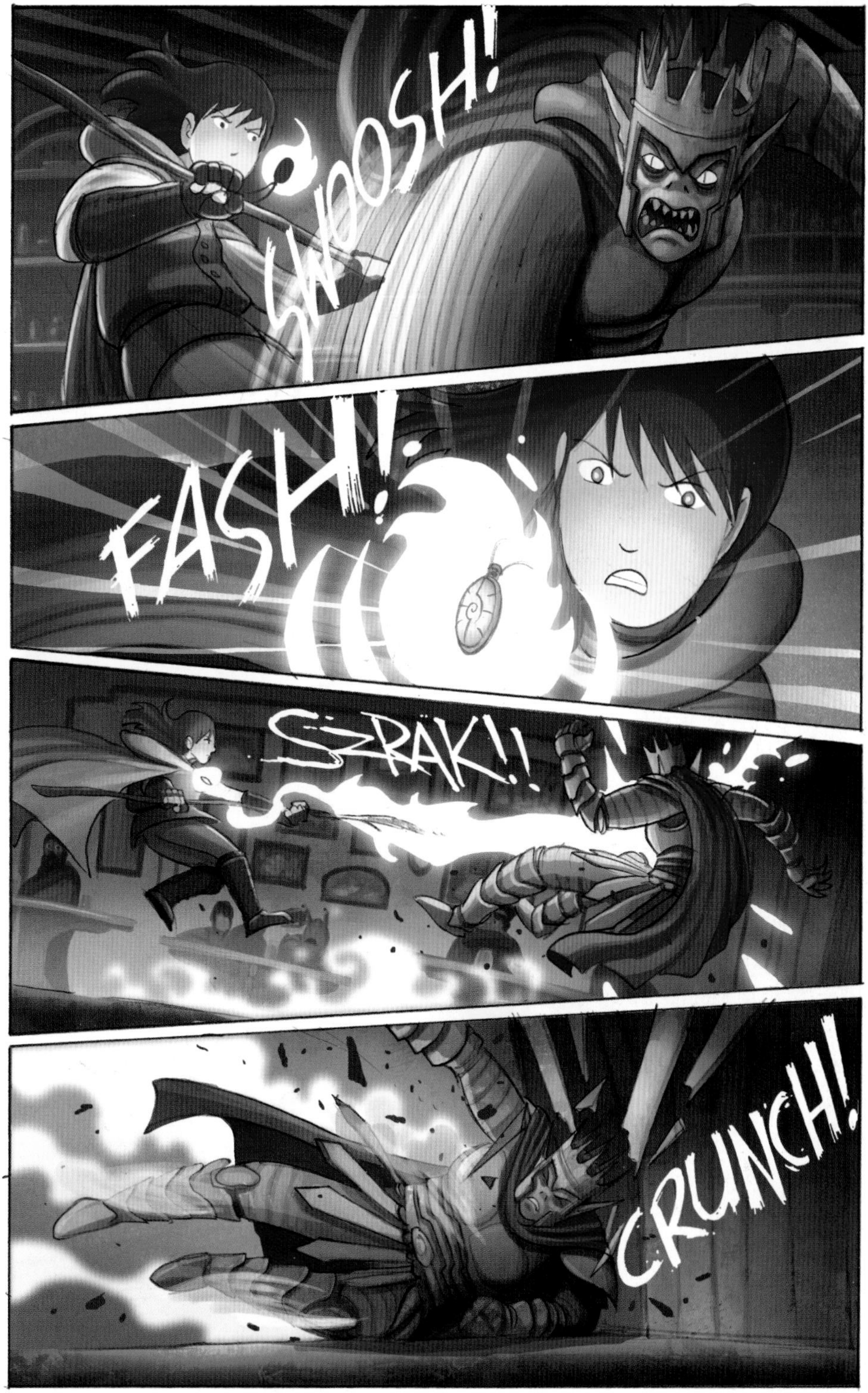
SWOOSH!
FASH!
SZRAK!!
CRUNCH!

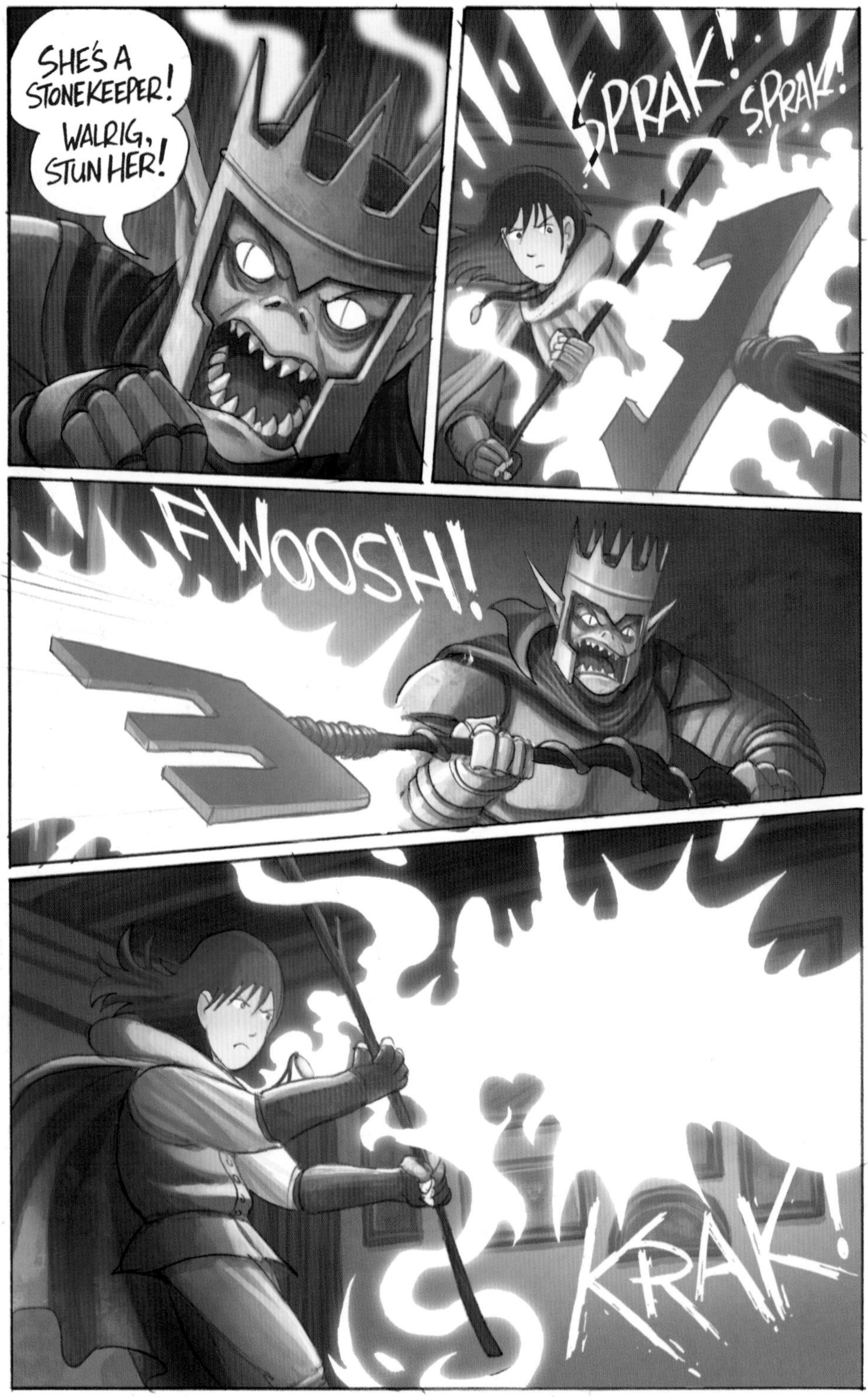
SHE'S A STONEKEEPER!
WALRIG, STUN HER!
SPRAK!
SPRAK!
FWOOSH!
KRAK!

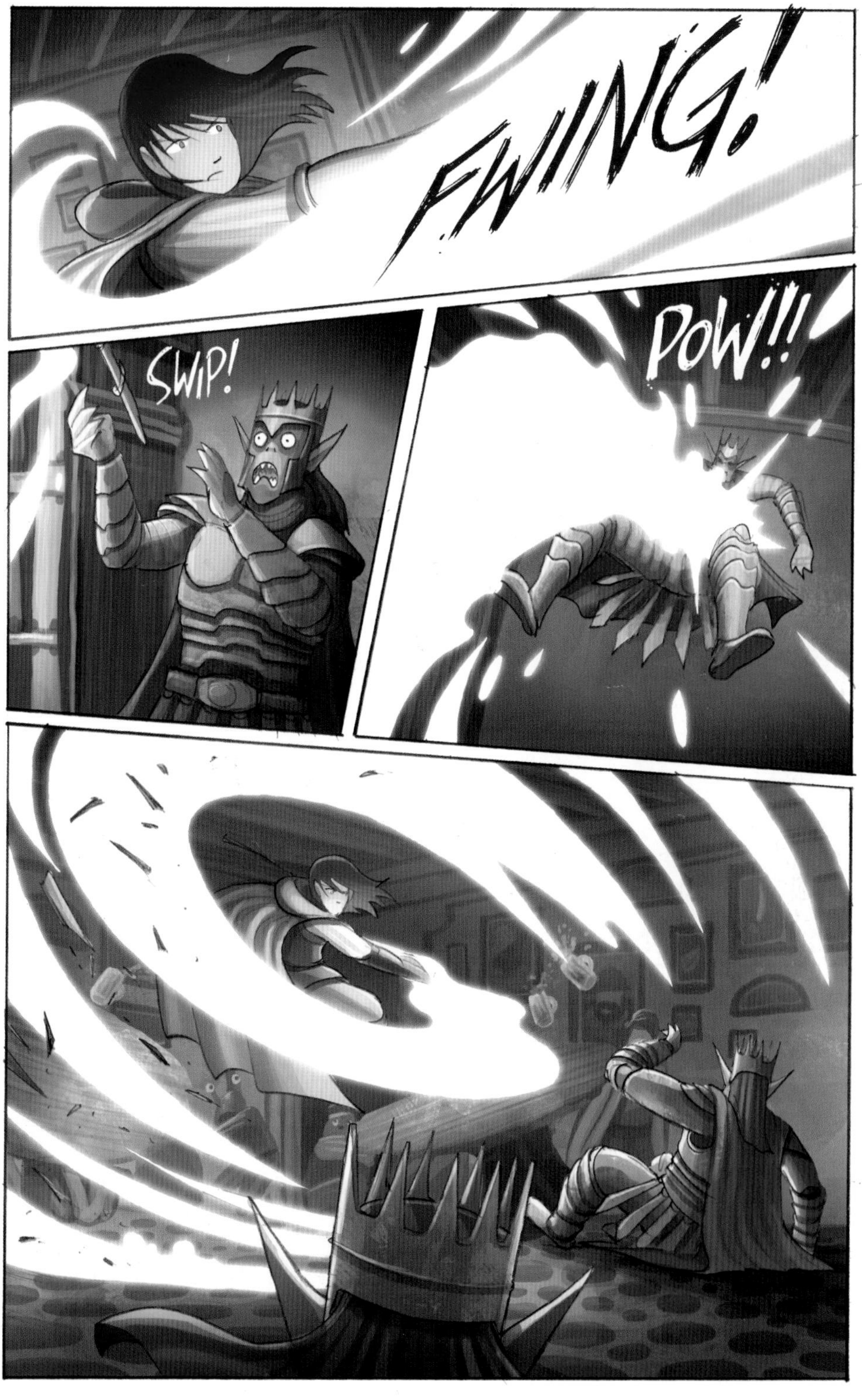
FWING!
SWIP!
POW!!

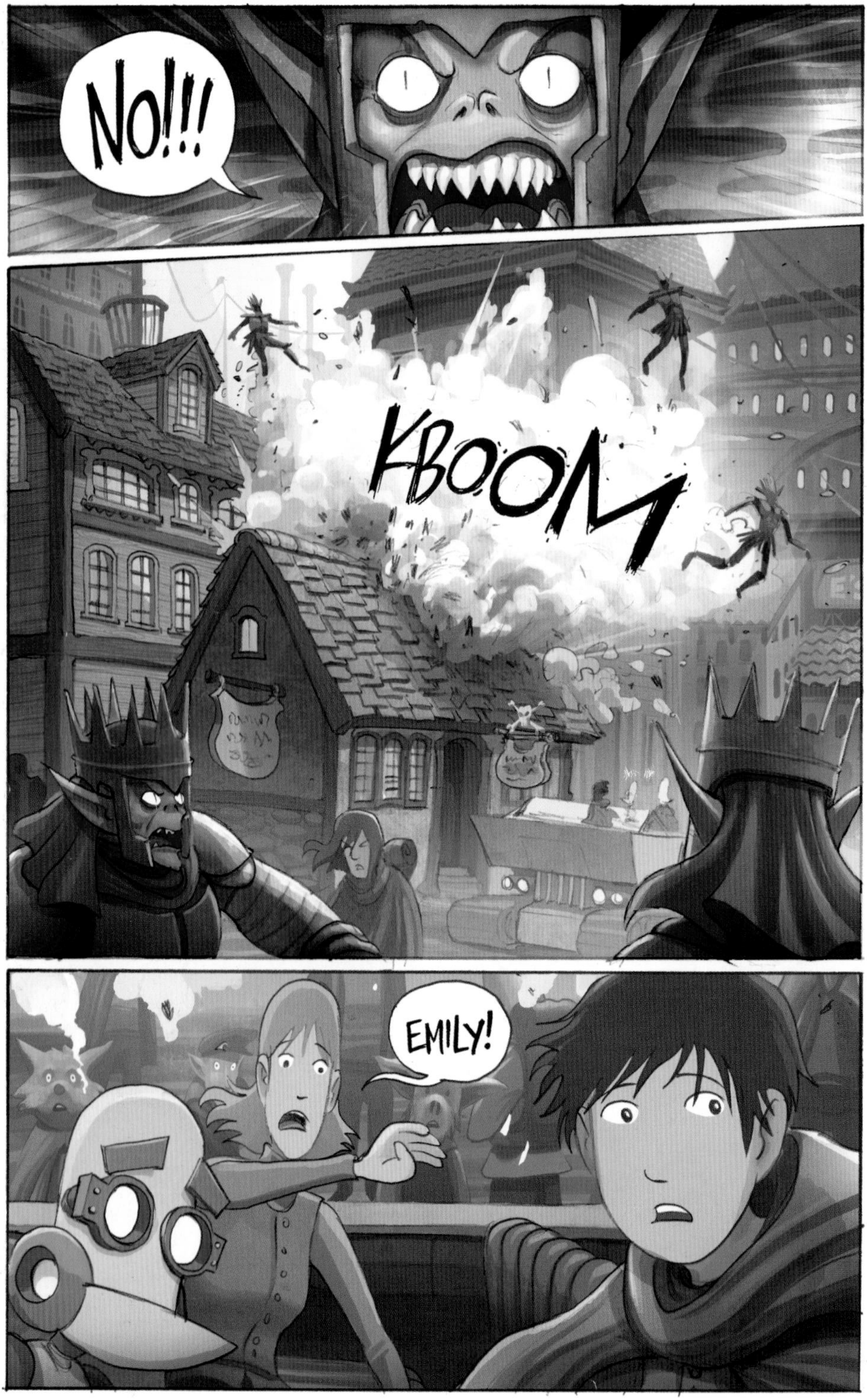
No!!!
KBOOM
EMILY!

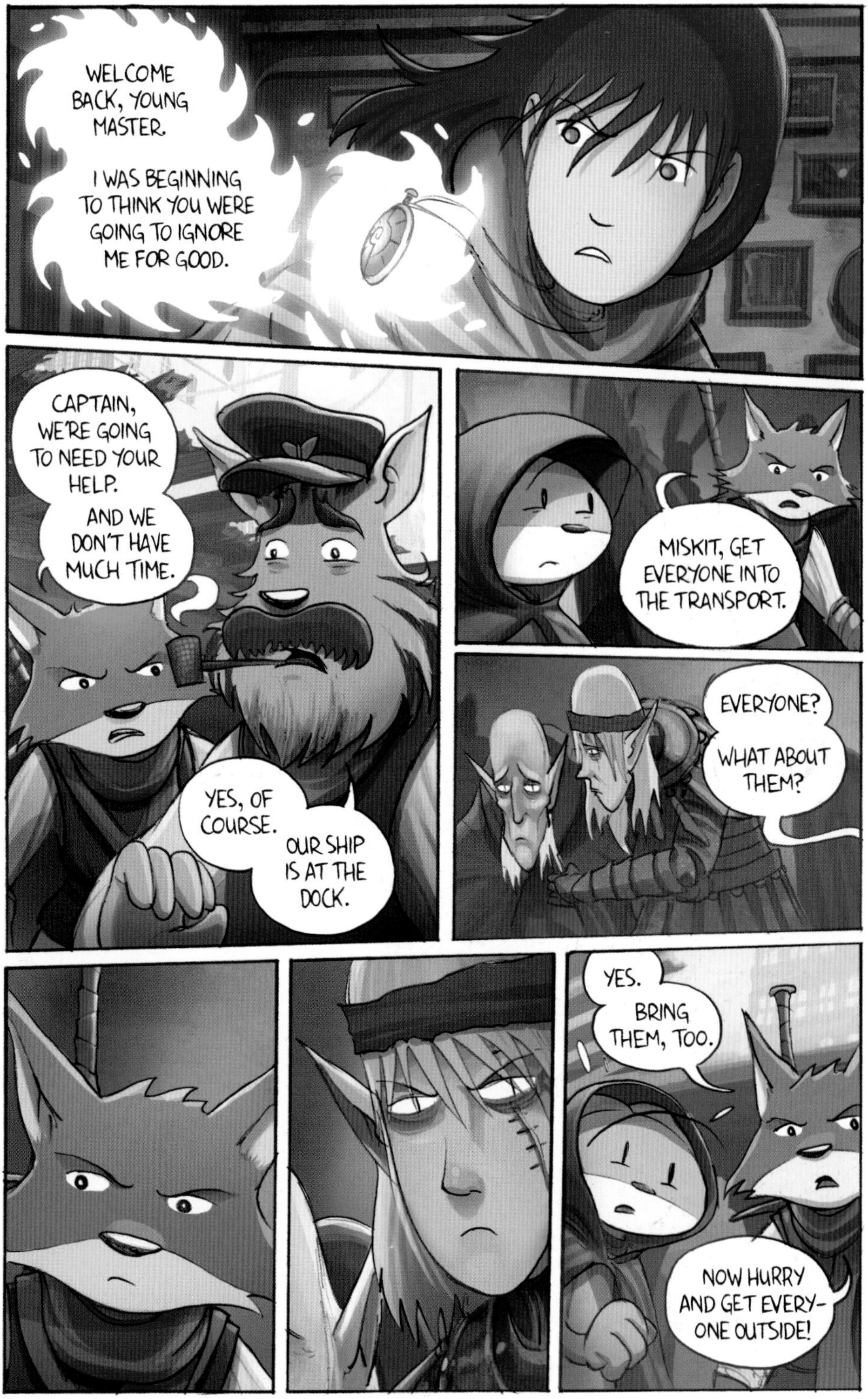
WELCOME BACK, YOUNG MASTER.
I WAS BEGINNING TO THINK YOU WERE GOING TO IGNORE ME FOR GOOD.
CAPTAIN, WE'RE GOING TO NEED YOUR HELP.
AND WE DON'T HAVE MUCH TIME.
YES, OF COURSE.
OUR SHIP IS AT THE DOCK.
MISKIT, GET EVERYONE INTO THE TRANSPORT.
EVERYONE?
WHAT ABOUT THEM?
YES.
BRING THEM, TOO.
NOW HURRY AND GET EVERY-ONE OUTSIDE!

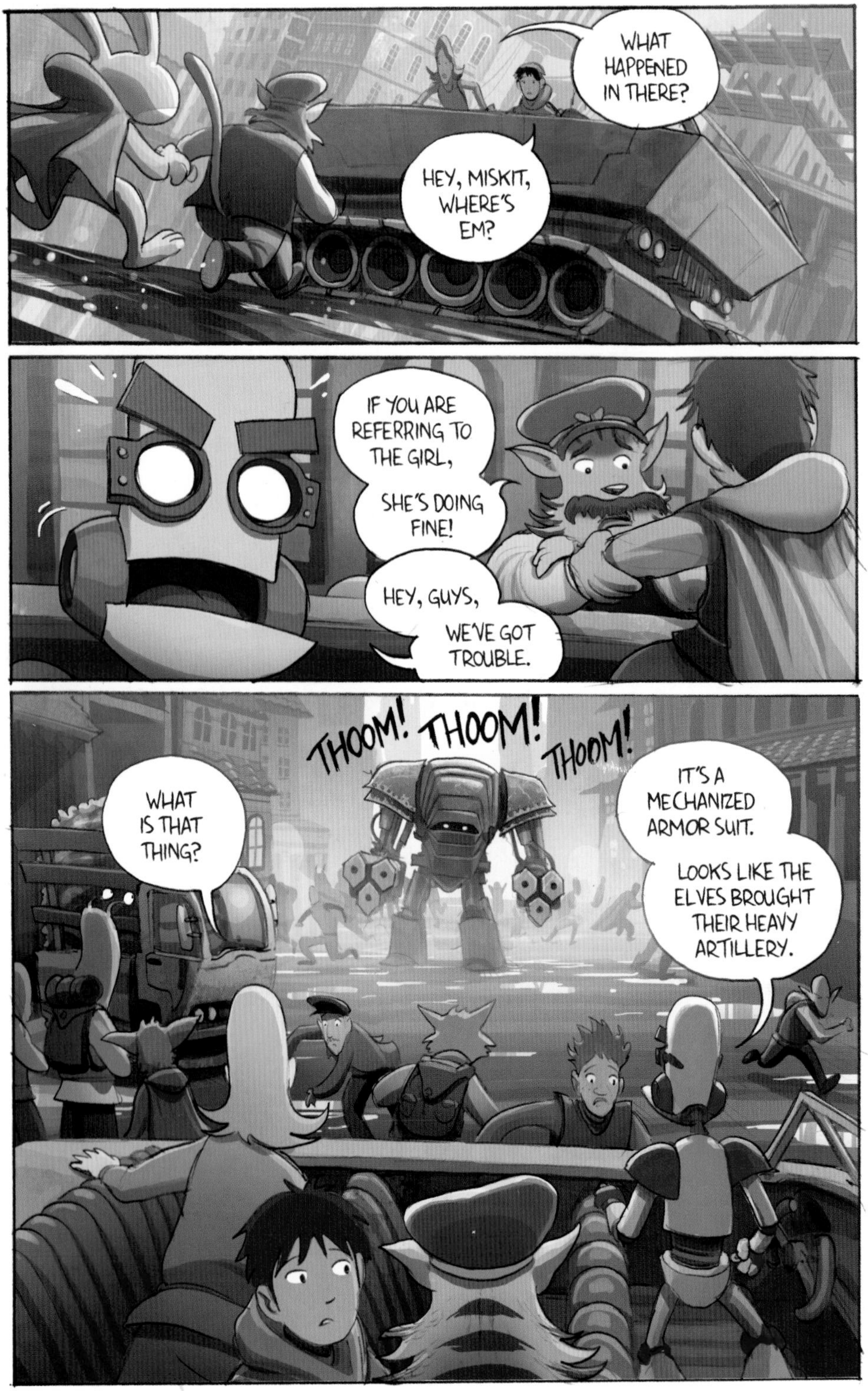
WHAT HAPPENED IN THERE?
HEY, MISKIT, WHERE'S EM?
IF YOU ARE REFERRING TO THE GIRL,
SHE'S DOING FINE!
HEY, GUYS,
WE'VE GOT TROUBLE.
THOOM! THOOM! THOOM!
WHAT IS THAT THING?
IT'S A MECHANIZED ARMOR SUIT.
LOOKS LIKE THE ELVES BROUGHT THEIR HEAVY ARTILLERY.

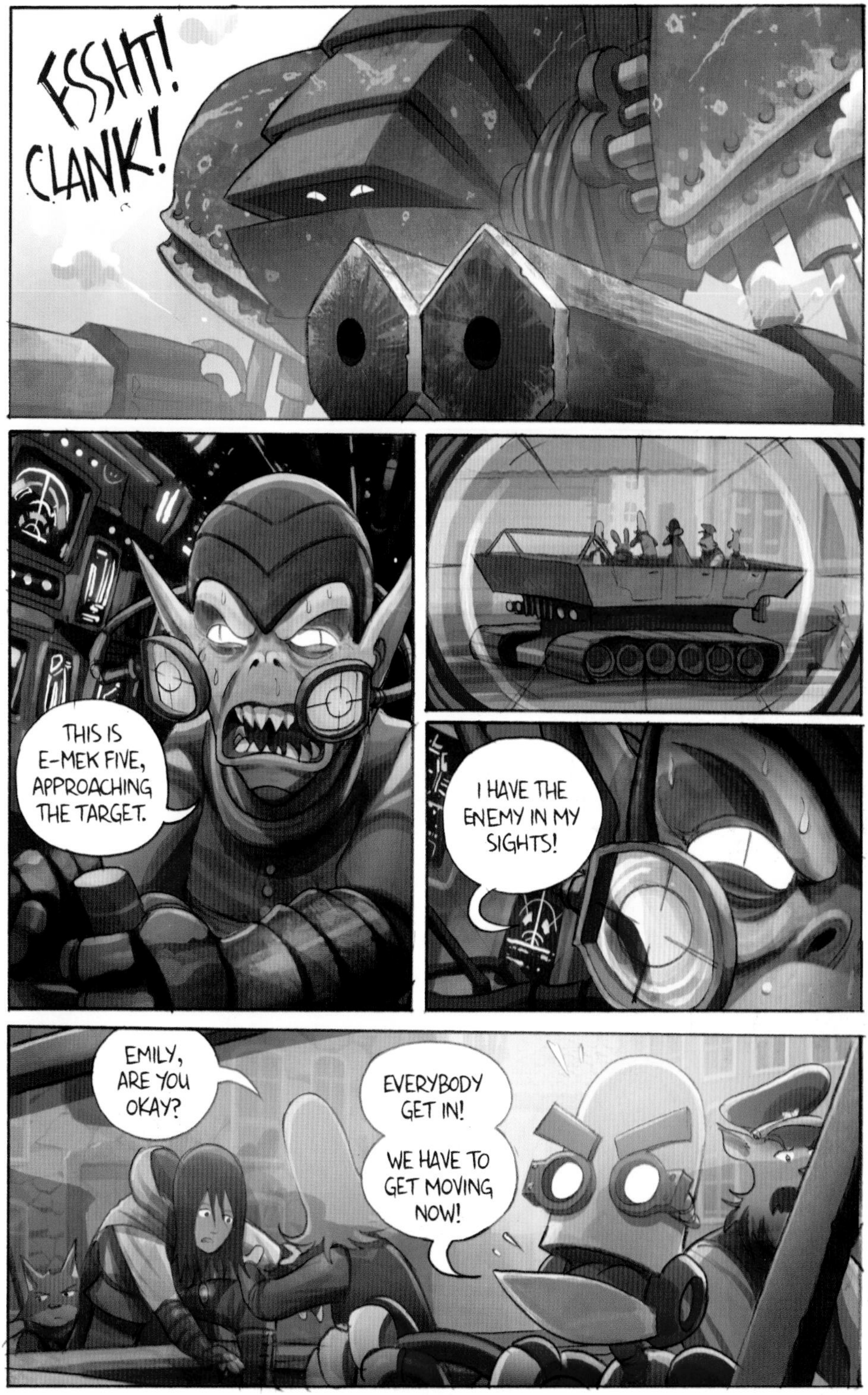
ESSHT! CLANK!
THIS IS E-MEK FIVE, APPROACHING THE TARGET.
I HAVE THE ENEMY IN MY SIGHTS!
EMILY, ARE YOU OKAY?
EVERYBODY GET IN!
WE HAVE TO GET MOVING NOW!

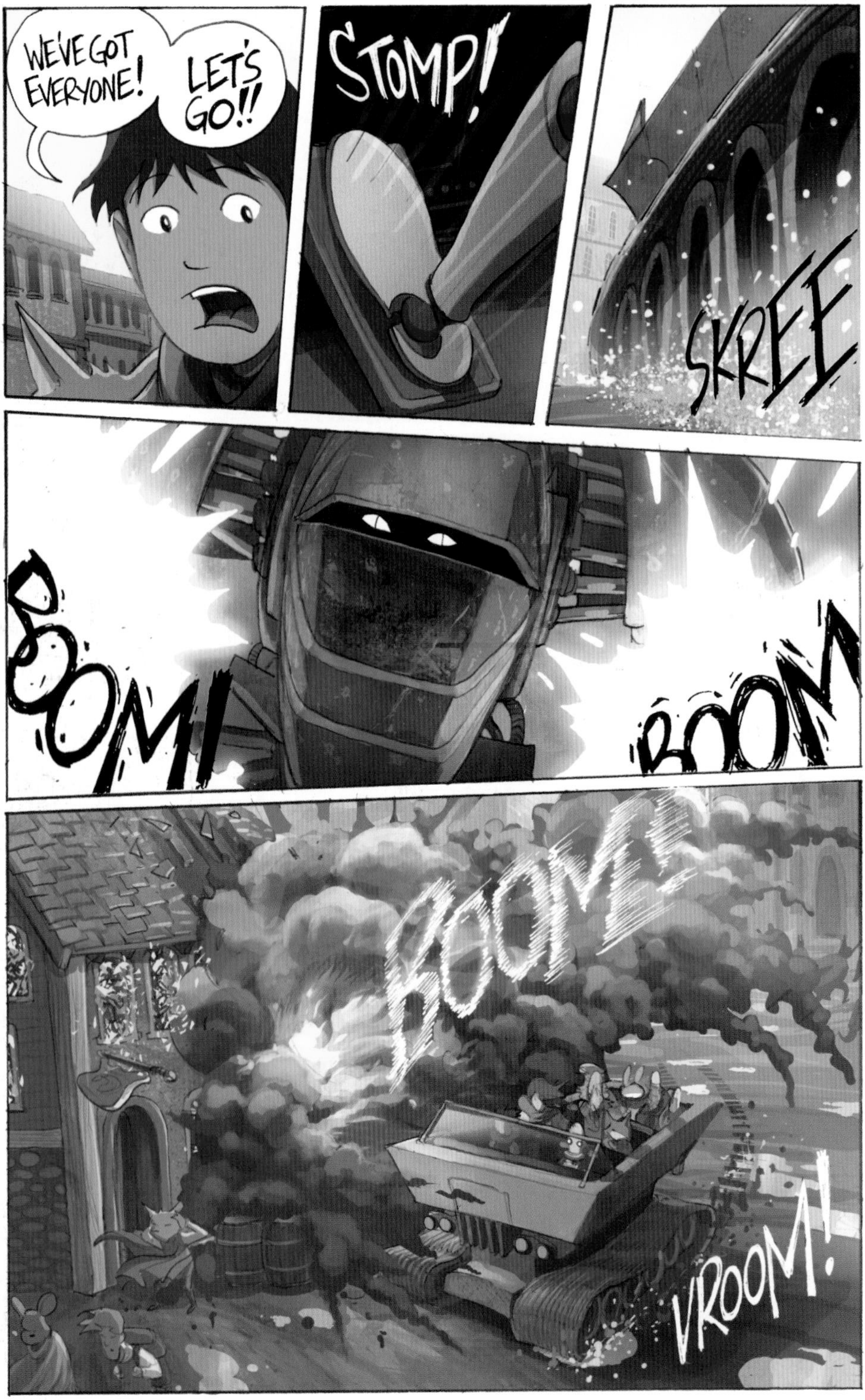
WE'VE GOT EVERYONE!
LET'S GO!!
STOMP!
SKREE
BOOM!
BOOM
BOOM!
VROOM!

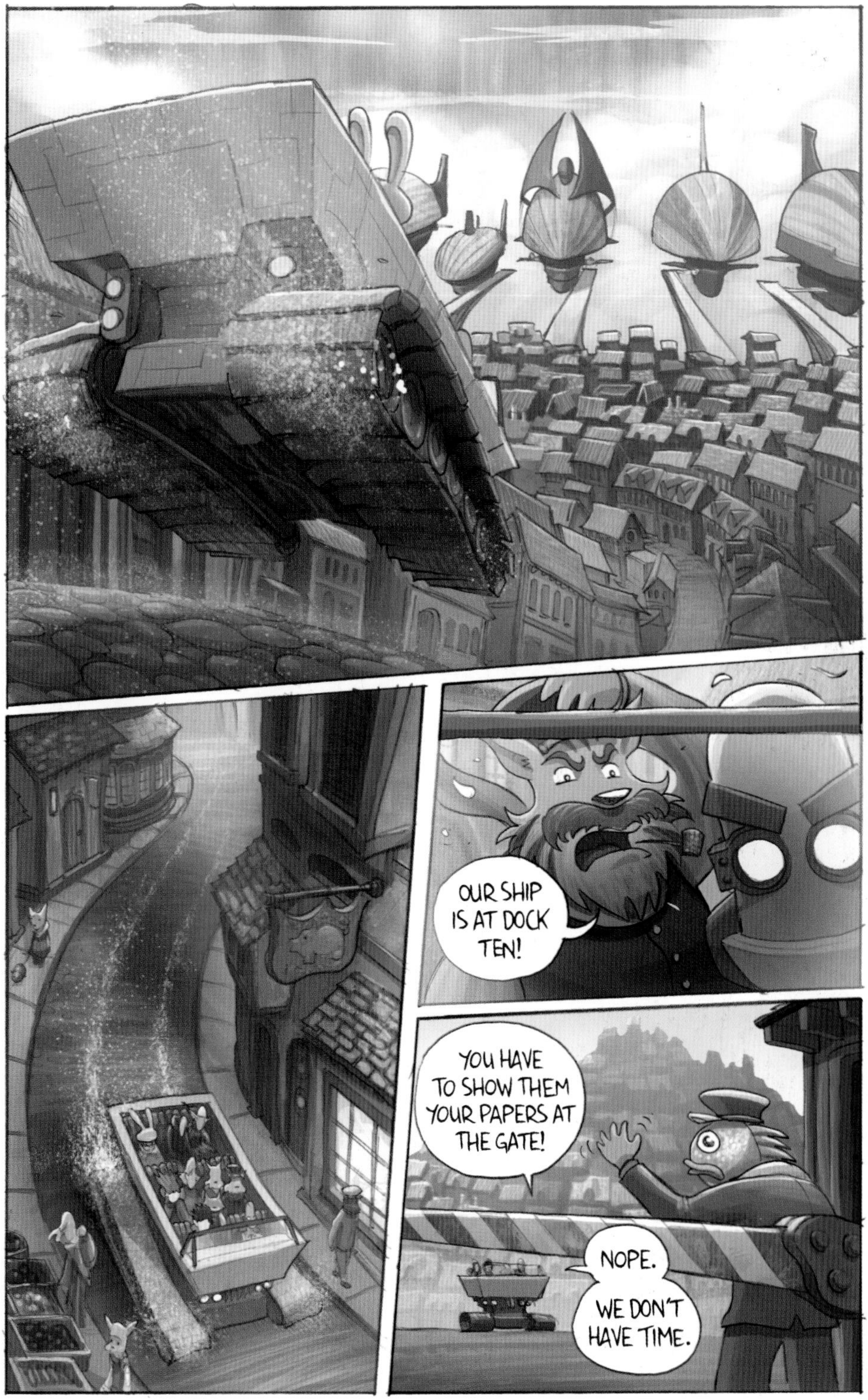
OUR SHIP IS AT DOCK TEN!
YOU HAVE TO SHOW THEM YOUR PAPERS AT THE GATE!
NOPE.
WE DON'T HAVE TIME.

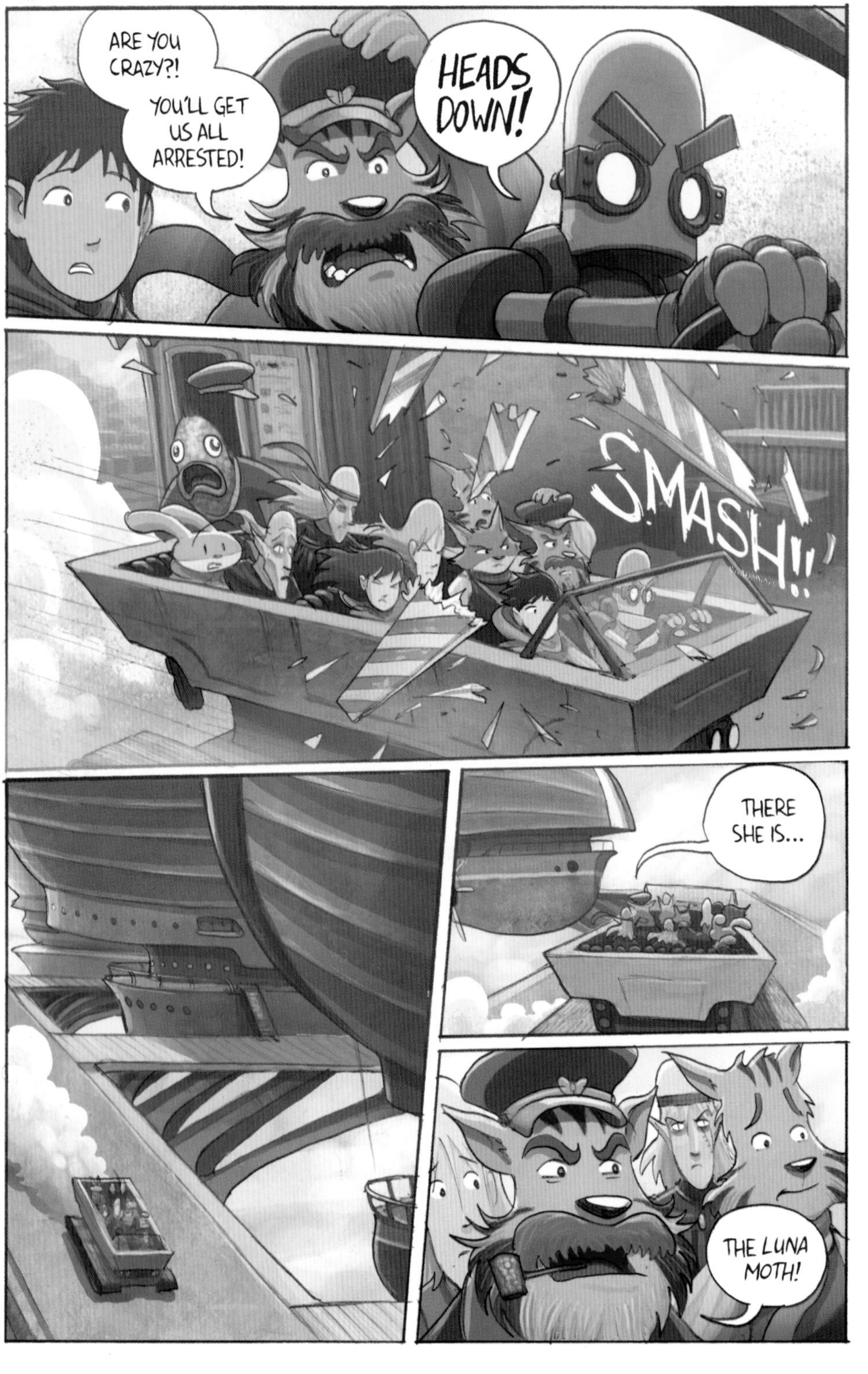
ARE YOU CRAZY?!
YOU'LL GET US ALL ARRESTED!
HEADS DOWN!
SMASH!!
THERE SHE IS...
THE LUNA MOTH!

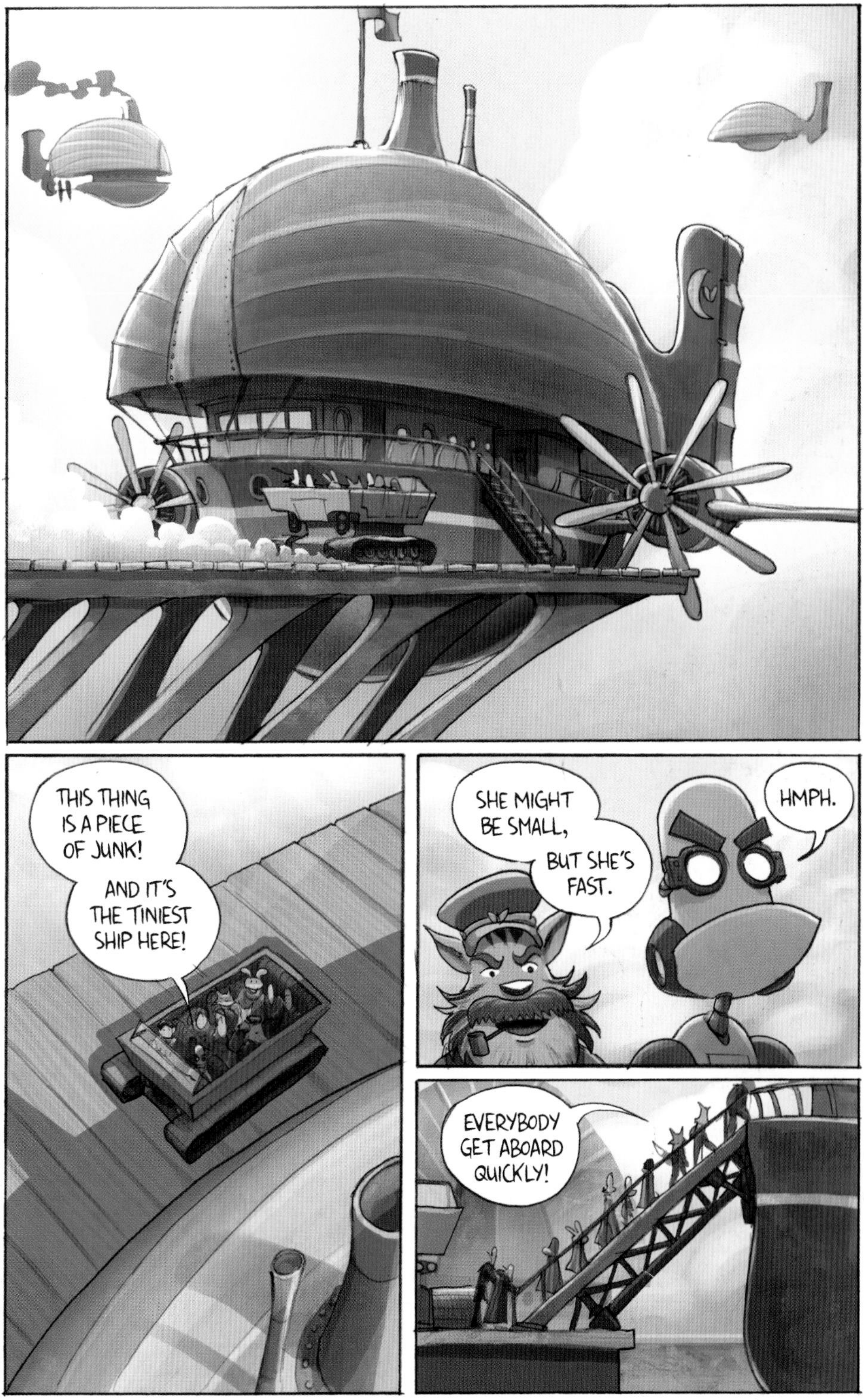
THIS THING IS A PIECE OF JUNK!
AND IT'S THE TINIEST SHIP HERE!
SHE MIGHT BE SMALL,
BUT SHE'S FAST.
HMPH.
EVERYBODY GET ABOARD QUICKLY!

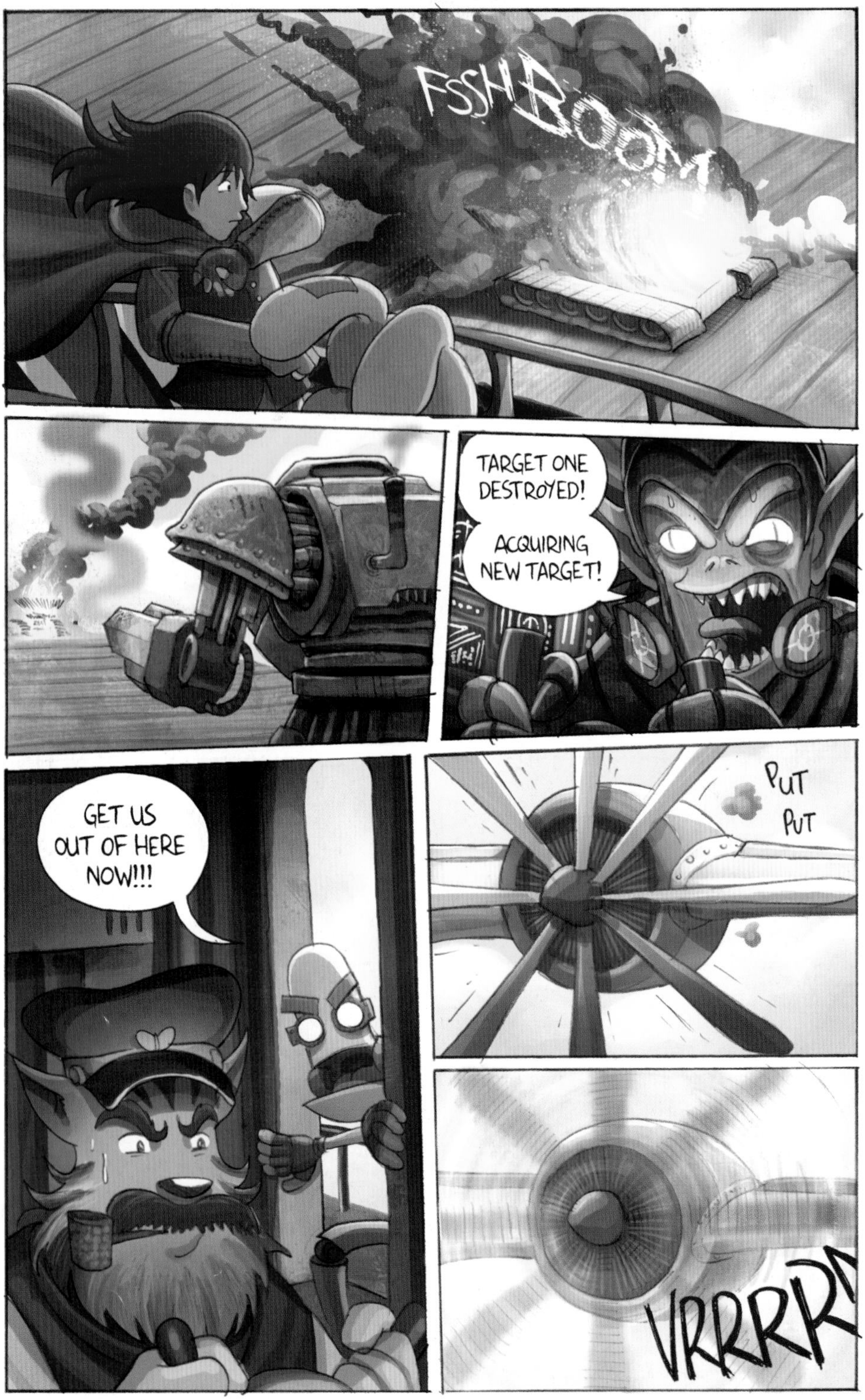
FSSHBOOM!
TARGET ONE DESTROYED!
ACQUIRING NEW TARGET!
GET US OUT OF HERE NOW!!!
PUT
PUT
VRRRR

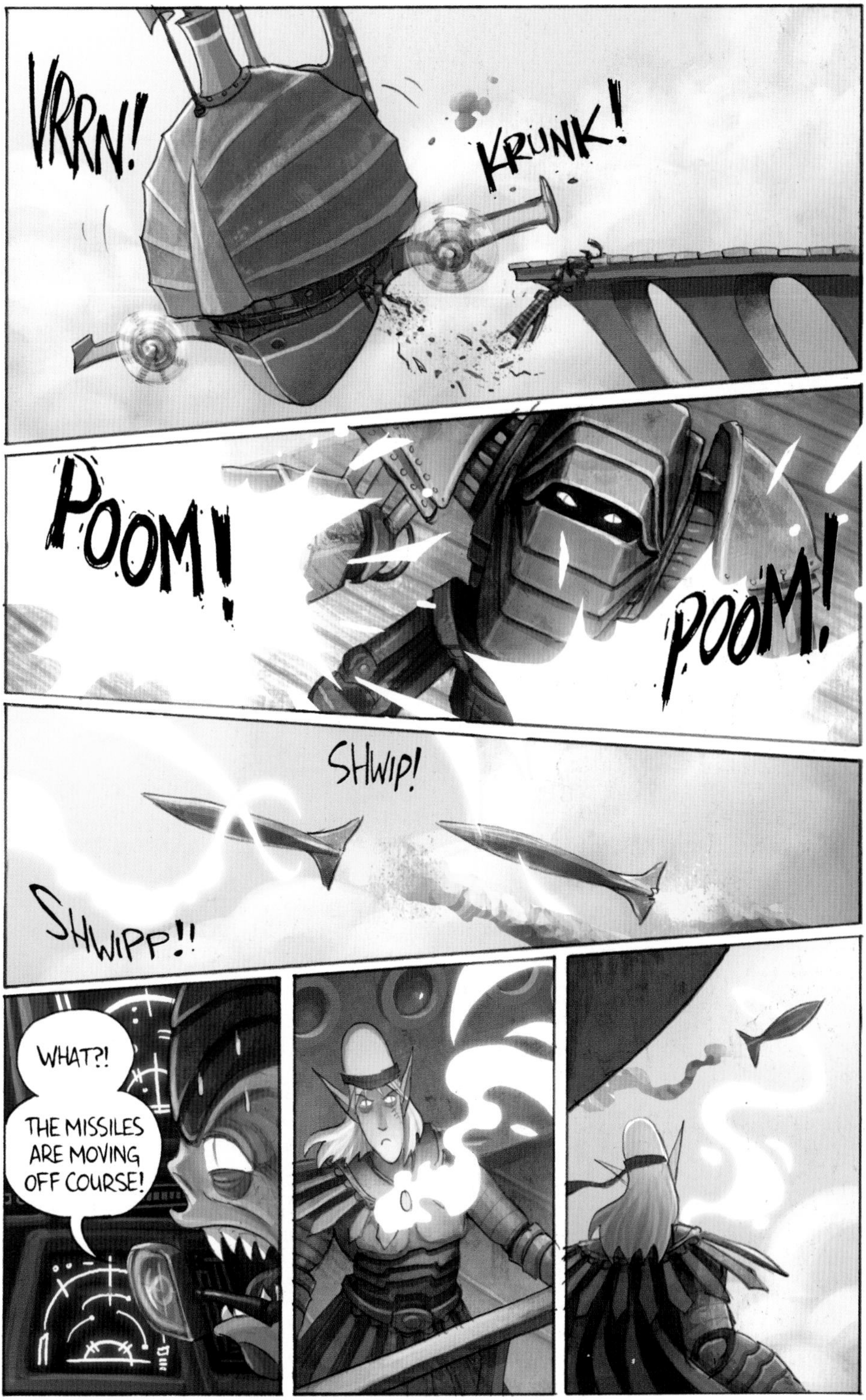
VRRN!
KRUNK!
POOM!
POOM!
SHWIP!
SHWIPP!!
WHAT?!
THE MISSILES ARE MOVING OFF COURSE!

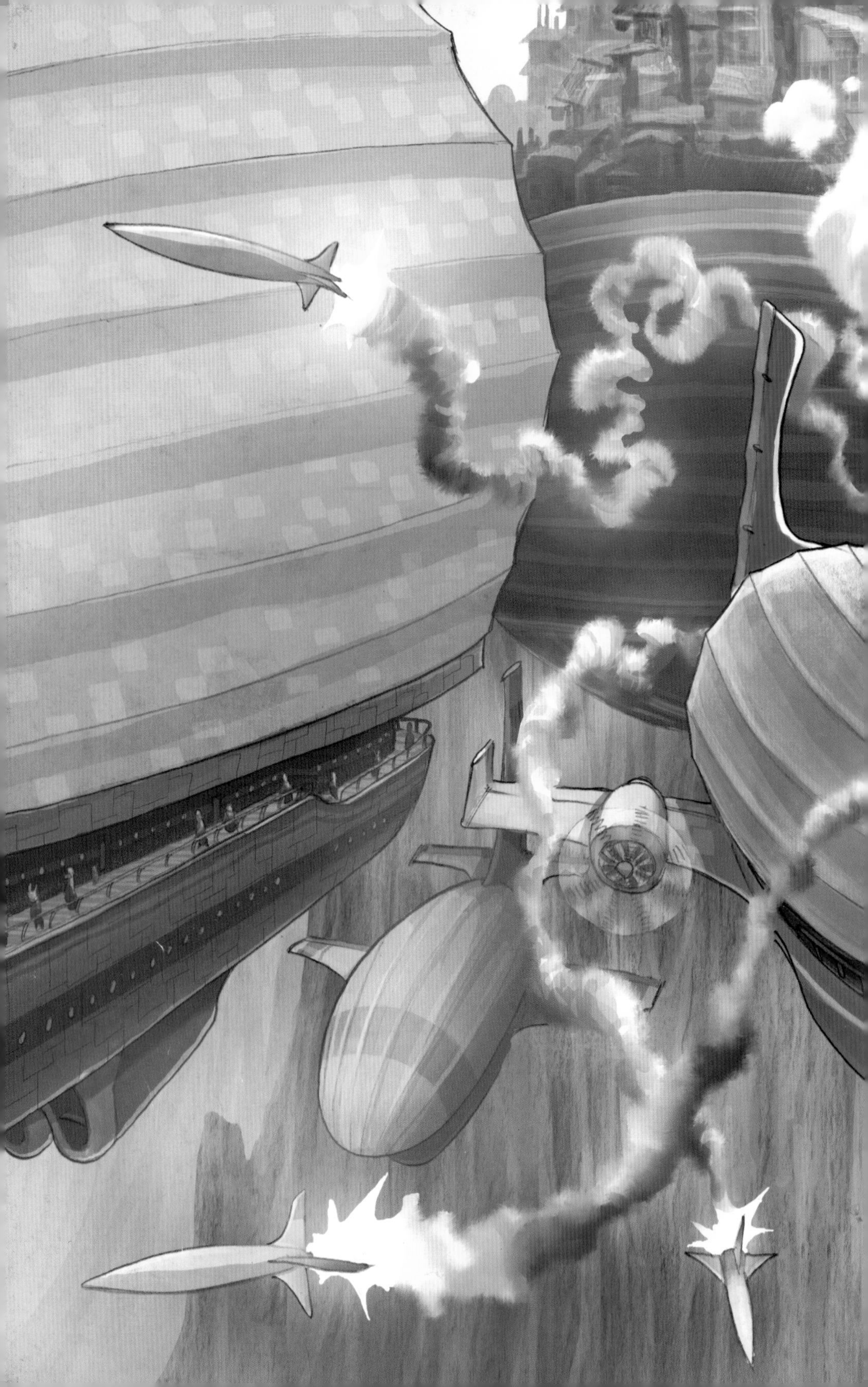

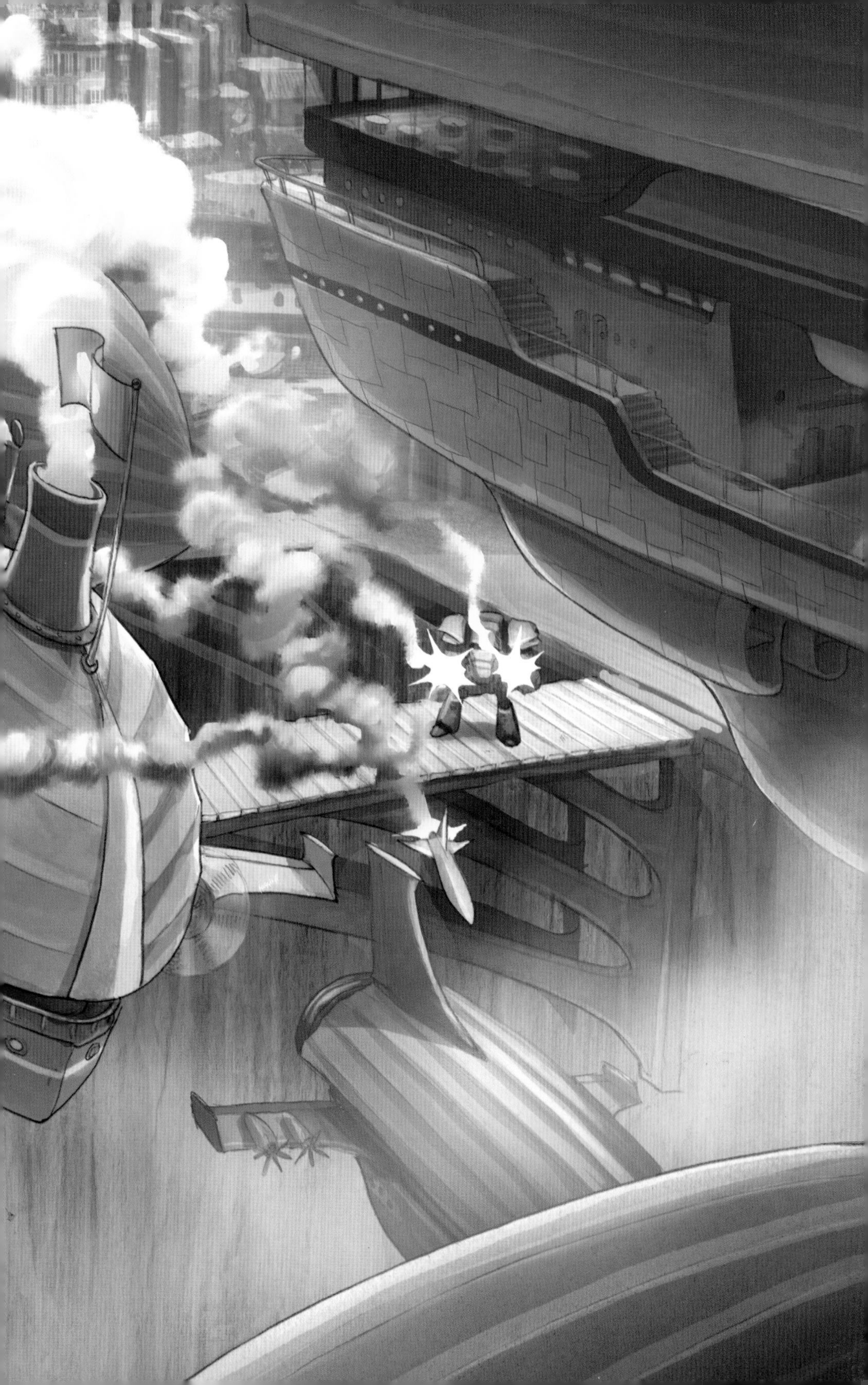

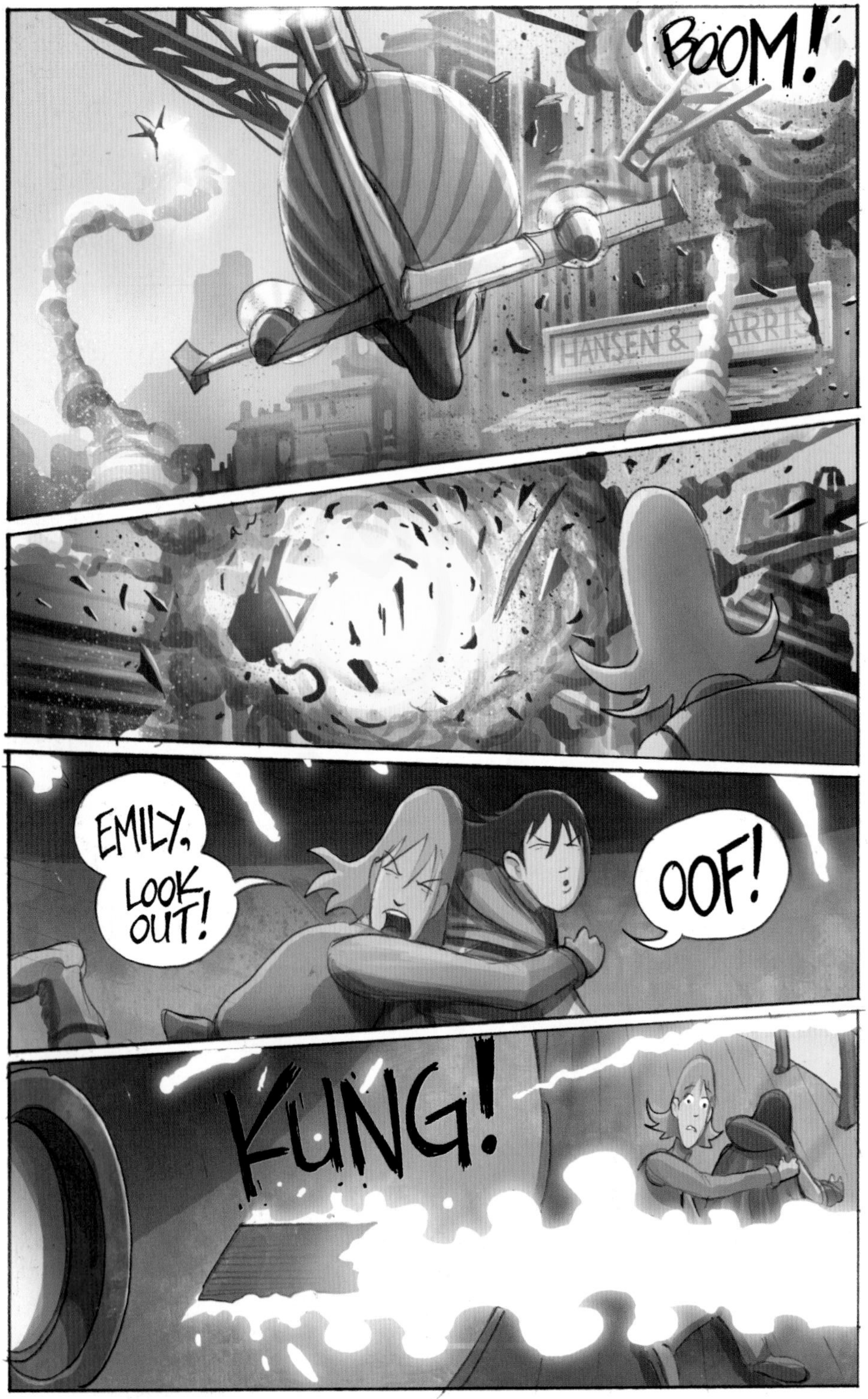
BOOM!
HANSEN &
EMILY, LOOK OUT!
OOF!
KUNG!

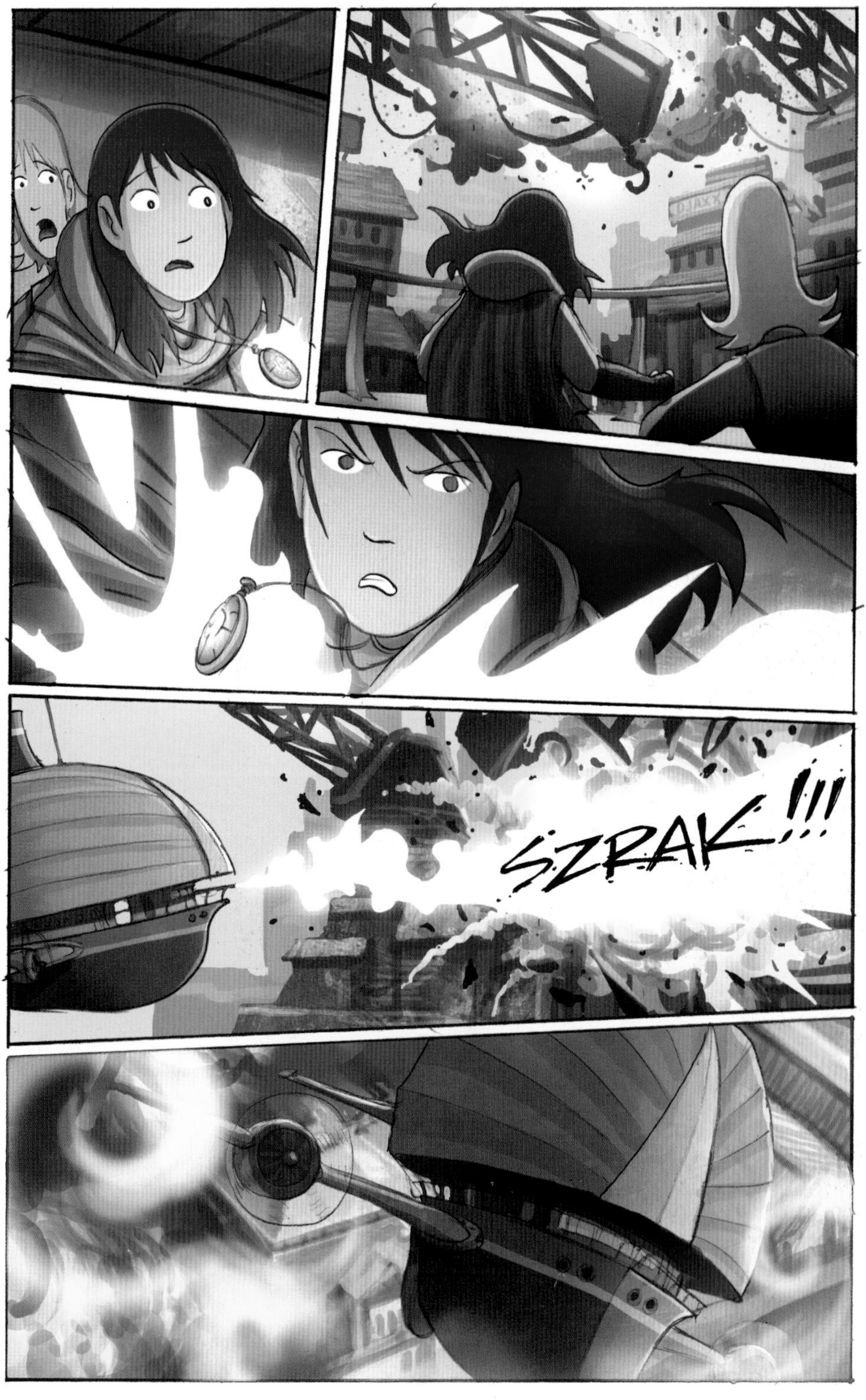
SZRAK!!!

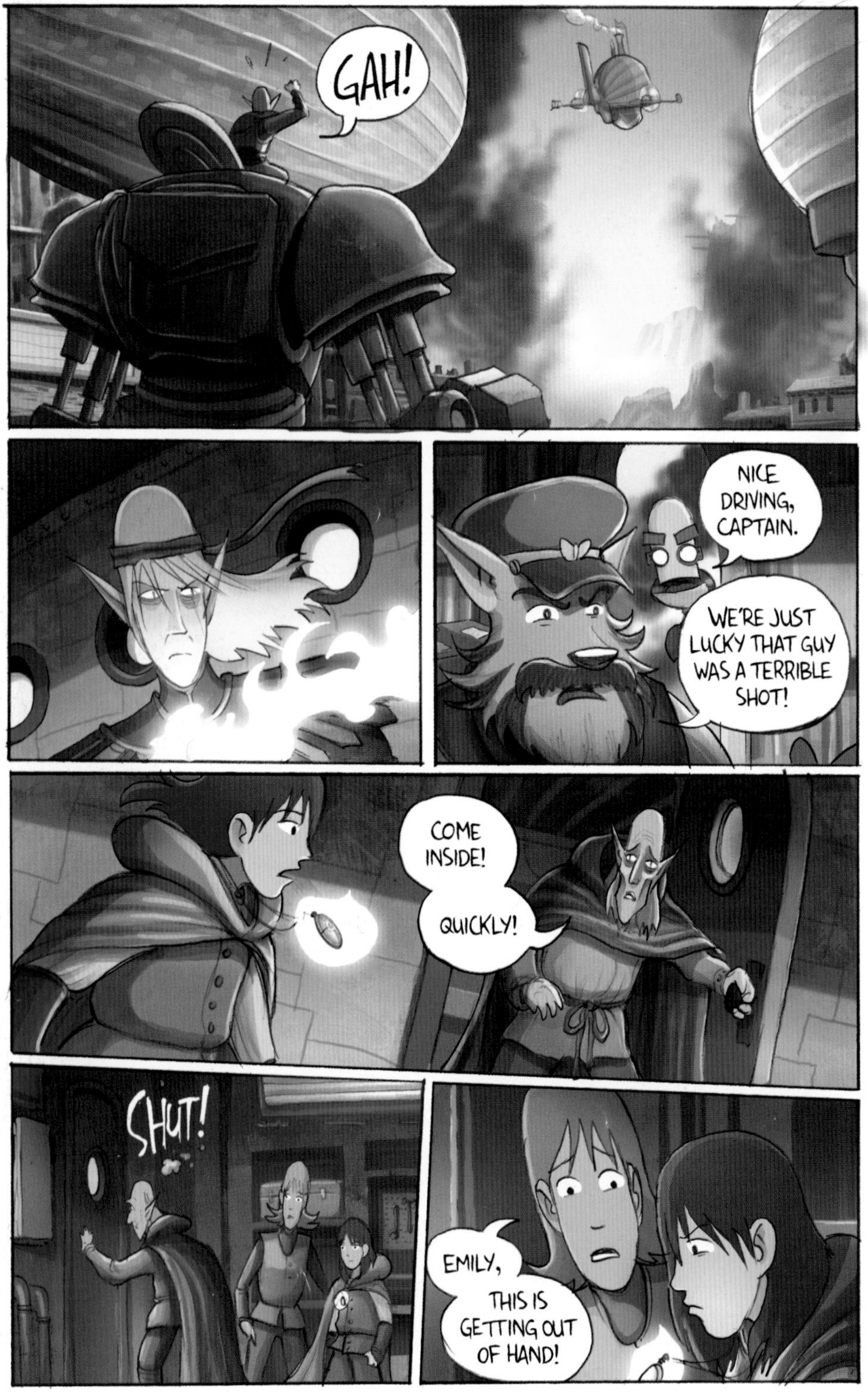
GAH!
NICE DRIVING, CAPTAIN.
WE'RE JUST LUCKY THAT GUY WAS A TERRIBLE SHOT!
COME INSIDE!
QUICKLY!
SHUT!
EMILY,
THIS IS GETTING OUT OF HAND!

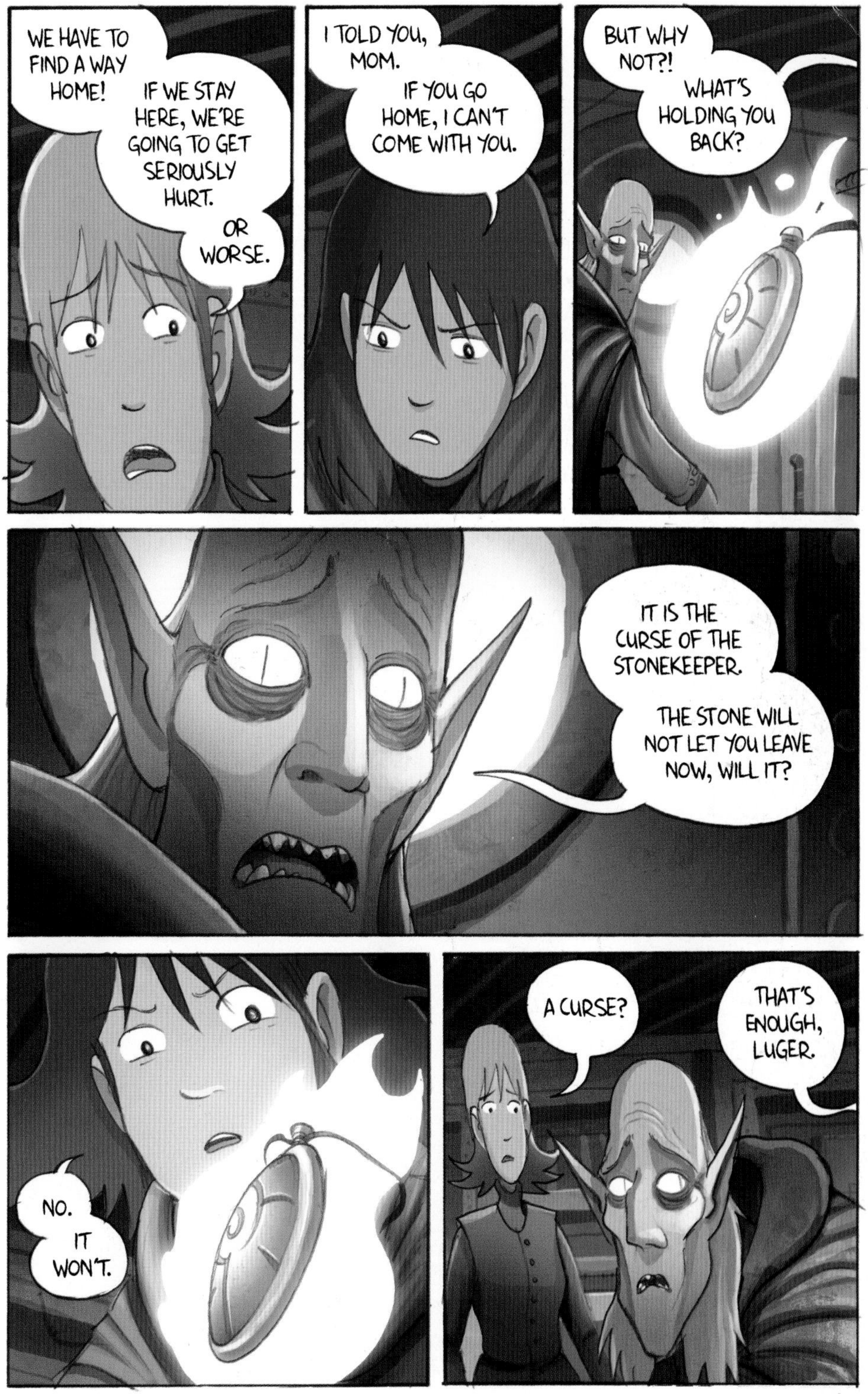
WE HAVE TO FIND A WAY HOME!
IF WE STAY HERE, WE'RE GOING TO GET SERIOUSLY HURT.
OR WORSE.
I TOLD YOU, MOM.
IF YOU GO HOME, I CAN'T COME WITH YOU.
BUT WHY NOT?!
WHAT'S HOLDING YOU BACK?
IT IS THE CURSE OF THE STONEKEEPER.
THE STONE WILL NOT LET YOU LEAVE NOW, WILL IT?
NO.
IT WON'T.
A CURSE?
THAT'S ENOUGH, LUGER.

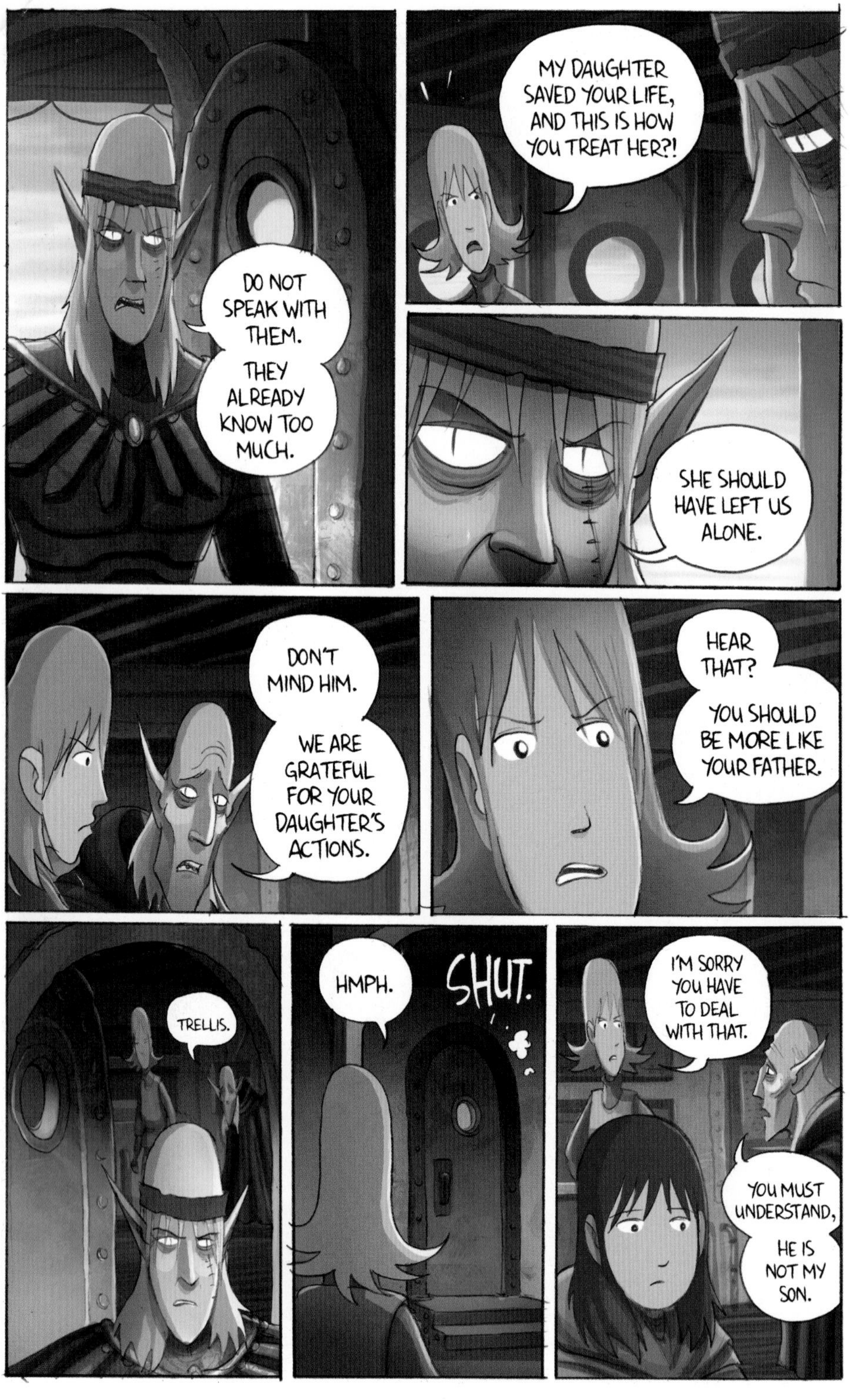
MY DAUGHTER SAVED YOUR LIFE, AND THIS IS HOW YOU TREAT HER?!
DO NOT SPEAK WITH THEM.
THEY ALREADY KNOW TOO MUCH.
SHE SHOULD HAVE LEFT US ALONE.
DON'T MIND HIM.
WE ARE GRATEFUL FOR YOUR DAUGHTER'S ACTIONS.
HEAR THAT?
YOU SHOULD BE MORE LIKE YOUR FATHER.
TRELLIS.
HMPH.
SHUT.
I'M SORRY YOU HAVE TO DEAL WITH THAT.
YOU MUST UNDERSTAND,
HE IS NOT MY SON.

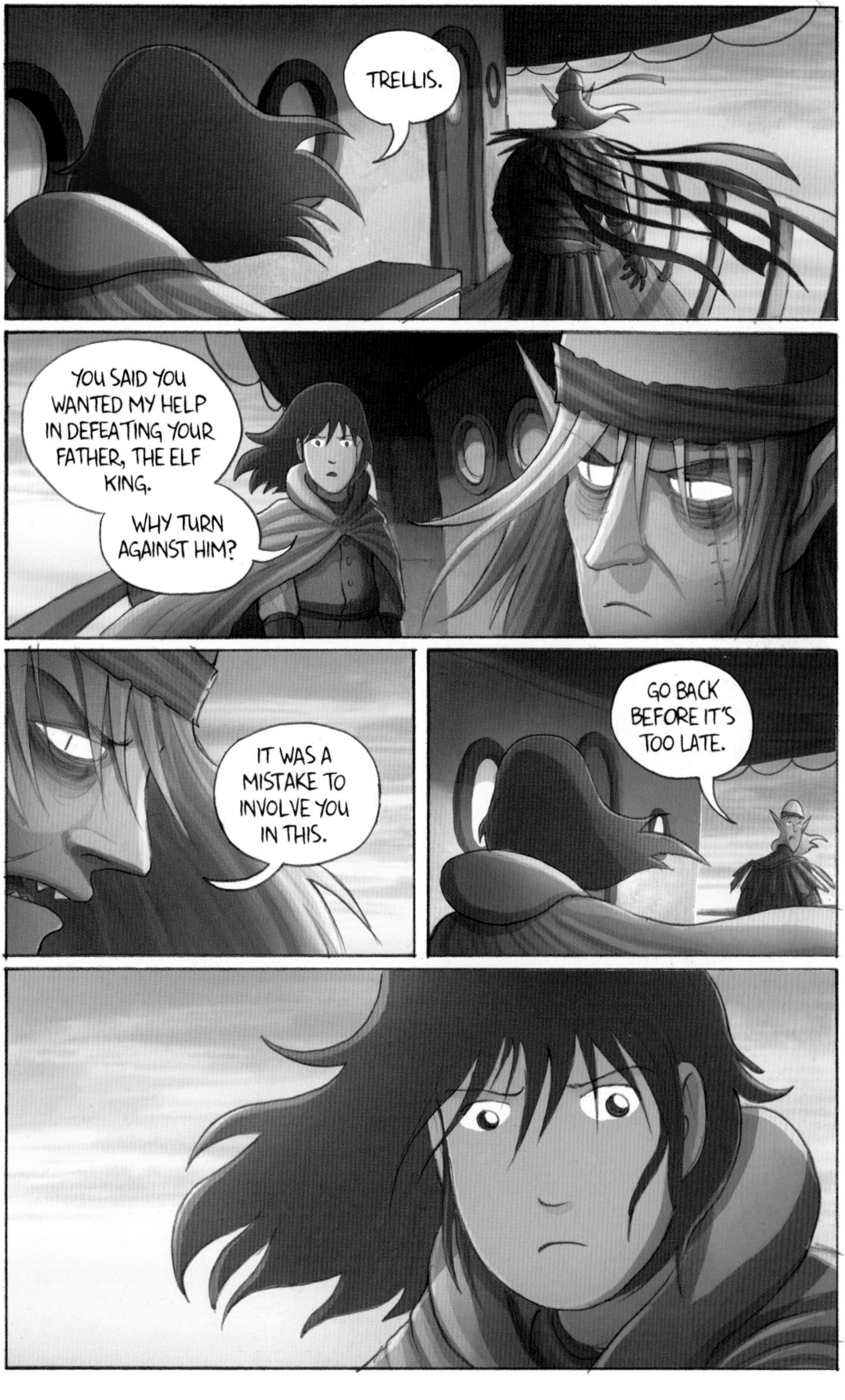
TRELLIS.
YOU SAID YOU WANTED MY HELP IN DEFEATING YOUR FATHER, THE ELF KING.
WHY TURN AGAINST HIM?
IT WAS A MISTAKE TO INVOLVE YOU IN THIS.
GO BACK BEFORE IT'S TOO LATE.

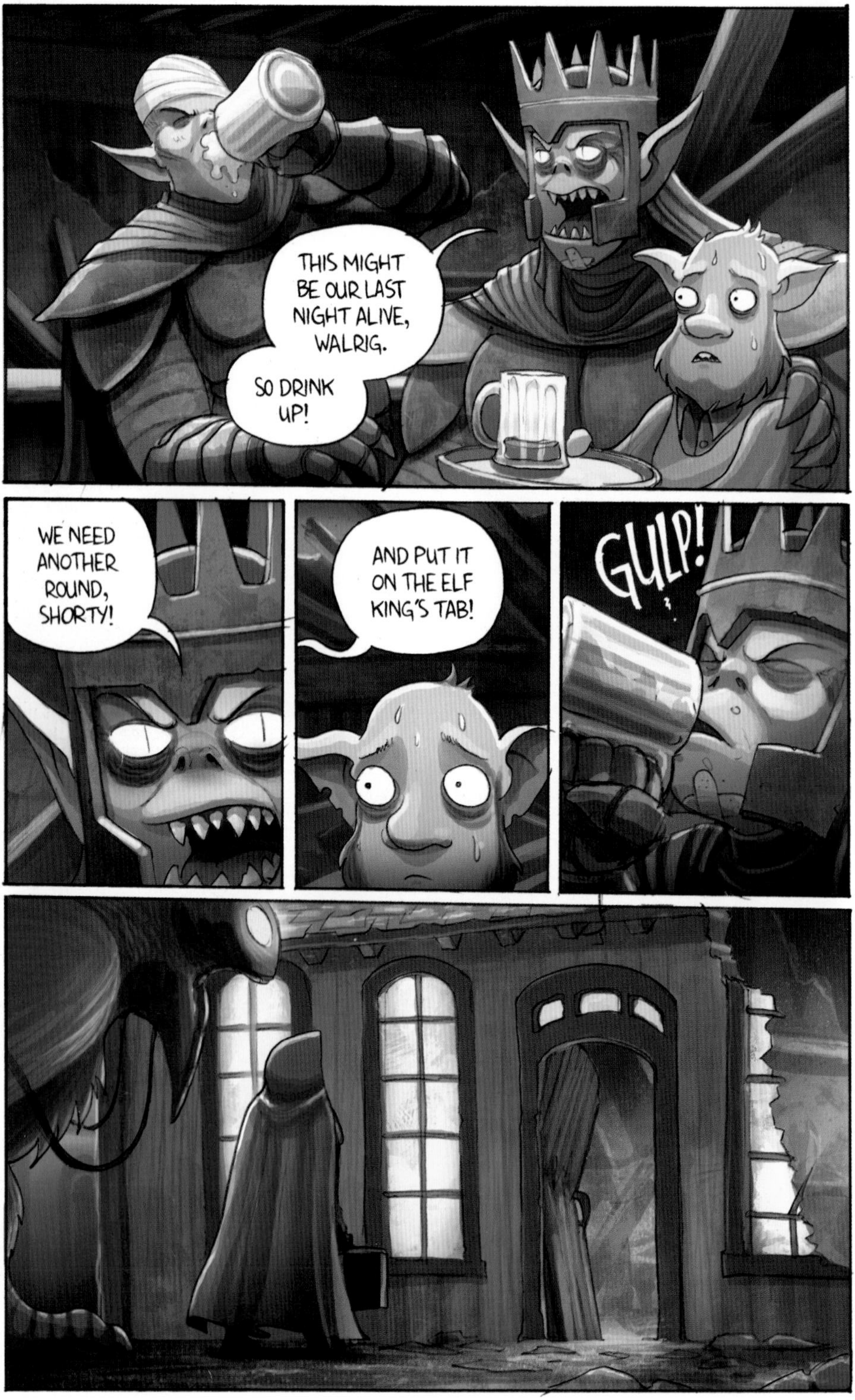
THIS MIGHT BE OUR LAST NIGHT ALIVE, WALRIG.
SO DRINK UP!
WE NEED ANOTHER ROUND, SHORTY!
AND PUT IT ON THE ELF KING'S TAB!
GULP!

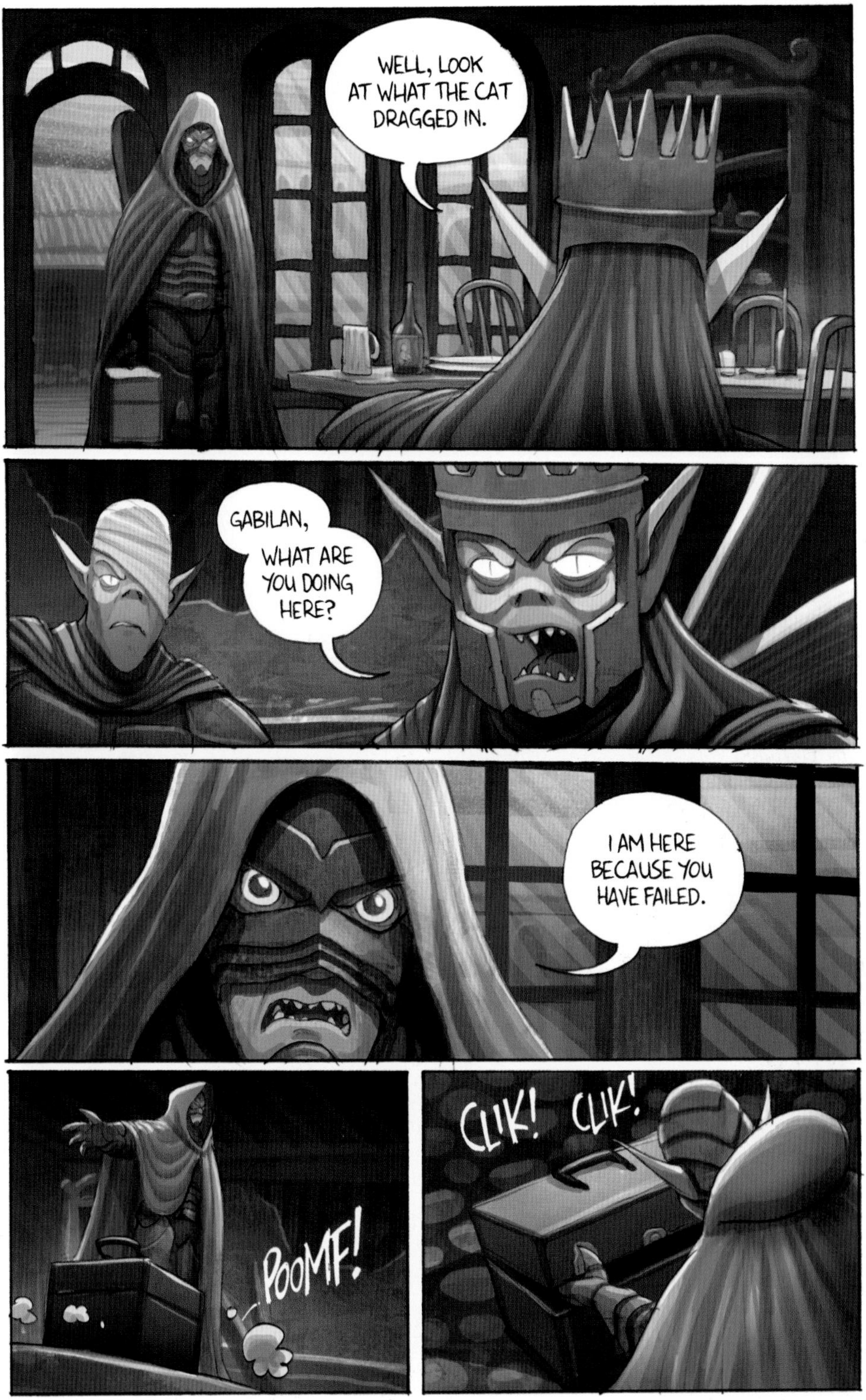
WELL, LOOK AT WHAT THE CAT DRAGGED IN.
GABILAN, WHAT ARE YOU DOING HERE?
I AM HERE BECAUSE YOU HAVE FAILED.
POOMF!
CLIK! CLIK!

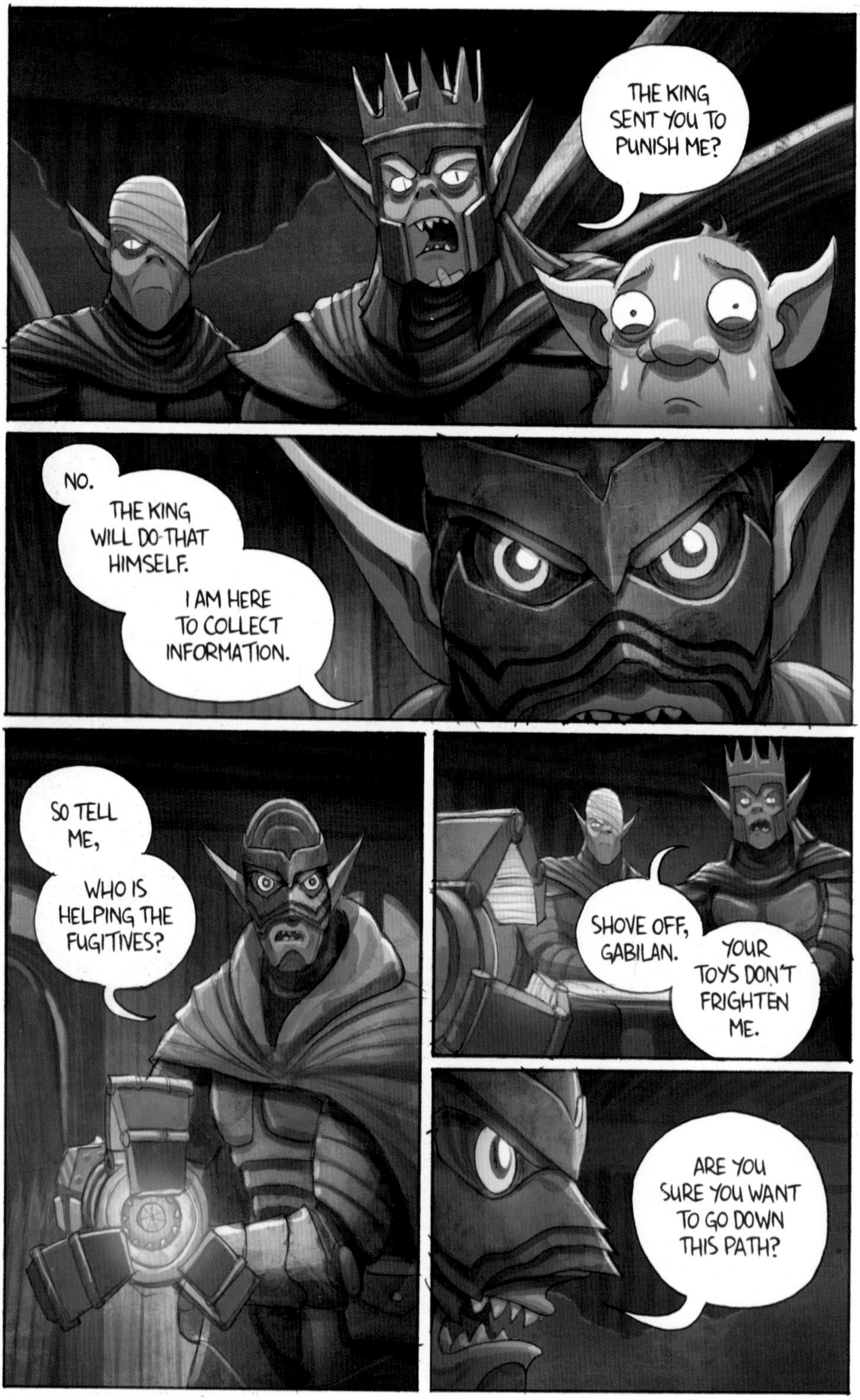
THE KING SENT YOU TO PUNISH ME?
NO.
THE KING WILL DO THAT HIMSELF.
I AM HERE TO COLLECT INFORMATION.
SO TELL ME,
WHO IS HELPING THE FUGITIVES?
SHOVE OFF, GABILAN.
YOUR TOYS DON'T FRIGHTEN ME.
ARE YOU SURE YOU WANT TO GO DOWN THIS PATH?

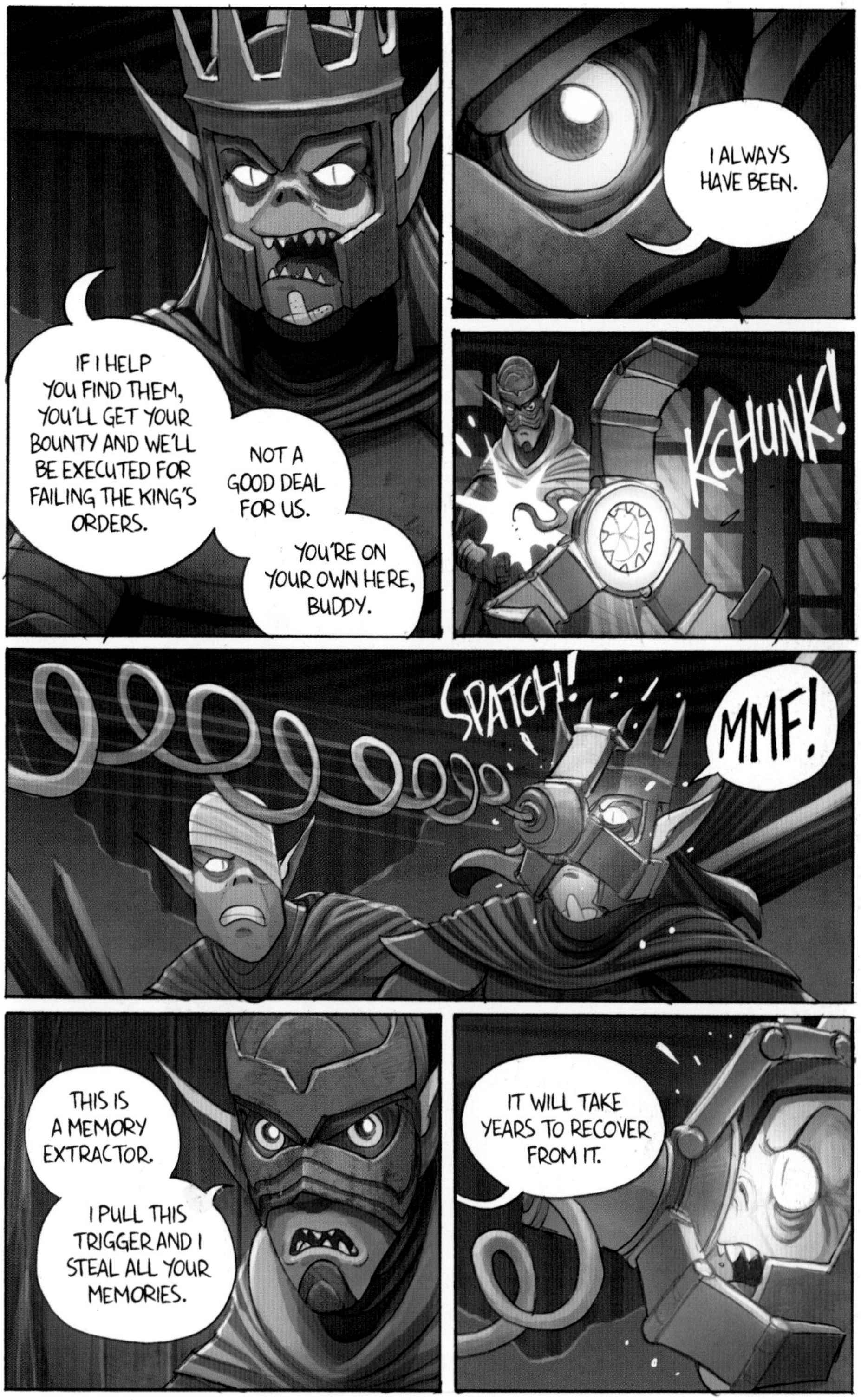
IF I HELP YOU FIND THEM, YOU'LL GET YOUR BOUNTY AND WE'LL BE EXECUTED FOR FAILING THE KING'S ORDERS.
NOT A GOOD DEAL FOR US.
YOU'RE ON YOUR OWN HERE, BUDDY.
I ALWAYS HAVE BEEN.
KCHUNK!
SPATCH!
MMF!
THIS IS A MEMORY EXTRACTOR.
I PULL THIS TRIGGER AND I STEAL ALL YOUR MEMORIES.
IT WILL TAKE YEARS TO RECOVER FROM IT.

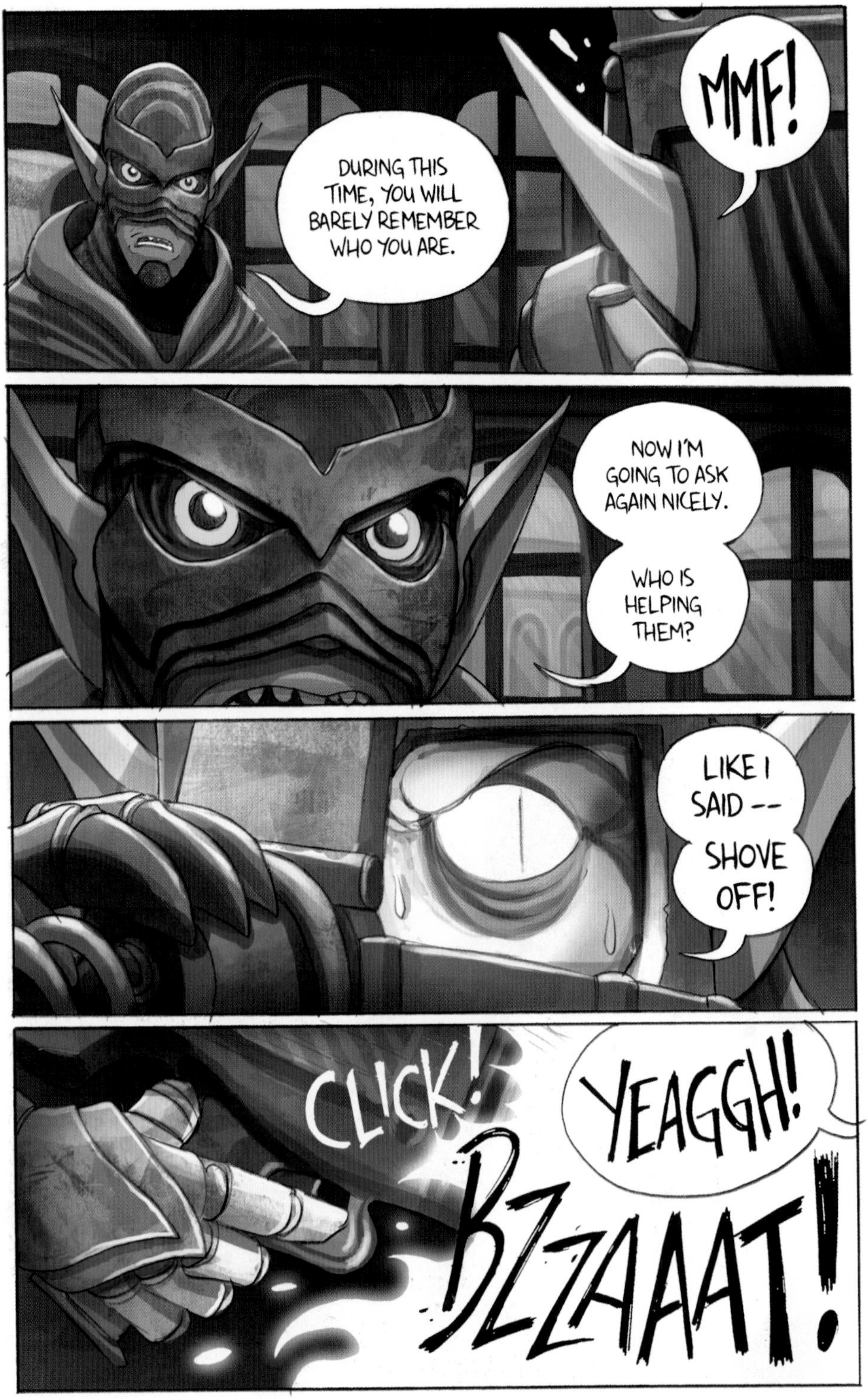
DURING THIS TIME, YOU WILL BARELY REMEMBER WHO YOU ARE.
MMF!
NOW I'M GOING TO ASK AGAIN NICELY.
WHO IS HELPING THEM?
LIKE I SAID --
SHOVE OFF!
CLICK!
YEAGGH!
BZZAAAT!

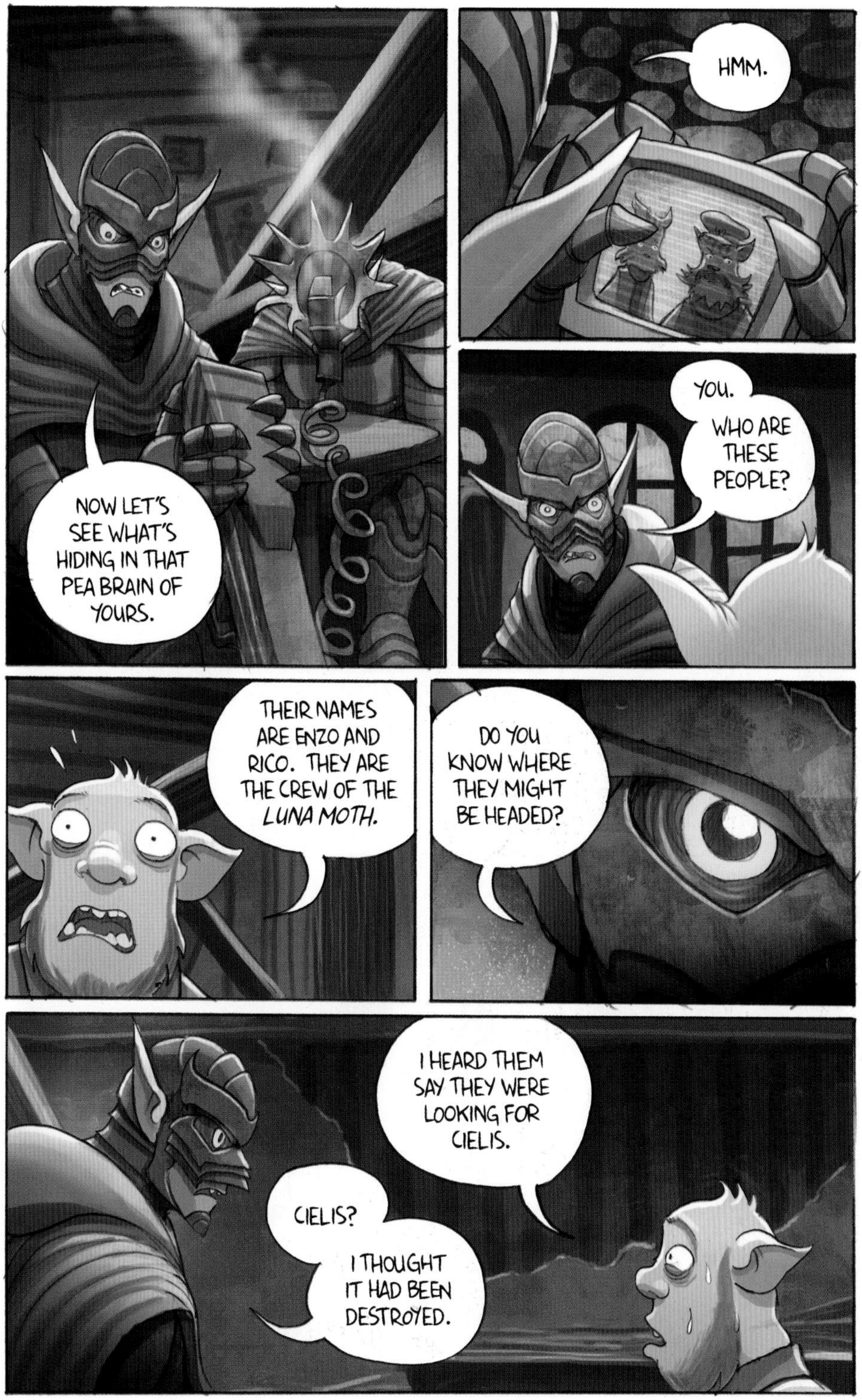
NOW LET'S SEE WHAT'S HIDING IN THAT PEA BRAIN OF YOURS.
HMM.
YOU.
WHO ARE THESE PEOPLE?
THEIR NAMES ARE ENZO AND RICO. THEY ARE THE CREW OF THE *LUNA MOTH*.
DO YOU KNOW WHERE THEY MIGHT BE HEADED?
I HEARD THEM SAY THEY WERE LOOKING FOR CIELIS.
CIELIS?
I THOUGHT IT HAD BEEN DESTROYED.

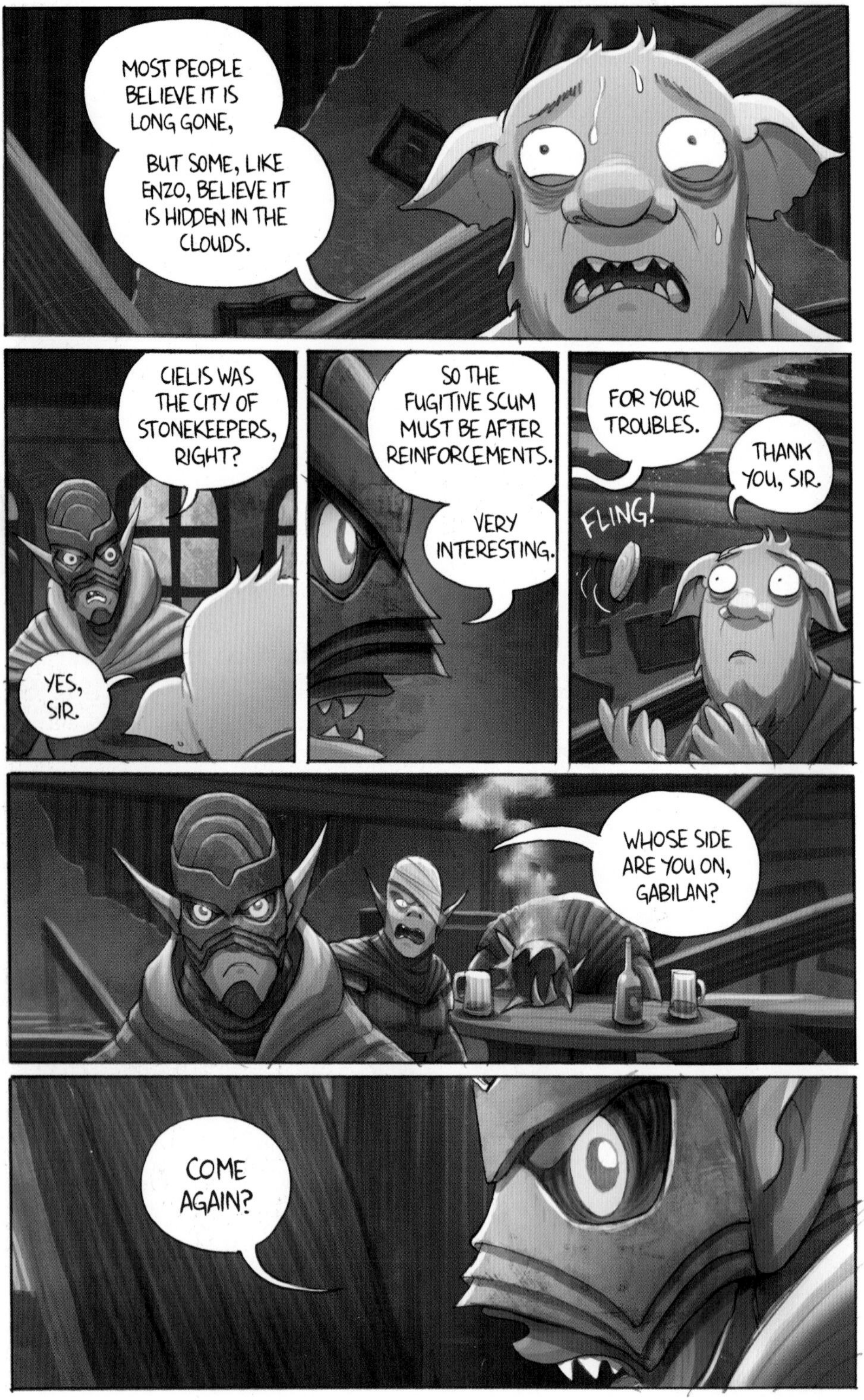
MOST PEOPLE BELIEVE IT IS LONG GONE,
BUT SOME, LIKE ENZO, BELIEVE IT IS HIDDEN IN THE CLOUDS.
CIELIS WAS THE CITY OF STONEKEEPERS, RIGHT?
YES, SIR.
SO THE FUGITIVE SCUM MUST BE AFTER REINFORCEMENTS.
VERY INTERESTING.
FOR YOUR TROUBLES.
FLING!
THANK YOU, SIR.
WHOSE SIDE ARE YOU ON, GABILAN?
COME AGAIN?

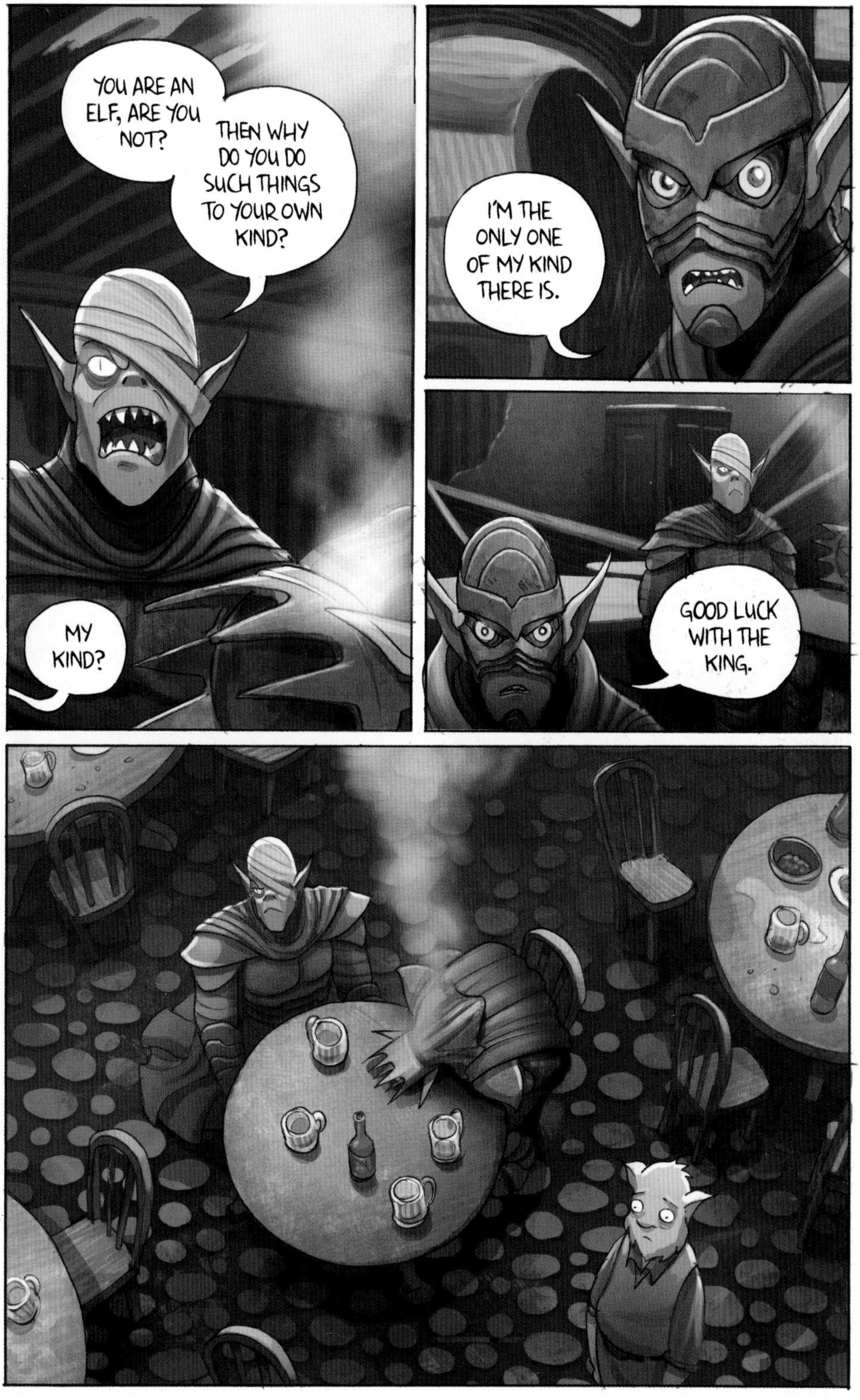
YOU ARE AN ELF, ARE YOU NOT?
THEN WHY DO YOU DO SUCH THINGS TO YOUR OWN KIND?
MY KIND?
I'M THE ONLY ONE OF MY KIND THERE IS.
GOOD LUCK WITH THE KING.

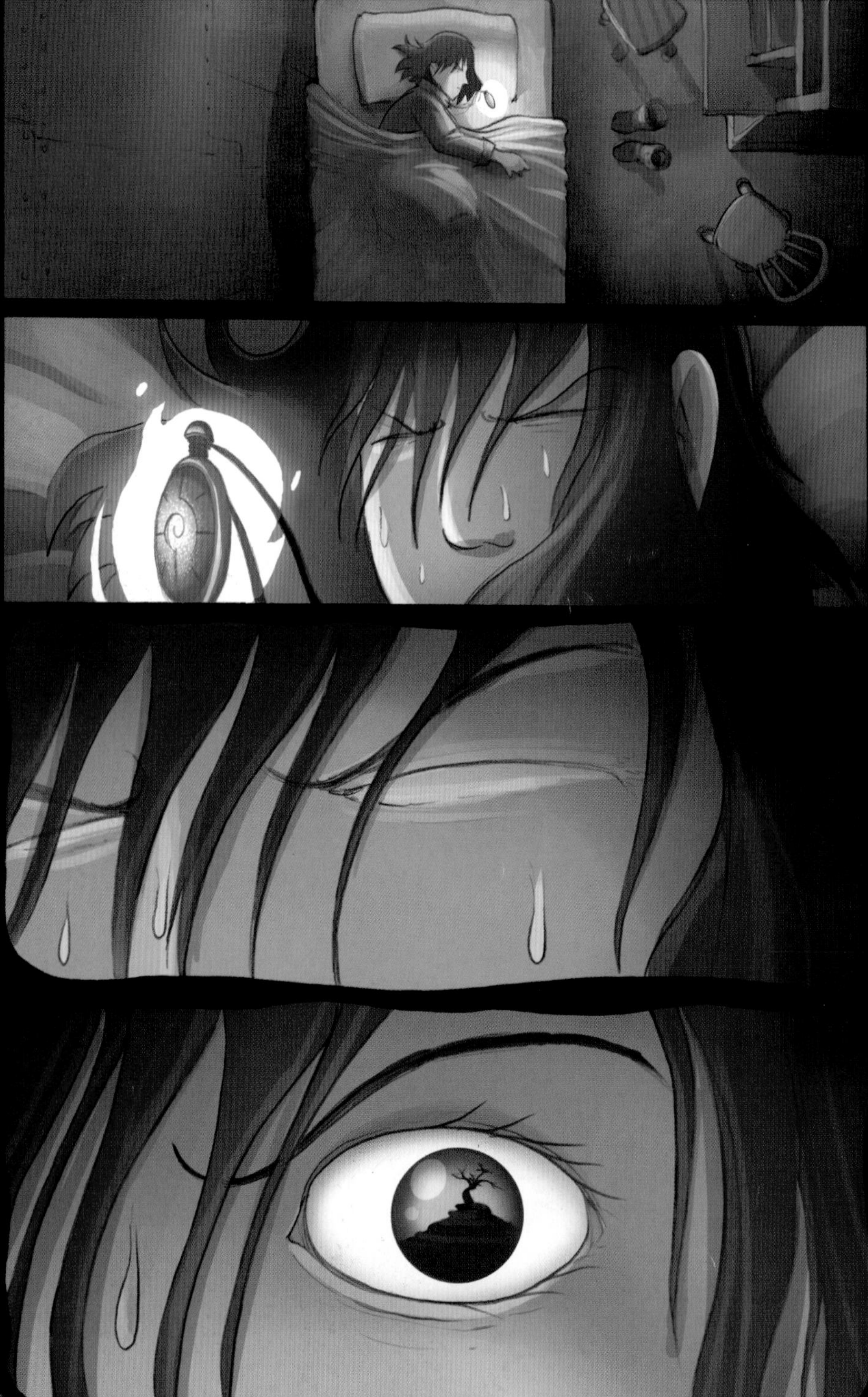

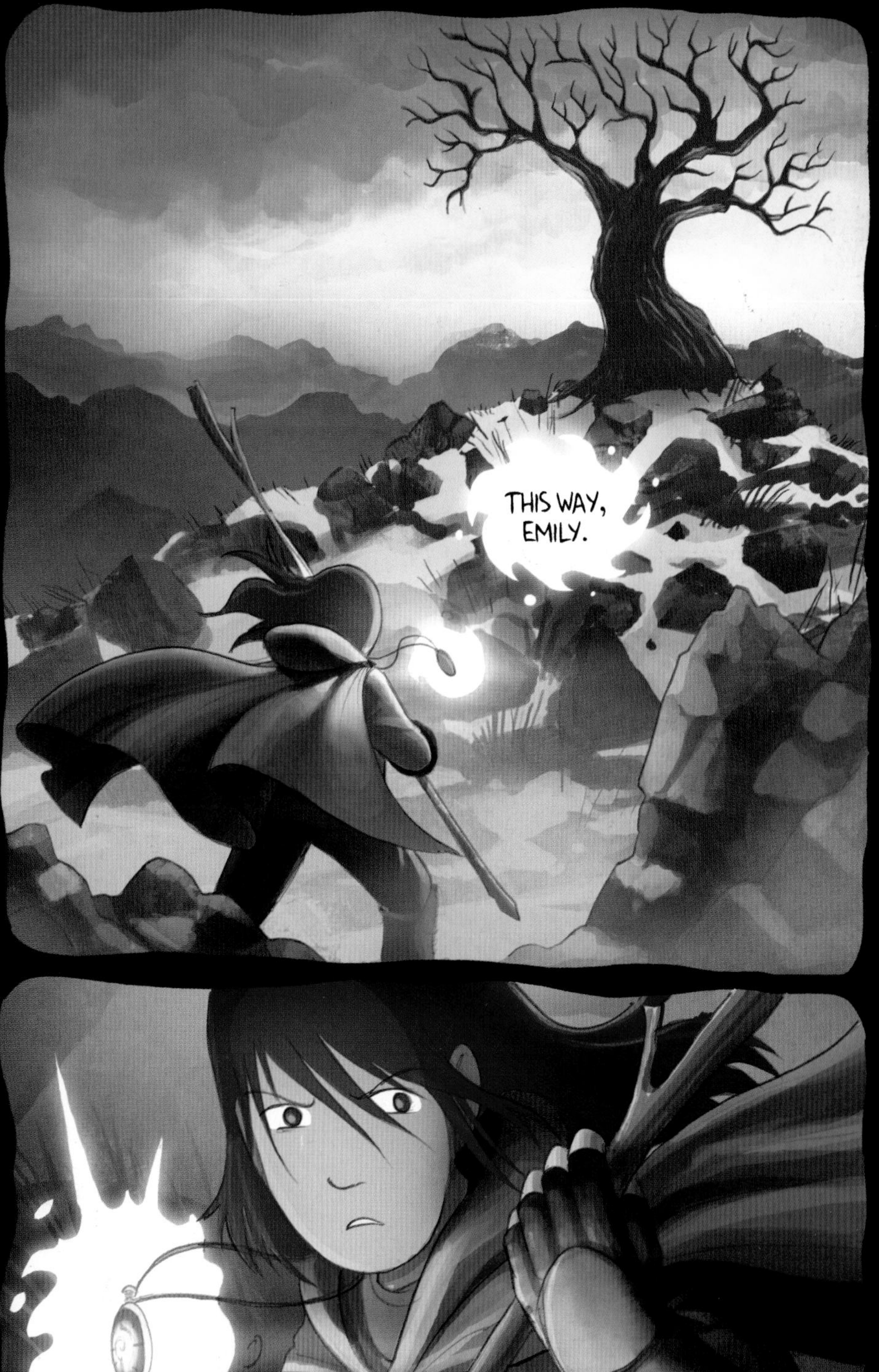
THIS WAY, EMILY.

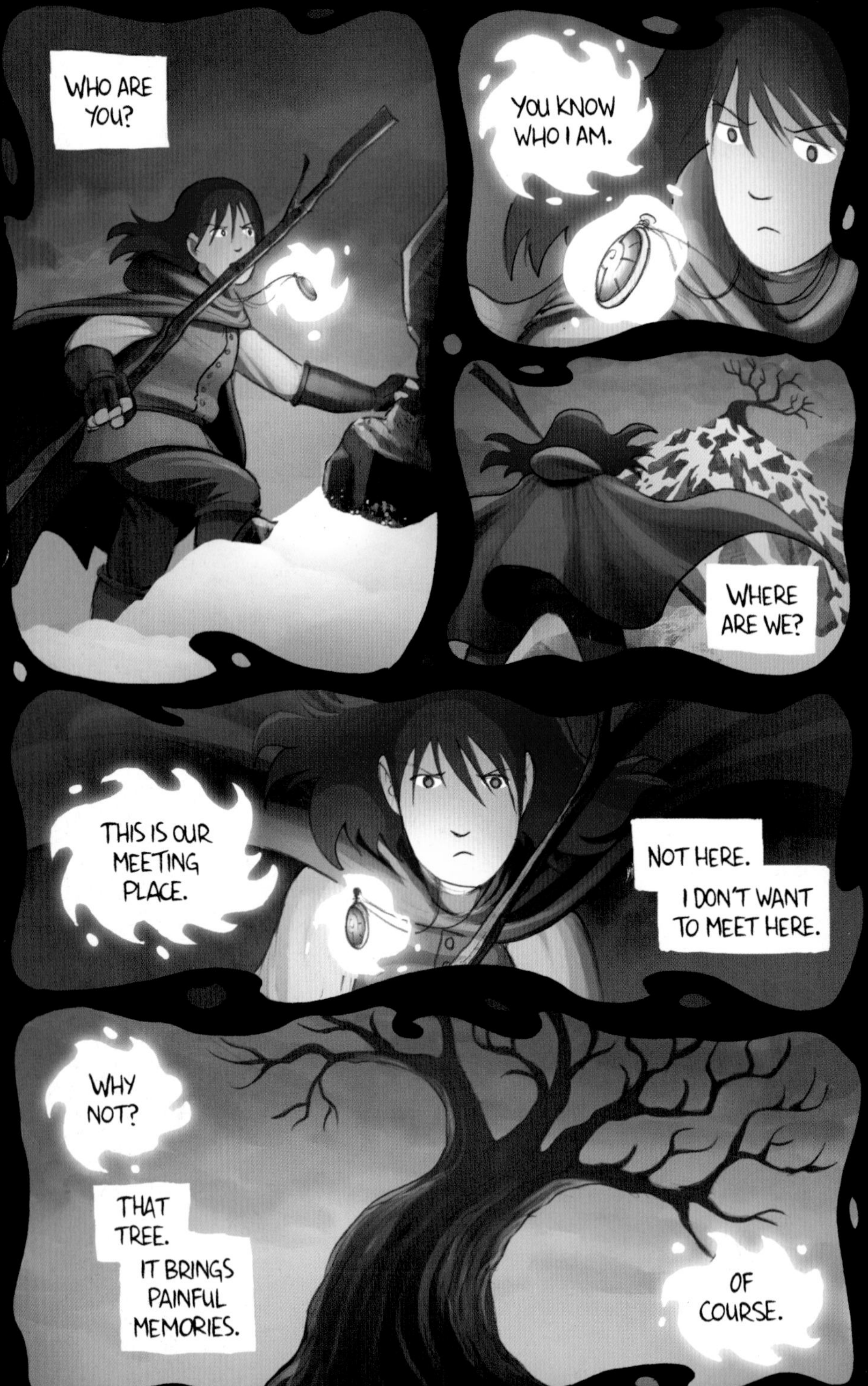
WHO ARE YOU?
YOU KNOW WHO I AM.
WHERE ARE WE?
THIS IS OUR MEETING PLACE.
NOT HERE.
I DON'T WANT TO MEET HERE.
WHY NOT?
THAT TREE.
IT BRINGS PAINFUL MEMORIES.
OF COURSE.

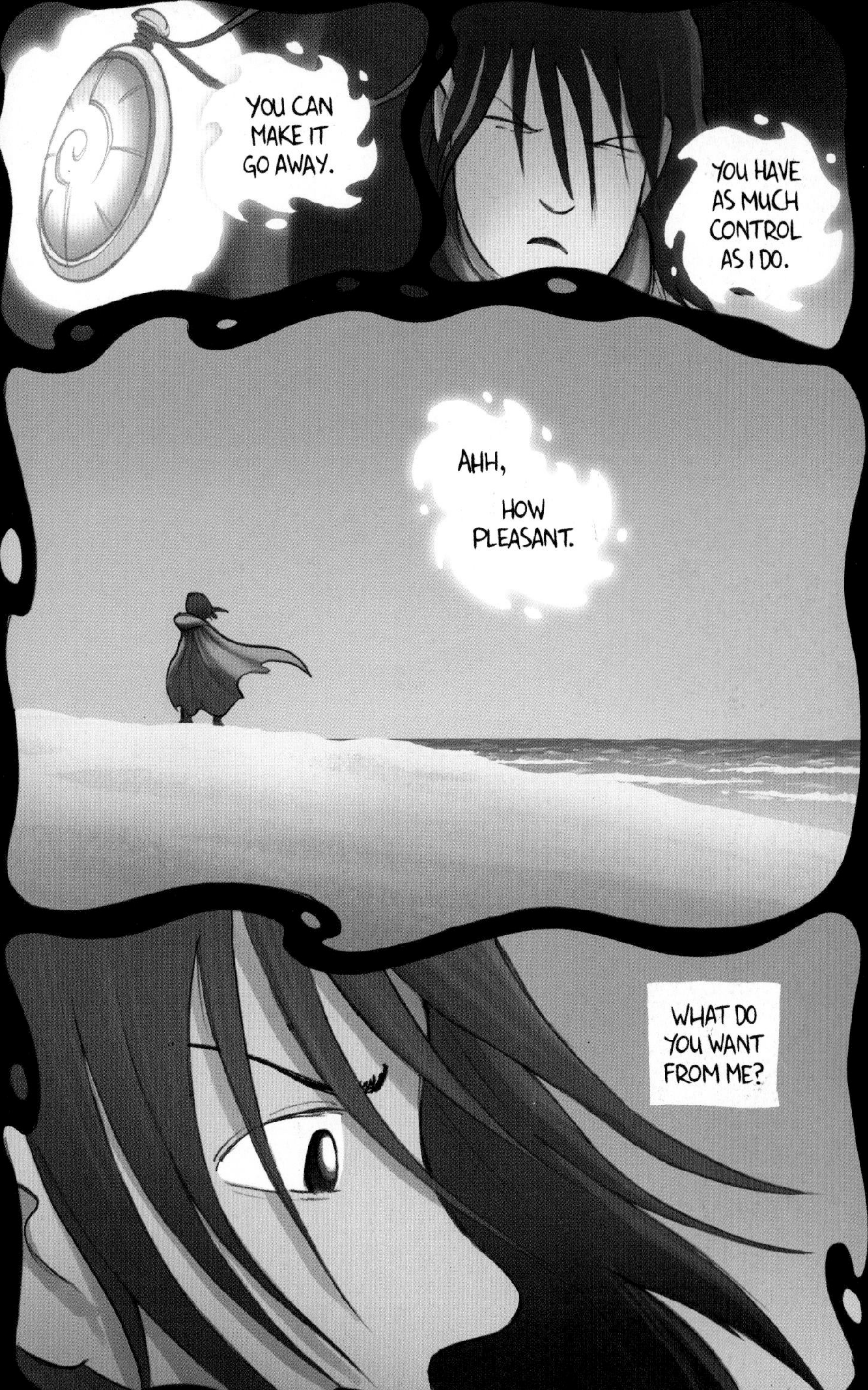
YOU CAN MAKE IT GO AWAY.
YOU HAVE AS MUCH CONTROL AS I DO.
AHH, HOW PLEASANT.
WHAT DO YOU WANT FROM ME?

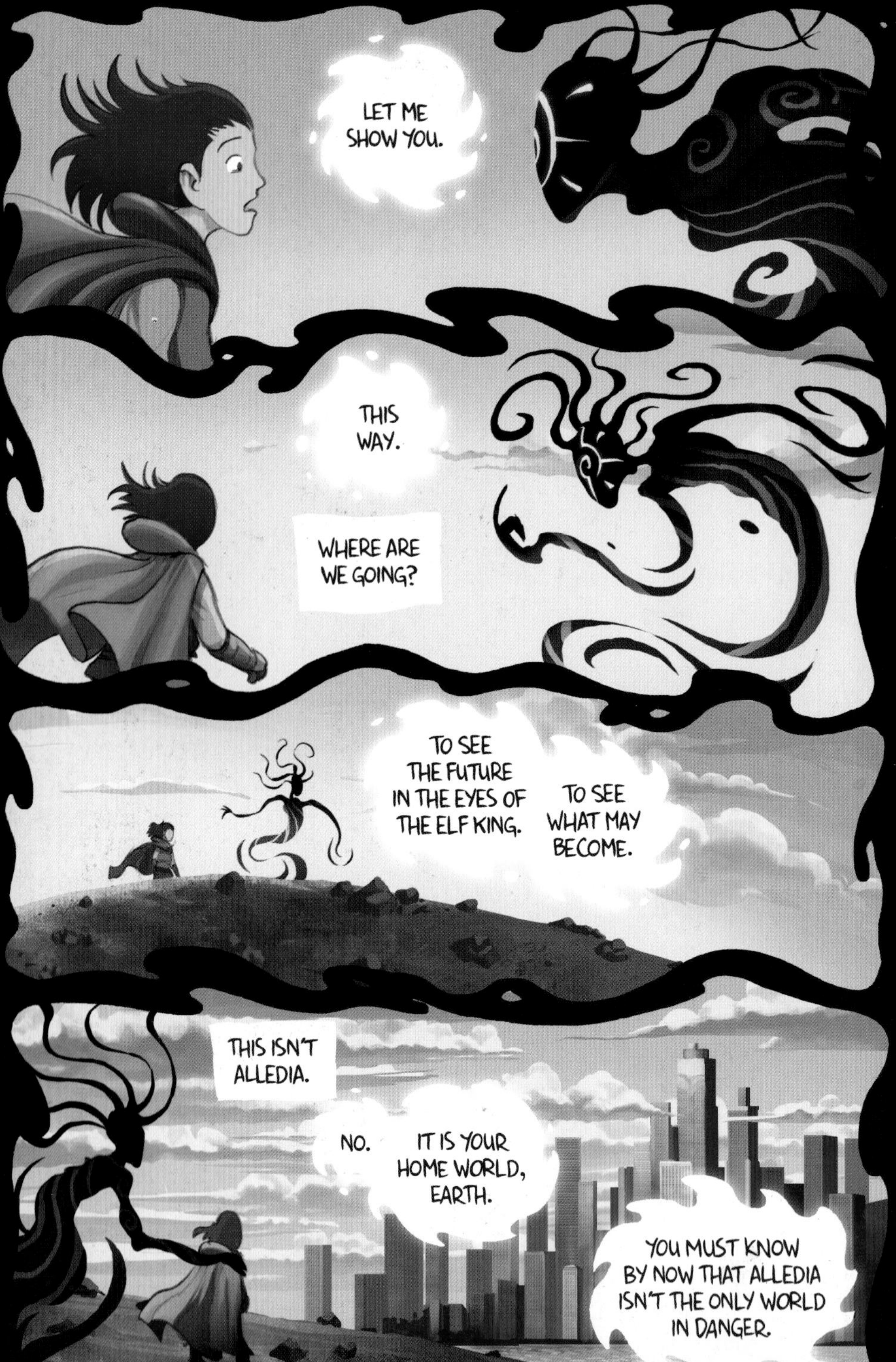
LET ME SHOW YOU.
THIS WAY.
WHERE ARE WE GOING?
TO SEE THE FUTURE IN THE EYES OF THE ELF KING.
TO SEE WHAT MAY BECOME.
THIS ISN'T ALLEDIA.
NO.
IT IS YOUR HOME WORLD, EARTH.
YOU MUST KNOW BY NOW THAT ALLEDIA ISN'T THE ONLY WORLD IN DANGER.

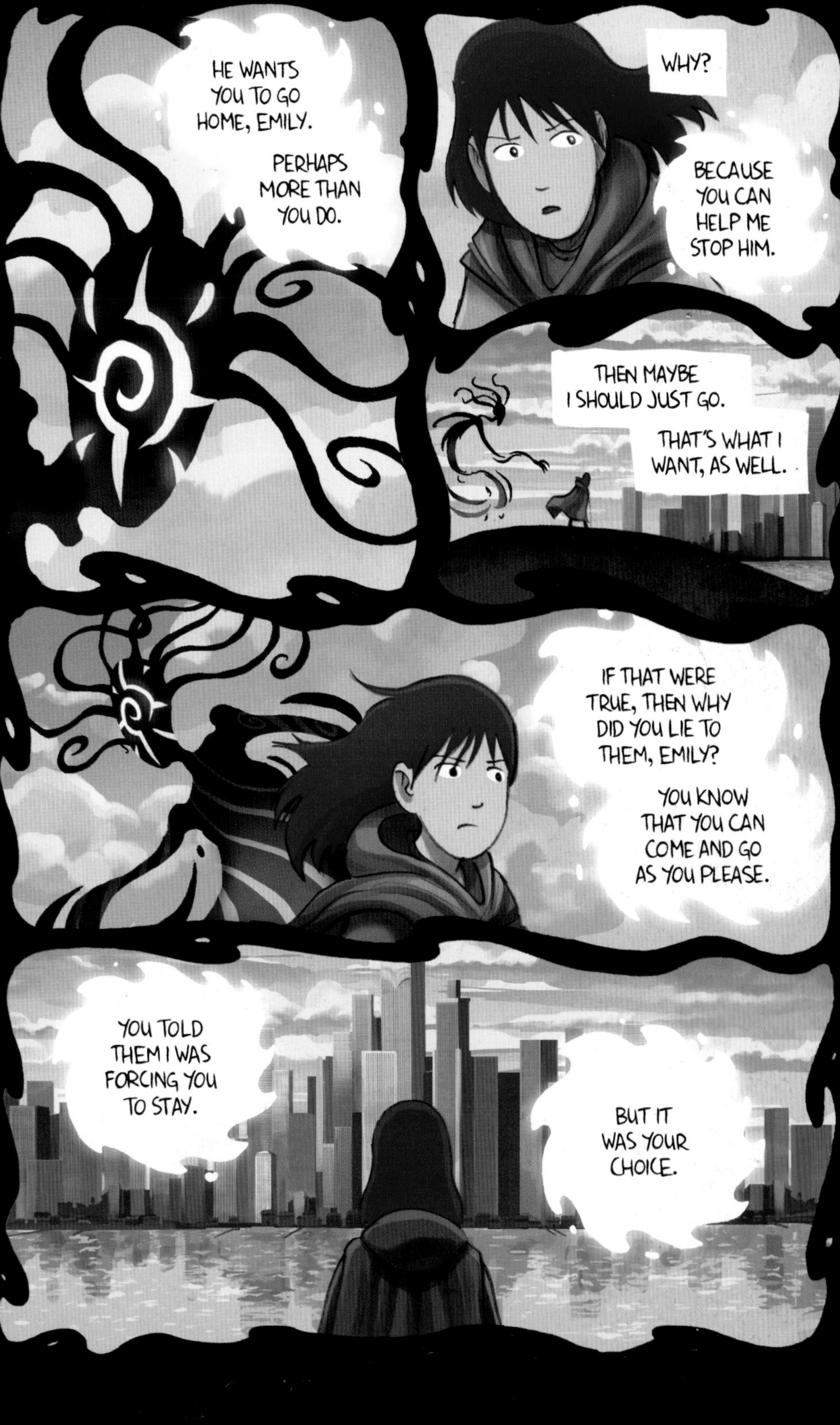
HE WANTS YOU TO GO HOME, EMILY.
PERHAPS MORE THAN YOU DO.
WHY?
BECAUSE YOU CAN HELP ME STOP HIM.
THEN MAYBE I SHOULD JUST GO.
THAT'S WHAT I WANT, AS WELL.
IF THAT WERE TRUE, THEN WHY DID YOU LIE TO THEM, EMILY?
YOU KNOW THAT YOU CAN COME AND GO AS YOU PLEASE.
YOU TOLD THEM I WAS FORCING YOU TO STAY.
BUT IT WAS YOUR CHOICE.

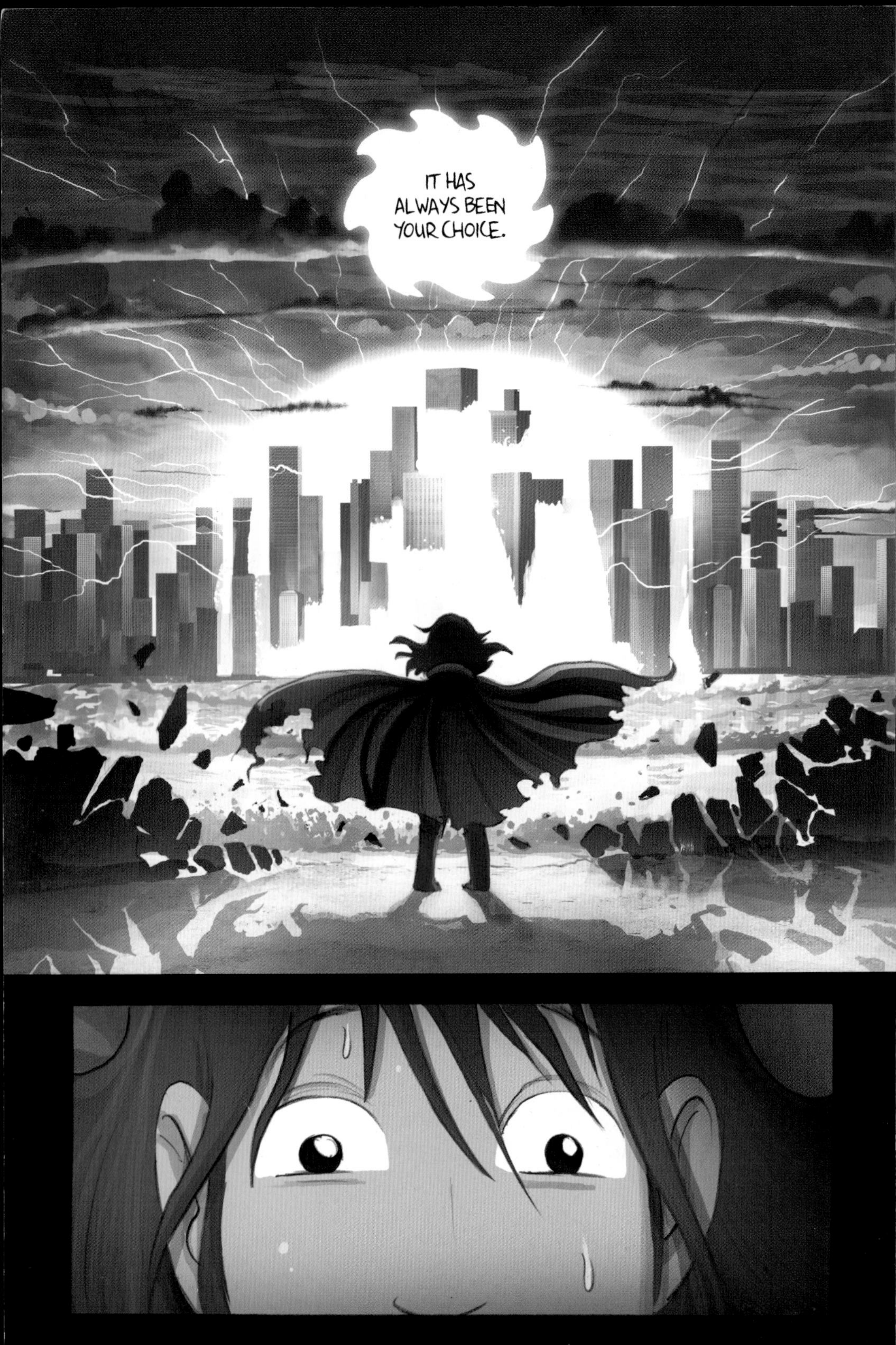
IT HAS
ALWAYS BEEN
YOUR CHOICE.

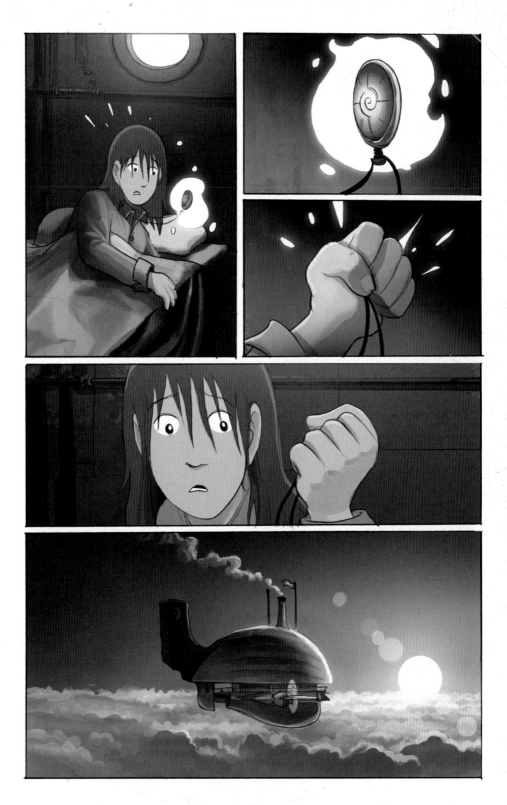

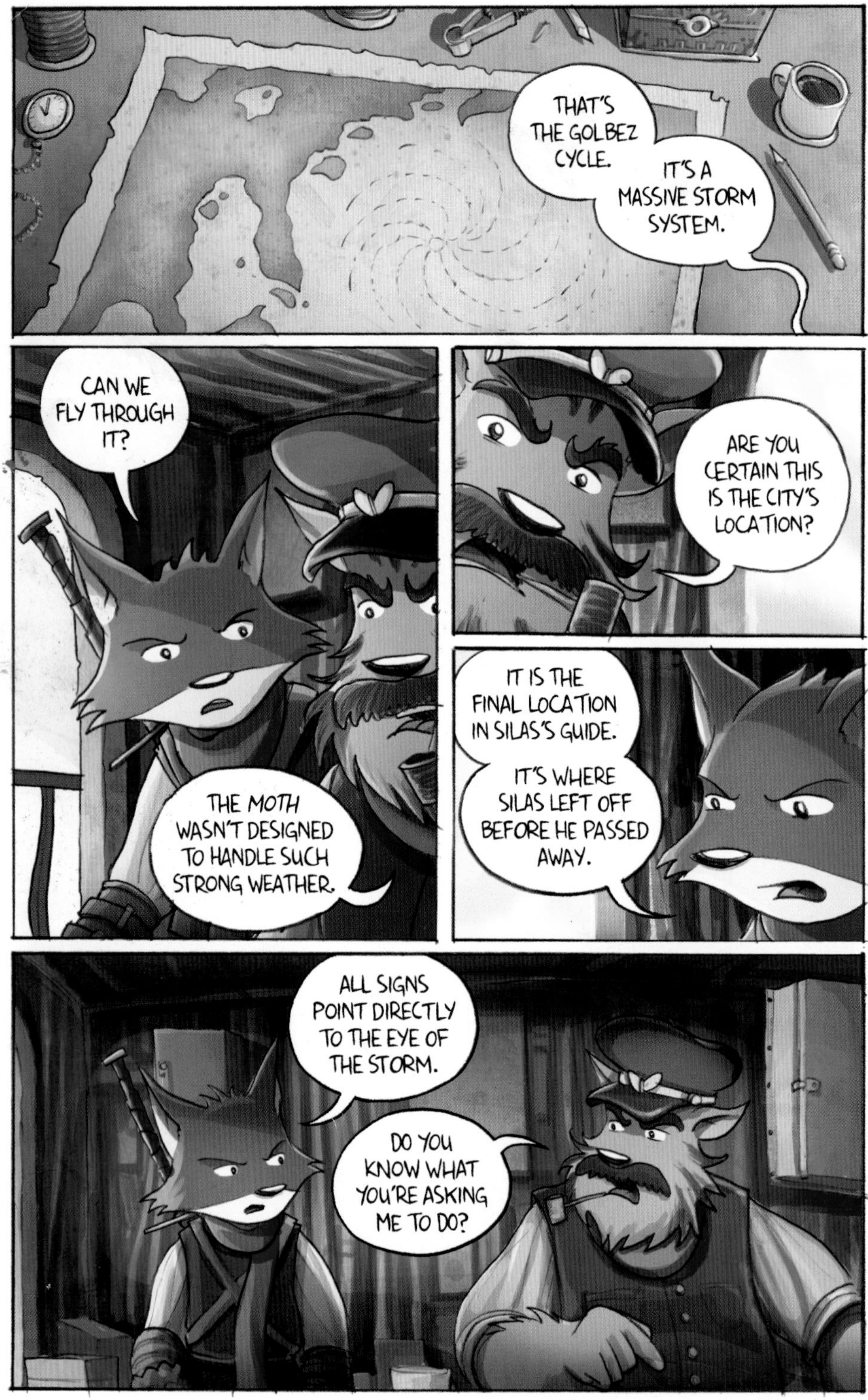
THAT'S THE GOLBEZ CYCLE.
IT'S A MASSIVE STORM SYSTEM.
CAN WE FLY THROUGH IT?
THE MOTH WASN'T DESIGNED TO HANDLE SUCH STRONG WEATHER.
ARE YOU CERTAIN THIS IS THE CITY'S LOCATION?
IT IS THE FINAL LOCATION IN SILAS'S GUIDE.
IT'S WHERE SILAS LEFT OFF BEFORE HE PASSED AWAY.
ALL SIGNS POINT DIRECTLY TO THE EYE OF THE STORM.
DO YOU KNOW WHAT YOU'RE ASKING ME TO DO?

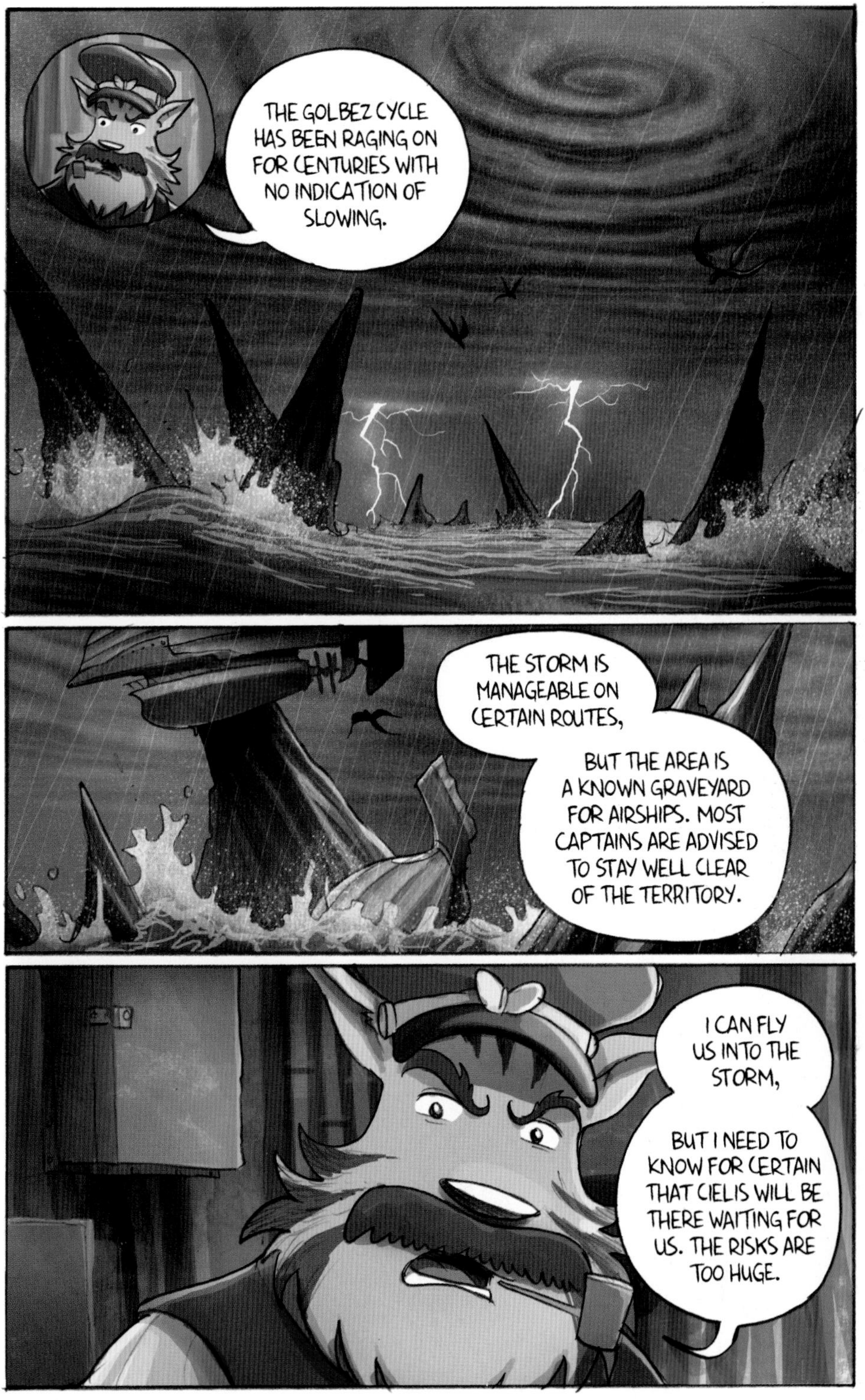
THE GOLBEZ CYCLE HAS BEEN RAGING ON FOR CENTURIES WITH NO INDICATION OF SLOWING.
THE STORM IS MANAGEABLE ON CERTAIN ROUTES,
BUT THE AREA IS A KNOWN GRAVEYARD FOR AIRSHIPS. MOST CAPTAINS ARE ADVISED TO STAY WELL CLEAR OF THE TERRITORY.
I CAN FLY US INTO THE STORM,
BUT I NEED TO KNOW FOR CERTAIN THAT CIELIS WILL BE THERE WAITING FOR US. THE RISKS ARE TOO HUGE.

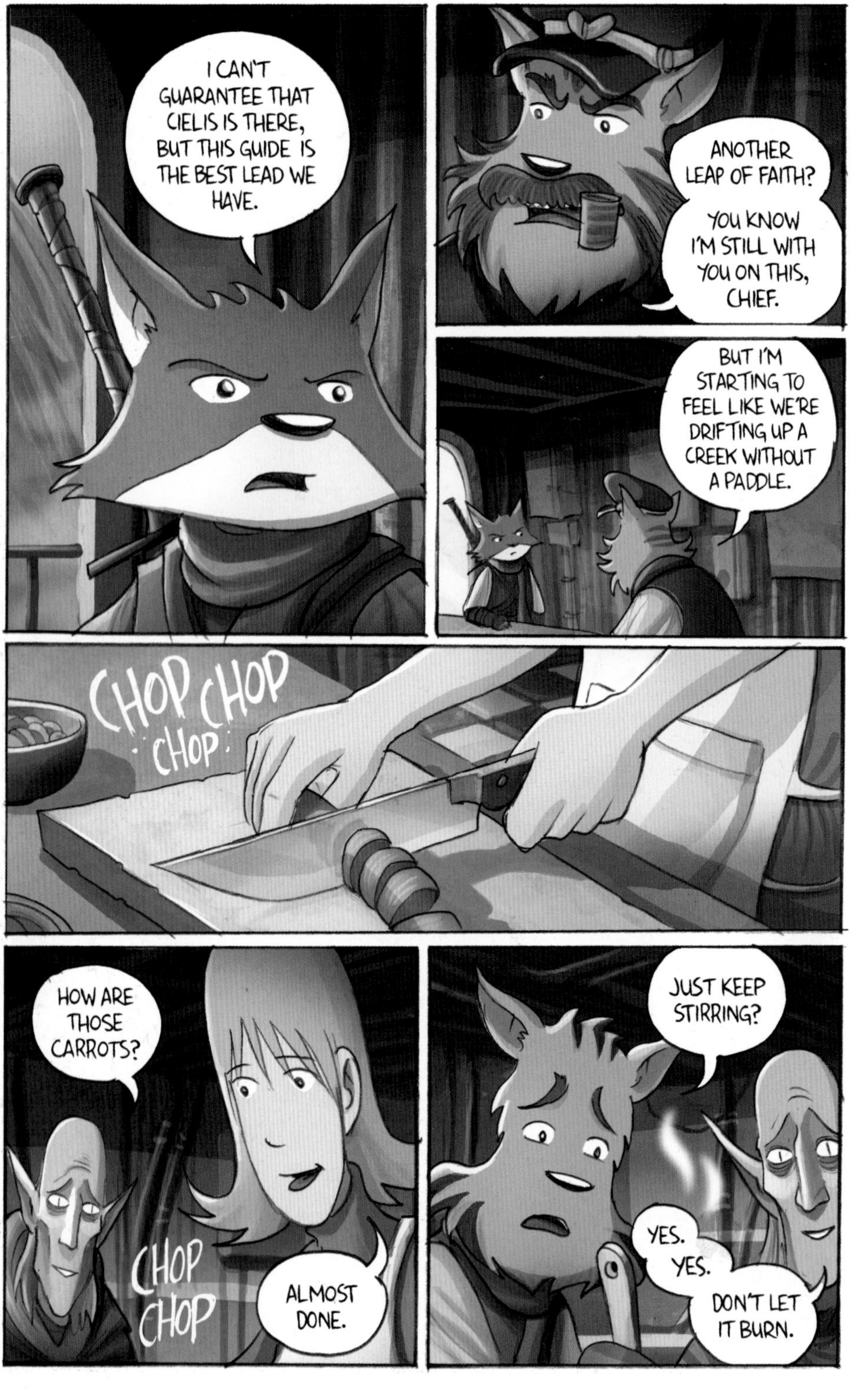
I CAN'T GUARANTEE THAT CIELIS IS THERE, BUT THIS GUIDE IS THE BEST LEAD WE HAVE.
ANOTHER LEAP OF FAITH?
YOU KNOW I'M STILL WITH YOU ON THIS, CHIEF.
BUT I'M STARTING TO FEEL LIKE WE'RE DRIFTING UP A CREEK WITHOUT A PADDLE.
CHOP CHOP
CHOP
HOW ARE THOSE CARROTS?
CHOP CHOP
ALMOST DONE.
JUST KEEP STIRRING?
YES.
YES.
DON'T LET IT BURN.

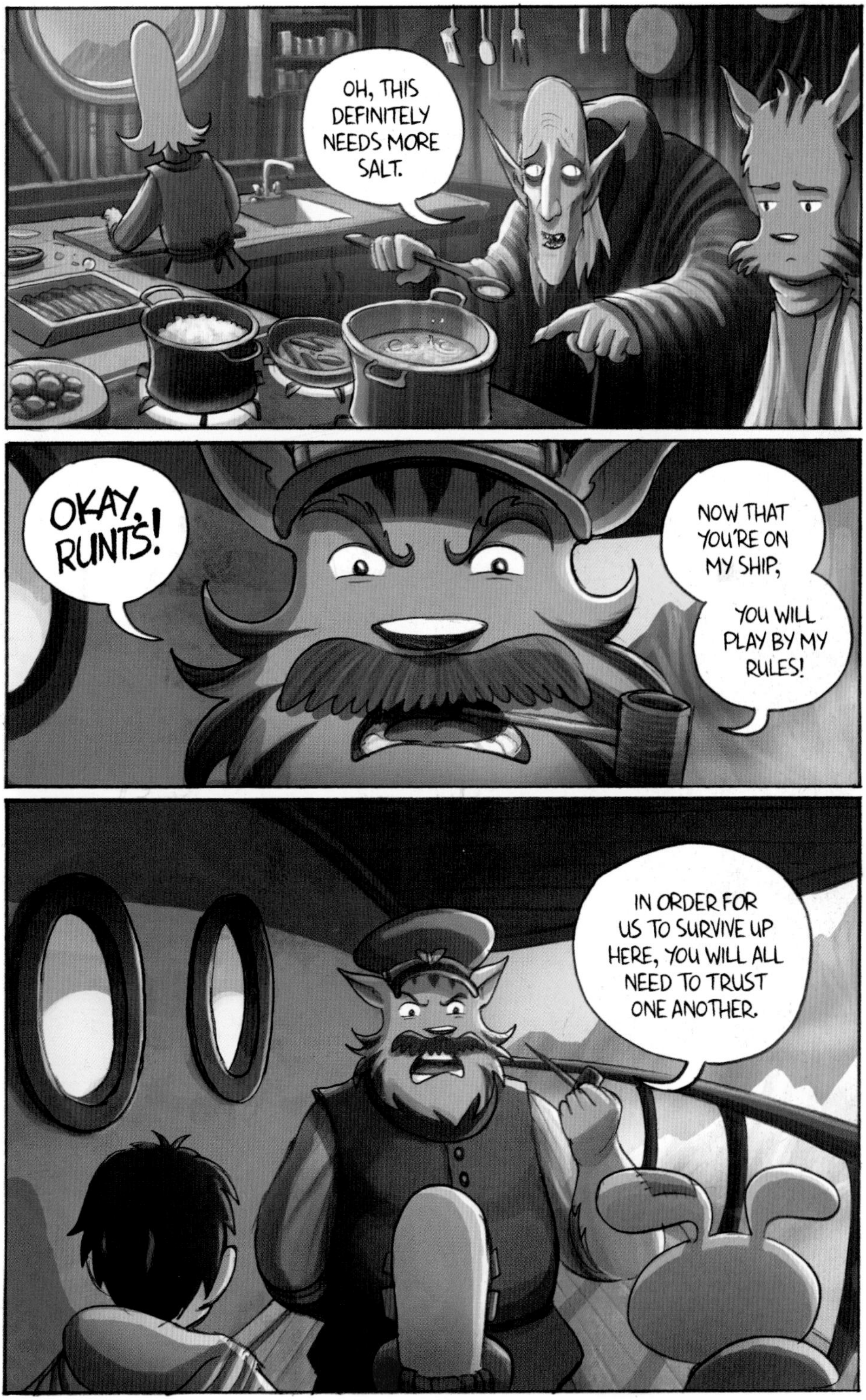
OH, THIS DEFINITELY NEEDS MORE SALT.
OKAY, RUNTS!
NOW THAT YOU'RE ON MY SHIP,
YOU WILL PLAY BY MY RULES!
IN ORDER FOR US TO SURVIVE UP HERE, YOU WILL ALL NEED TO TRUST ONE ANOTHER.

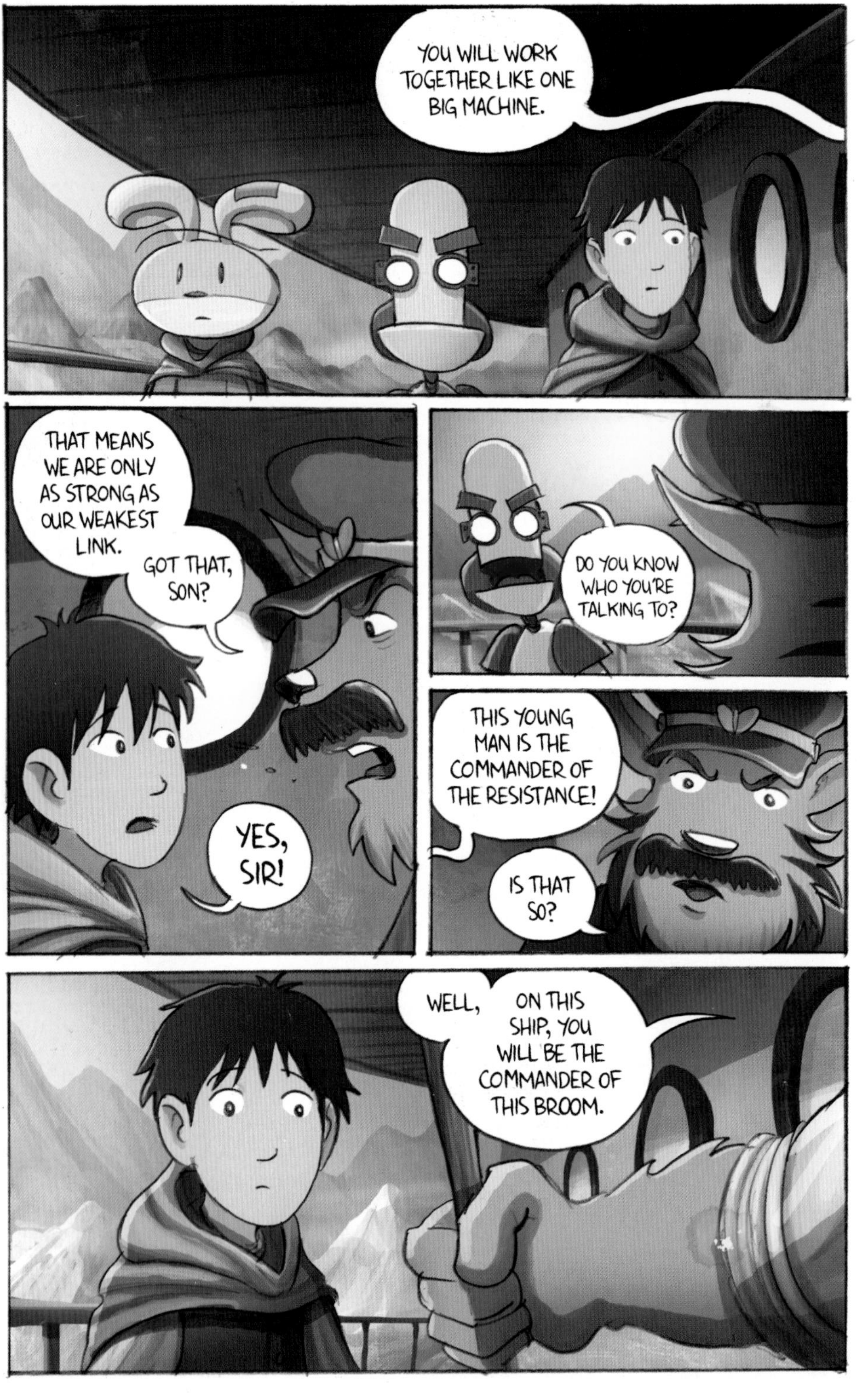
YOU WILL WORK TOGETHER LIKE ONE BIG MACHINE.
THAT MEANS WE ARE ONLY AS STRONG AS OUR WEAKEST LINK.
GOT THAT, SON?
YES, SIR!
DO YOU KNOW WHO YOU'RE TALKING TO?
THIS YOUNG MAN IS THE COMMANDER OF THE RESISTANCE!
IS THAT SO?
WELL,
ON THIS SHIP, YOU WILL BE THE COMMANDER OF THIS BROOM.

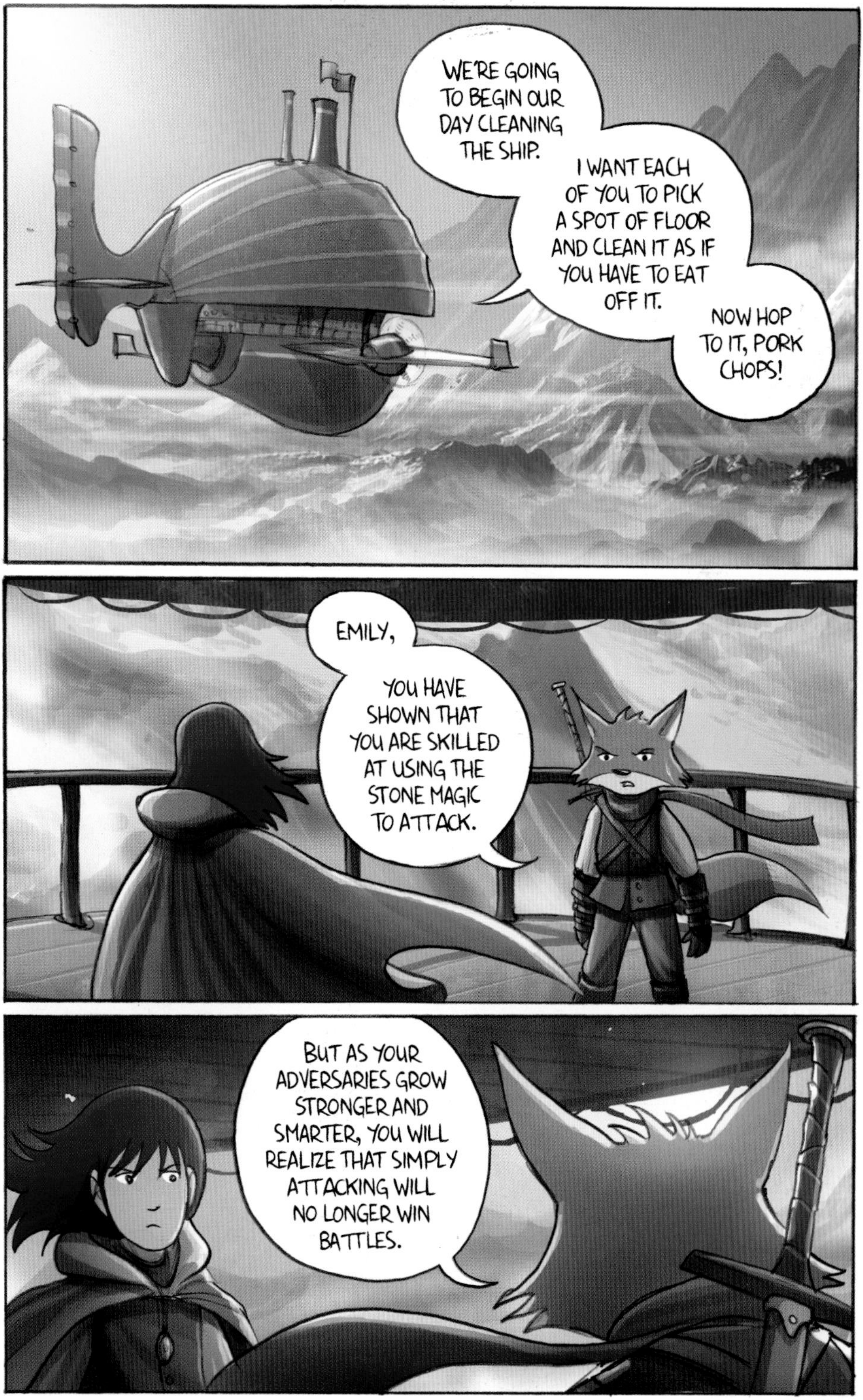

WE'RE GOING TO BEGIN OUR DAY CLEANING THE SHIP.
I WANT EACH OF YOU TO PICK A SPOT OF FLOOR AND CLEAN IT AS IF YOU HAVE TO EAT OFF IT.
NOW HOP TO IT, PORK CHOPS!
EMILY,
YOU HAVE SHOWN THAT YOU ARE SKILLED AT USING THE STONE MAGIC TO ATTACK.
BUT AS YOUR ADVERSARIES GROW STRONGER AND SMARTER, YOU WILL REALIZE THAT SIMPLY ATTACKING WILL NO LONGER WIN BATTLES.

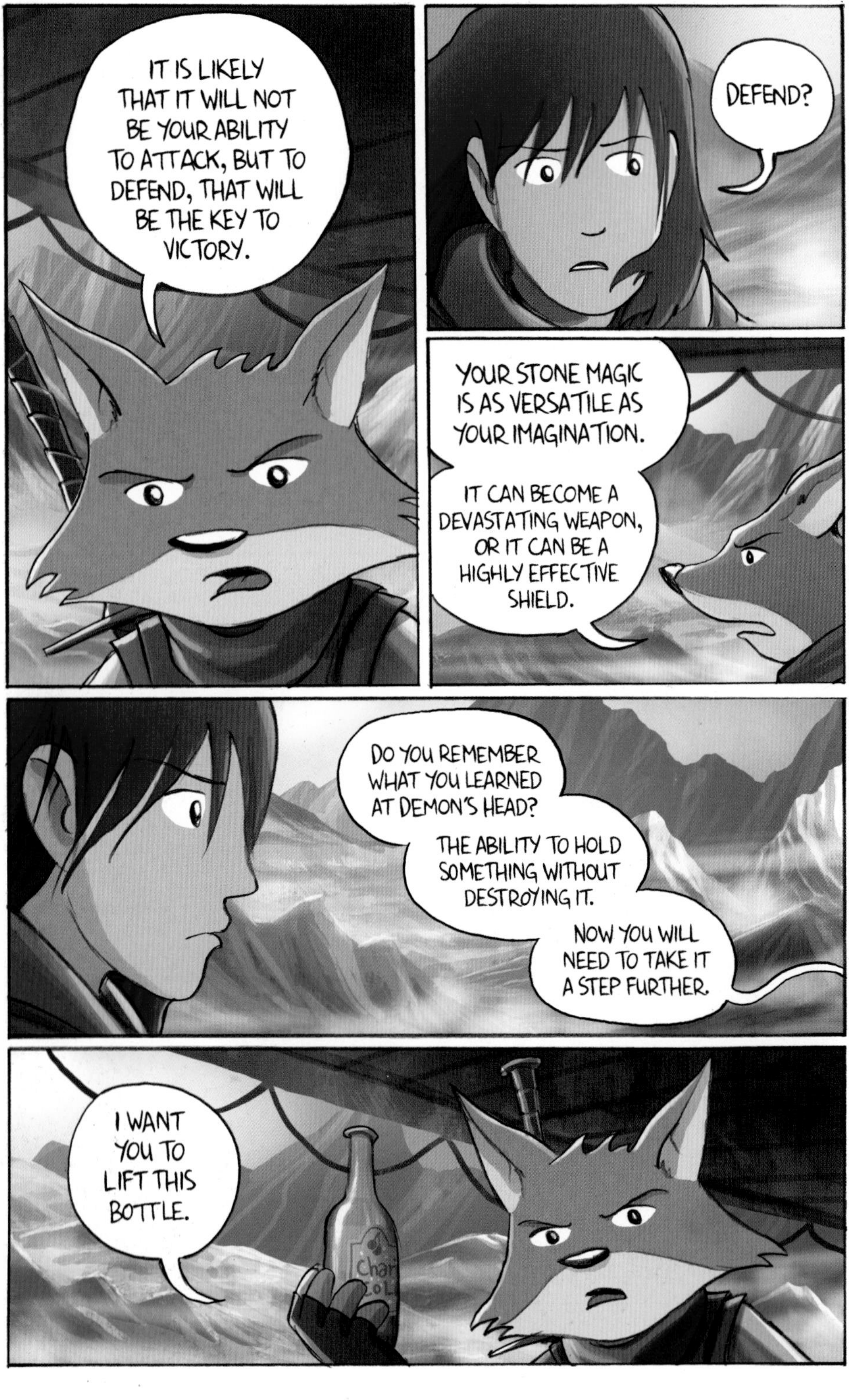
IT IS LIKELY THAT IT WILL NOT BE YOUR ABILITY TO ATTACK, BUT TO DEFEND, THAT WILL BE THE KEY TO VICTORY.
DEFEND?
YOUR STONE MAGIC IS AS VERSATILE AS YOUR IMAGINATION.
IT CAN BECOME A DEVASTATING WEAPON, OR IT CAN BE A HIGHLY EFFECTIVE SHIELD.
DO YOU REMEMBER WHAT YOU LEARNED AT DEMON'S HEAD?
THE ABILITY TO HOLD SOMETHING WITHOUT DESTROYING IT.
NOW YOU WILL NEED TO TAKE IT A STEP FURTHER.
I WANT YOU TO LIFT THIS BOTTLE.

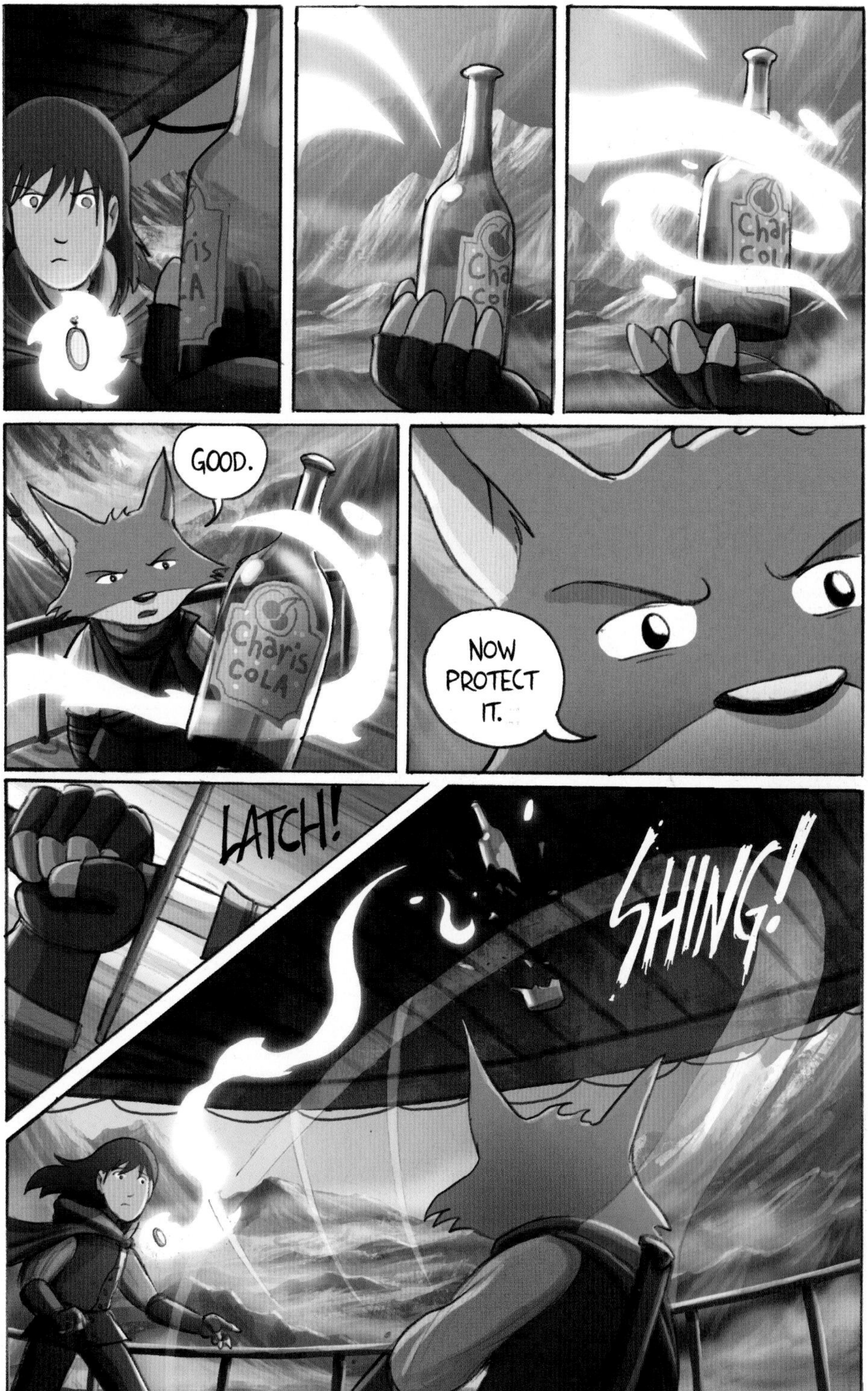
Char's COLA
GOOD.
NOW PROTECT IT.
LATCH!
SHING!

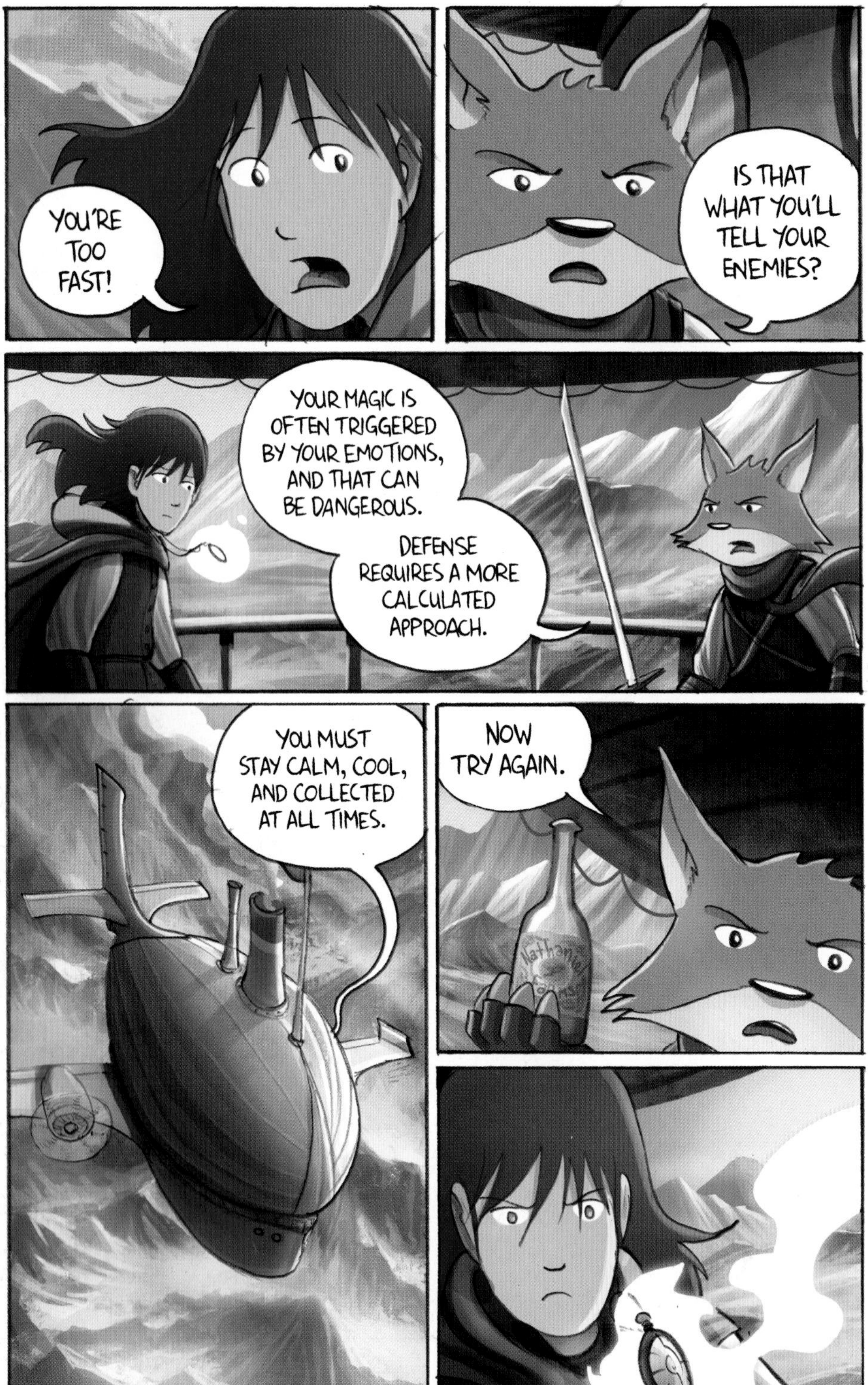
YOU'RE TOO FAST!
IS THAT WHAT YOU'LL TELL YOUR ENEMIES?
YOUR MAGIC IS OFTEN TRIGGERED BY YOUR EMOTIONS, AND THAT CAN BE DANGEROUS.
DEFENSE REQUIRES A MORE CALCULATED APPROACH.
YOU MUST STAY CALM, COOL, AND COLLECTED AT ALL TIMES.
NOW TRY AGAIN.

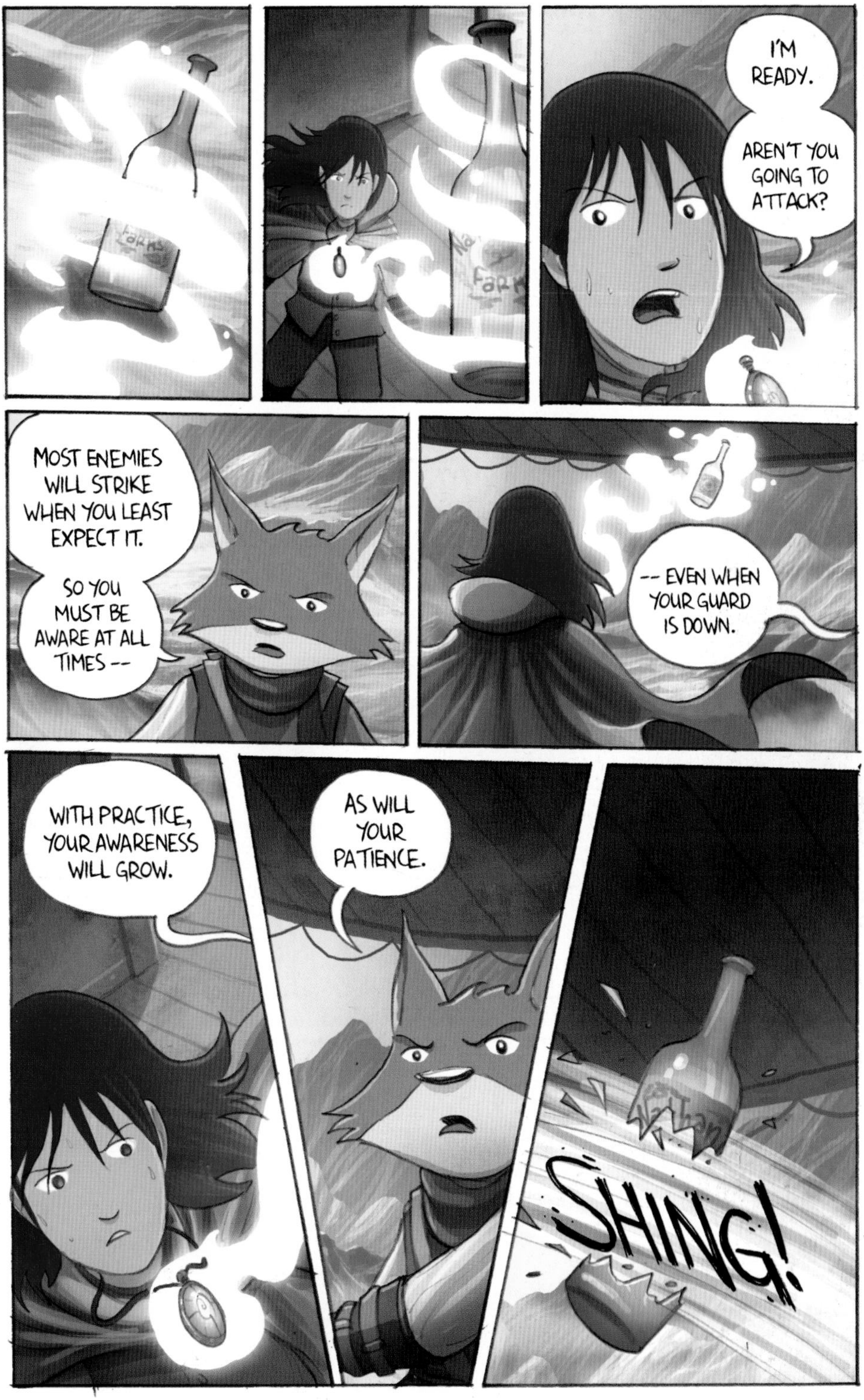
I'M READY.
AREN'T YOU GOING TO ATTACK?
MOST ENEMIES WILL STRIKE WHEN YOU LEAST EXPECT IT.
SO YOU MUST BE AWARE AT ALL TIMES --
-- EVEN WHEN YOUR GUARD IS DOWN.
WITH PRACTICE, YOUR AWARENESS WILL GROW.
AS WILL YOUR PATIENCE.
SHING!

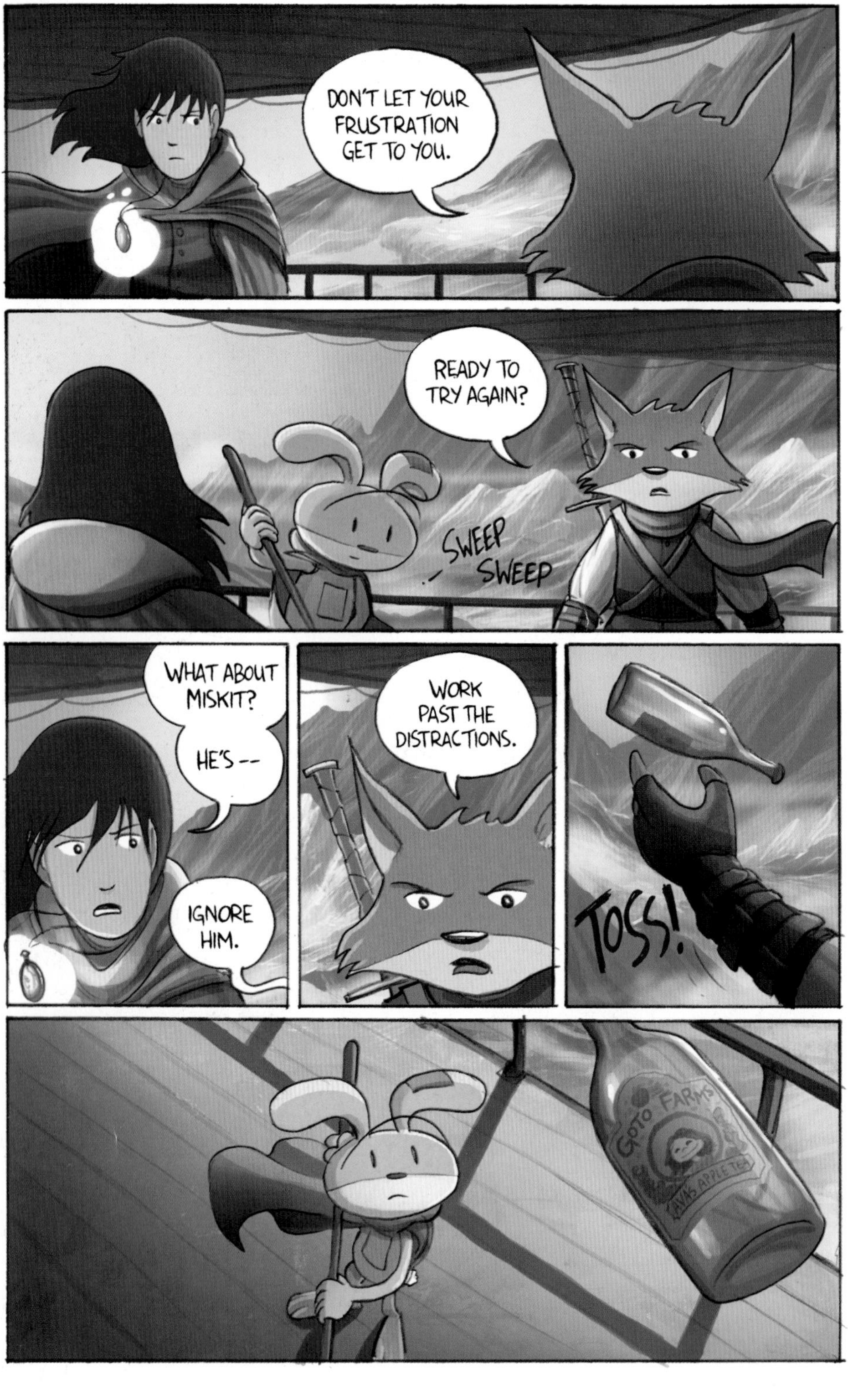
DON'T LET YOUR FRUSTRATION GET TO YOU.
READY TO TRY AGAIN?
SWEEP SWEEP
WHAT ABOUT MISKIT?
HE'S --
IGNORE HIM.
WORK PAST THE DISTRACTIONS.
TOSS!
GOTO FARMS
AVA'S APPLE TEA

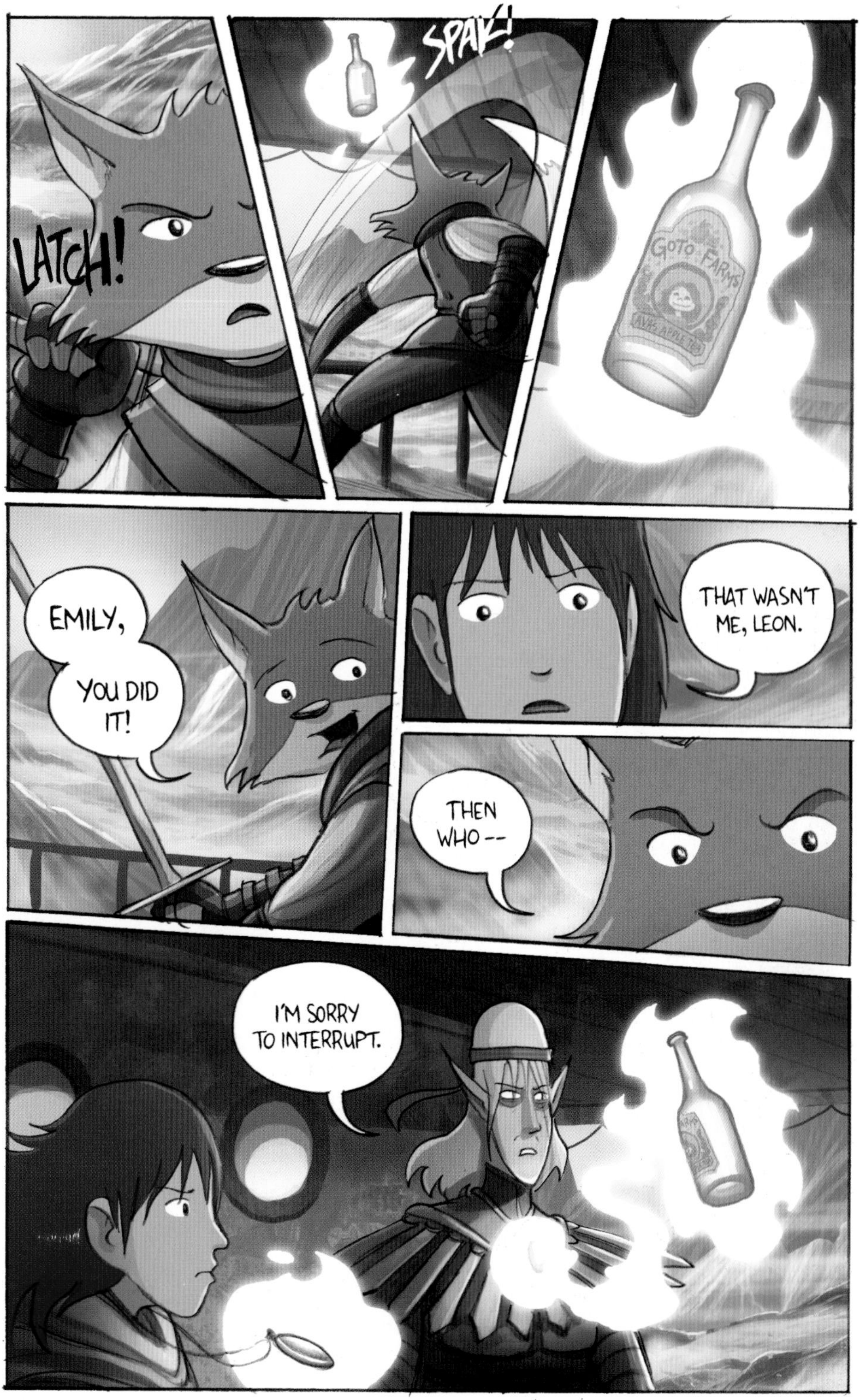
LATCH!
SPAK!
GOTO FARMS
AVA'S APPLE TEA
EMILY,
YOU DID IT!
THAT WASN'T ME, LEON.
THEN WHO --
I'M SORRY TO INTERRUPT.

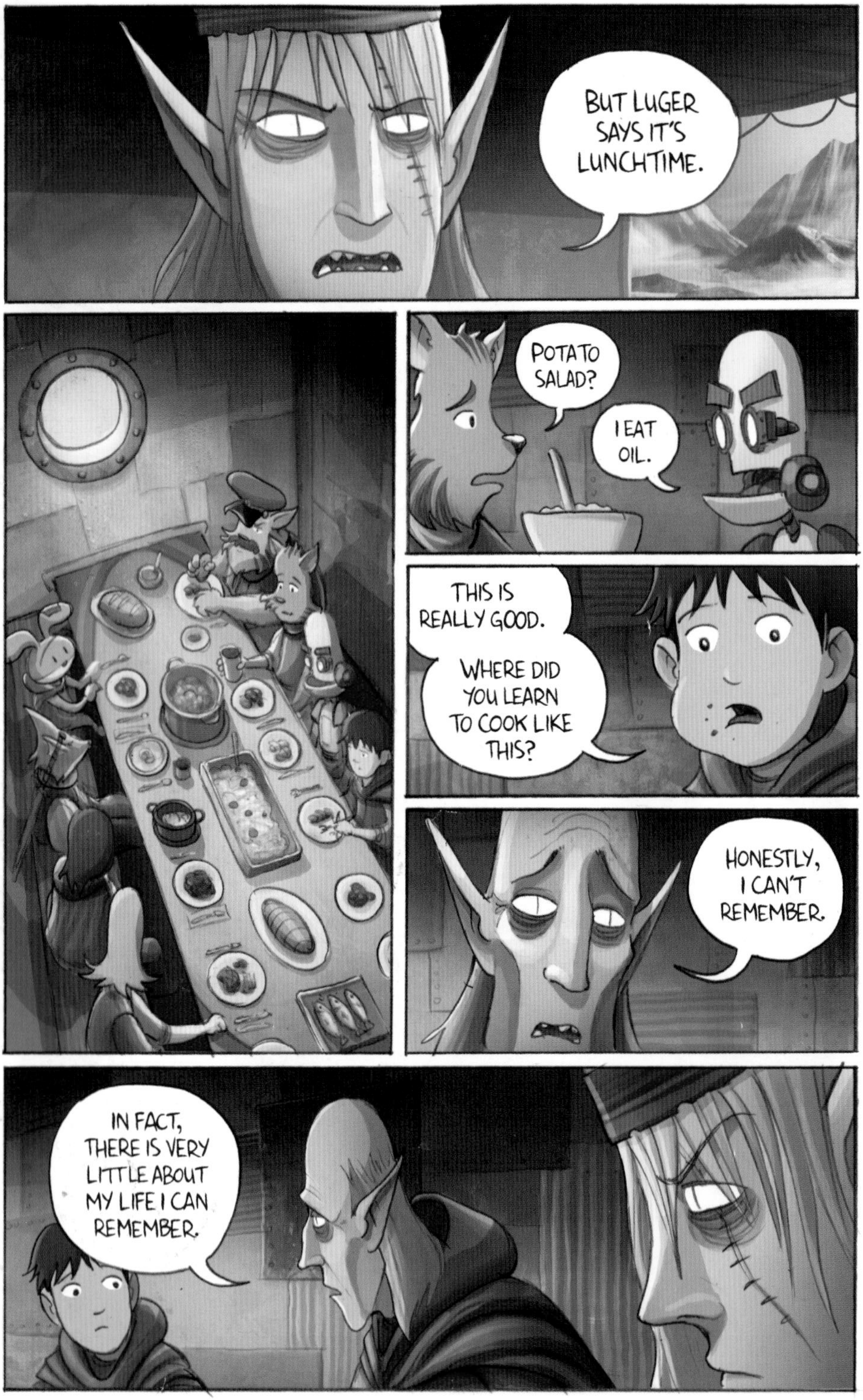
BUT LUGER SAYS IT'S LUNCHTIME.
POTATO SALAD?
I EAT OIL.
THIS IS REALLY GOOD.
WHERE DID YOU LEARN TO COOK LIKE THIS?
HONESTLY, I CAN'T REMEMBER.
IN FACT, THERE IS VERY LITTLE ABOUT MY LIFE I CAN REMEMBER.

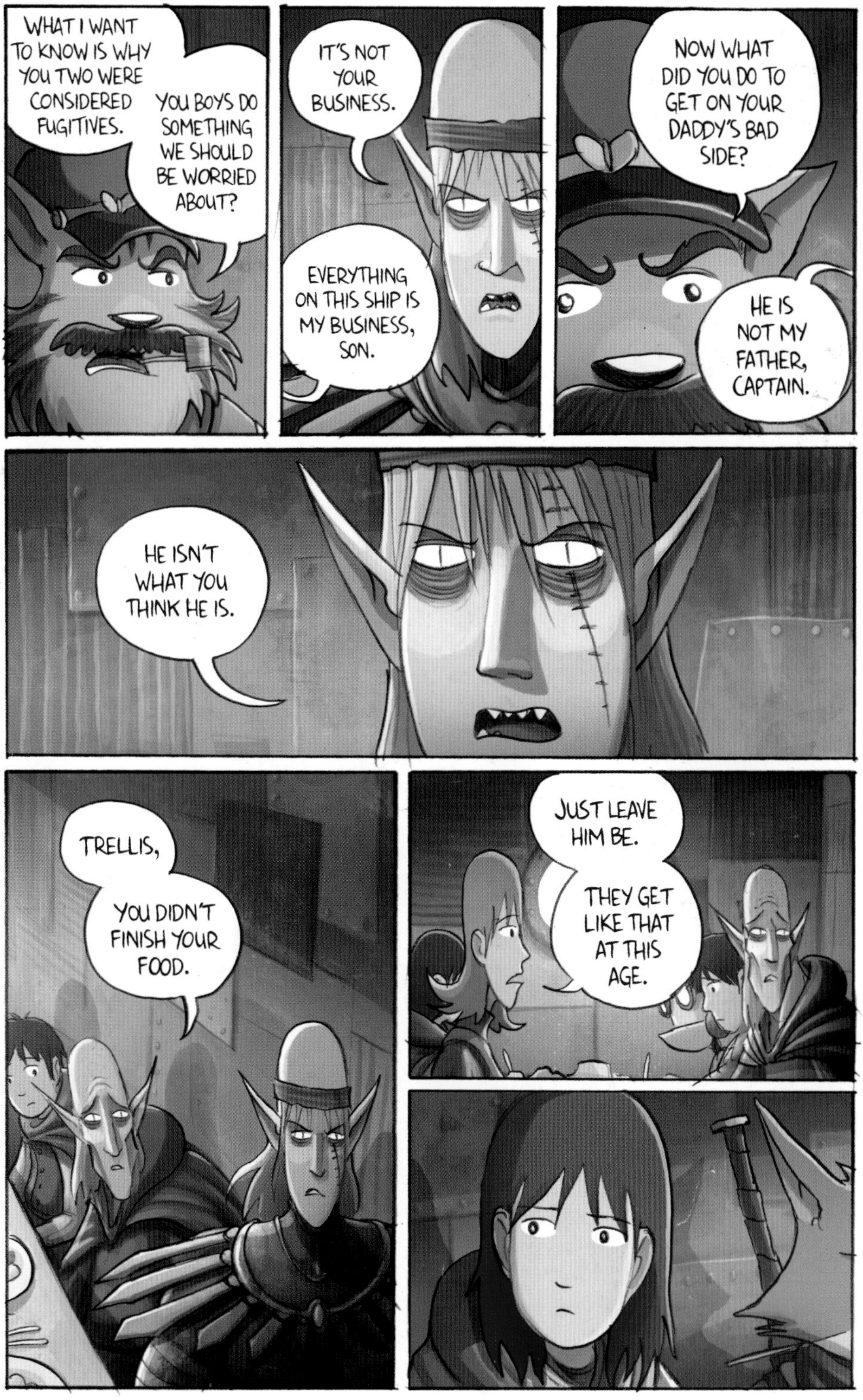
WHAT I WANT TO KNOW IS WHY YOU TWO WERE CONSIDERED FUGITIVES.
YOU BOYS DO SOMETHING WE SHOULD BE WORRIED ABOUT?
IT'S NOT YOUR BUSINESS.
EVERYTHING ON THIS SHIP IS MY BUSINESS, SON.
NOW WHAT DID YOU DO TO GET ON YOUR DADDY'S BAD SIDE?
HE IS NOT MY FATHER, CAPTAIN.
HE ISN'T WHAT YOU THINK HE IS.
TRELLIS,
YOU DIDN'T FINISH YOUR FOOD.
JUST LEAVE HIM BE.
THEY GET LIKE THAT AT THIS AGE.

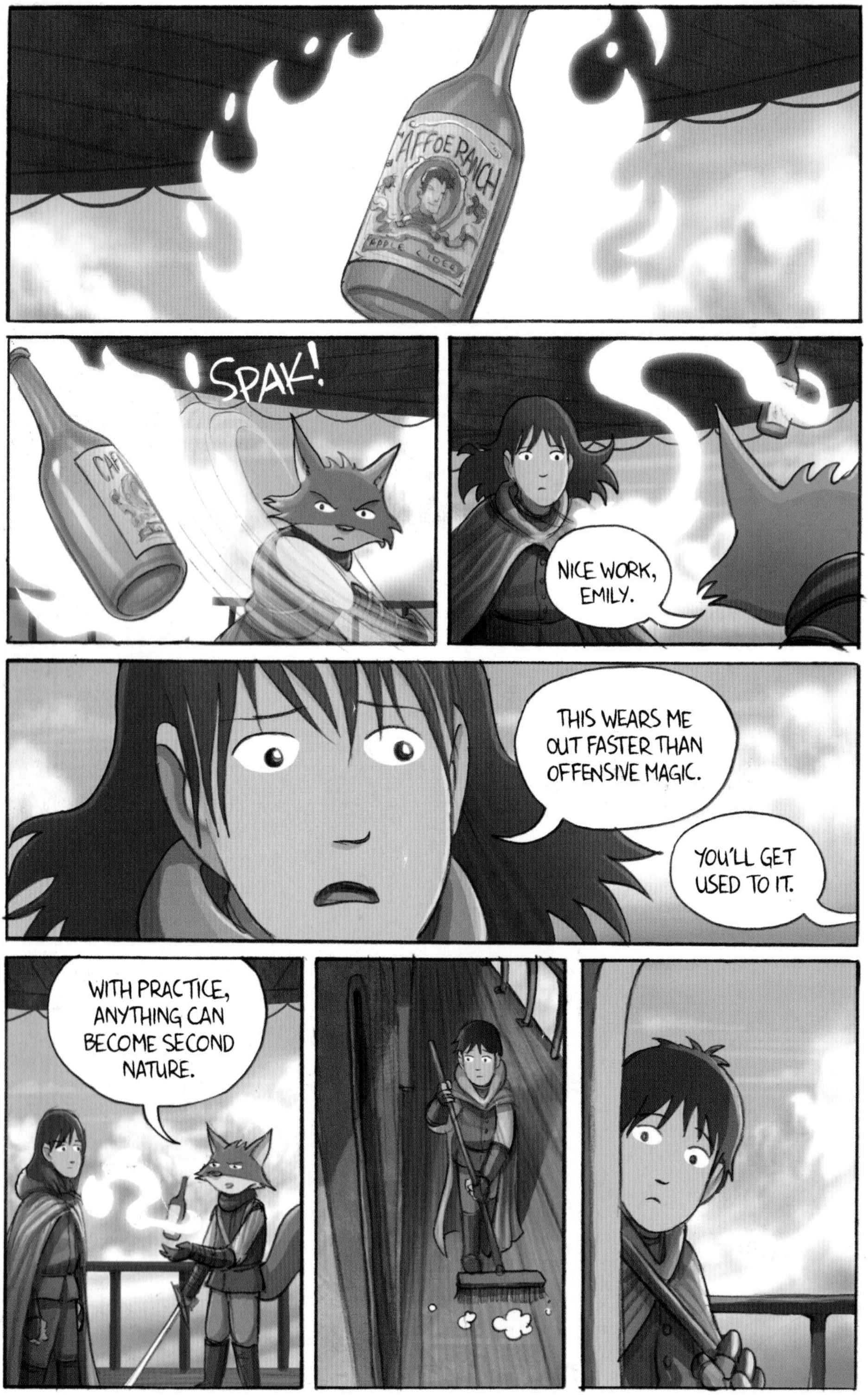
CAFFOE RANCH
APPLE CIDER
SPAK!
NICE WORK, EMILY.
THIS WEARS ME OUT FASTER THAN OFFENSIVE MAGIC.
YOU'LL GET USED TO IT.
WITH PRACTICE, ANYTHING CAN BECOME SECOND NATURE.

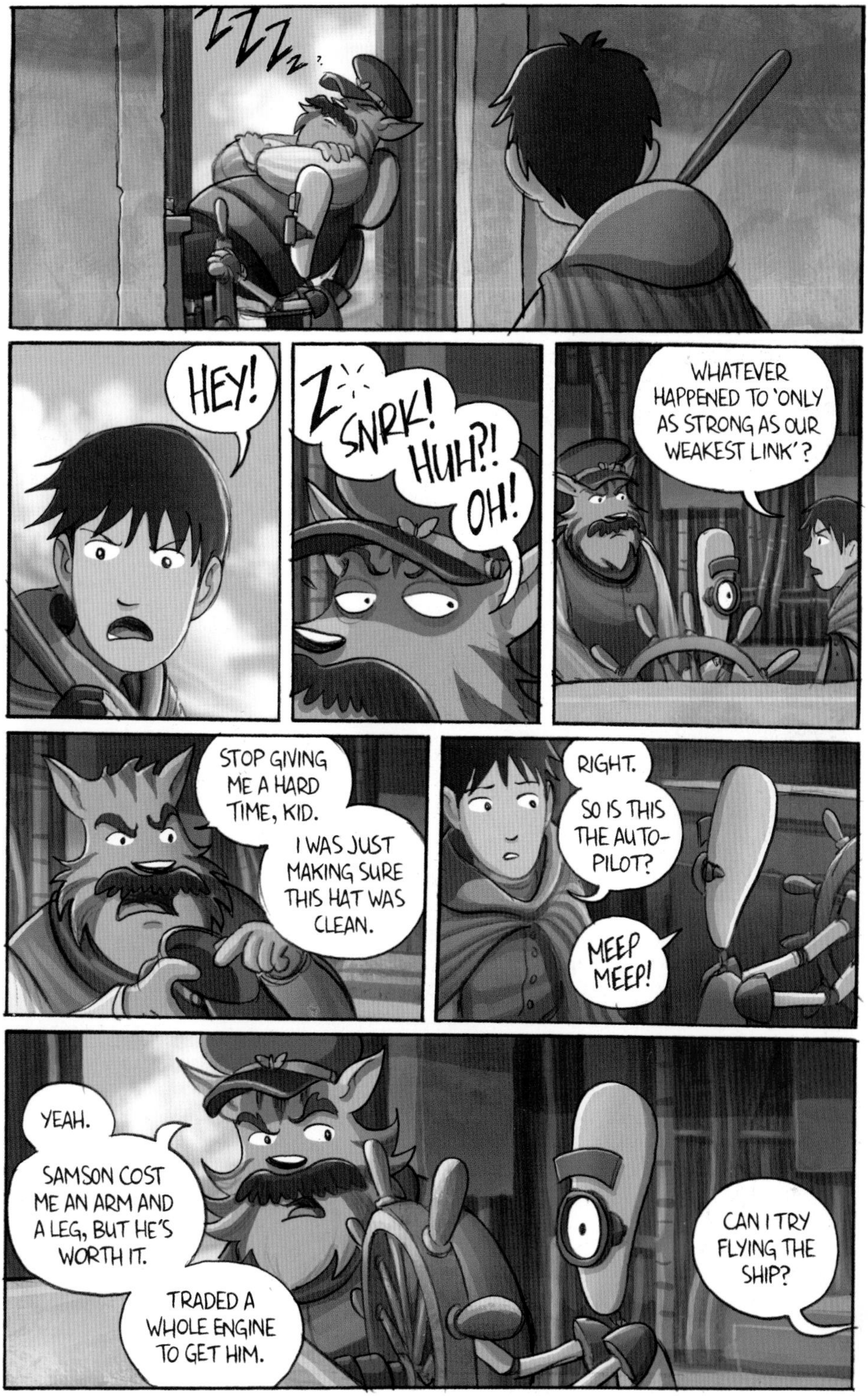
ZZZZ
HEY!
Z SNRK! HUH?! OH!
WHATEVER HAPPENED TO 'ONLY AS STRONG AS OUR WEAKEST LINK'?
STOP GIVING ME A HARD TIME, KID.
I WAS JUST MAKING SURE THIS HAT WAS CLEAN.
RIGHT.
SO IS THIS THE AUTO-PILOT?
MEEP MEEP!
YEAH.
SAMSON COST ME AN ARM AND A LEG, BUT HE'S WORTH IT.
TRADED A WHOLE ENGINE TO GET HIM.
CAN I TRY FLYING THE SHIP?

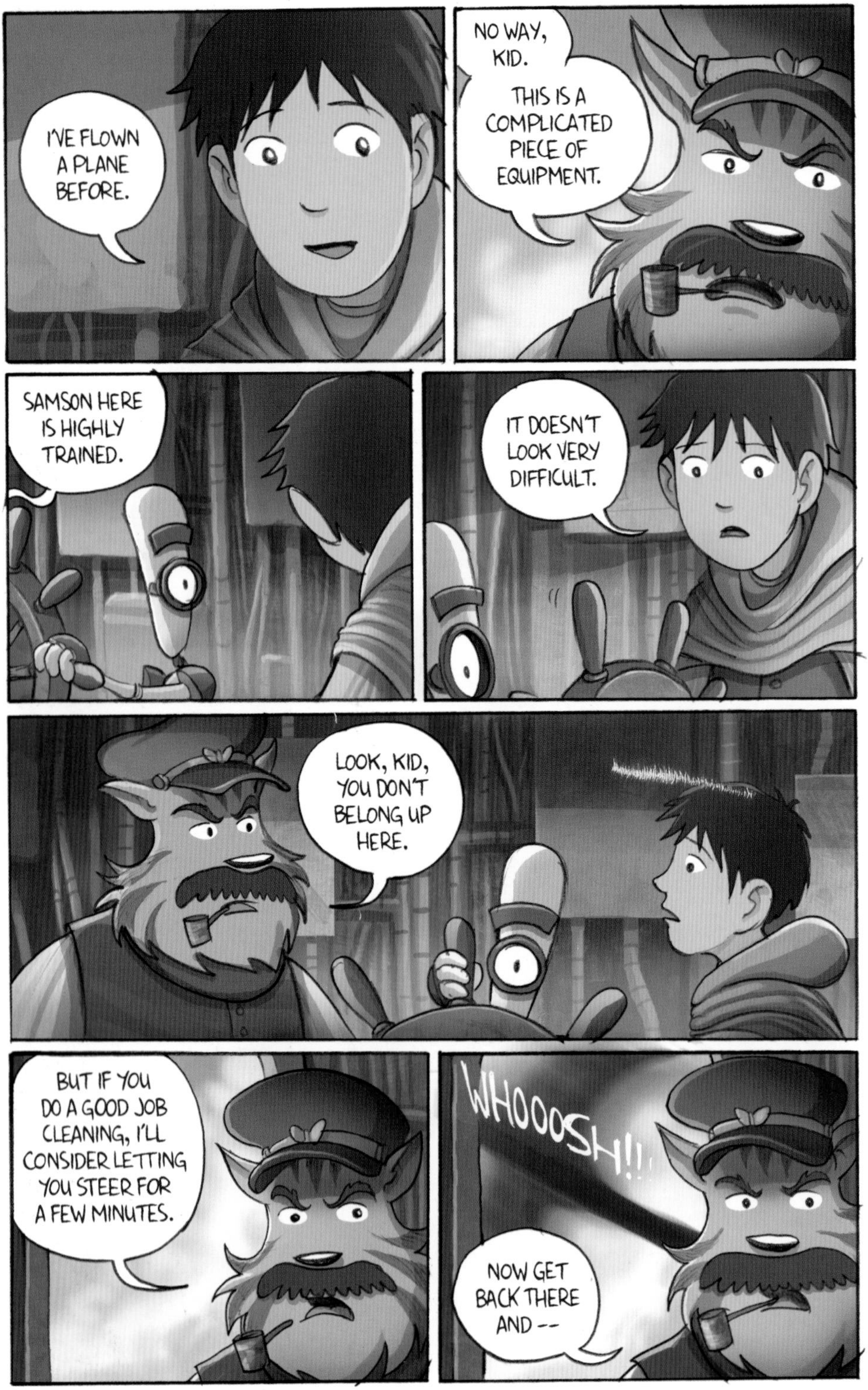
I'VE FLOWN A PLANE BEFORE.
NO WAY, KID.
THIS IS A COMPLICATED PIECE OF EQUIPMENT.
SAMSON HERE IS HIGHLY TRAINED.
IT DOESN'T LOOK VERY DIFFICULT.
LOOK, KID, YOU DON'T BELONG UP HERE.
BUT IF YOU DO A GOOD JOB CLEANING, I'LL CONSIDER LETTING YOU STEER FOR A FEW MINUTES.
WHOOOSH!!!
NOW GET BACK THERE AND --

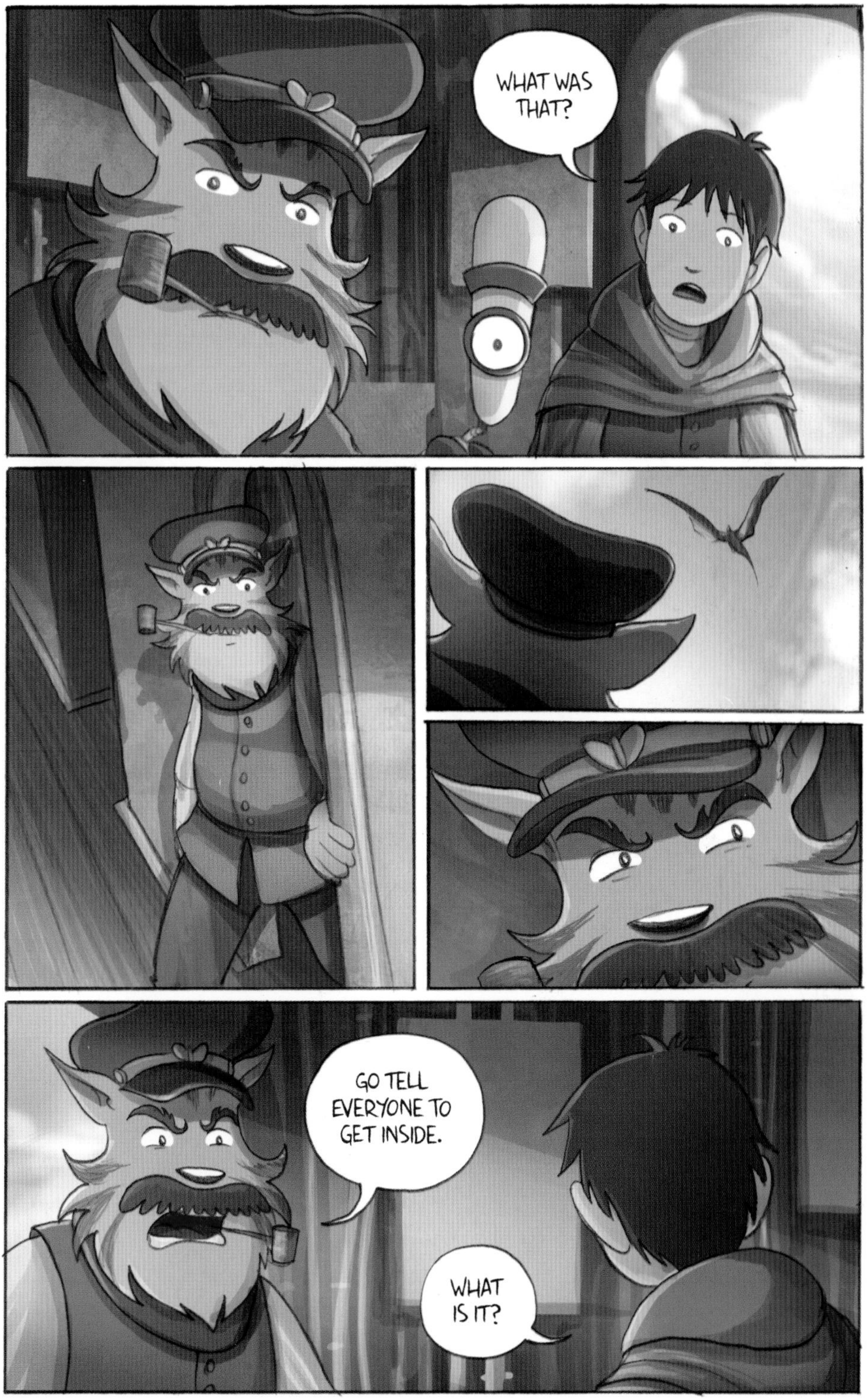
WHAT WAS THAT?
GO TELL EVERYONE TO GET INSIDE.
WHAT IS IT?

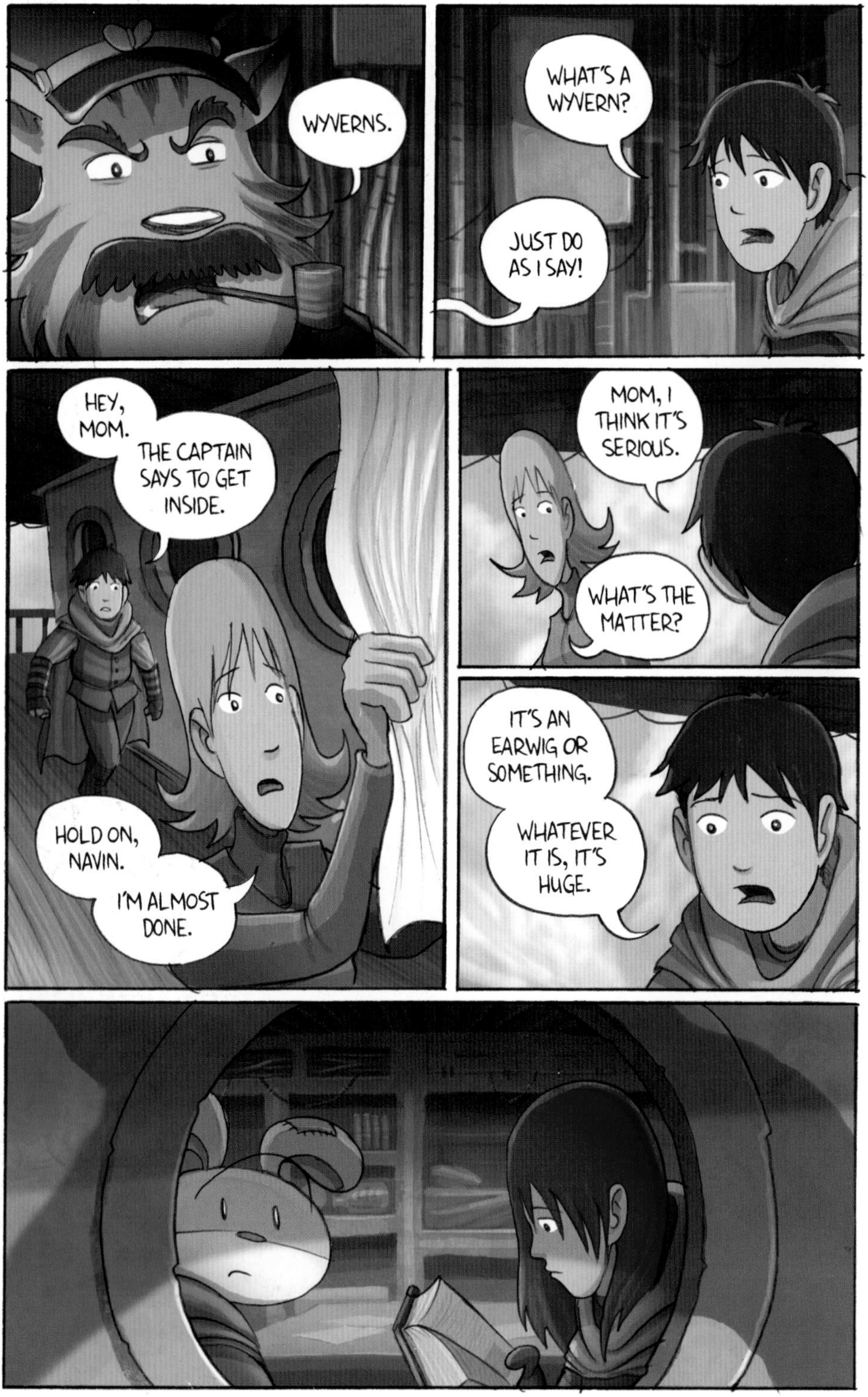
WYVERNS.
WHAT'S A WYVERN?
JUST DO AS I SAY!
HEY, MOM.
THE CAPTAIN SAYS TO GET INSIDE.
HOLD ON, NAVIN.
I'M ALMOST DONE.
MOM, I THINK IT'S SERIOUS.
WHAT'S THE MATTER?
IT'S AN EARWIG OR SOMETHING.
WHATEVER IT IS, IT'S HUGE.

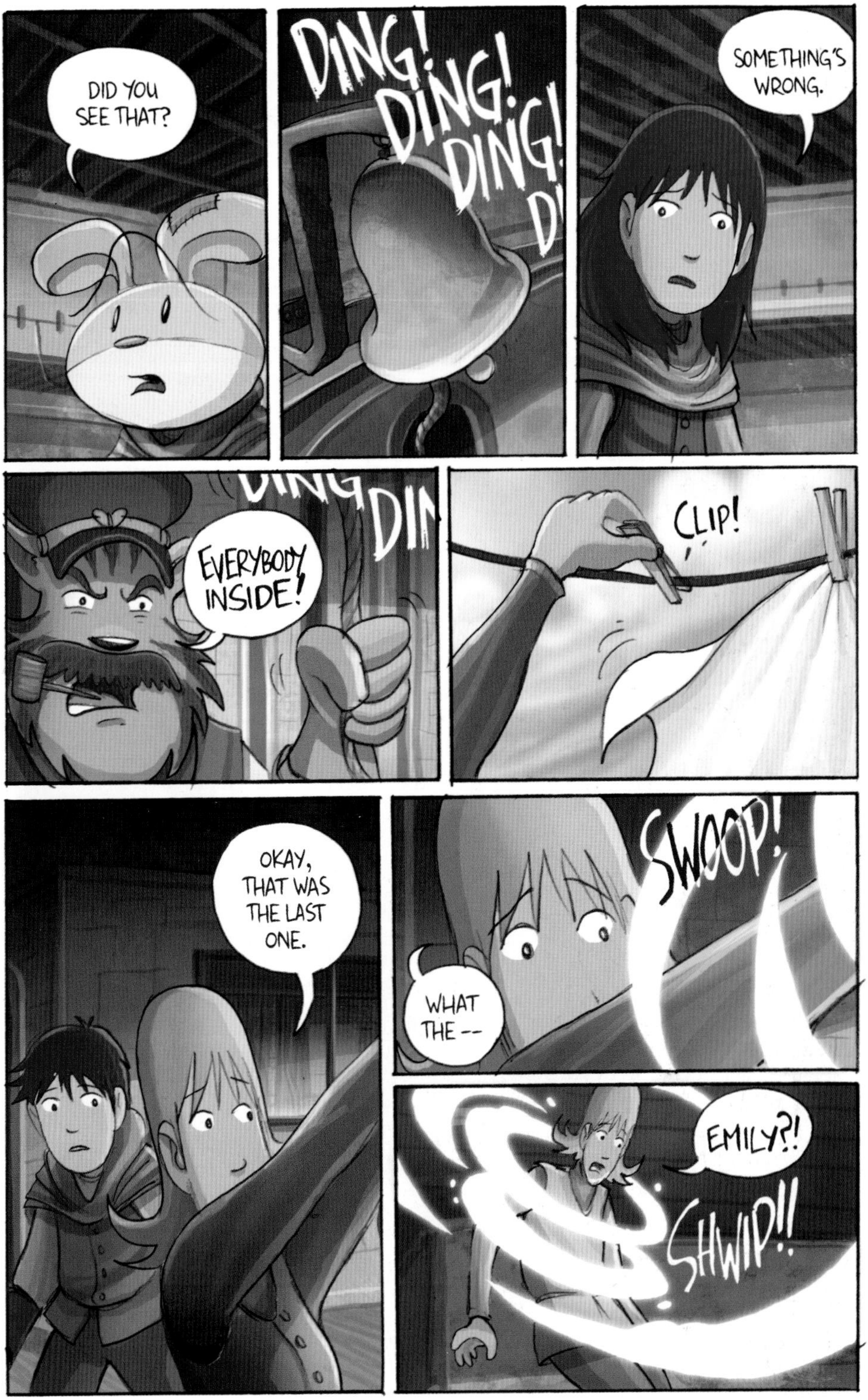
DID YOU SEE THAT?
DING! DING! DING! DI
SOMETHING'S WRONG.
DING DIN
EVERYBODY INSIDE!
CLIP!
OKAY, THAT WAS THE LAST ONE.
SWOOP!
WHAT THE --
EMILY?!
SHWIP!!

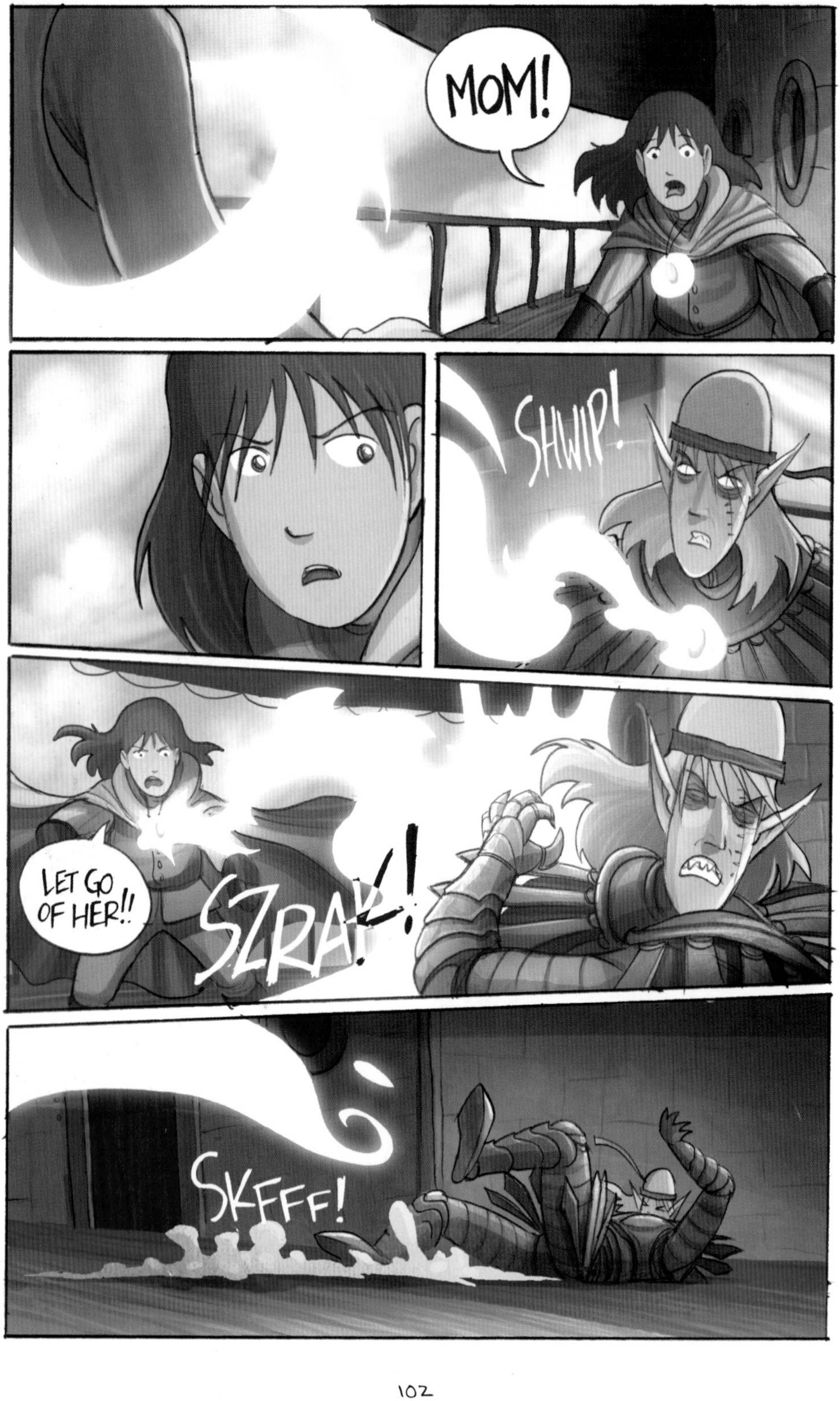
MOM!
SHWIP!
LET GO OF HER!!
SZRAK!
SKFFF!

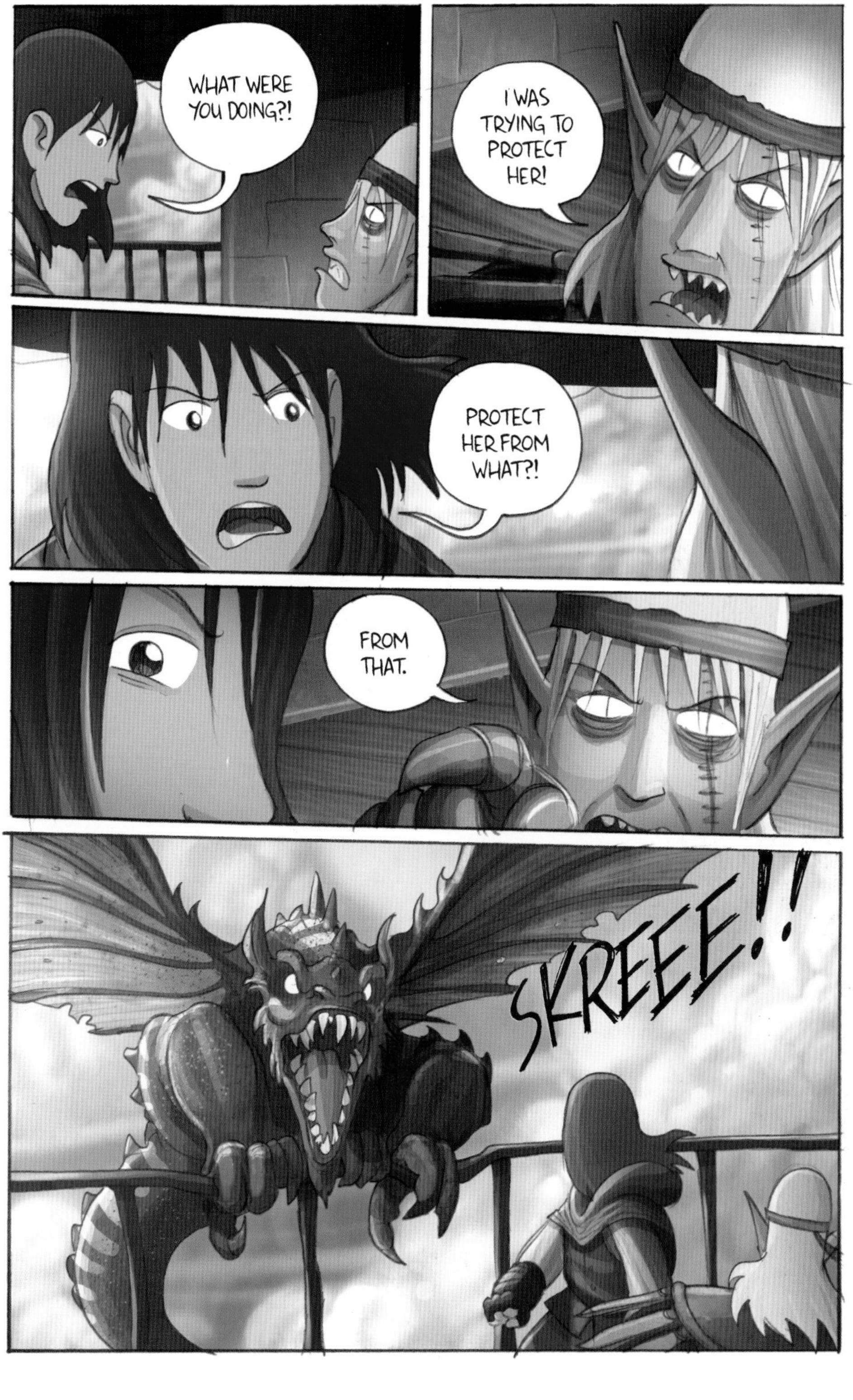
WHAT WERE YOU DOING?!
I WAS TRYING TO PROTECT HER!
PROTECT HER FROM WHAT?!
FROM THAT.
SKREEE!!

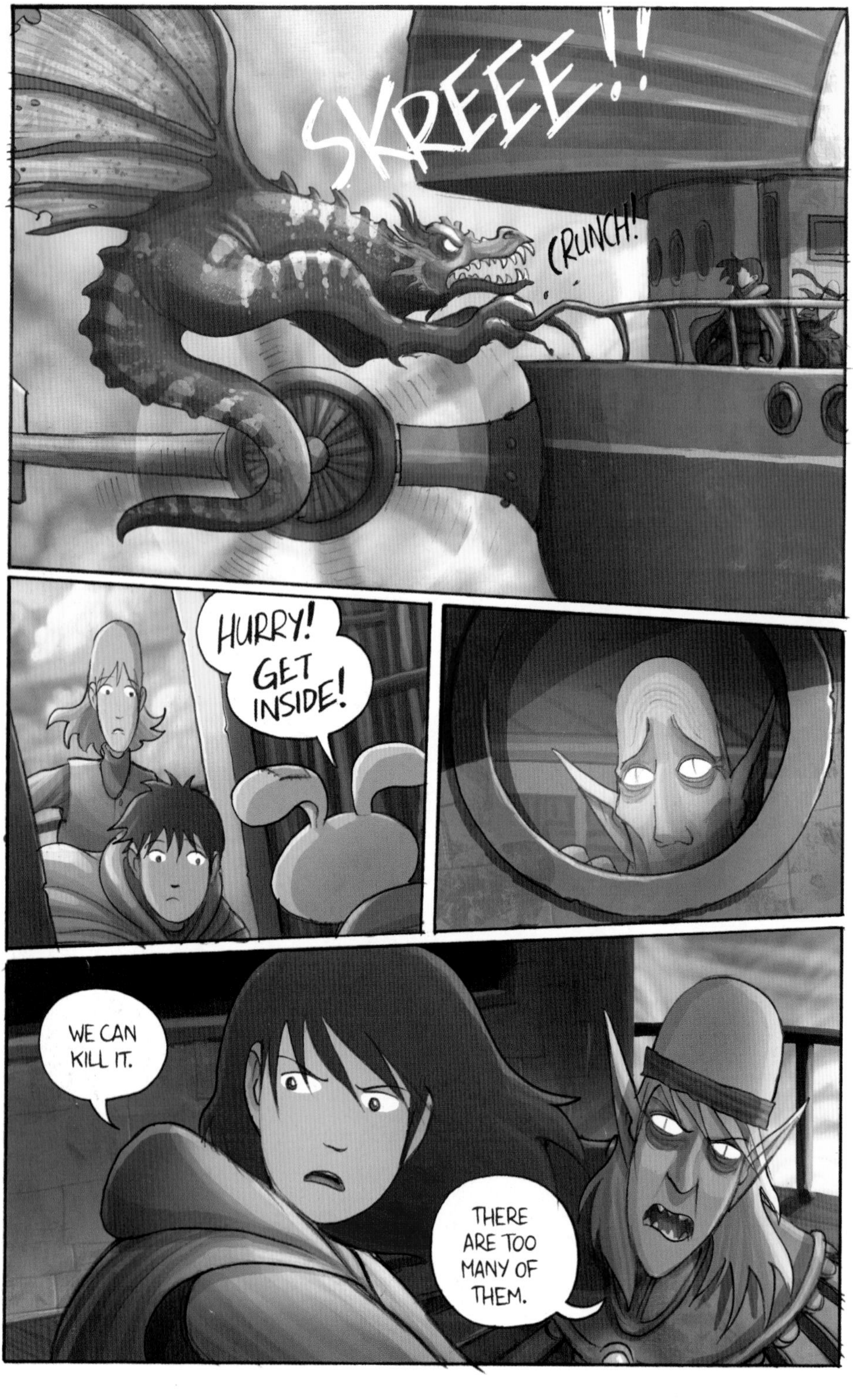
SKREEE!!
CRUNCH!
HURRY! GET INSIDE!
WE CAN KILL IT.
THERE ARE TOO MANY OF THEM.

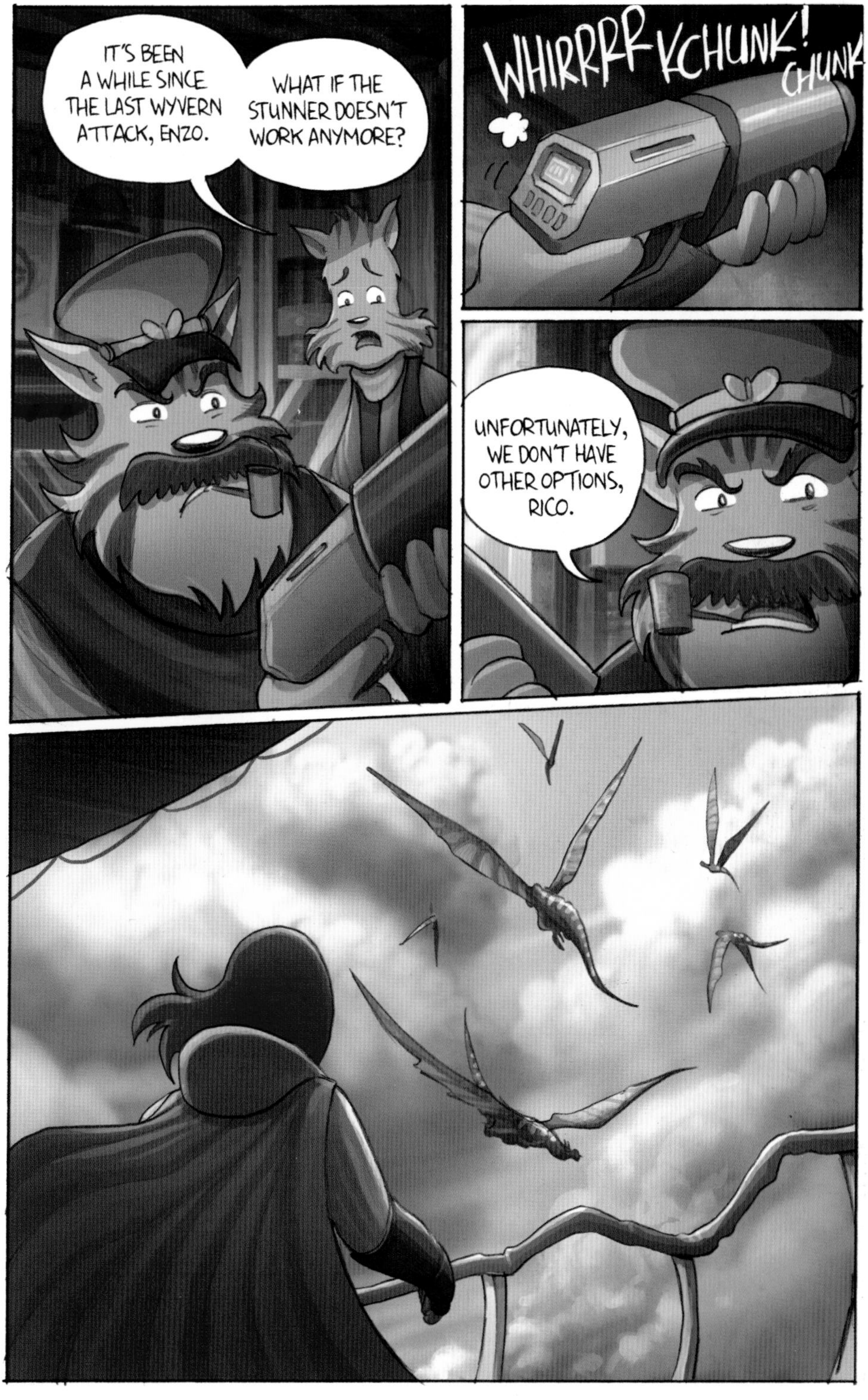
IT'S BEEN A WHILE SINCE THE LAST WYVERN ATTACK, ENZO.
WHAT IF THE STUNNER DOESN'T WORK ANYMORE?
WHIRRRR KCHUNK!
CHUNK
UNFORTUNATELY, WE DON'T HAVE OTHER OPTIONS, RICO.

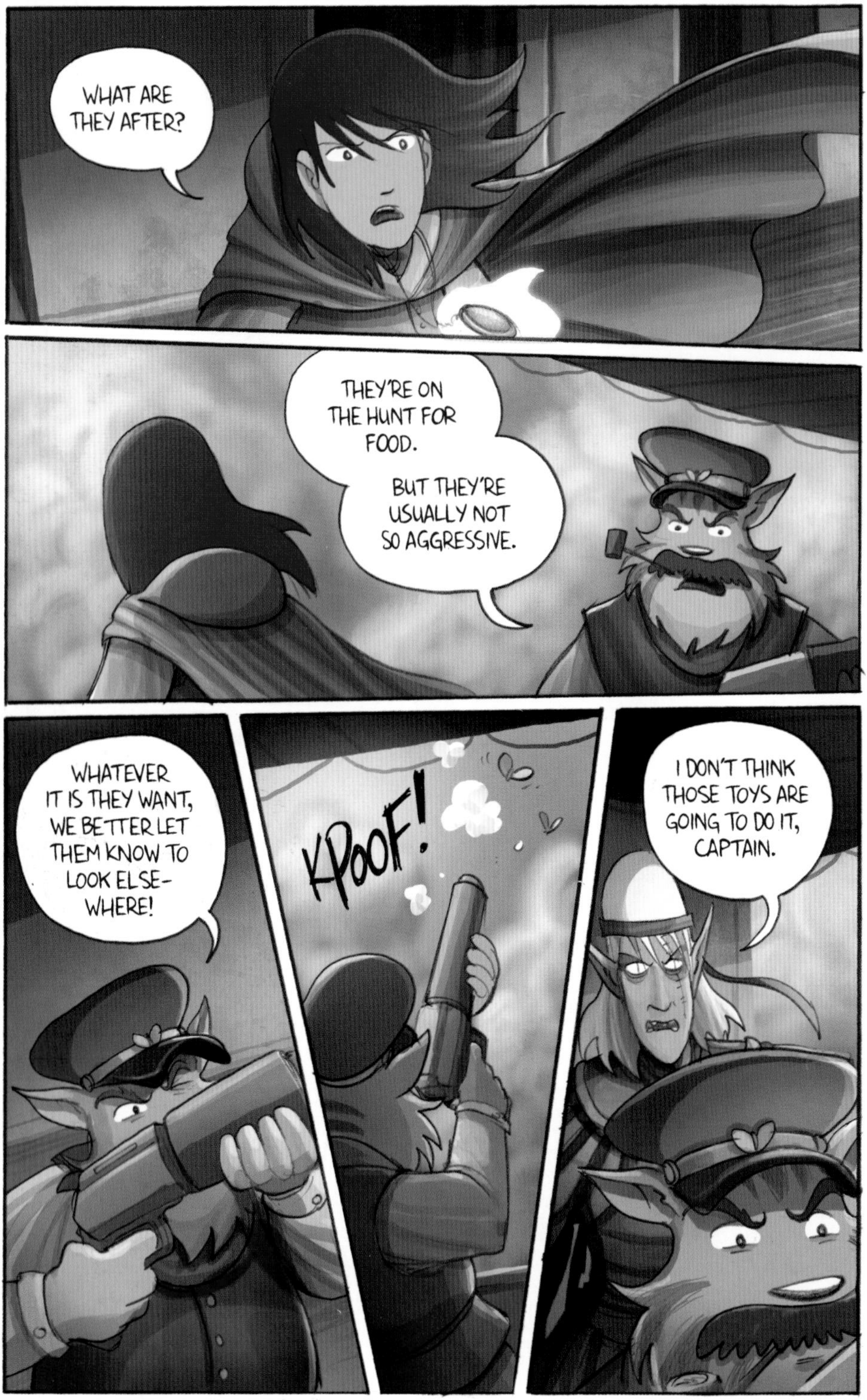
WHAT ARE THEY AFTER?
THEY'RE ON THE HUNT FOR FOOD.
BUT THEY'RE USUALLY NOT SO AGGRESSIVE.
WHATEVER IT IS THEY WANT, WE BETTER LET THEM KNOW TO LOOK ELSE-WHERE!
KPOOF!
I DON'T THINK THOSE TOYS ARE GOING TO DO IT, CAPTAIN.

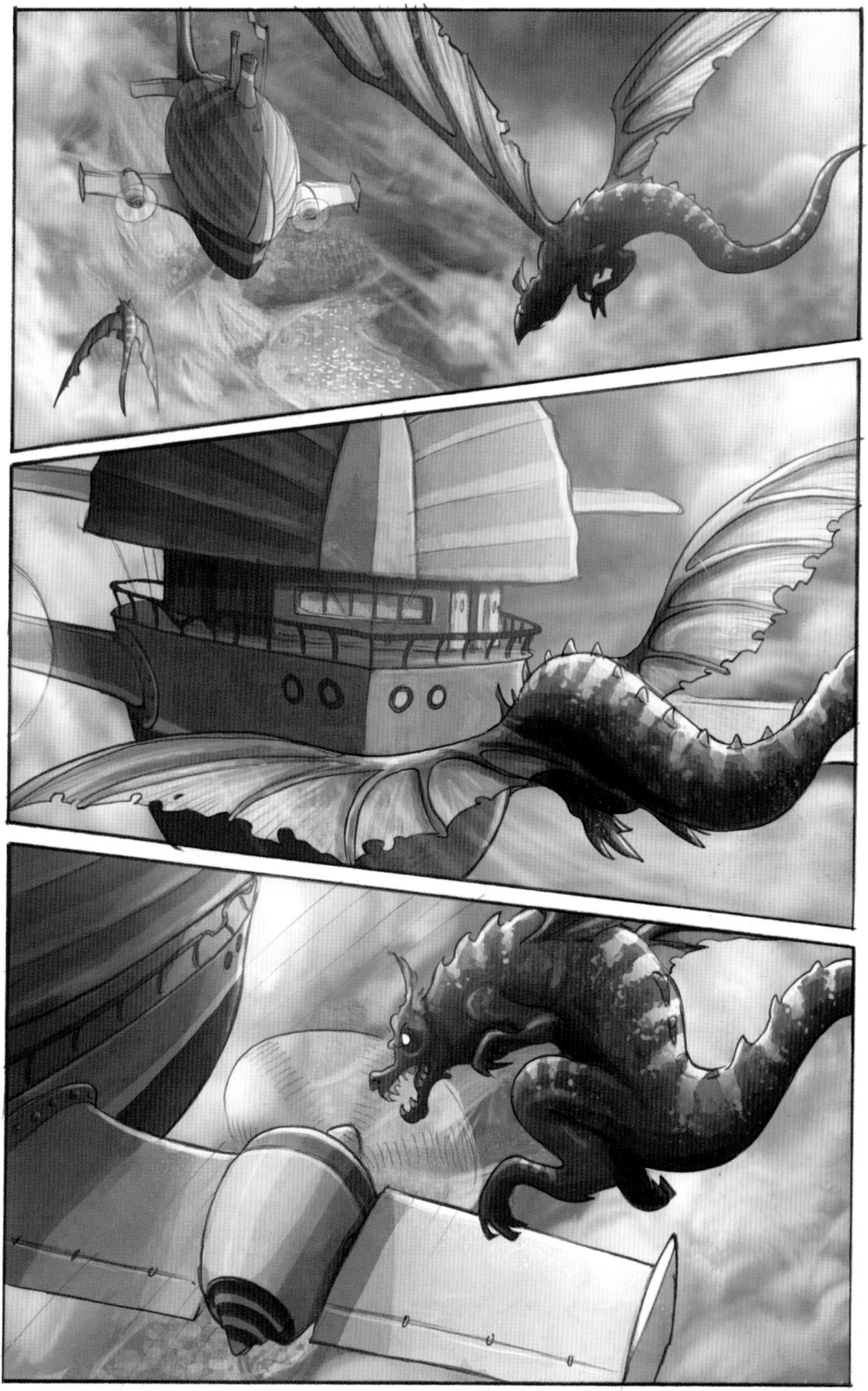

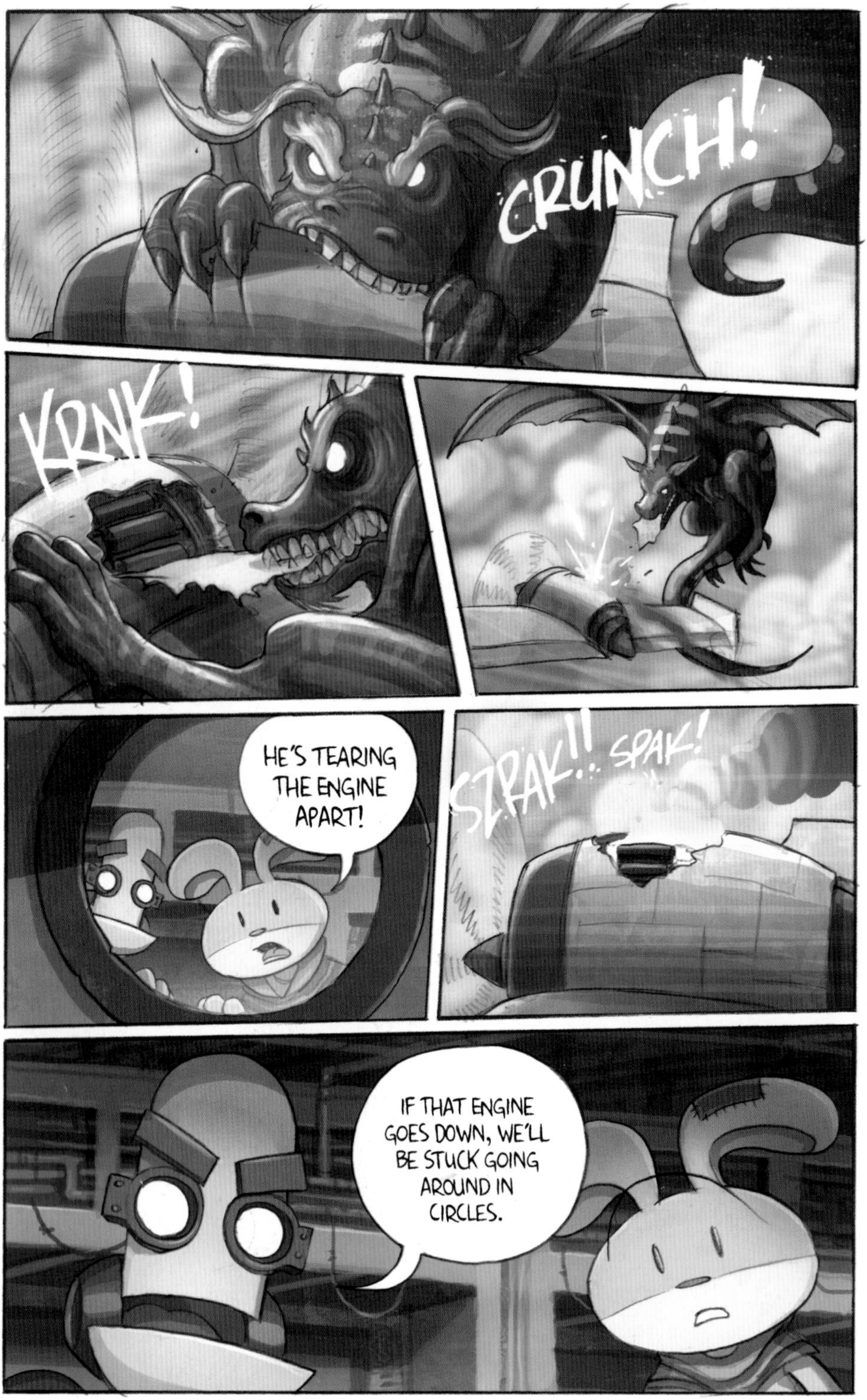
CRUNCH!
KRNK!
HE'S TEARING THE ENGINE APART!
SZRAK!! SPAK!
IF THAT ENGINE GOES DOWN, WE'LL BE STUCK GOING AROUND IN CIRCLES.

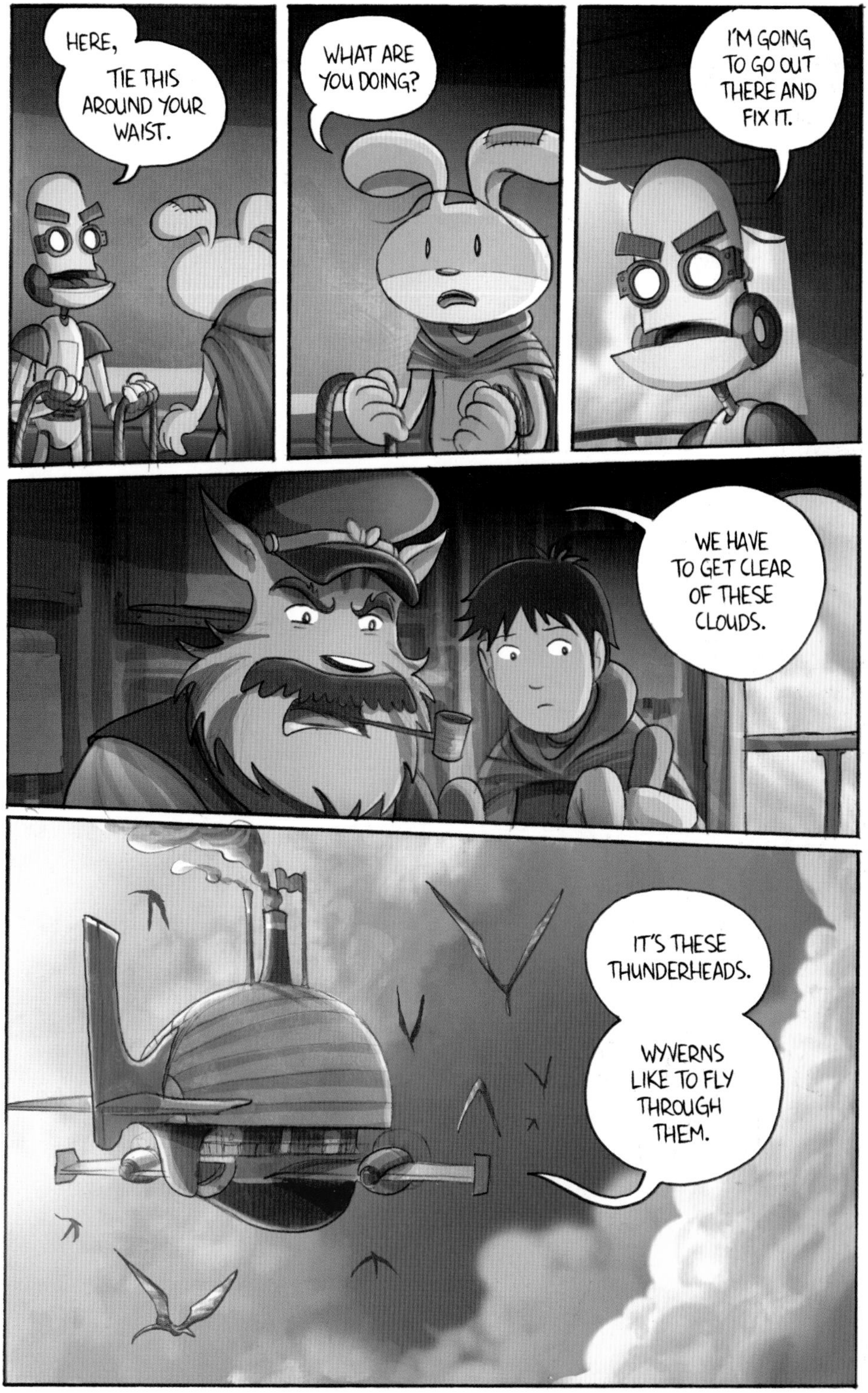
HERE, TIE THIS AROUND YOUR WAIST.
WHAT ARE YOU DOING?
I'M GOING TO GO OUT THERE AND FIX IT.
WE HAVE TO GET CLEAR OF THESE CLOUDS.
IT'S THESE THUNDERHEADS.
WYVERNS LIKE TO FLY THROUGH THEM.

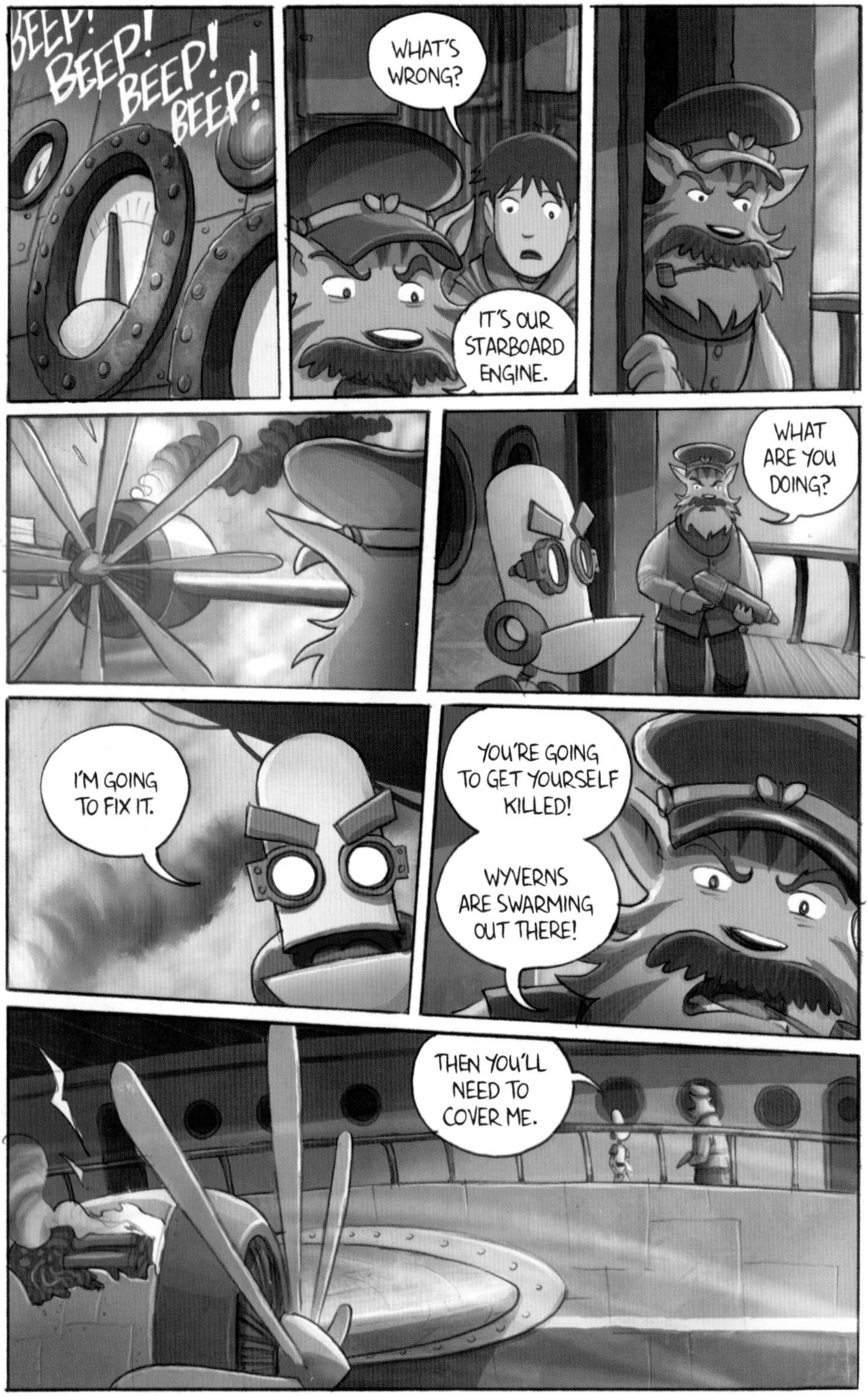
BEEP! BEEP! BEEP! BEEP!
WHAT'S WRONG?
IT'S OUR STARBOARD ENGINE.
WHAT ARE YOU DOING?
I'M GOING TO FIX IT.
YOU'RE GOING TO GET YOURSELF KILLED!
WYVERNS ARE SWARMING OUT THERE!
THEN YOU'LL NEED TO COVER ME.

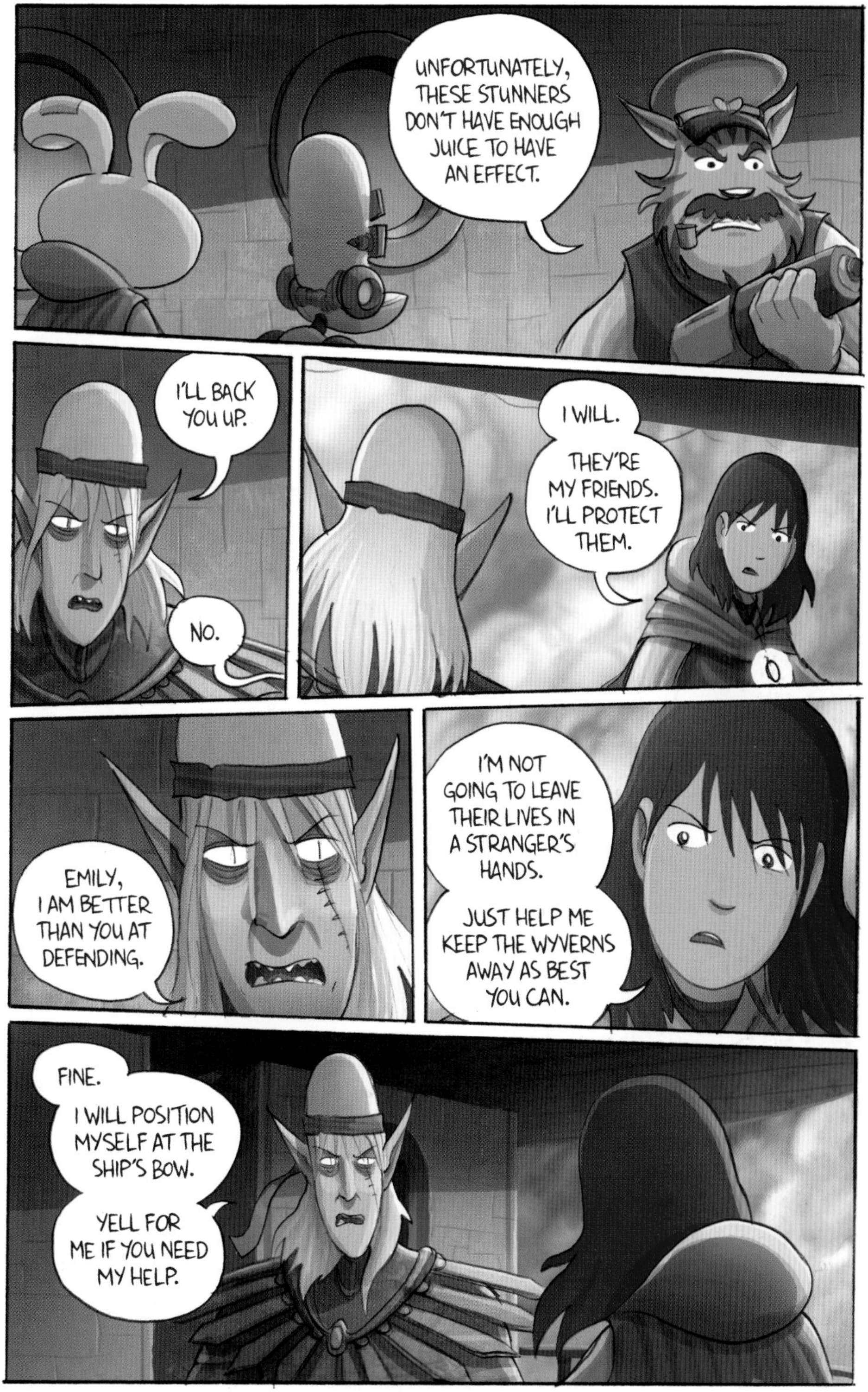
UNFORTUNATELY, THESE STUNNERS DON'T HAVE ENOUGH JUICE TO HAVE AN EFFECT.
I'LL BACK YOU UP.
NO.
I WILL.
THEY'RE MY FRIENDS. I'LL PROTECT THEM.
EMILY, I AM BETTER THAN YOU AT DEFENDING.
I'M NOT GOING TO LEAVE THEIR LIVES IN A STRANGER'S HANDS.
JUST HELP ME KEEP THE WYVERNS AWAY AS BEST YOU CAN.
FINE.
I WILL POSITION MYSELF AT THE SHIP'S BOW.
YELL FOR ME IF YOU NEED MY HELP.

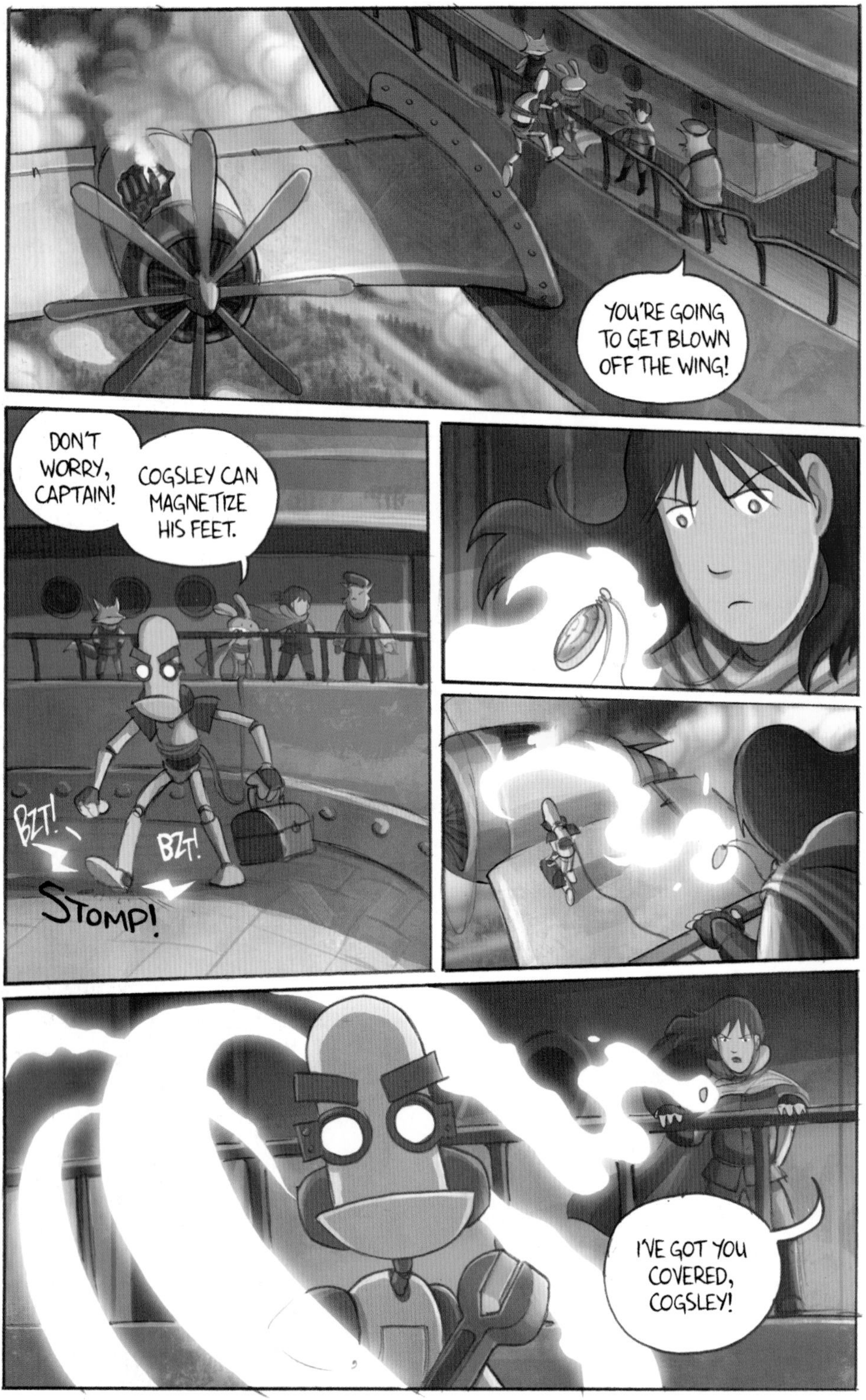
YOU'RE GOING TO GET BLOWN OFF THE WING!
DON'T WORRY, CAPTAIN!
COGSLEY CAN MAGNETIZE HIS FEET.
BZT!
BZT!
STOMP!
I'VE GOT YOU COVERED, COGSLEY!

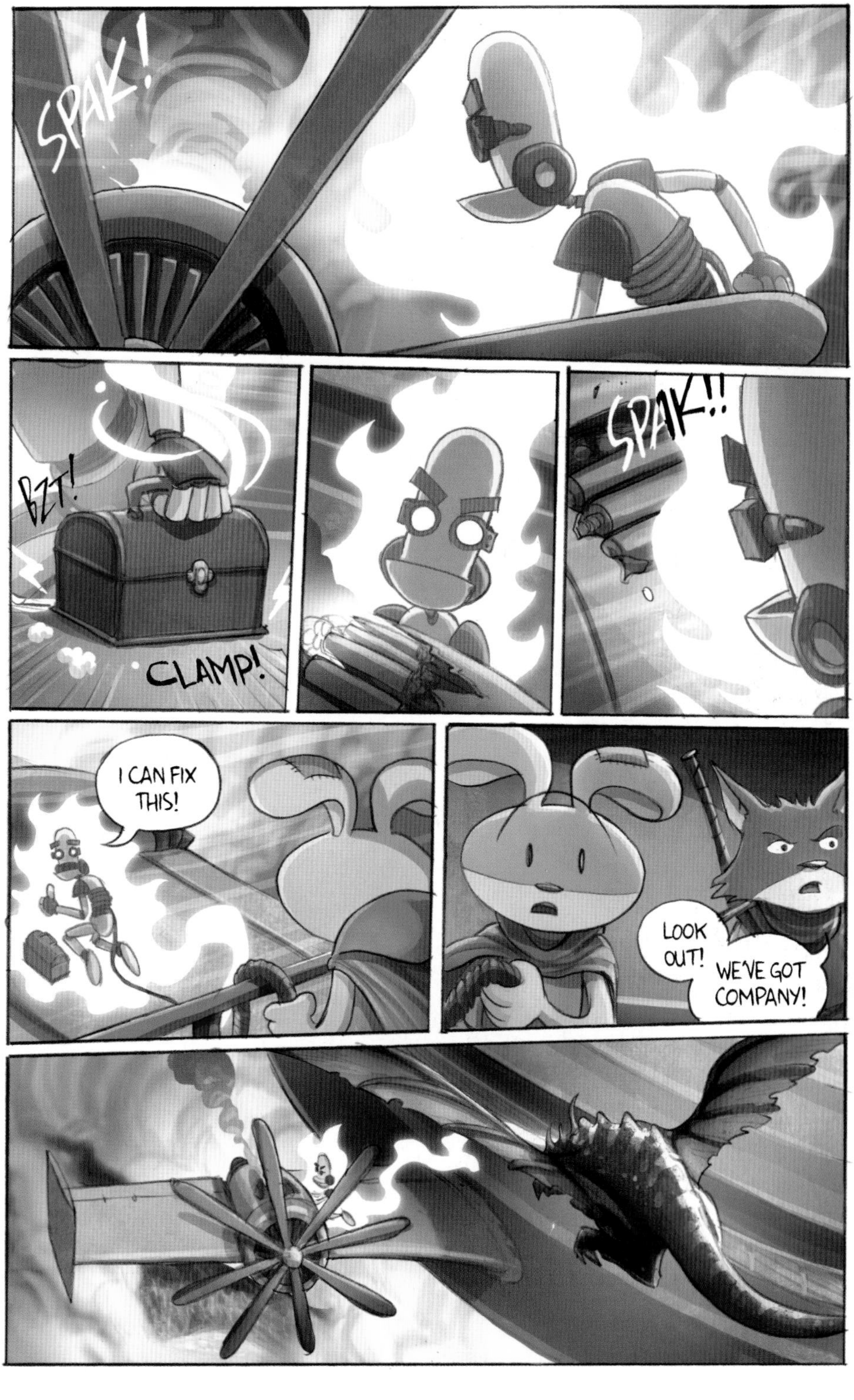
SPAK!
BZT!
CLAMP!
SPAK!!
I CAN FIX THIS!
LOOK OUT!
WE'VE GOT COMPANY!

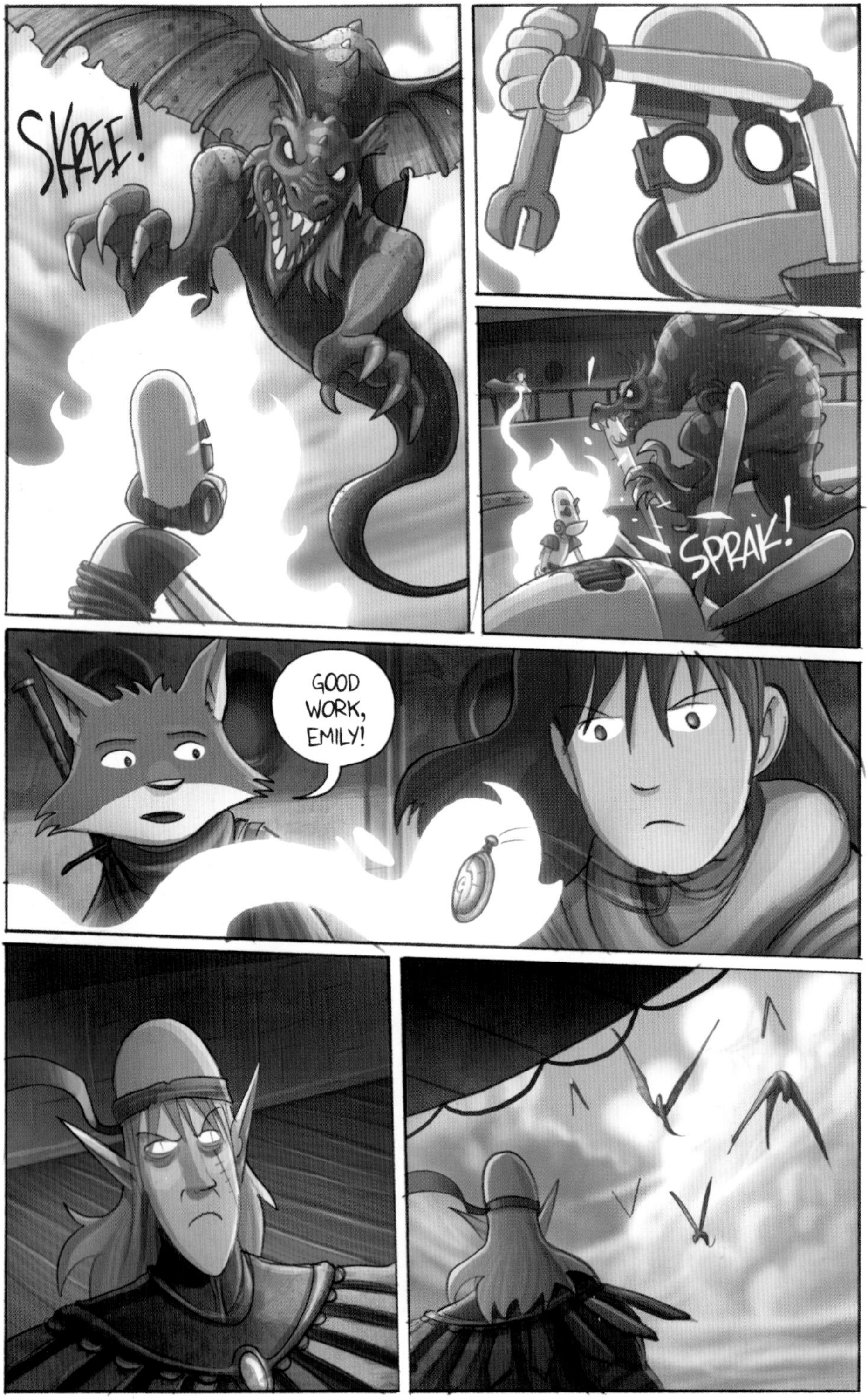
SKREE!
SPRAK!
GOOD WORK, EMILY!

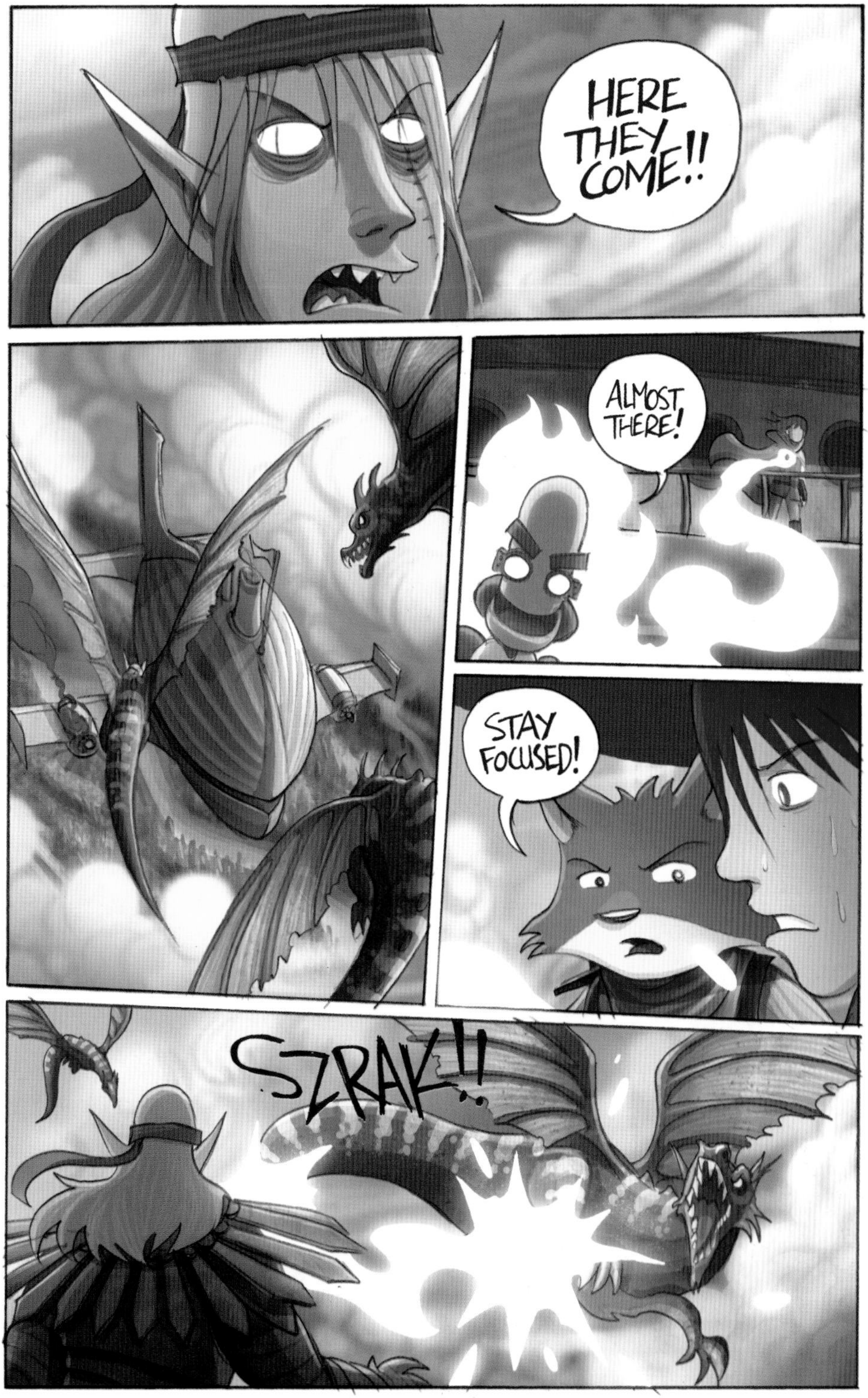
HERE THEY COME!!
ALMOST THERE!
STAY FOCUSED!
SZRAK!!

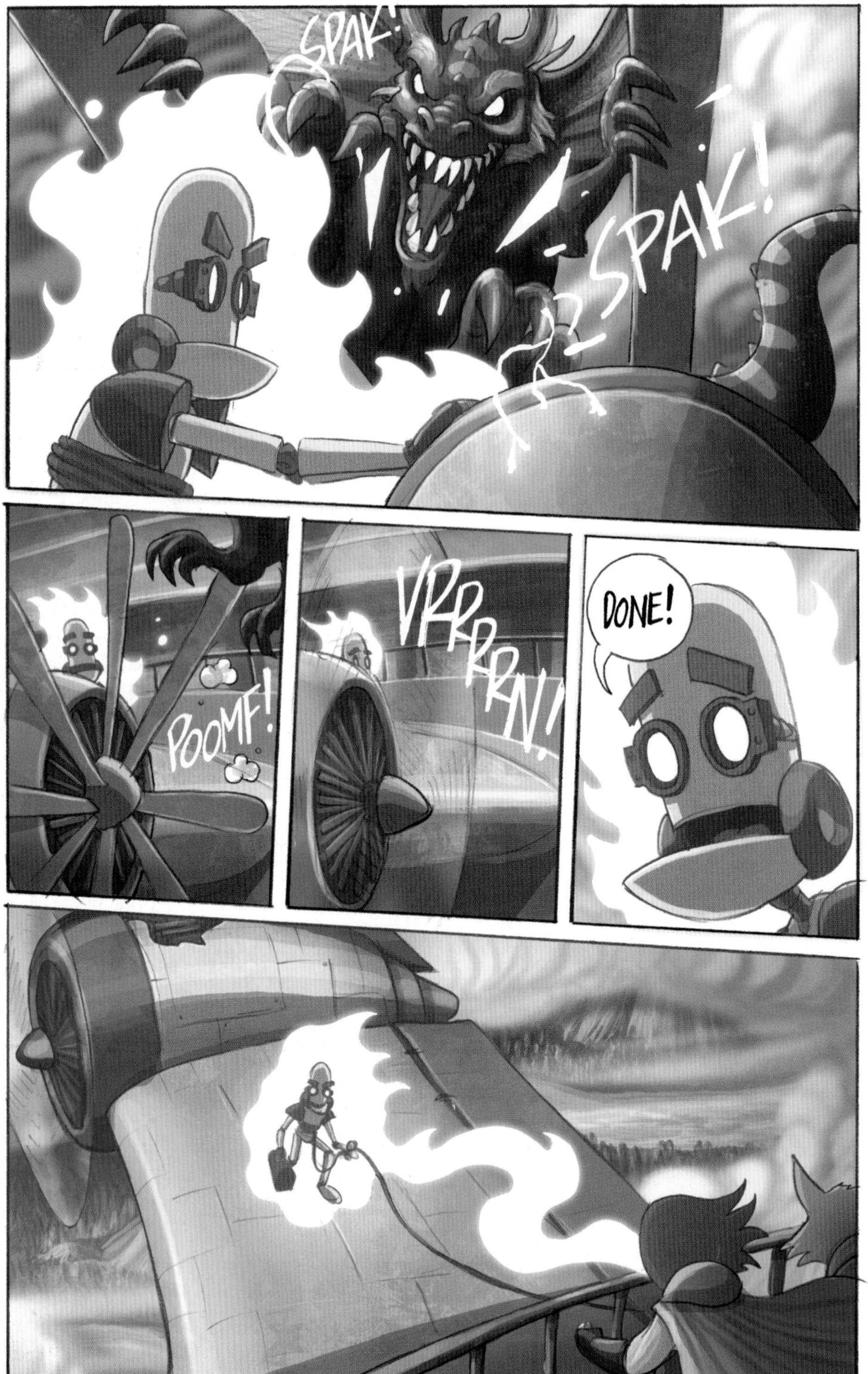
SPAK!
SPAK!
POOMF!
VRRRRRN!
DONE!

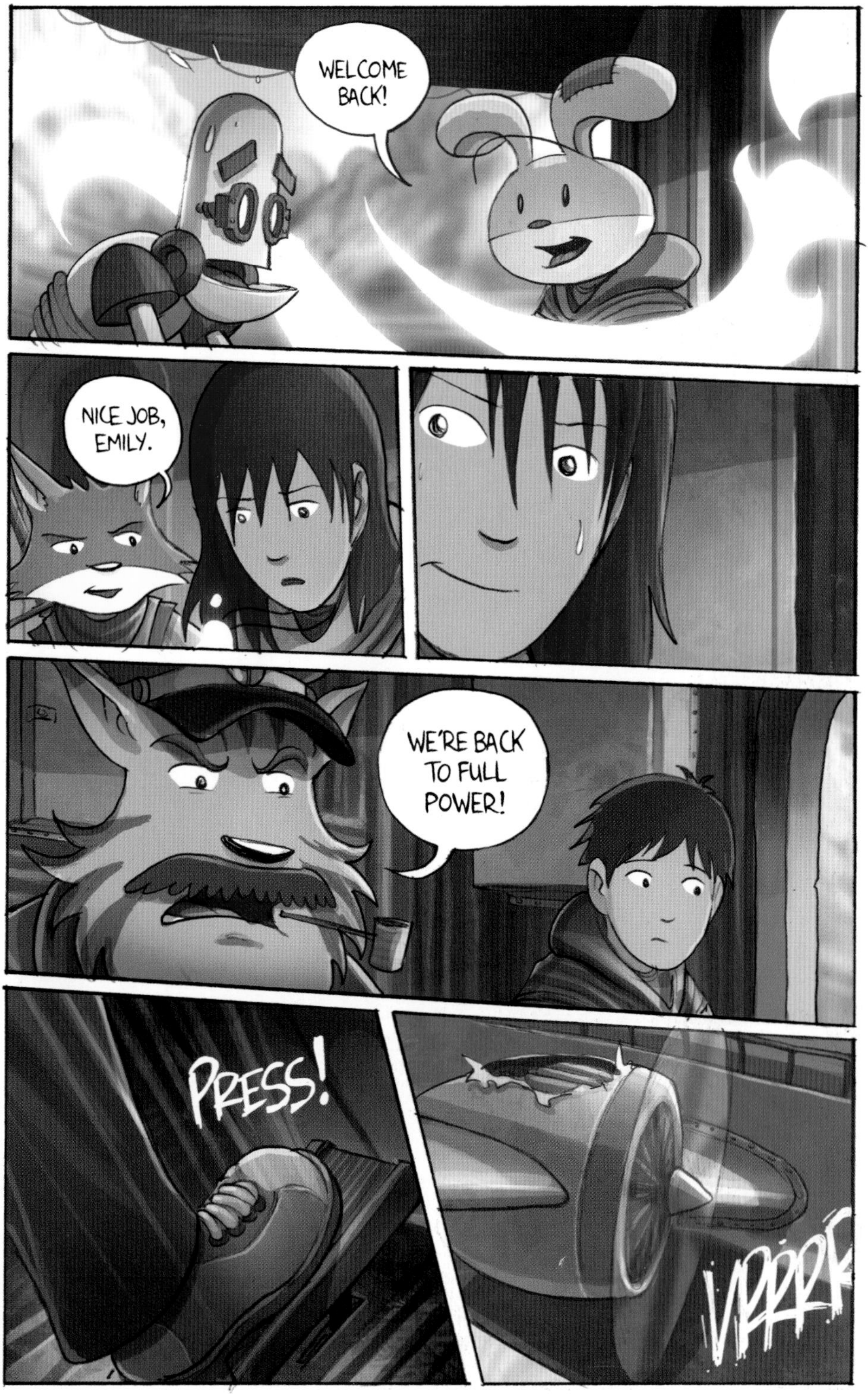
WELCOME BACK!
NICE JOB, EMILY.
WE'RE BACK TO FULL POWER!
PRESS!
VRRRR

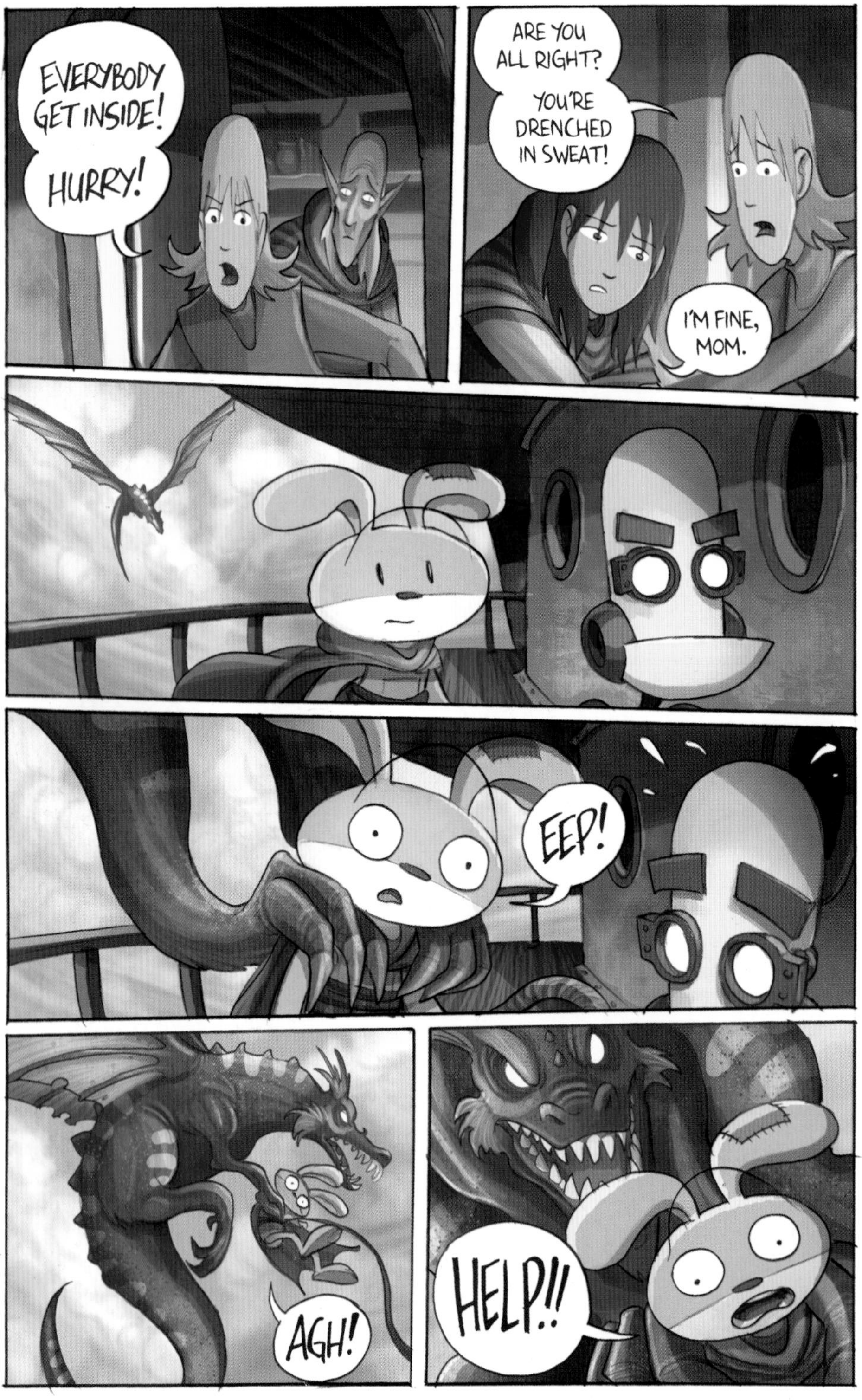
EVERYBODY GET INSIDE!
HURRY!
ARE YOU ALL RIGHT?
YOU'RE DRENCHED IN SWEAT!
I'M FINE, MOM.
EEP!
AGH!
HELP!!

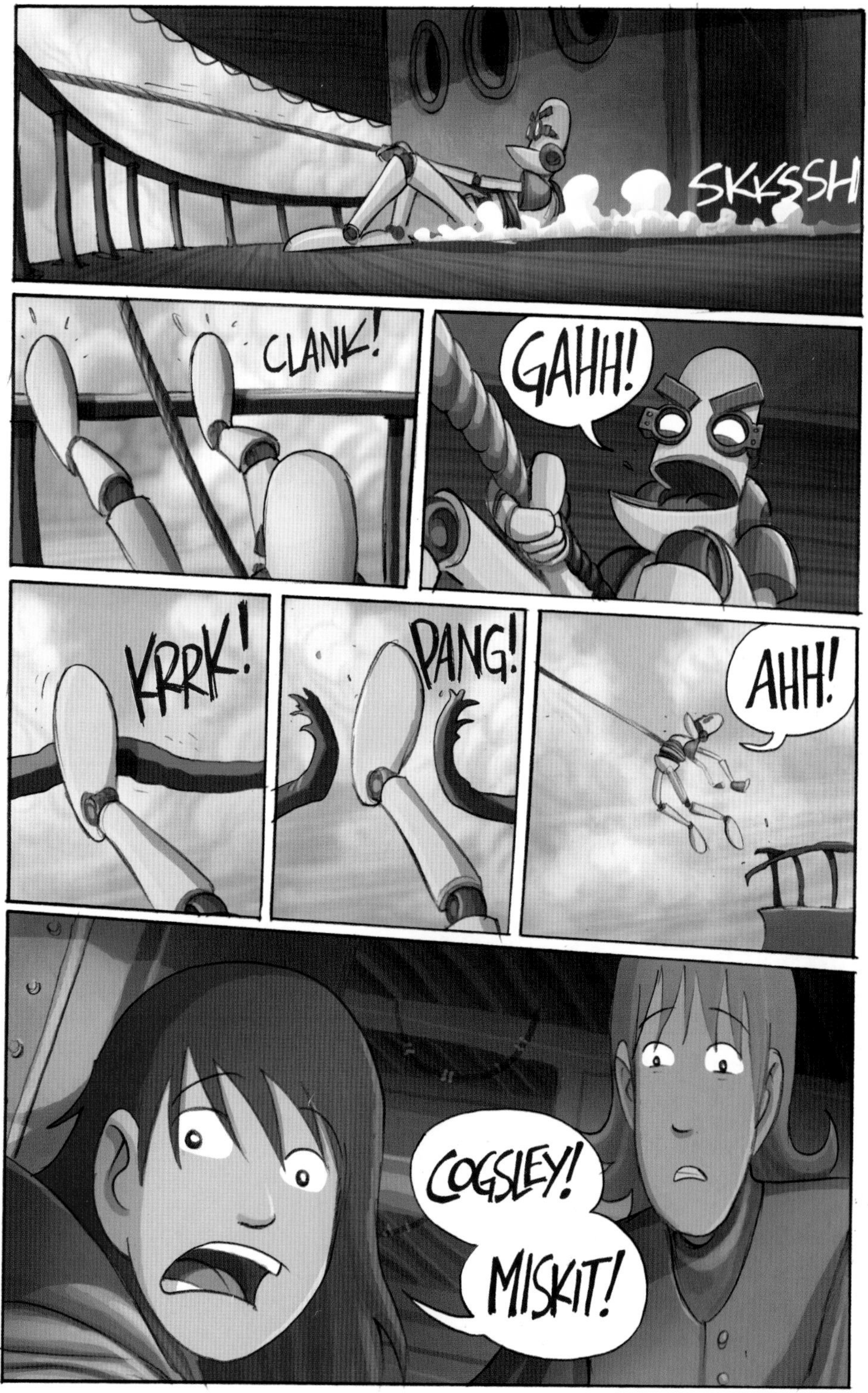
SKKSSH
CLANK!
GAHH!
KRRK!
PANG!
AHH!
COGSLEY!
MISKIT!

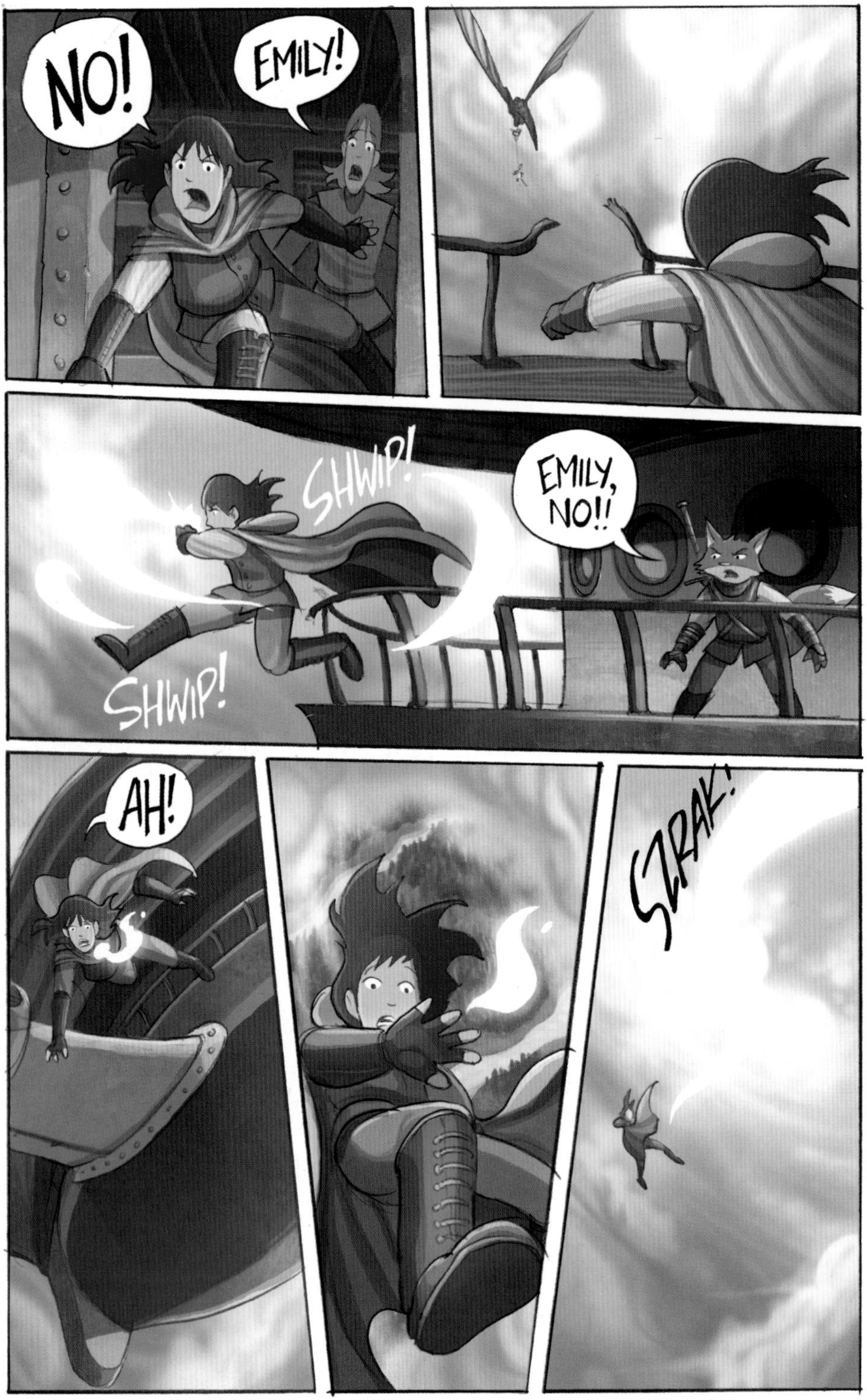
NO!
EMILY!
SHWIP!
EMILY, NO!!
SHWIP!
AH!
SZRAK!

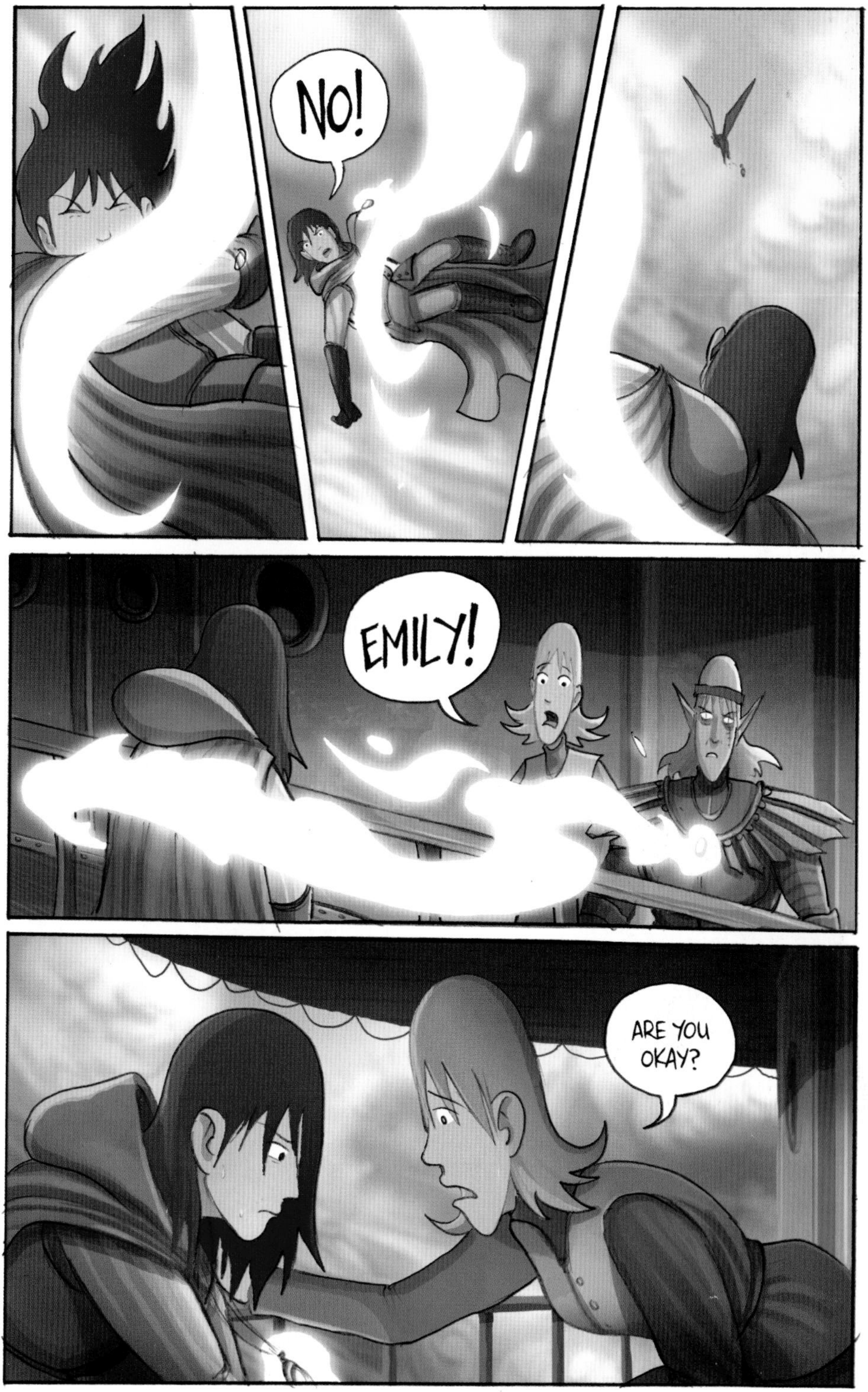
NO!
EMILY!
ARE YOU OKAY?

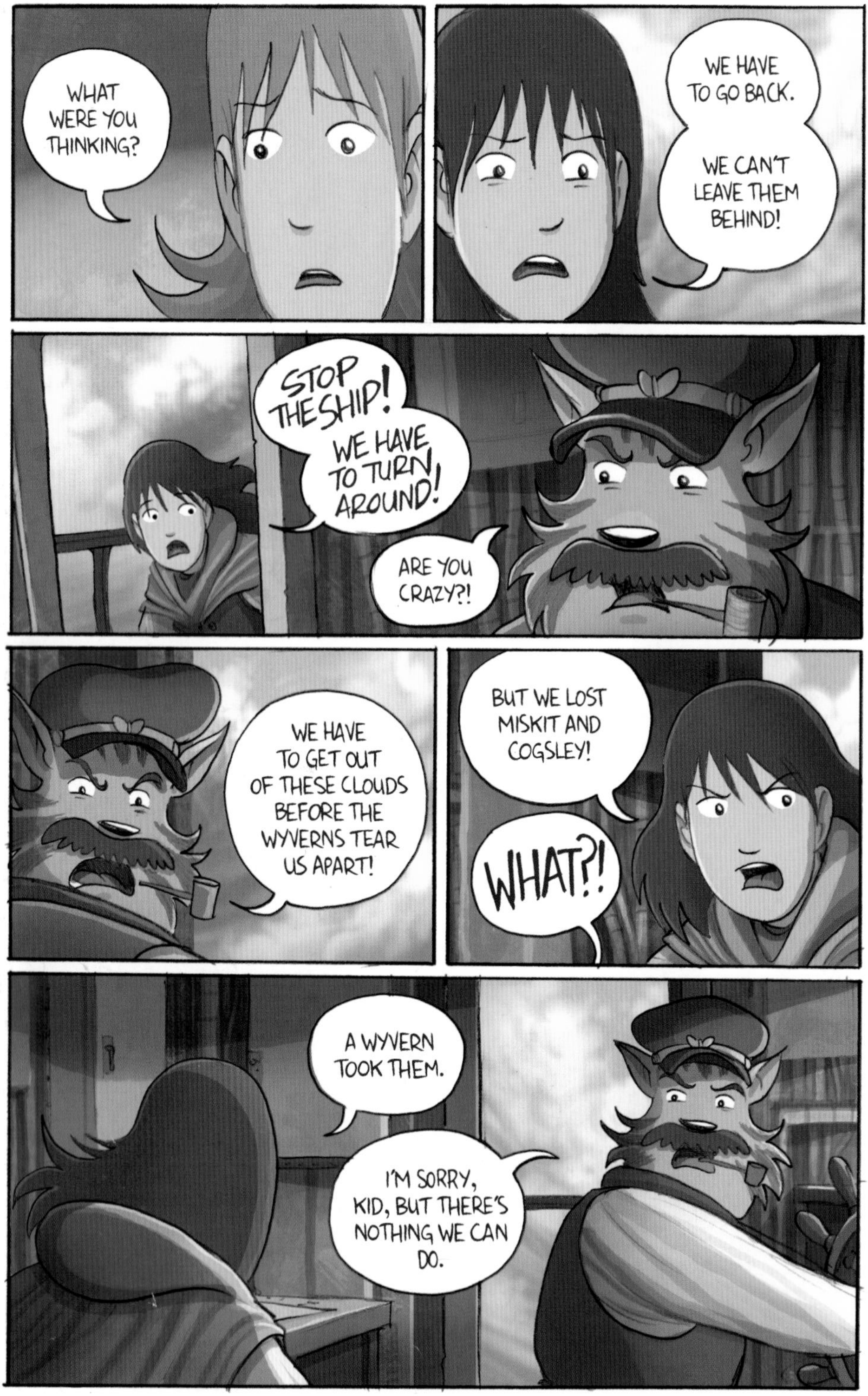
WHAT WERE YOU THINKING?
WE HAVE TO GO BACK.
WE CAN'T LEAVE THEM BEHIND!
STOP THE SHIP! WE HAVE TO TURN AROUND!
ARE YOU CRAZY?!
WE HAVE TO GET OUT OF THESE CLOUDS BEFORE THE WYVERNS TEAR US APART!
BUT WE LOST MISKIT AND COGSLEY!
WHAT?!
A WYVERN TOOK THEM.
I'M SORRY, KID, BUT THERE'S NOTHING WE CAN DO.

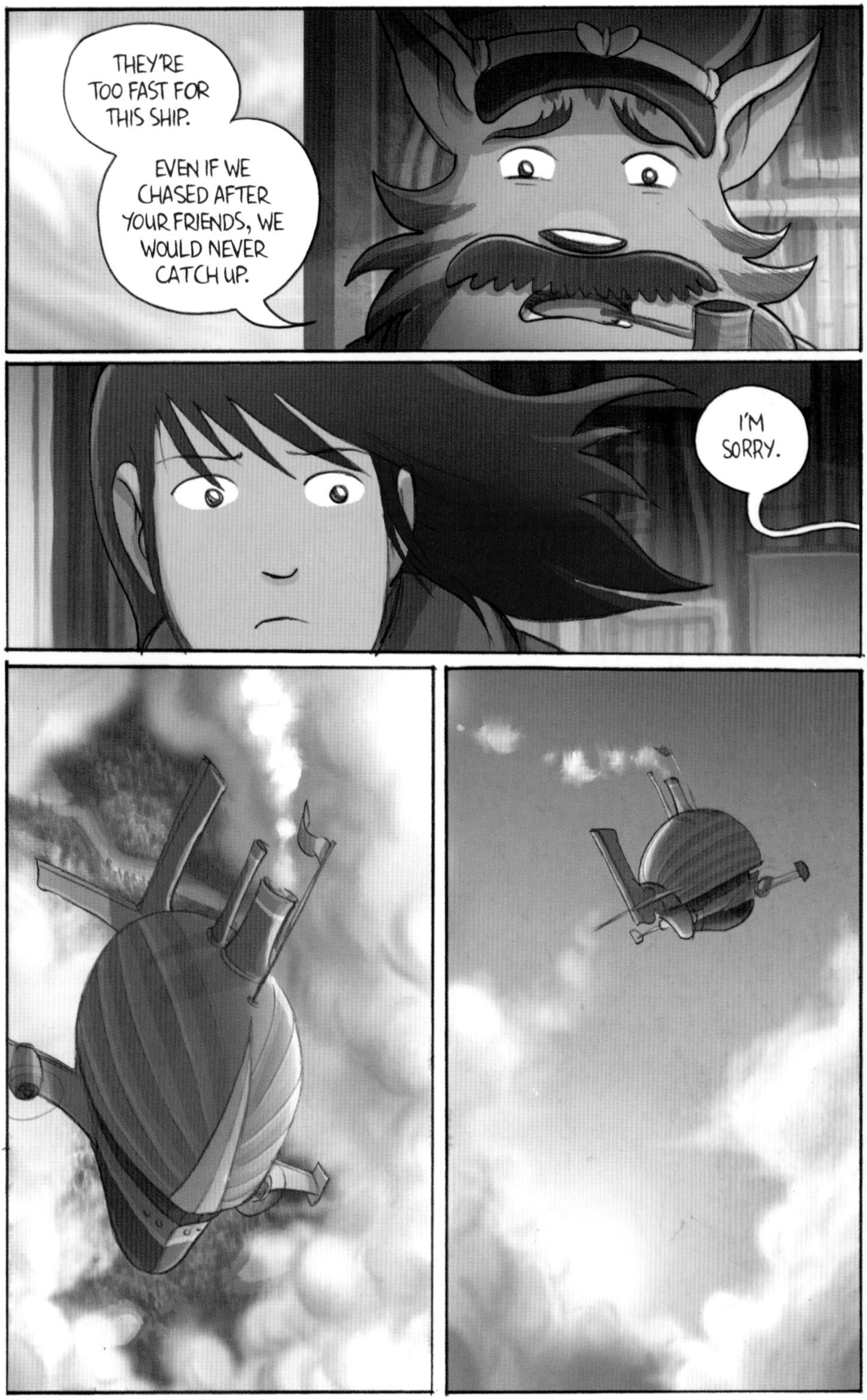
THEY'RE TOO FAST FOR THIS SHIP.
EVEN IF WE CHASED AFTER YOUR FRIENDS, WE WOULD NEVER CATCH UP.
I'M SORRY.

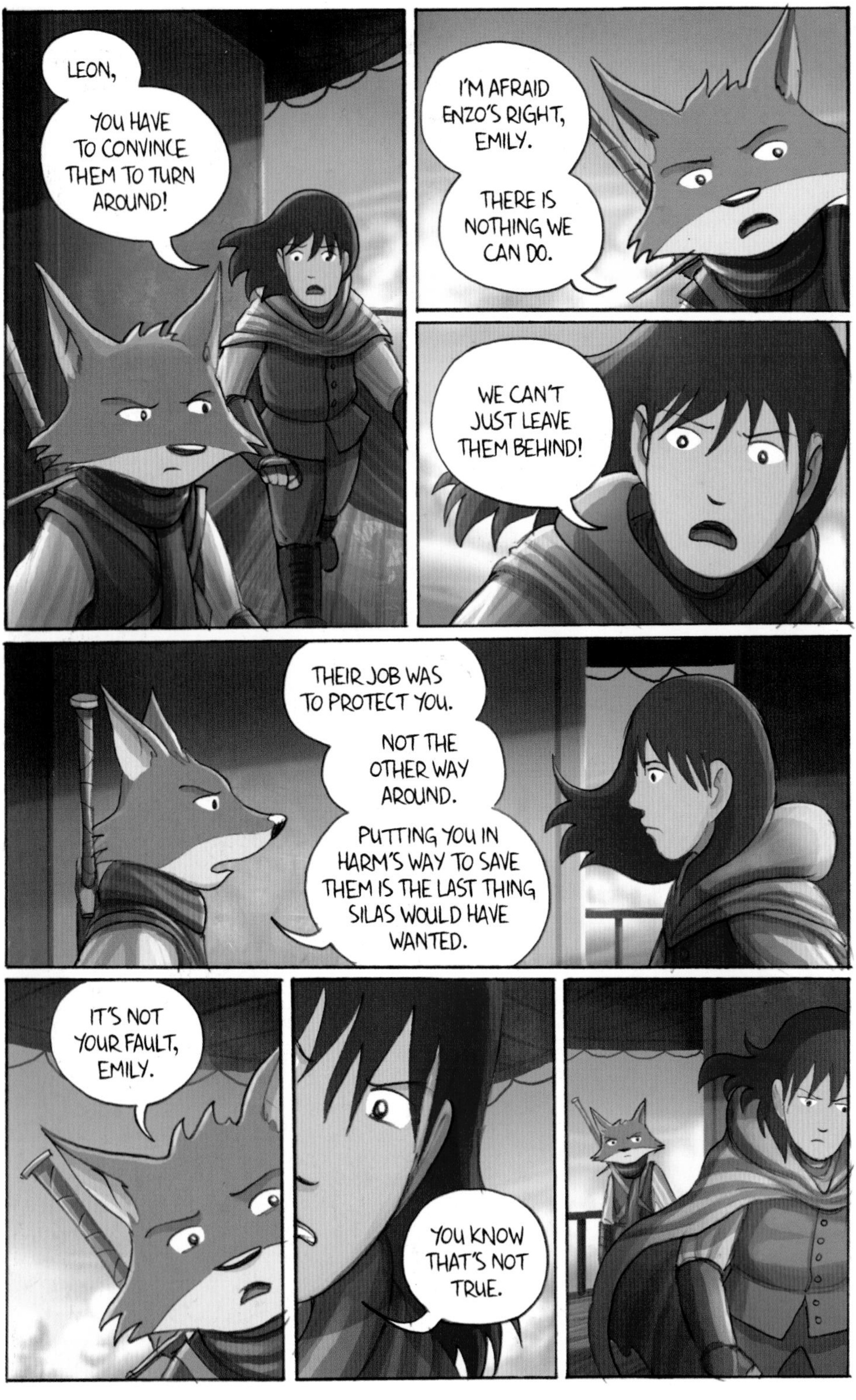
LEON,
YOU HAVE TO CONVINCE THEM TO TURN AROUND!
I'M AFRAID ENZO'S RIGHT, EMILY.
THERE IS NOTHING WE CAN DO.
WE CAN'T JUST LEAVE THEM BEHIND!
THEIR JOB WAS TO PROTECT YOU.
NOT THE OTHER WAY AROUND.
PUTTING YOU IN HARM'S WAY TO SAVE THEM IS THE LAST THING SILAS WOULD HAVE WANTED.
IT'S NOT YOUR FAULT, EMILY.
YOU KNOW THAT'S NOT TRUE.

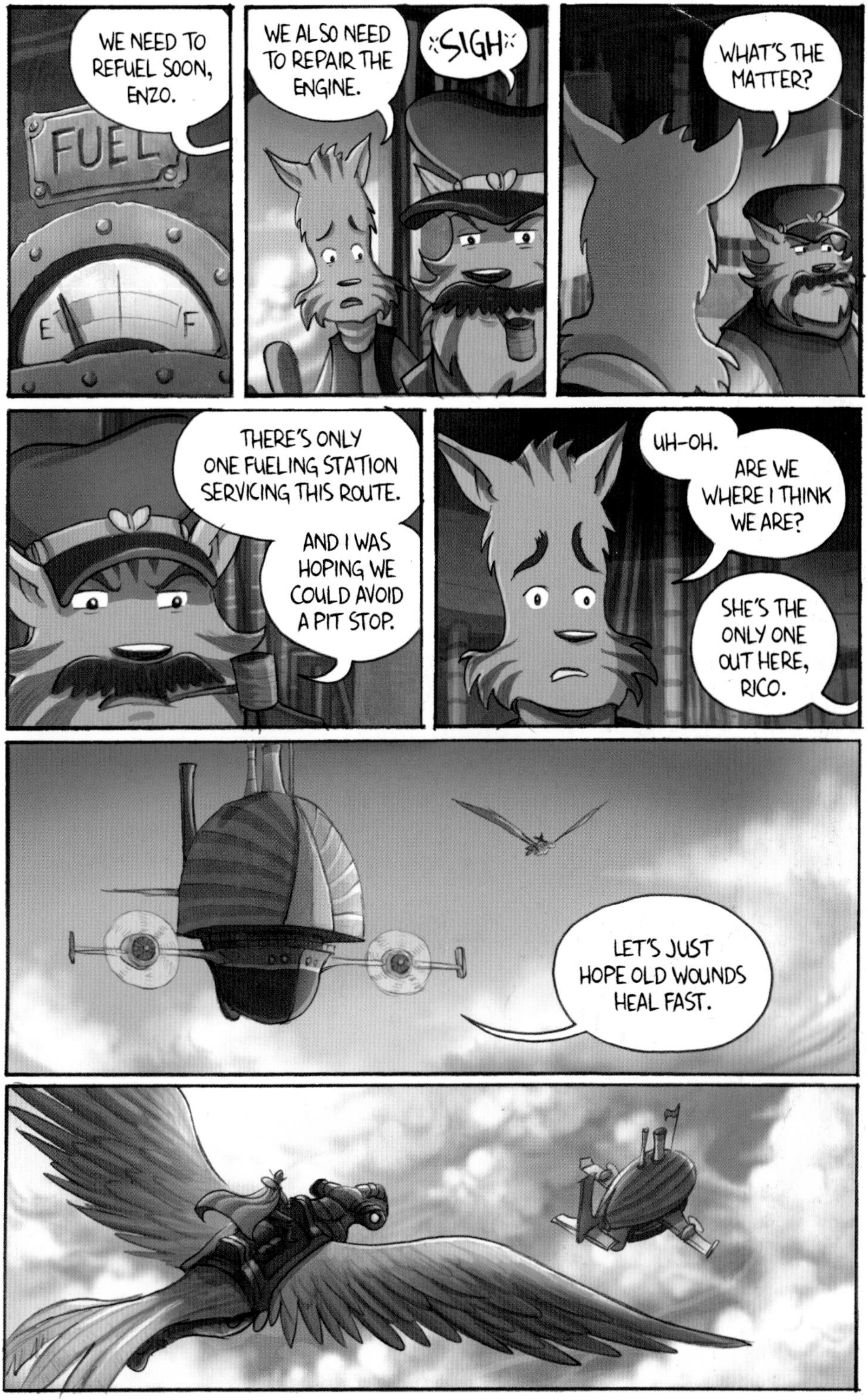
WE NEED TO REFUEL SOON, ENZO.
FUEL
E
F
WE ALSO NEED TO REPAIR THE ENGINE.
SIGH
WHAT'S THE MATTER?
THERE'S ONLY ONE FUELING STATION SERVICING THIS ROUTE.
AND I WAS HOPING WE COULD AVOID A PIT STOP.
UH-OH.
ARE WE WHERE I THINK WE ARE?
SHE'S THE ONLY ONE OUT HERE, RICO.
LET'S JUST HOPE OLD WOUNDS HEAL FAST.

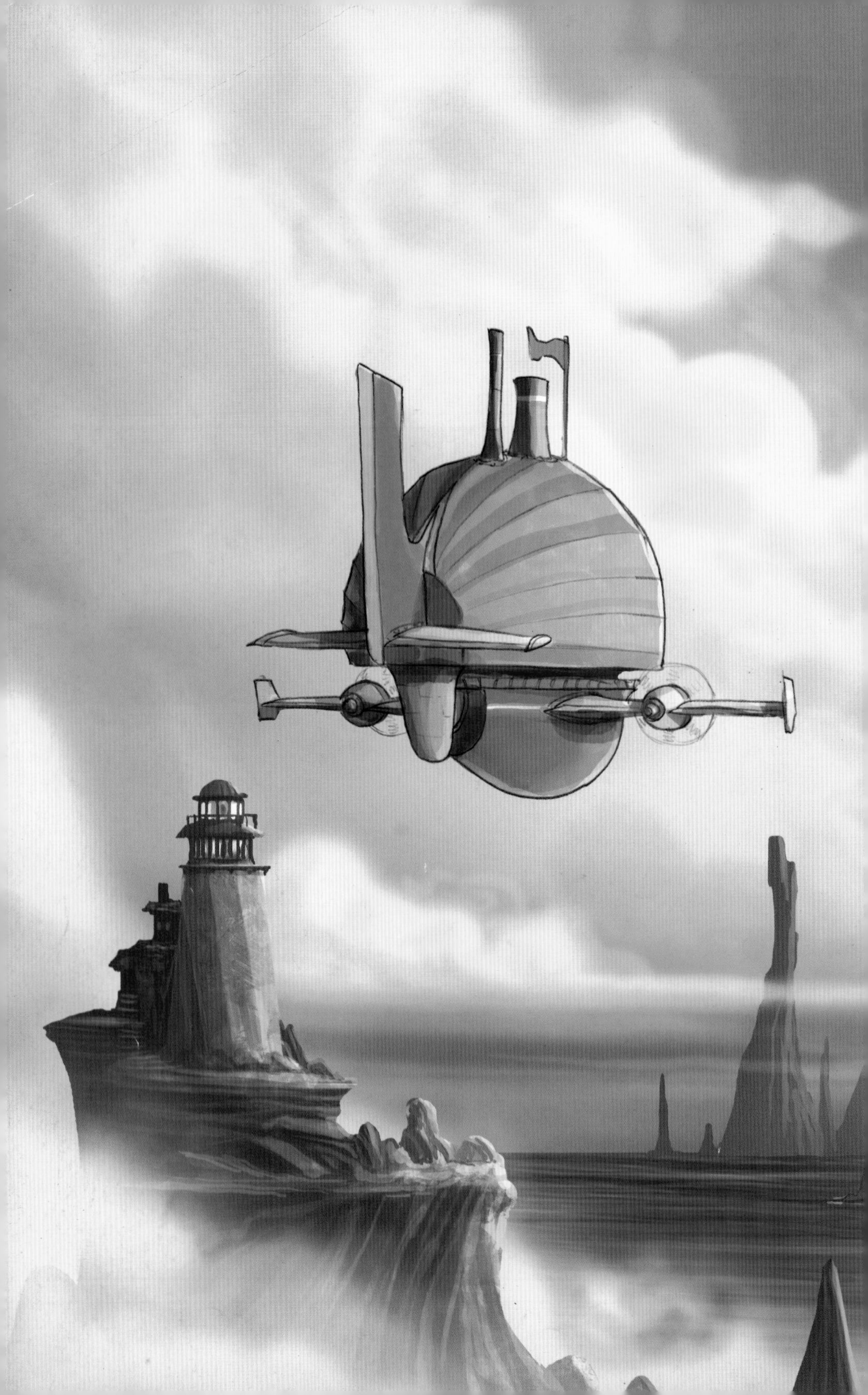

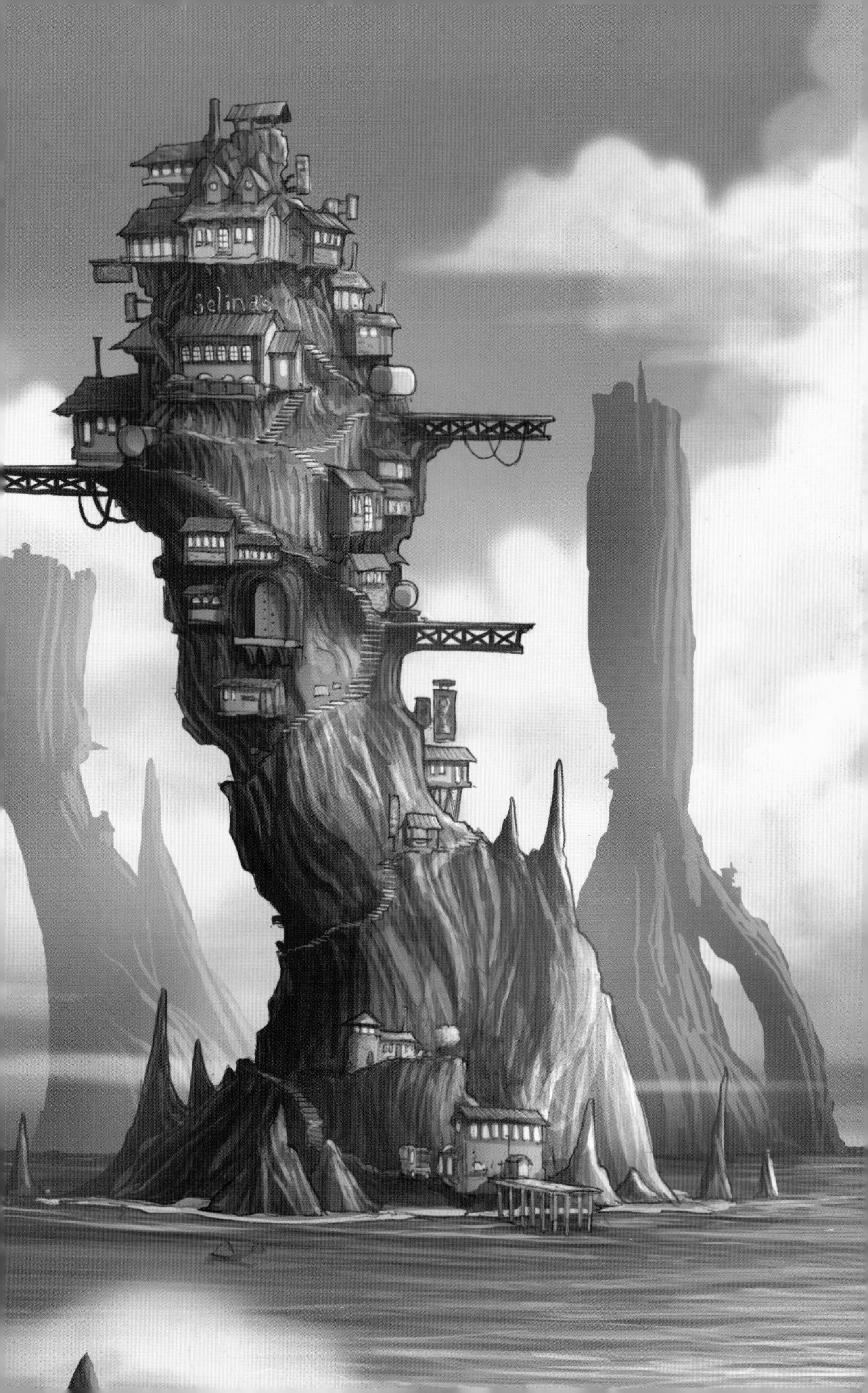
Selina's

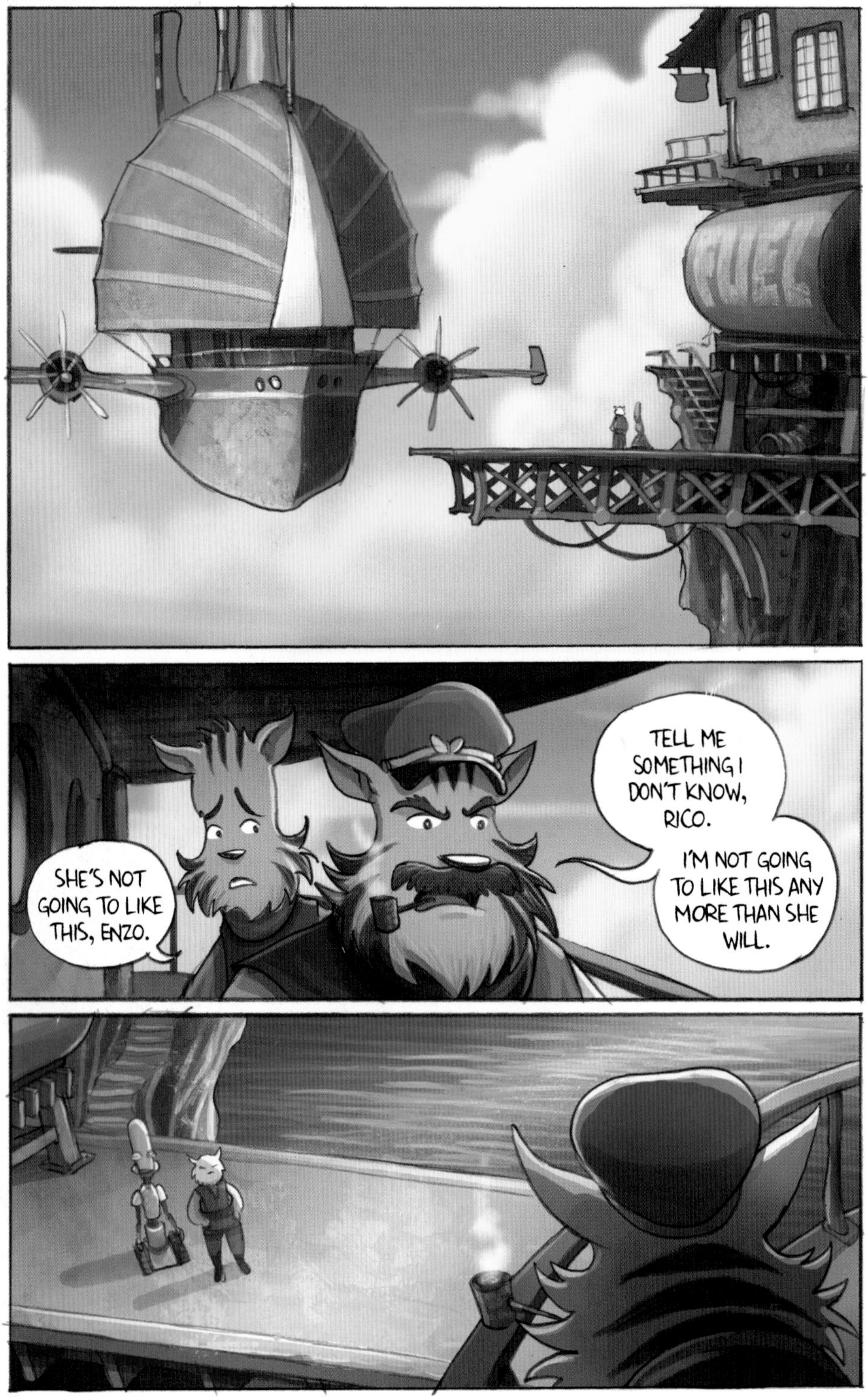
SHE'S NOT GOING TO LIKE THIS, ENZO.
TELL ME SOMETHING I DON'T KNOW, RICO.
I'M NOT GOING TO LIKE THIS ANY MORE THAN SHE WILL.

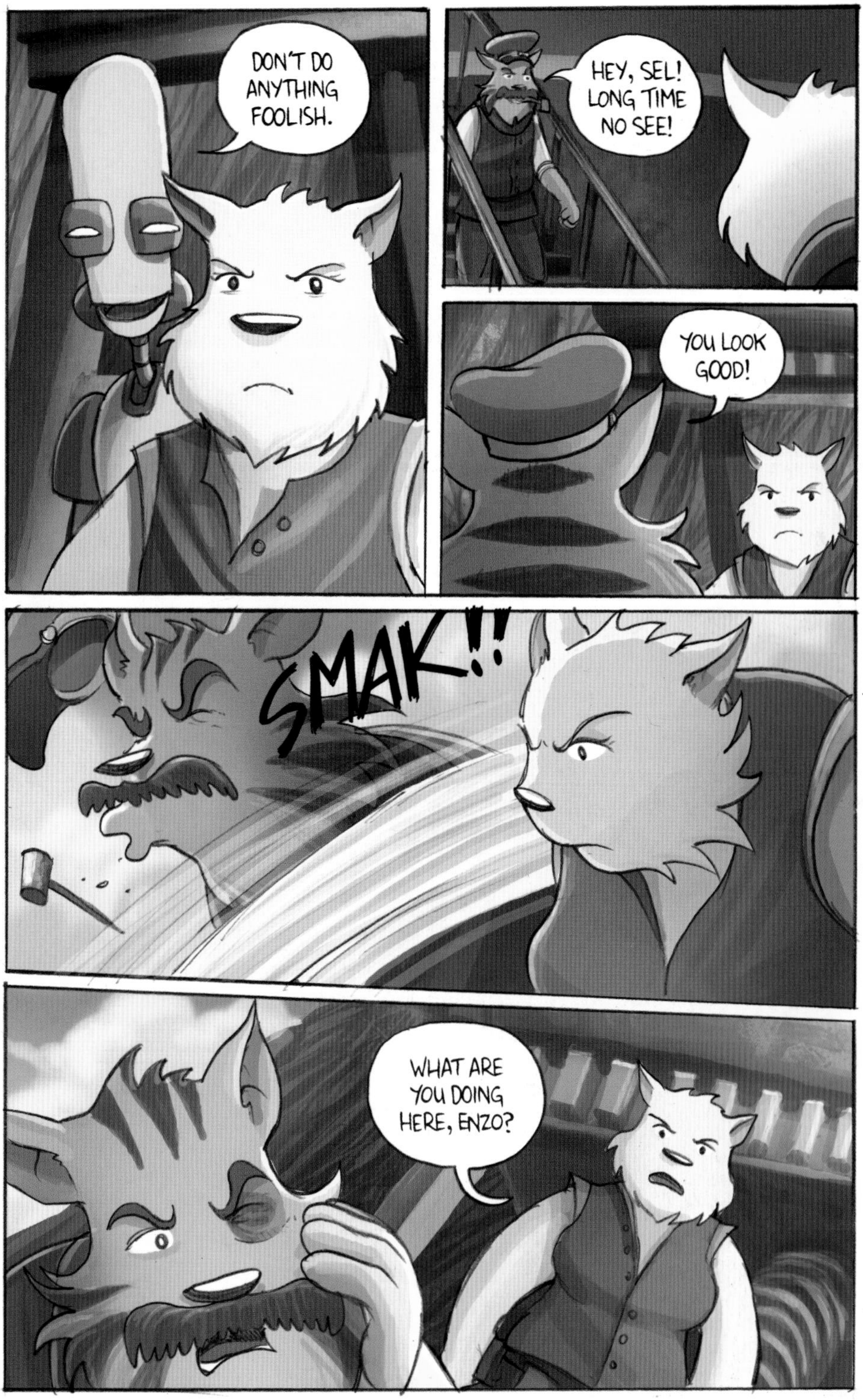
DON'T DO ANYTHING FOOLISH.
HEY, SEL! LONG TIME NO SEE!
YOU LOOK GOOD!
SMAK!!
WHAT ARE YOU DOING HERE, ENZO?

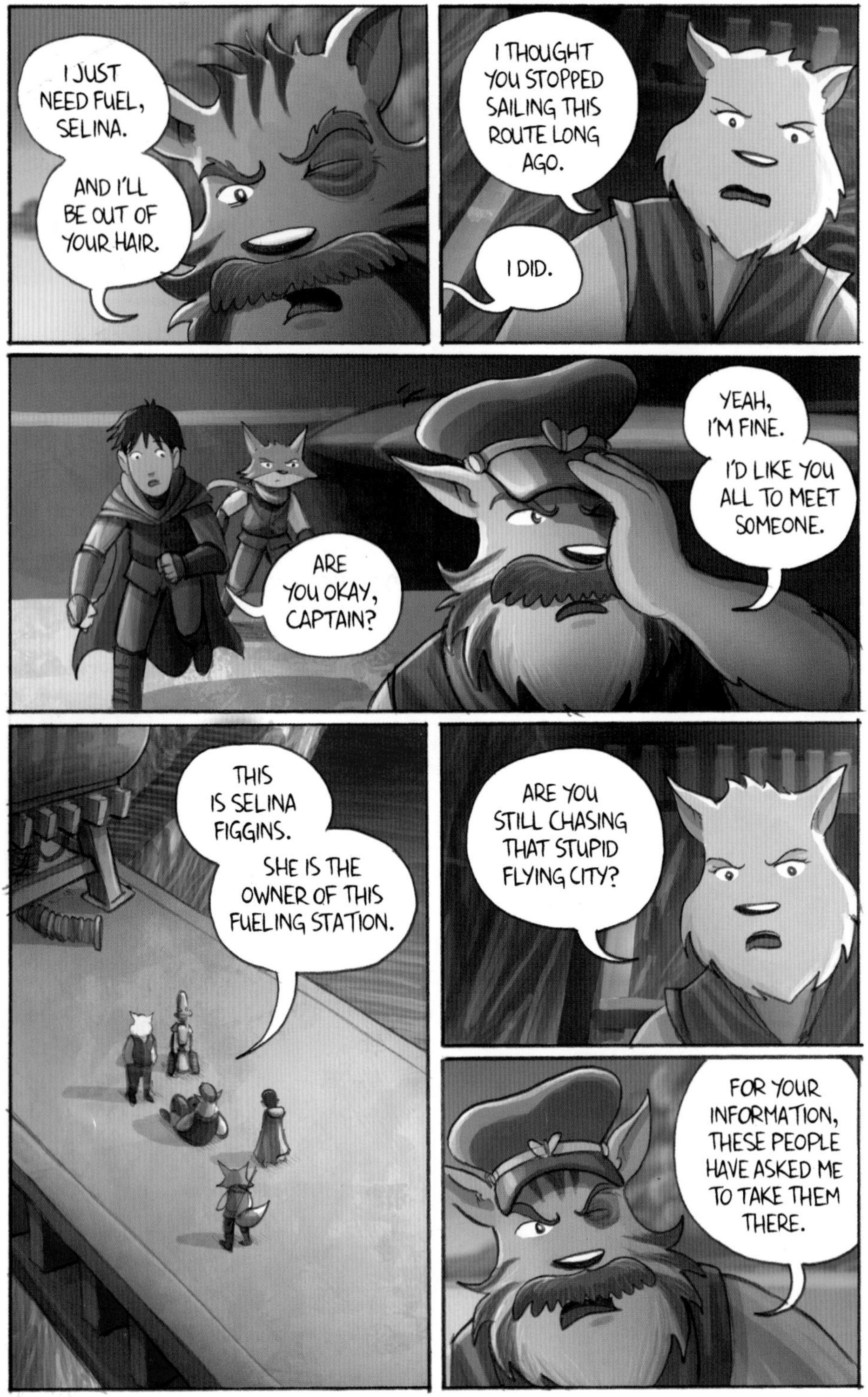
I JUST NEED FUEL, SELINA.
AND I'LL BE OUT OF YOUR HAIR.
I THOUGHT YOU STOPPED SAILING THIS ROUTE LONG AGO.
I DID.
ARE YOU OKAY, CAPTAIN?
YEAH, I'M FINE.
I'D LIKE YOU ALL TO MEET SOMEONE.
THIS IS SELINA FIGGINS.
SHE IS THE OWNER OF THIS FUELING STATION.
ARE YOU STILL CHASING THAT STUPID FLYING CITY?
FOR YOUR INFORMATION, THESE PEOPLE HAVE ASKED ME TO TAKE THEM THERE.

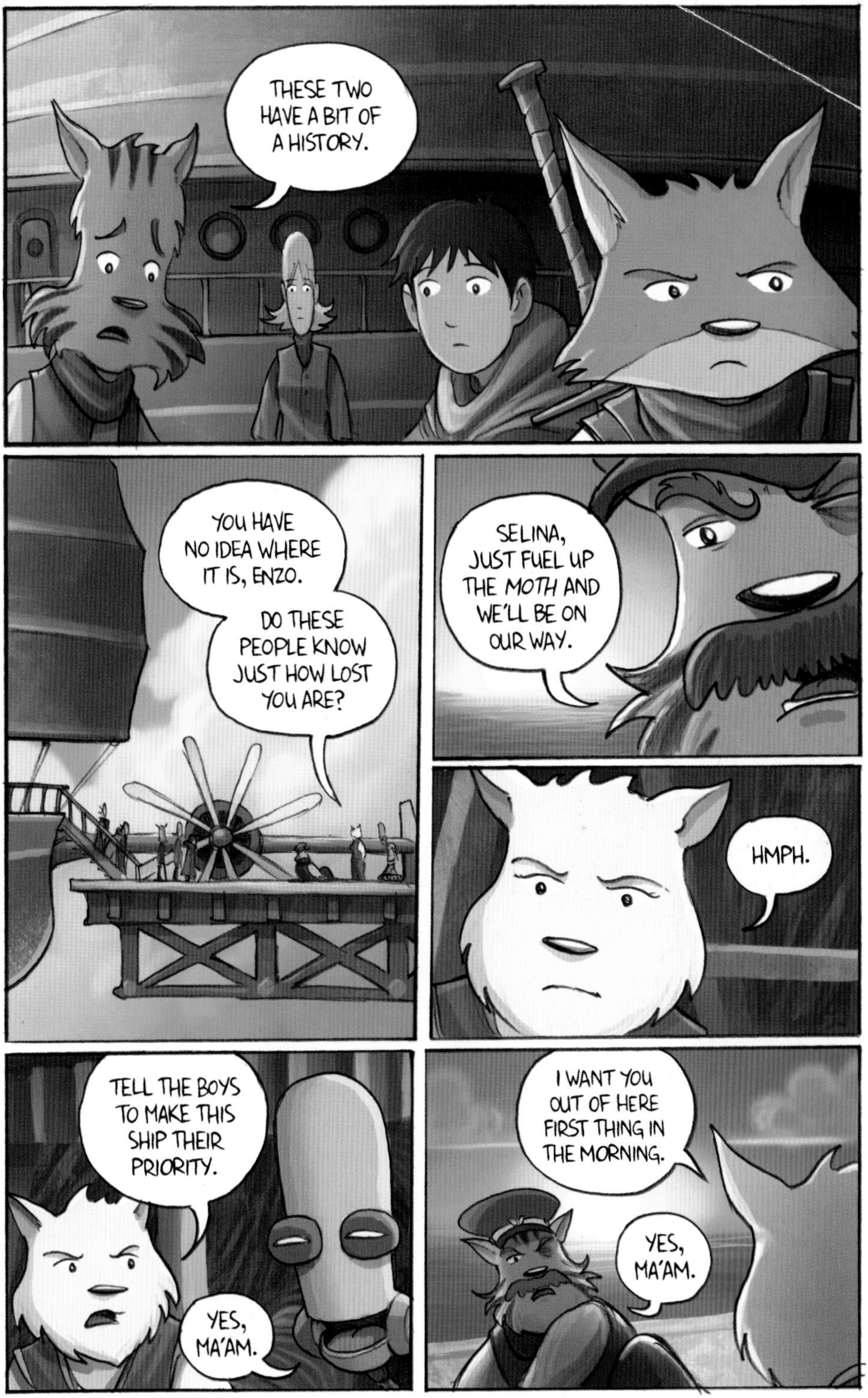
THESE TWO HAVE A BIT OF A HISTORY.
YOU HAVE NO IDEA WHERE IT IS, ENZO.
DO THESE PEOPLE KNOW JUST HOW LOST YOU ARE?
SELINA, JUST FUEL UP THE *MOTH* AND WE'LL BE ON OUR WAY.
HMPH.
TELL THE BOYS TO MAKE THIS SHIP THEIR PRIORITY.
YES, MA'AM.
I WANT YOU OUT OF HERE FIRST THING IN THE MORNING.
YES, MA'AM.

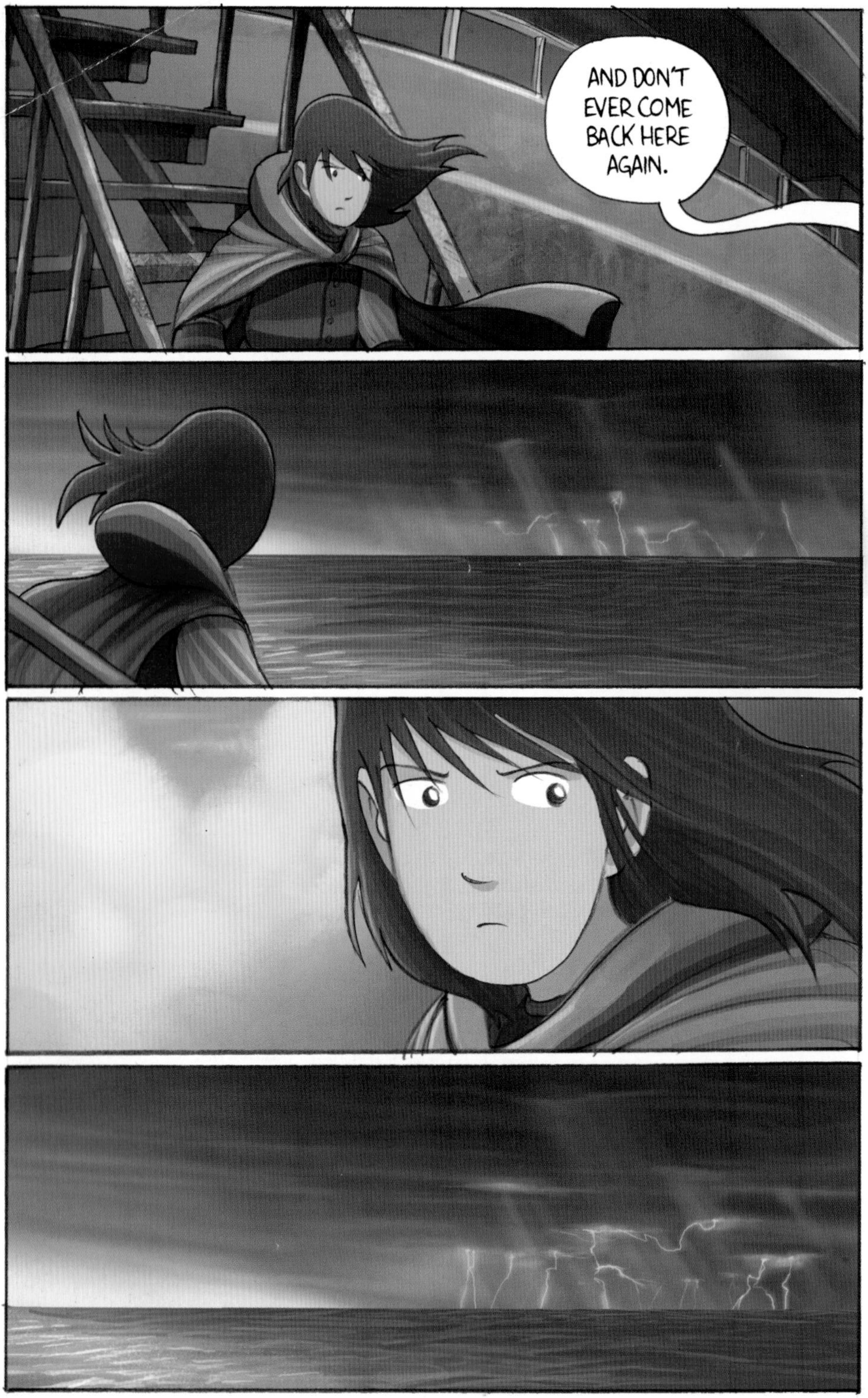
AND DON'T EVER COME BACK HERE AGAIN.

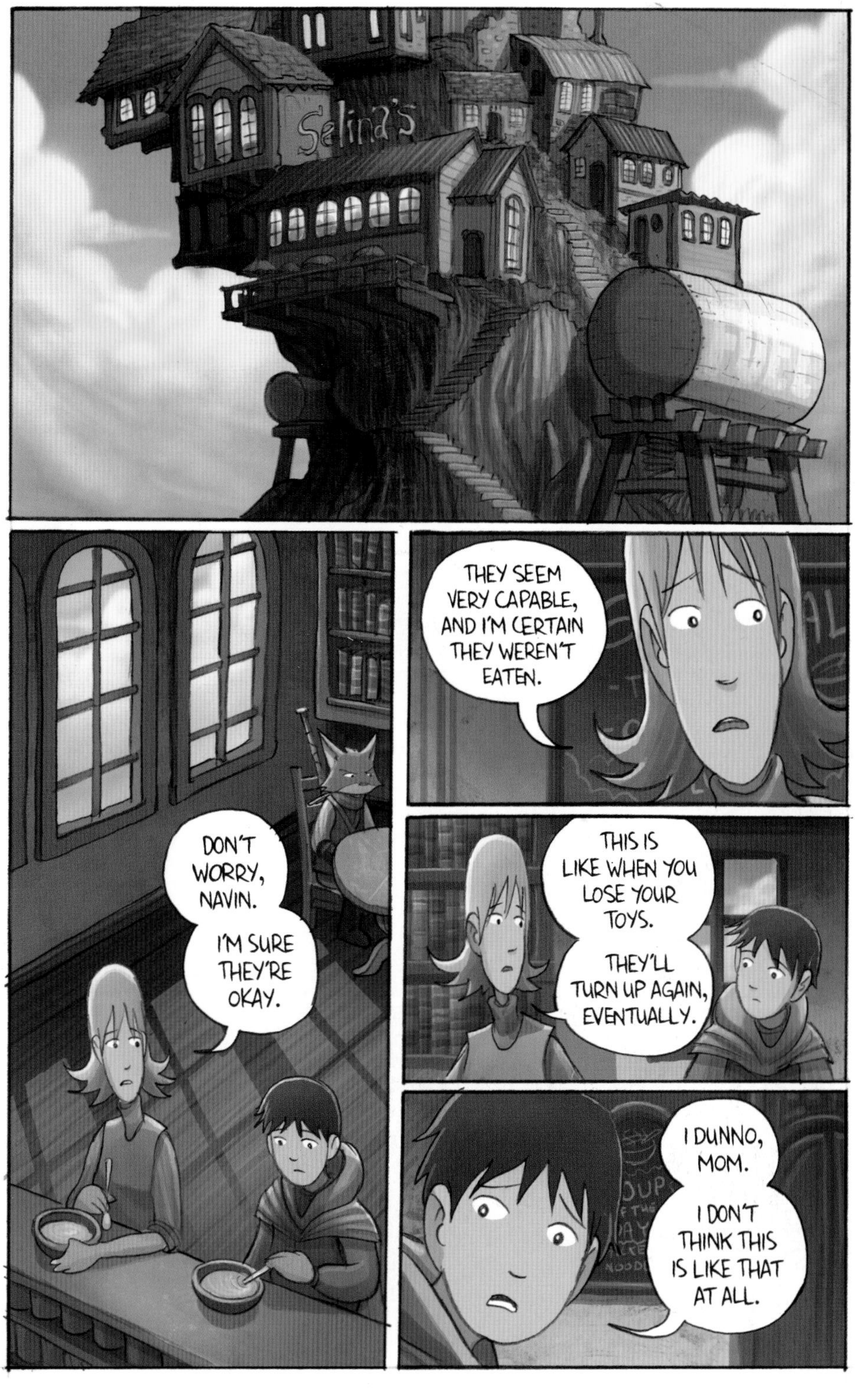
Selina's
DON'T WORRY, NAVIN.
I'M SURE THEY'RE OKAY.
THEY SEEM VERY CAPABLE, AND I'M CERTAIN THEY WEREN'T EATEN.
THIS IS LIKE WHEN YOU LOSE YOUR TOYS.
THEY'LL TURN UP AGAIN, EVENTUALLY.
I DUNNO, MOM.
I DON'T THINK THIS IS LIKE THAT AT ALL.

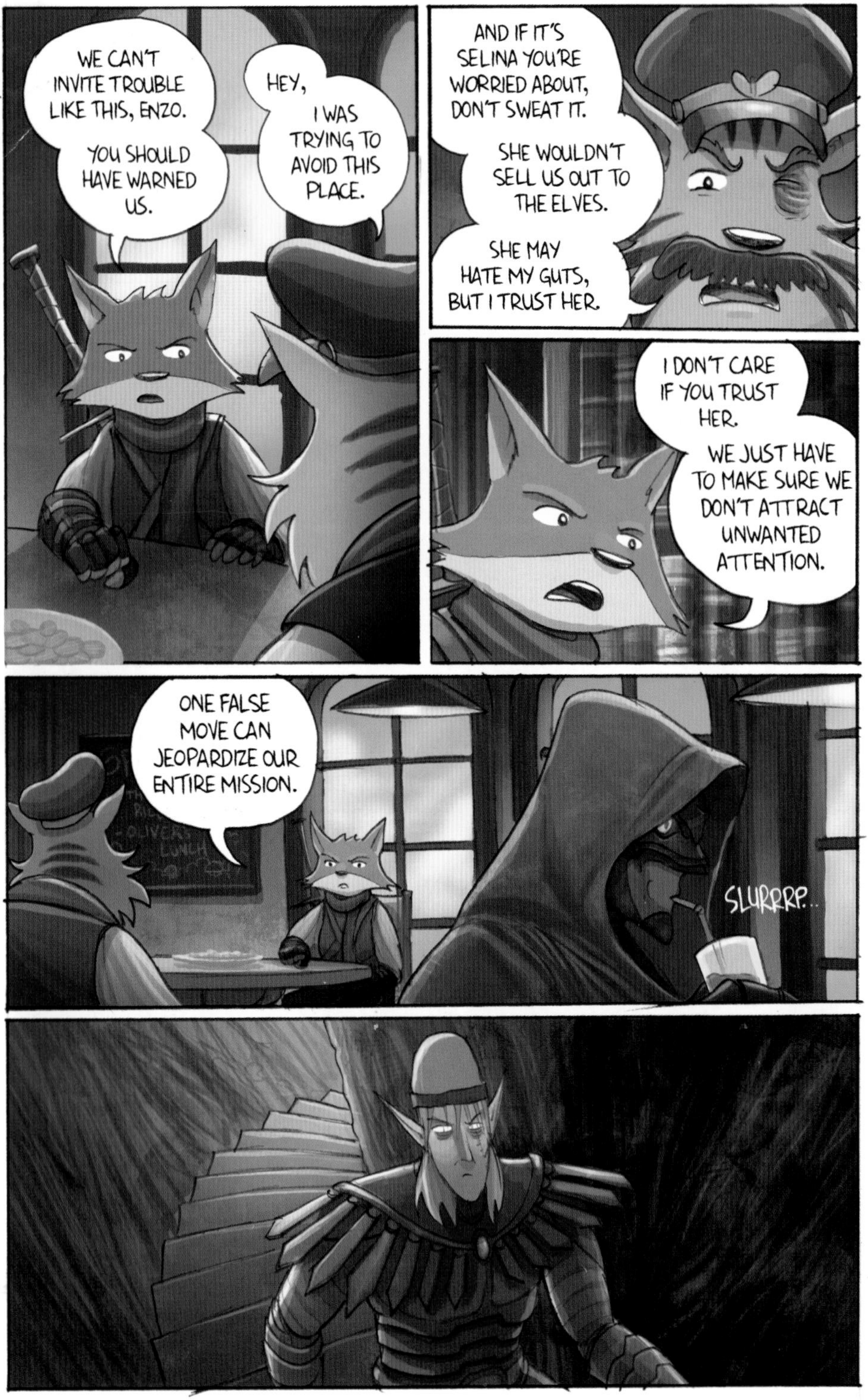
WE CAN'T INVITE TROUBLE LIKE THIS, ENZO.
YOU SHOULD HAVE WARNED US.
HEY,
I WAS TRYING TO AVOID THIS PLACE.
AND IF IT'S SELINA YOU'RE WORRIED ABOUT, DON'T SWEAT IT.
SHE WOULDN'T SELL US OUT TO THE ELVES.
SHE MAY HATE MY GUTS, BUT I TRUST HER.
I DON'T CARE IF YOU TRUST HER.
WE JUST HAVE TO MAKE SURE WE DON'T ATTRACT UNWANTED ATTENTION.
ONE FALSE MOVE CAN JEOPARDIZE OUR ENTIRE MISSION.
SLURRRP...

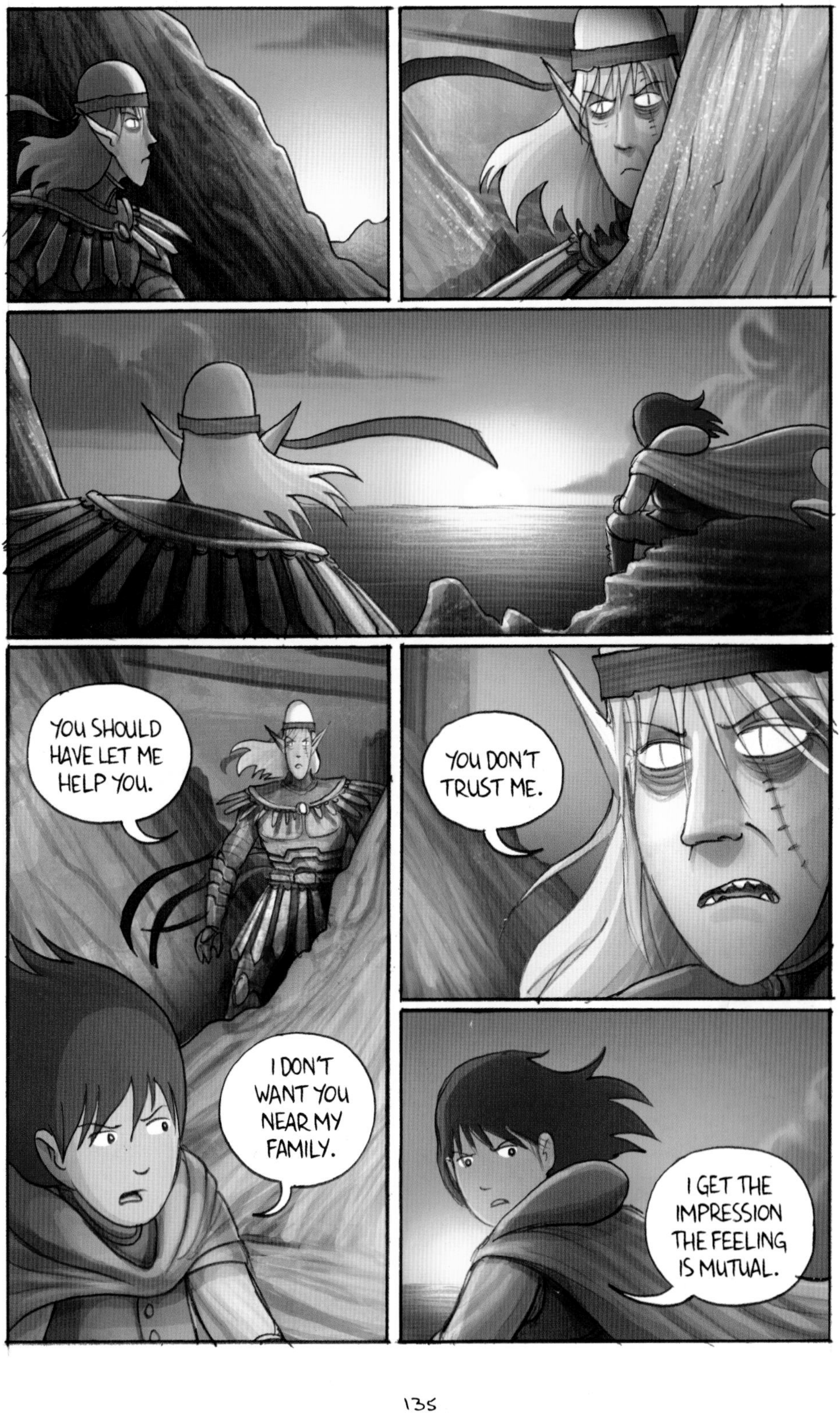
YOU SHOULD HAVE LET ME HELP YOU.
YOU DON'T TRUST ME.
I DON'T WANT YOU NEAR MY FAMILY.
I GET THE IMPRESSION THE FEELING IS MUTUAL.

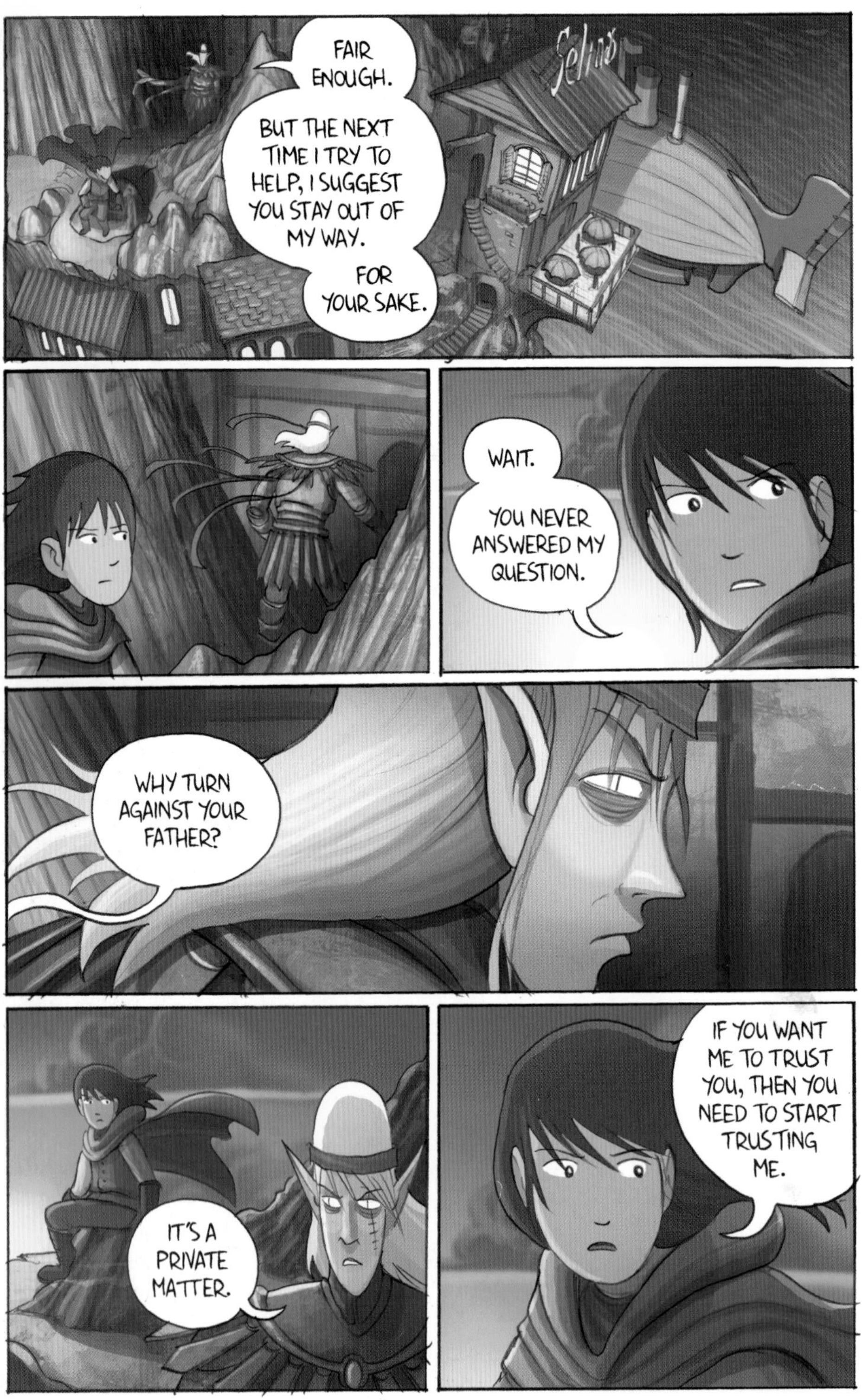
FAIR ENOUGH.
BUT THE NEXT TIME I TRY TO HELP, I SUGGEST YOU STAY OUT OF MY WAY.
FOR YOUR SAKE.
WAIT.
YOU NEVER ANSWERED MY QUESTION.
WHY TURN AGAINST YOUR FATHER?
IT'S A PRIVATE MATTER.
IF YOU WANT ME TO TRUST YOU, THEN YOU NEED TO START TRUSTING ME.

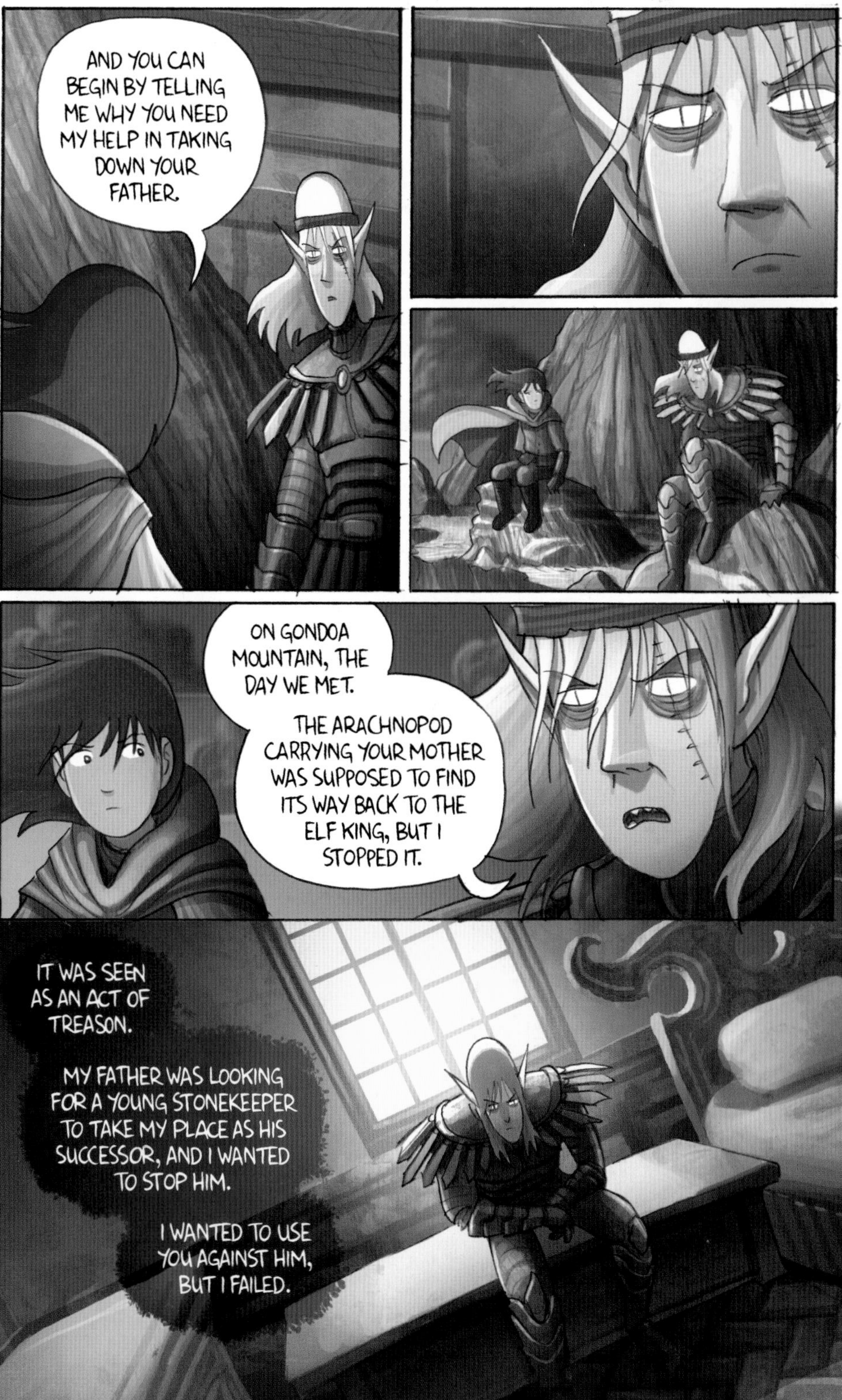
AND YOU CAN BEGIN BY TELLING ME WHY YOU NEED MY HELP IN TAKING DOWN YOUR FATHER.
ON GONDOA MOUNTAIN, THE DAY WE MET.
THE ARACHNOPOD CARRYING YOUR MOTHER WAS SUPPOSED TO FIND ITS WAY BACK TO THE ELF KING, BUT I STOPPED IT.
IT WAS SEEN AS AN ACT OF TREASON.
MY FATHER WAS LOOKING FOR A YOUNG STONEKEEPER TO TAKE MY PLACE AS HIS SUCCESSOR, AND I WANTED TO STOP HIM.
I WANTED TO USE YOU AGAINST HIM, BUT I FAILED.

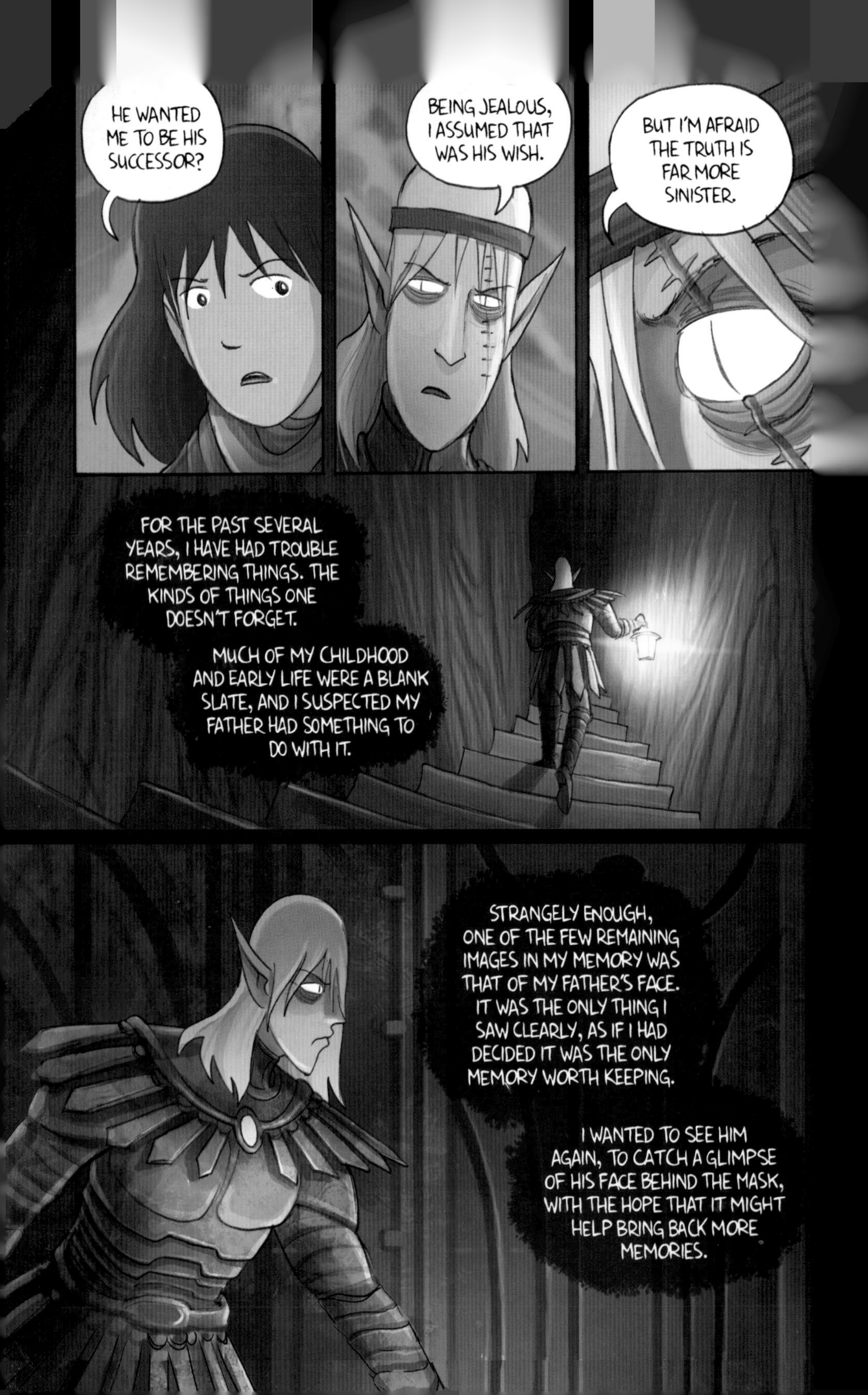
HE WANTED ME TO BE HIS SUCCESSOR?
BEING JEALOUS, I ASSUMED THAT WAS HIS WISH.
BUT I'M AFRAID THE TRUTH IS FAR MORE SINISTER.
FOR THE PAST SEVERAL YEARS, I HAVE HAD TROUBLE REMEMBERING THINGS. THE KINDS OF THINGS ONE DOESN'T FORGET.
MUCH OF MY CHILDHOOD AND EARLY LIFE WERE A BLANK SLATE, AND I SUSPECTED MY FATHER HAD SOMETHING TO DO WITH IT.
STRANGELY ENOUGH, ONE OF THE FEW REMAINING IMAGES IN MY MEMORY WAS THAT OF MY FATHER'S FACE. IT WAS THE ONLY THING I SAW CLEARLY, AS IF I HAD DECIDED IT WAS THE ONLY MEMORY WORTH KEEPING.
I WANTED TO SEE HIM AGAIN, TO CATCH A GLIMPSE OF HIS FACE BEHIND THE MASK, WITH THE HOPE THAT IT MIGHT HELP BRING BACK MORE MEMORIES.

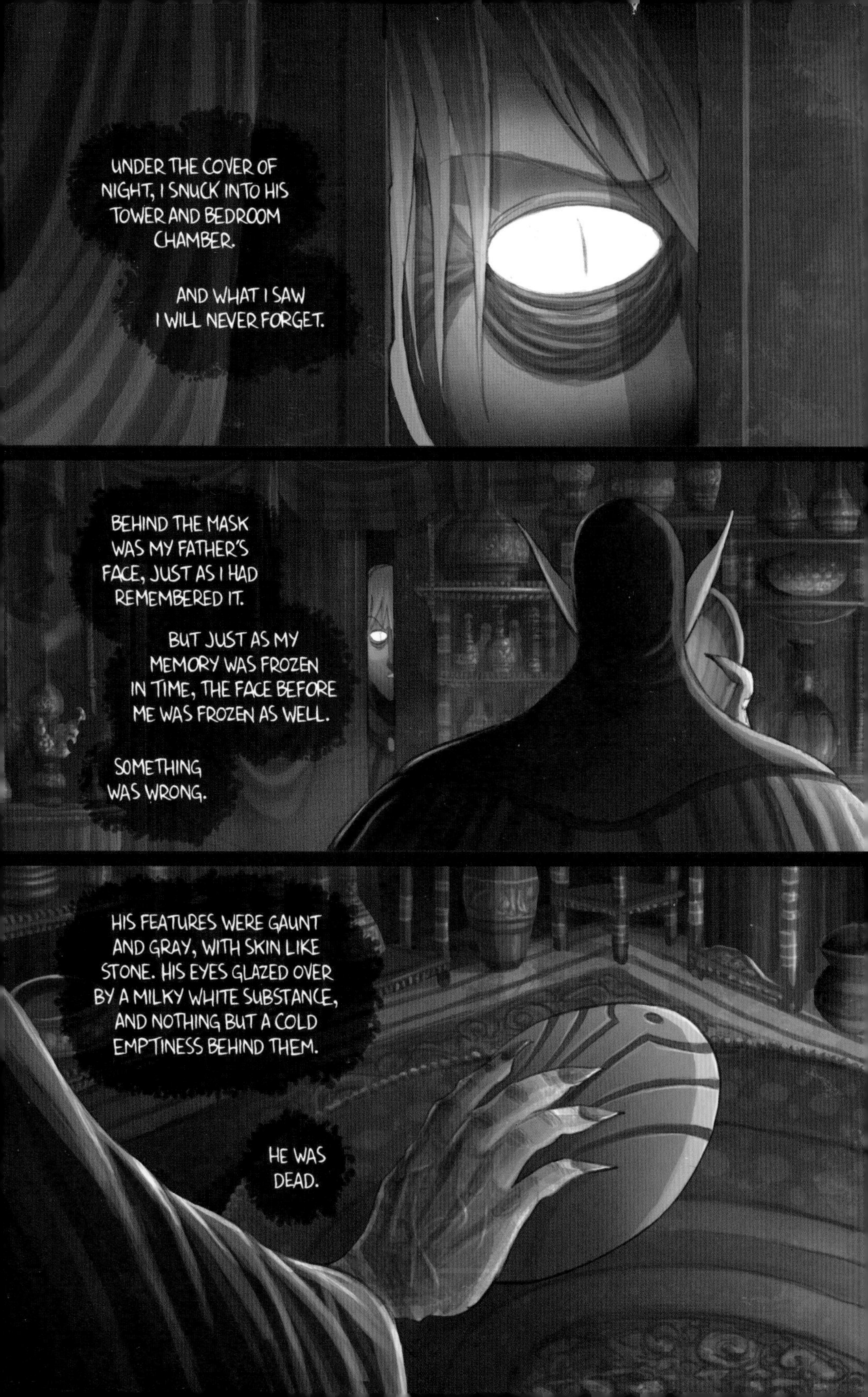
UNDER THE COVER OF NIGHT, I SNUCK INTO HIS TOWER AND BEDROOM CHAMBER.
AND WHAT I SAW I WILL NEVER FORGET.
BEHIND THE MASK WAS MY FATHER'S FACE, JUST AS I HAD REMEMBERED IT.
BUT JUST AS MY MEMORY WAS FROZEN IN TIME, THE FACE BEFORE ME WAS FROZEN AS WELL.
SOMETHING WAS WRONG.
HIS FEATURES WERE GAUNT AND GRAY, WITH SKIN LIKE STONE. HIS EYES GLAZED OVER BY A MILKY WHITE SUBSTANCE, AND NOTHING BUT A COLD EMPTINESS BEHIND THEM.
HE WAS DEAD.

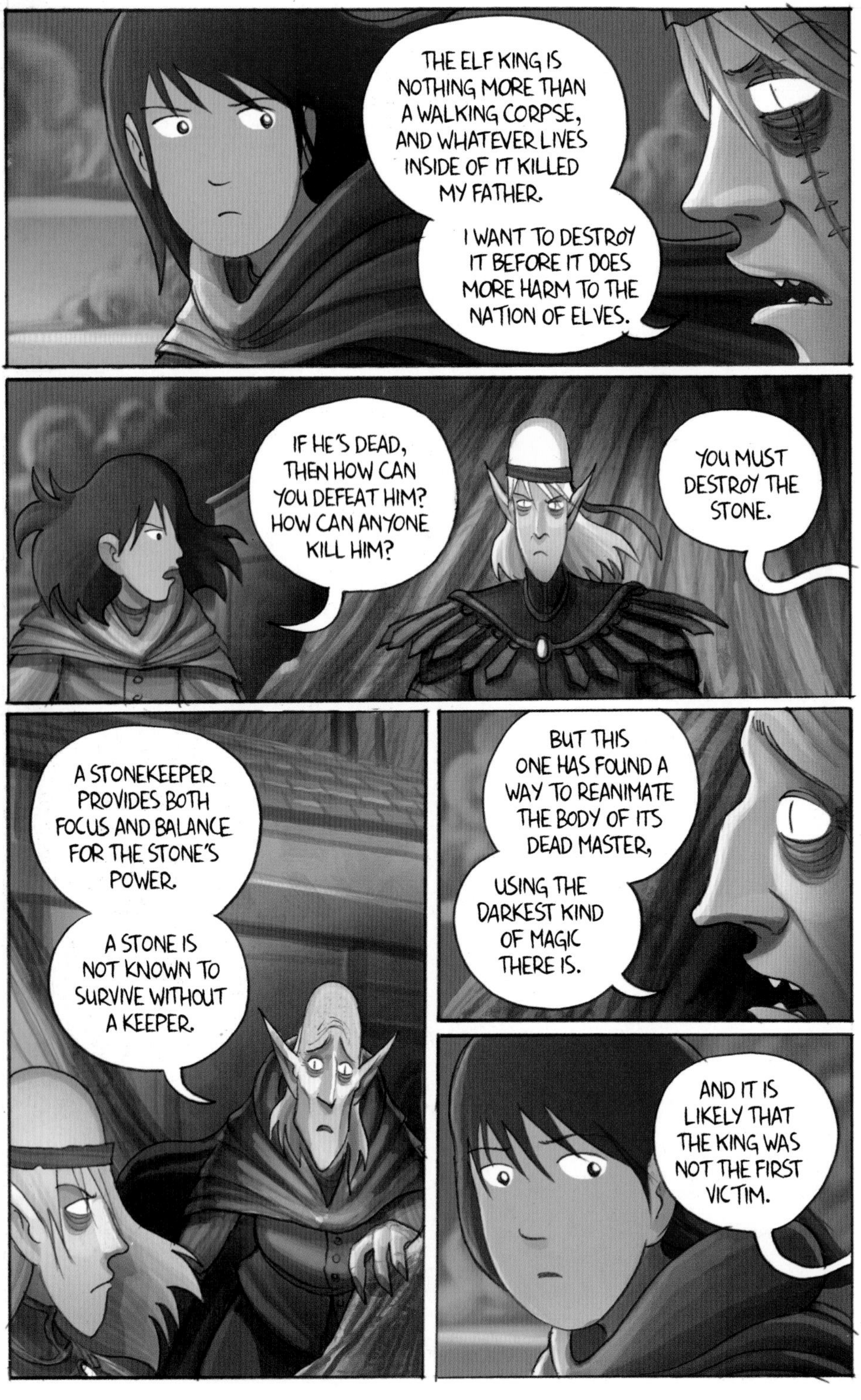
THE ELF KING IS NOTHING MORE THAN A WALKING CORPSE, AND WHATEVER LIVES INSIDE OF IT KILLED MY FATHER.
I WANT TO DESTROY IT BEFORE IT DOES MORE HARM TO THE NATION OF ELVES.
IF HE'S DEAD, THEN HOW CAN YOU DEFEAT HIM? HOW CAN ANYONE KILL HIM?
YOU MUST DESTROY THE STONE.
A STONEKEEPER PROVIDES BOTH FOCUS AND BALANCE FOR THE STONE'S POWER.
A STONE IS NOT KNOWN TO SURVIVE WITHOUT A KEEPER.
BUT THIS ONE HAS FOUND A WAY TO REANIMATE THE BODY OF ITS DEAD MASTER,
USING THE DARKEST KIND OF MAGIC THERE IS.
AND IT IS LIKELY THAT THE KING WAS NOT THE FIRST VICTIM.

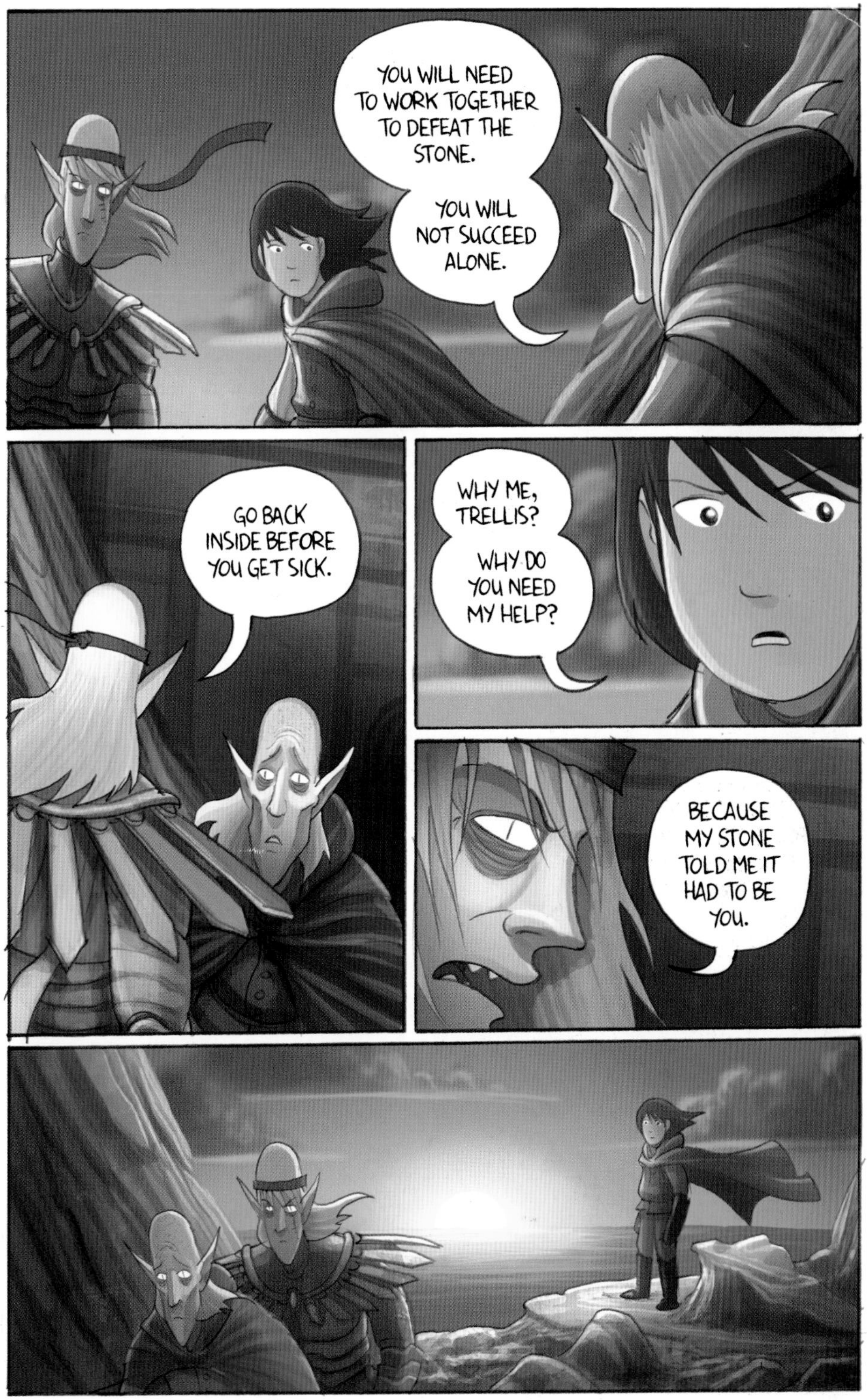
YOU WILL NEED TO WORK TOGETHER TO DEFEAT THE STONE.
YOU WILL NOT SUCCEED ALONE.
GO BACK INSIDE BEFORE YOU GET SICK.
WHY ME, TRELLIS?
WHY DO YOU NEED MY HELP?
BECAUSE MY STONE TOLD ME IT HAD TO BE YOU.

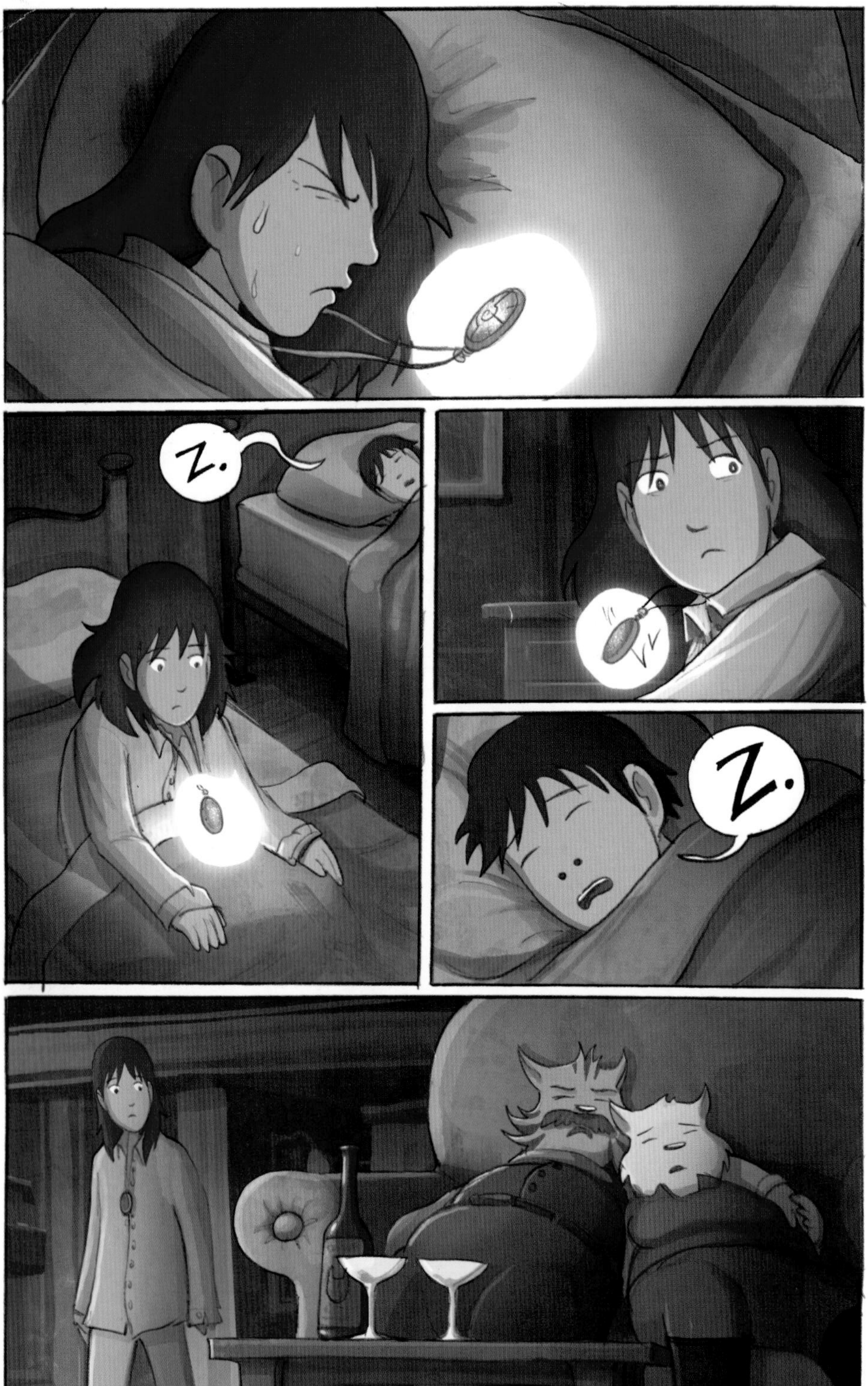
Z.
Z.

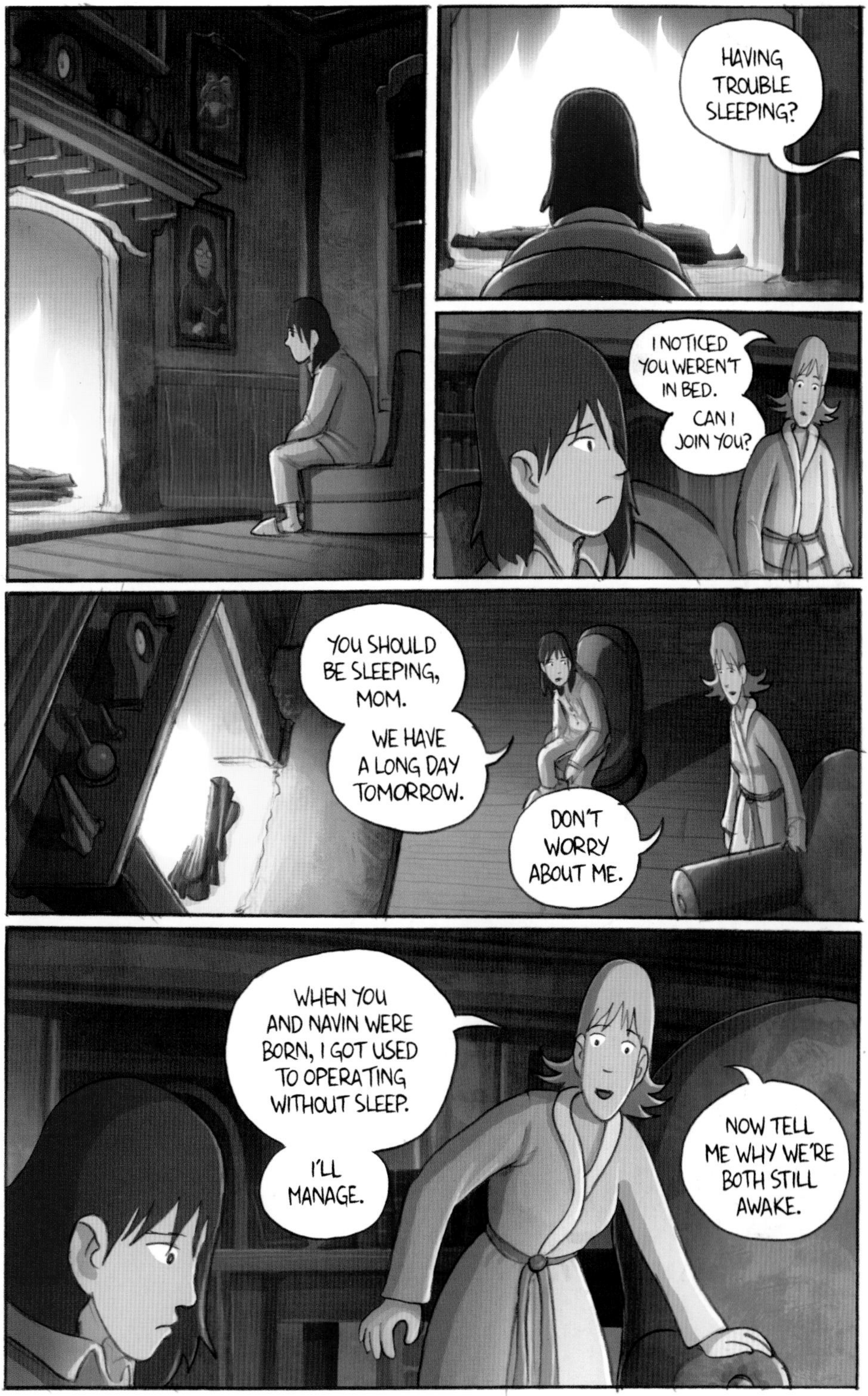
HAVING TROUBLE SLEEPING?
I NOTICED YOU WEREN'T IN BED.
CAN I JOIN YOU?
YOU SHOULD BE SLEEPING, MOM.
WE HAVE A LONG DAY TOMORROW.
DON'T WORRY ABOUT ME.
WHEN YOU AND NAVIN WERE BORN, I GOT USED TO OPERATING WITHOUT SLEEP.
I'LL MANAGE.
NOW TELL ME WHY WE'RE BOTH STILL AWAKE.

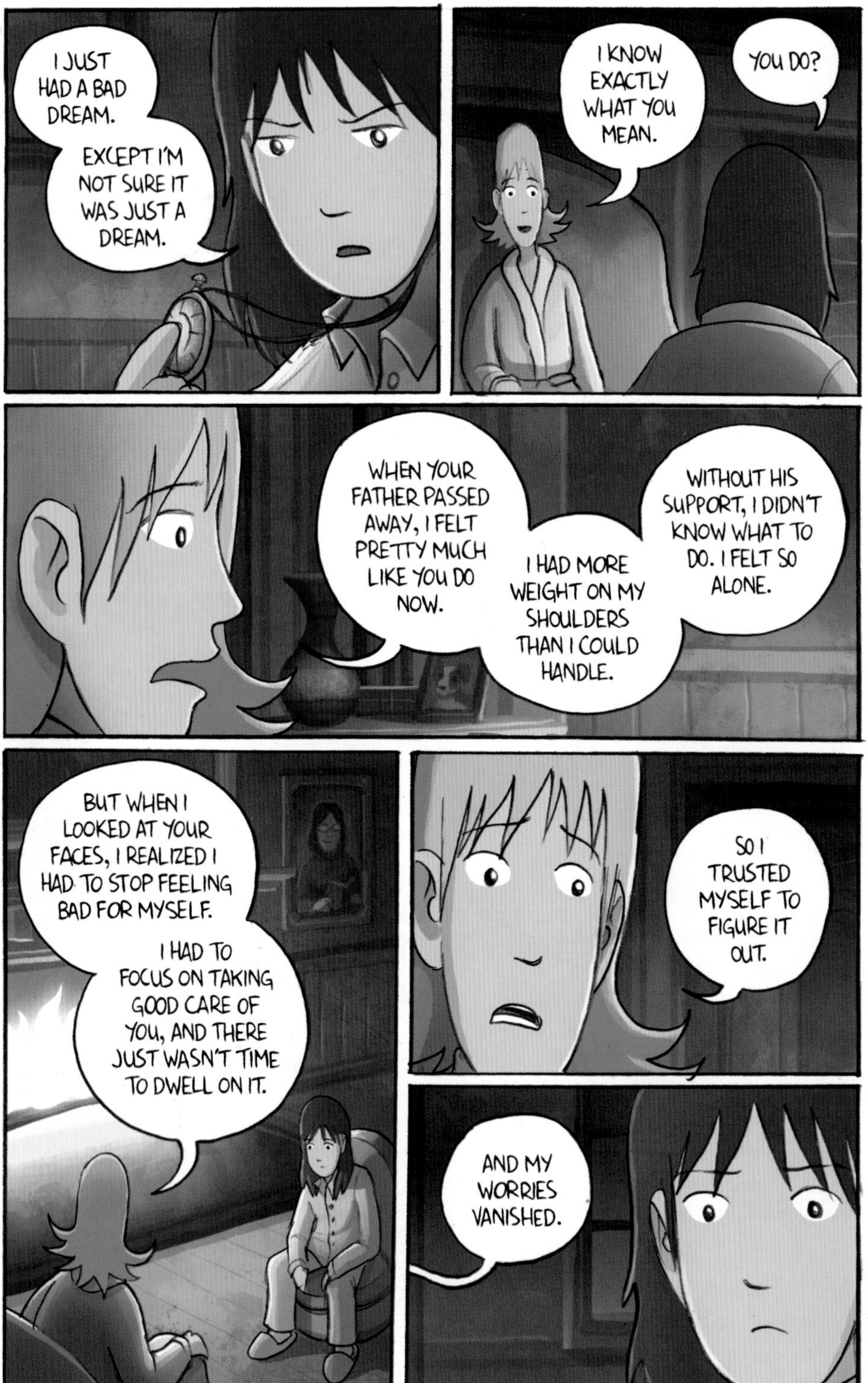
I JUST HAD A BAD DREAM.
EXCEPT I'M NOT SURE IT WAS JUST A DREAM.
I KNOW EXACTLY WHAT YOU MEAN.
YOU DO?
WHEN YOUR FATHER PASSED AWAY, I FELT PRETTY MUCH LIKE YOU DO NOW.
I HAD MORE WEIGHT ON MY SHOULDERS THAN I COULD HANDLE.
WITHOUT HIS SUPPORT, I DIDN'T KNOW WHAT TO DO. I FELT SO ALONE.
BUT WHEN I LOOKED AT YOUR FACES, I REALIZED I HAD TO STOP FEELING BAD FOR MYSELF.
I HAD TO FOCUS ON TAKING GOOD CARE OF YOU, AND THERE JUST WASN'T TIME TO DWELL ON IT.
SO I TRUSTED MYSELF TO FIGURE IT OUT.
AND MY WORRIES VANISHED.

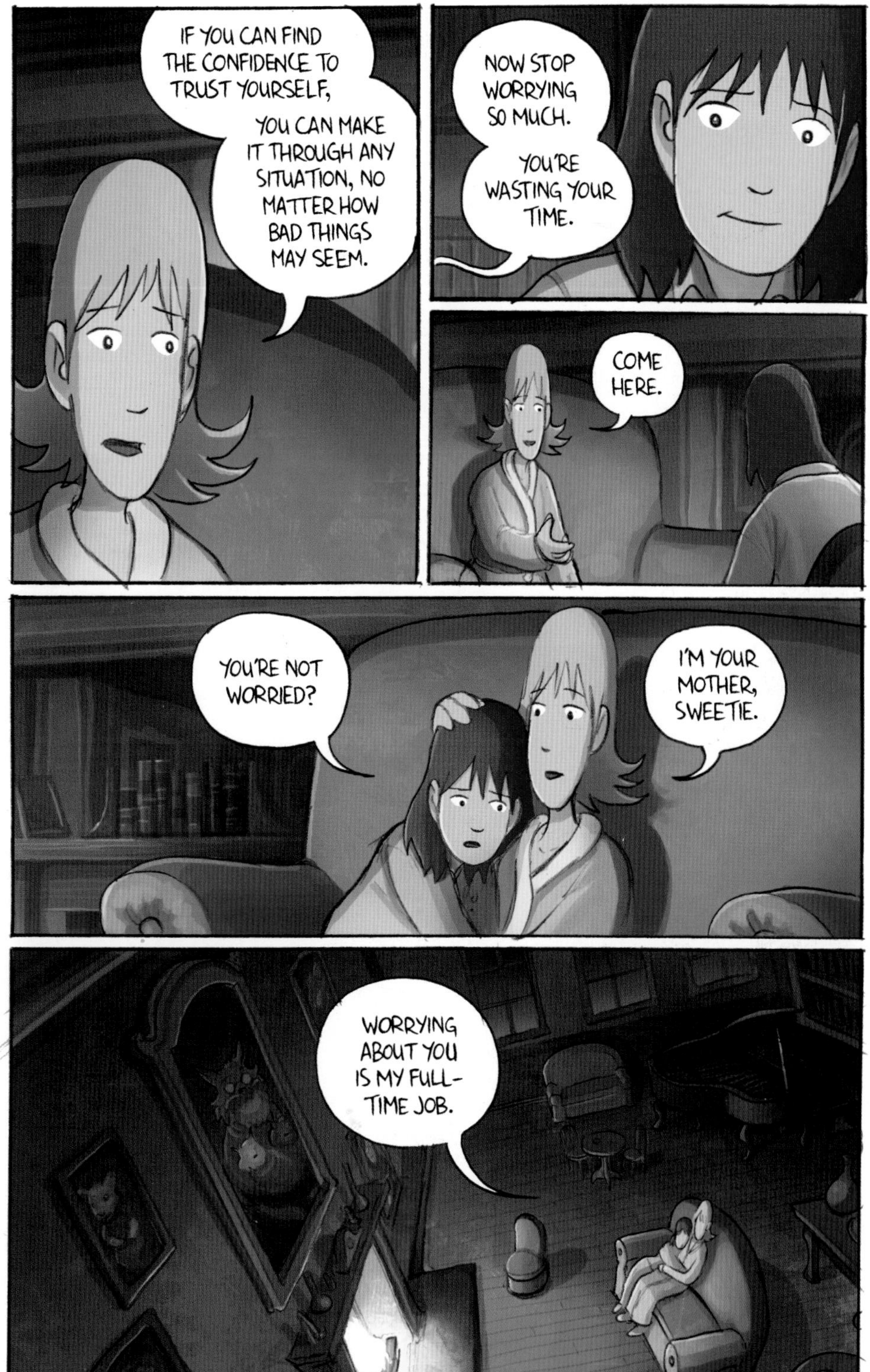
IF YOU CAN FIND THE CONFIDENCE TO TRUST YOURSELF,
YOU CAN MAKE IT THROUGH ANY SITUATION, NO MATTER HOW BAD THINGS MAY SEEM.
NOW STOP WORRYING SO MUCH.
YOU'RE WASTING YOUR TIME.
COME HERE.
YOU'RE NOT WORRIED?
I'M YOUR MOTHER, SWEETIE.
WORRYING ABOUT YOU IS MY FULL-TIME JOB.

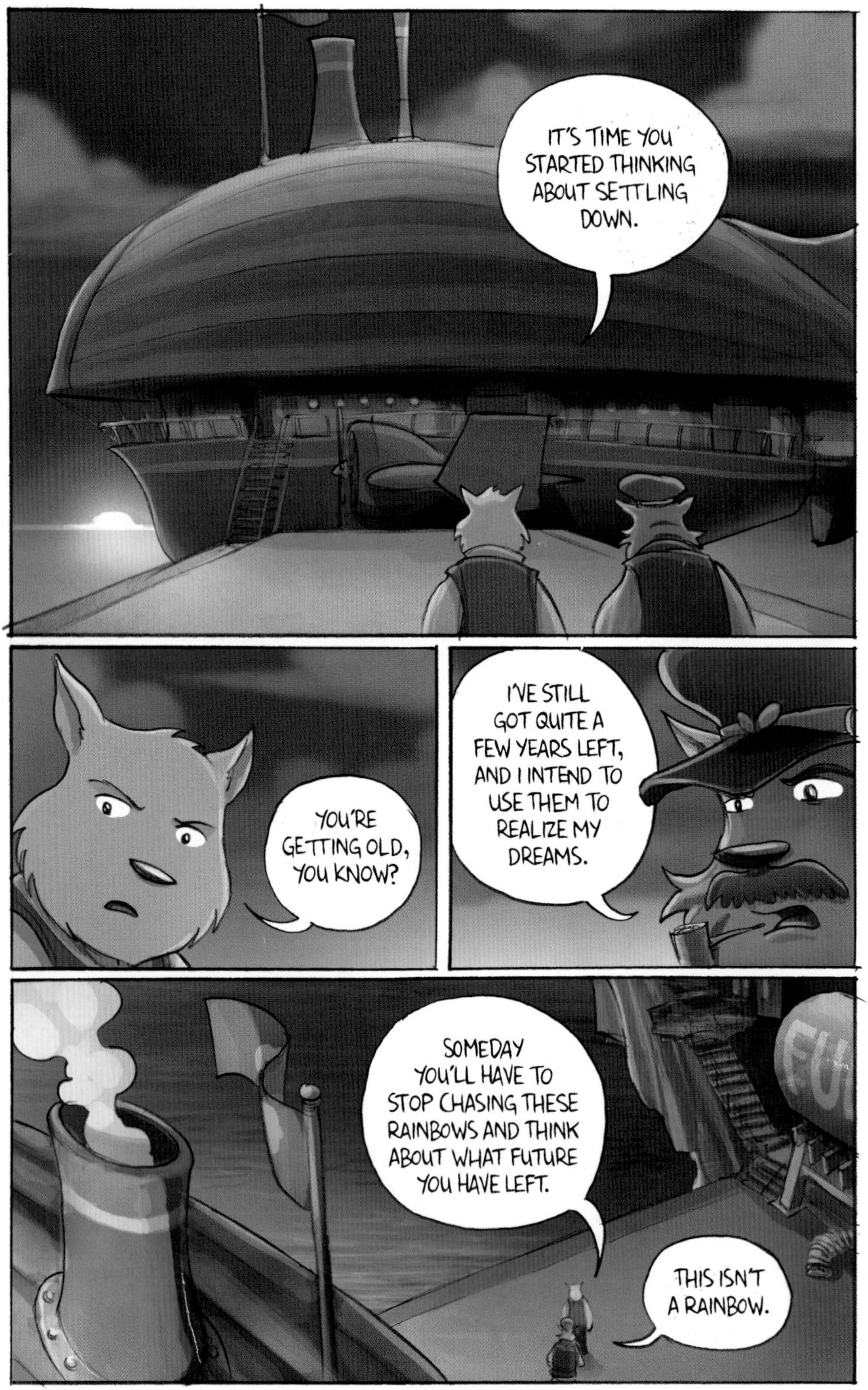
IT'S TIME YOU STARTED THINKING ABOUT SETTLING DOWN.
YOU'RE GETTING OLD, YOU KNOW?
I'VE STILL GOT QUITE A FEW YEARS LEFT, AND I INTEND TO USE THEM TO REALIZE MY DREAMS.
SOMEDAY YOU'LL HAVE TO STOP CHASING THESE RAINBOWS AND THINK ABOUT WHAT FUTURE YOU HAVE LEFT.
THIS ISN'T A RAINBOW.

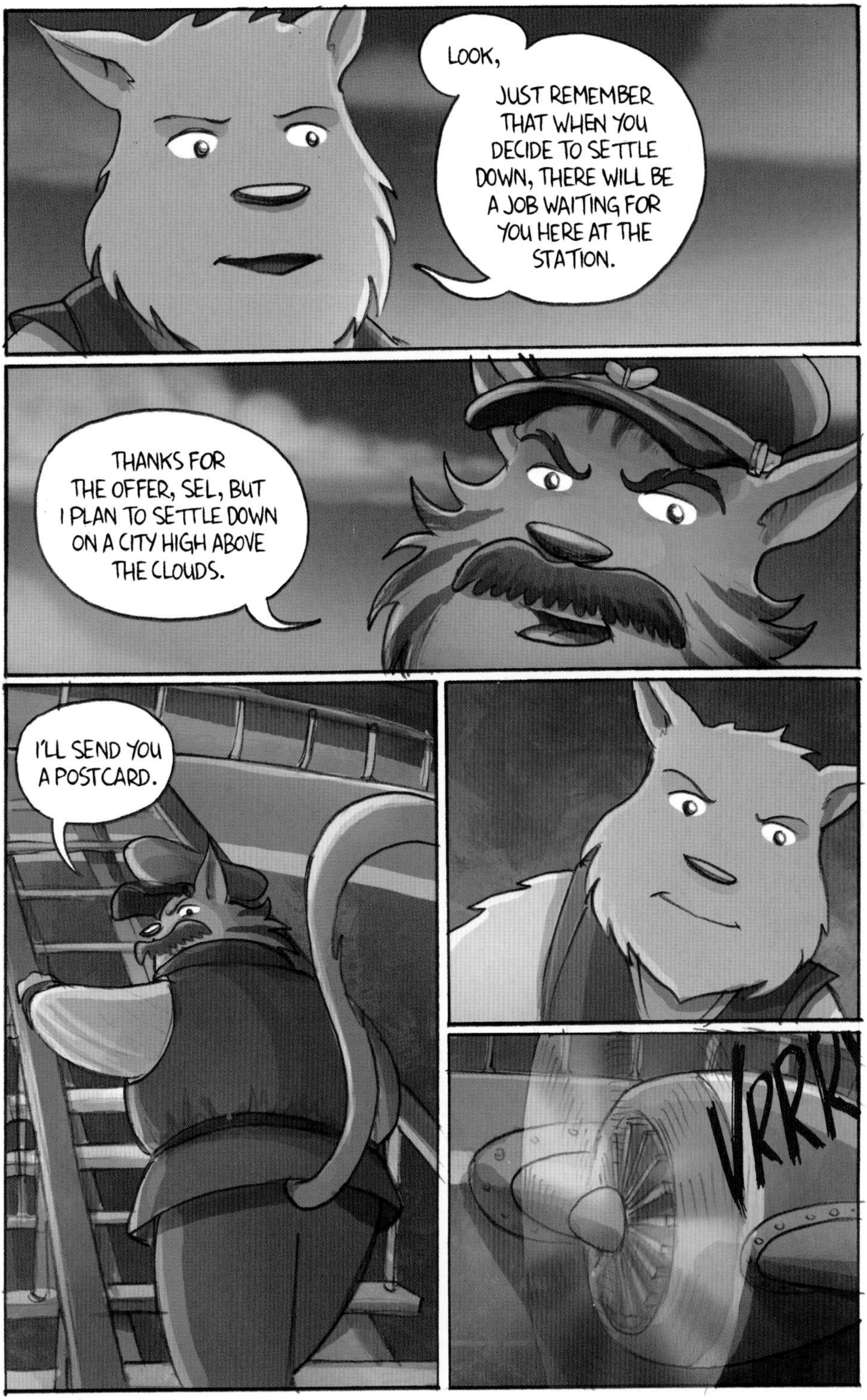
LOOK,
JUST REMEMBER THAT WHEN YOU DECIDE TO SETTLE DOWN, THERE WILL BE A JOB WAITING FOR YOU HERE AT THE STATION.
THANKS FOR THE OFFER, SEL, BUT I PLAN TO SETTLE DOWN ON A CITY HIGH ABOVE THE CLOUDS.
I'LL SEND YOU A POSTCARD.
VRRR

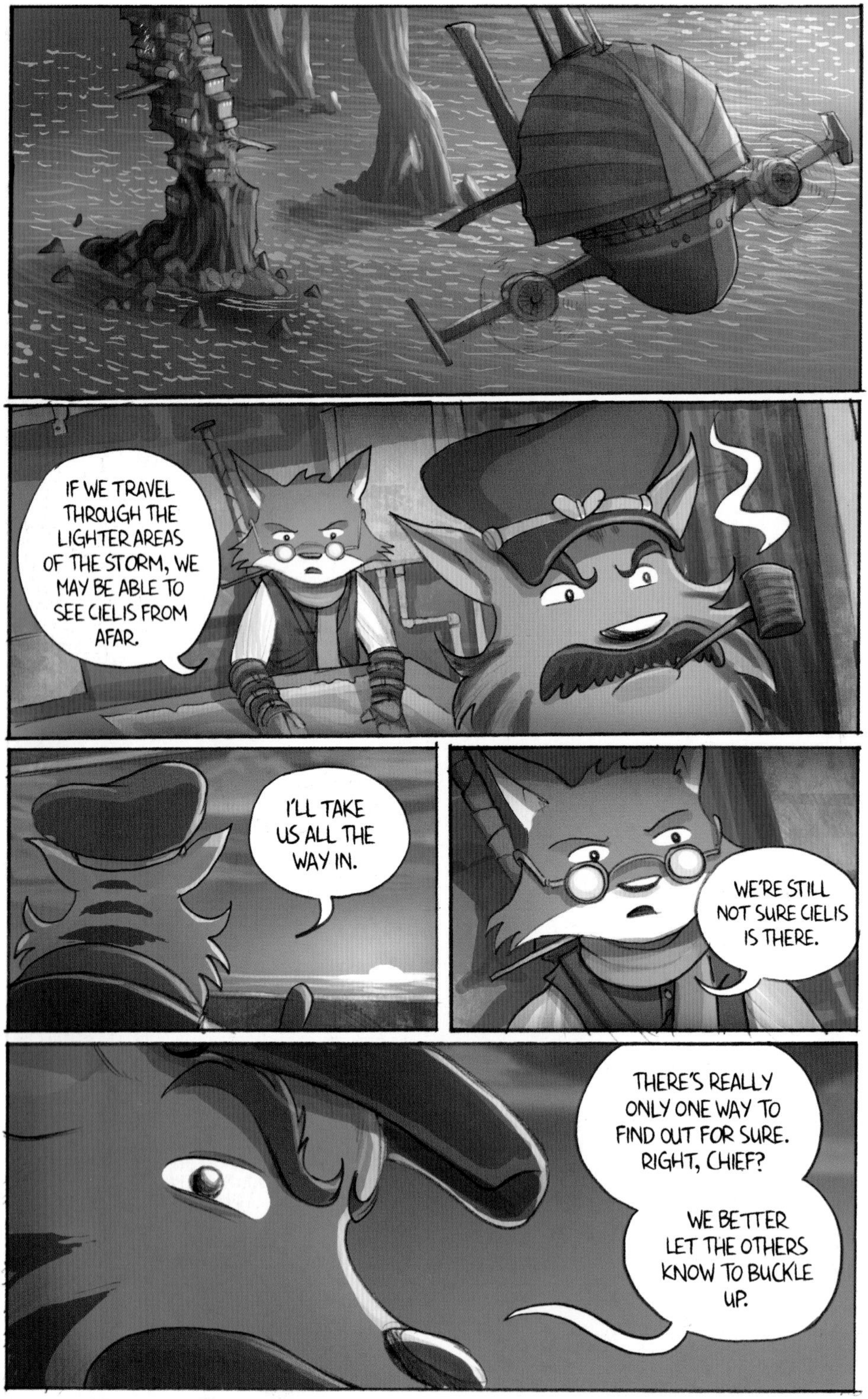
IF WE TRAVEL THROUGH THE LIGHTER AREAS OF THE STORM, WE MAY BE ABLE TO SEE CIELIS FROM AFAR.
I'LL TAKE US ALL THE WAY IN.
WE'RE STILL NOT SURE CIELIS IS THERE.
THERE'S REALLY ONLY ONE WAY TO FIND OUT FOR SURE. RIGHT, CHIEF?
WE BETTER LET THE OTHERS KNOW TO BUCKLE UP.

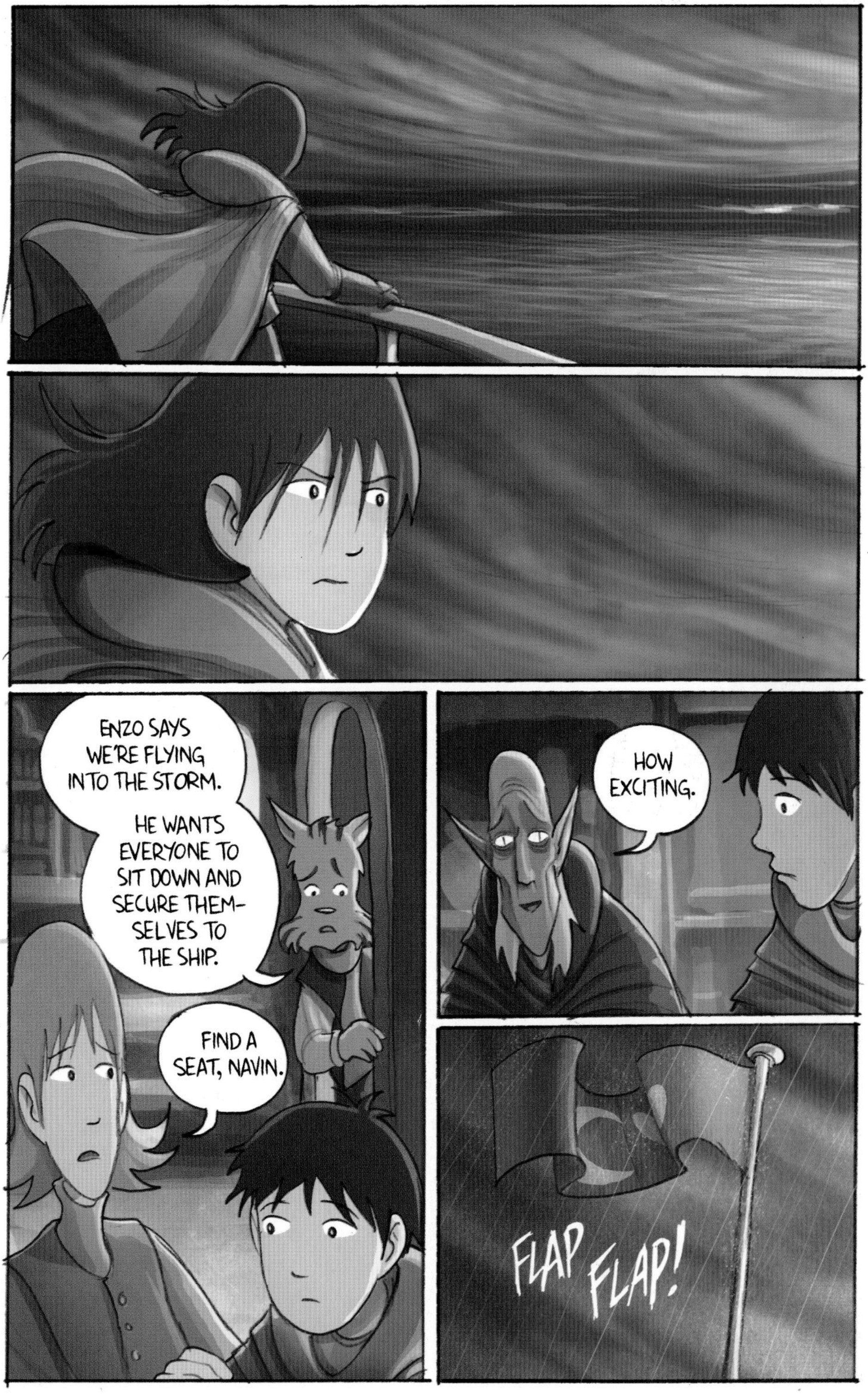
ENZO SAYS WE'RE FLYING INTO THE STORM.
HE WANTS EVERYONE TO SIT DOWN AND SECURE THEM-SELVES TO THE SHIP.
FIND A SEAT, NAVIN.
HOW EXCITING.
FLAP FLAP!

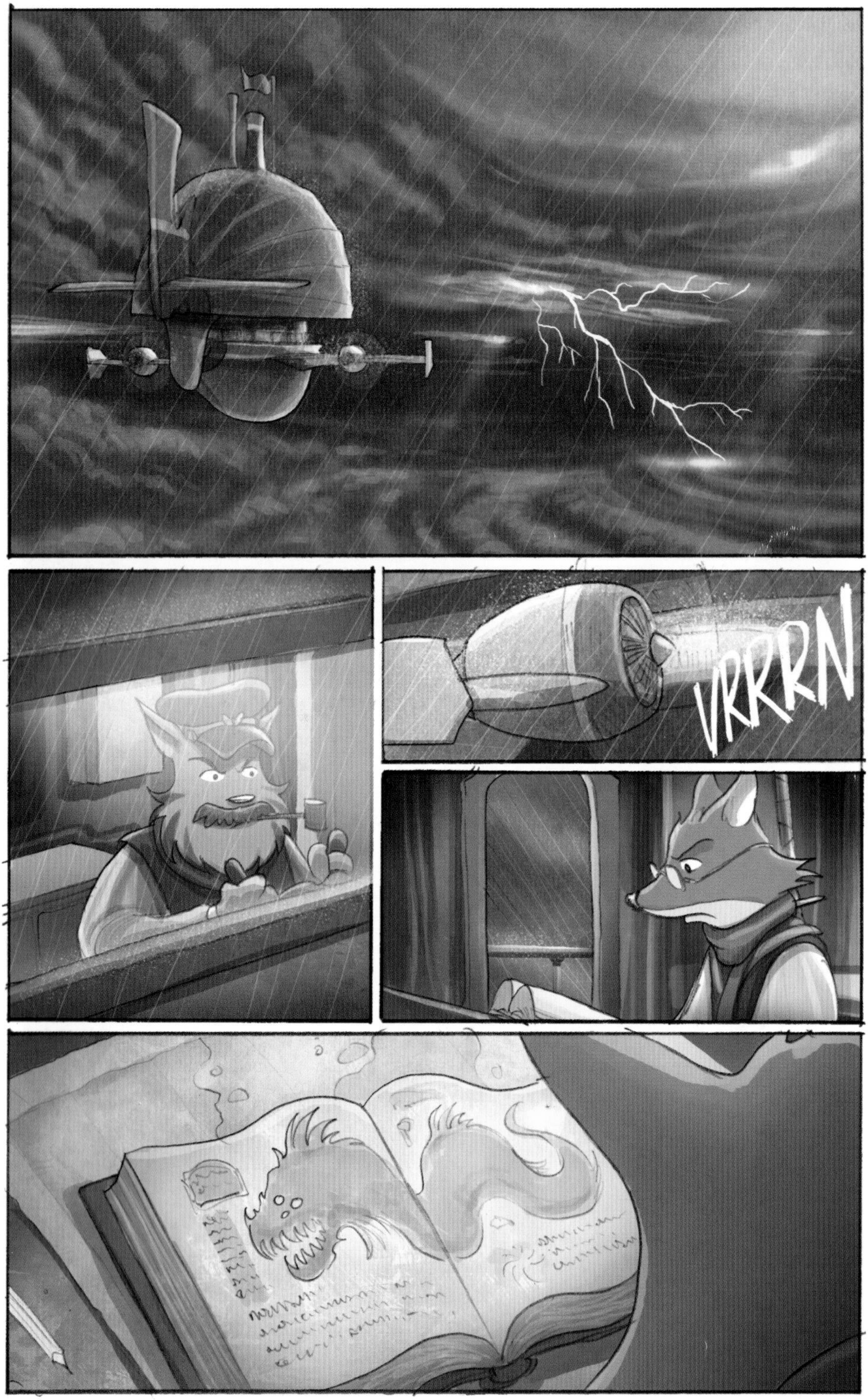
VRRRN

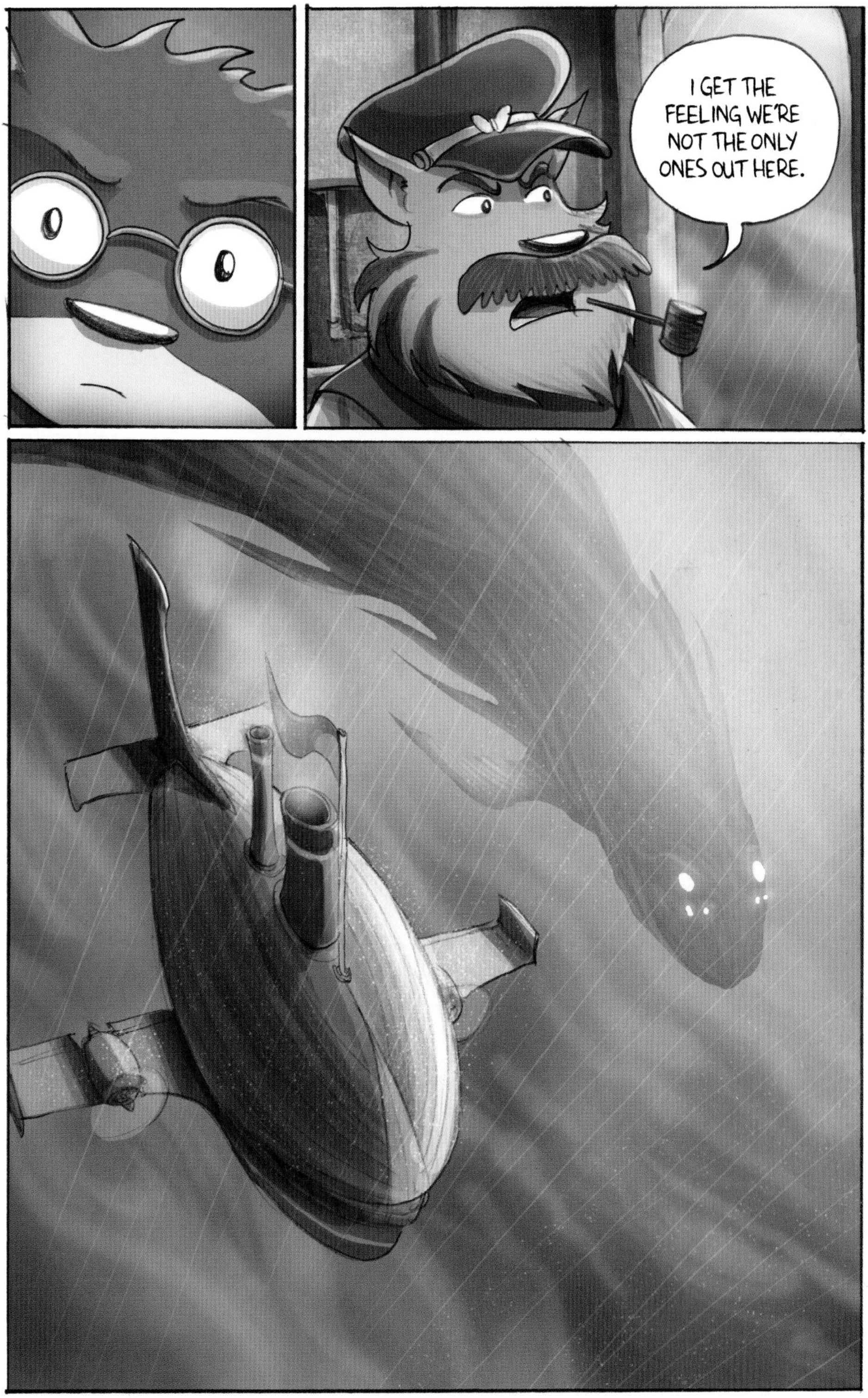
I GET THE FEELING WE'RE NOT THE ONLY ONES OUT HERE.

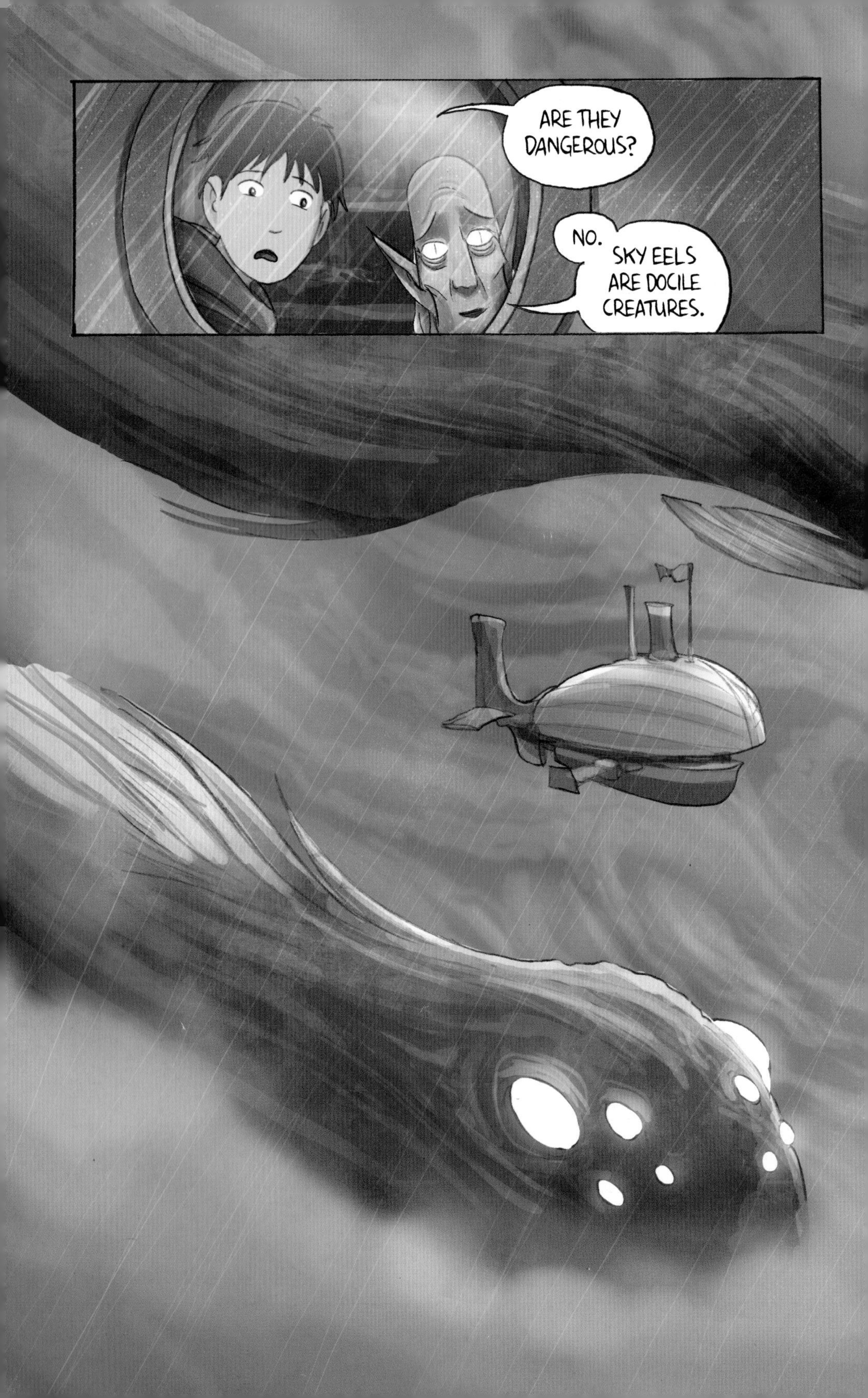
ARE THEY DANGEROUS?
NO.
SKY EELS ARE DOCILE CREATURES.

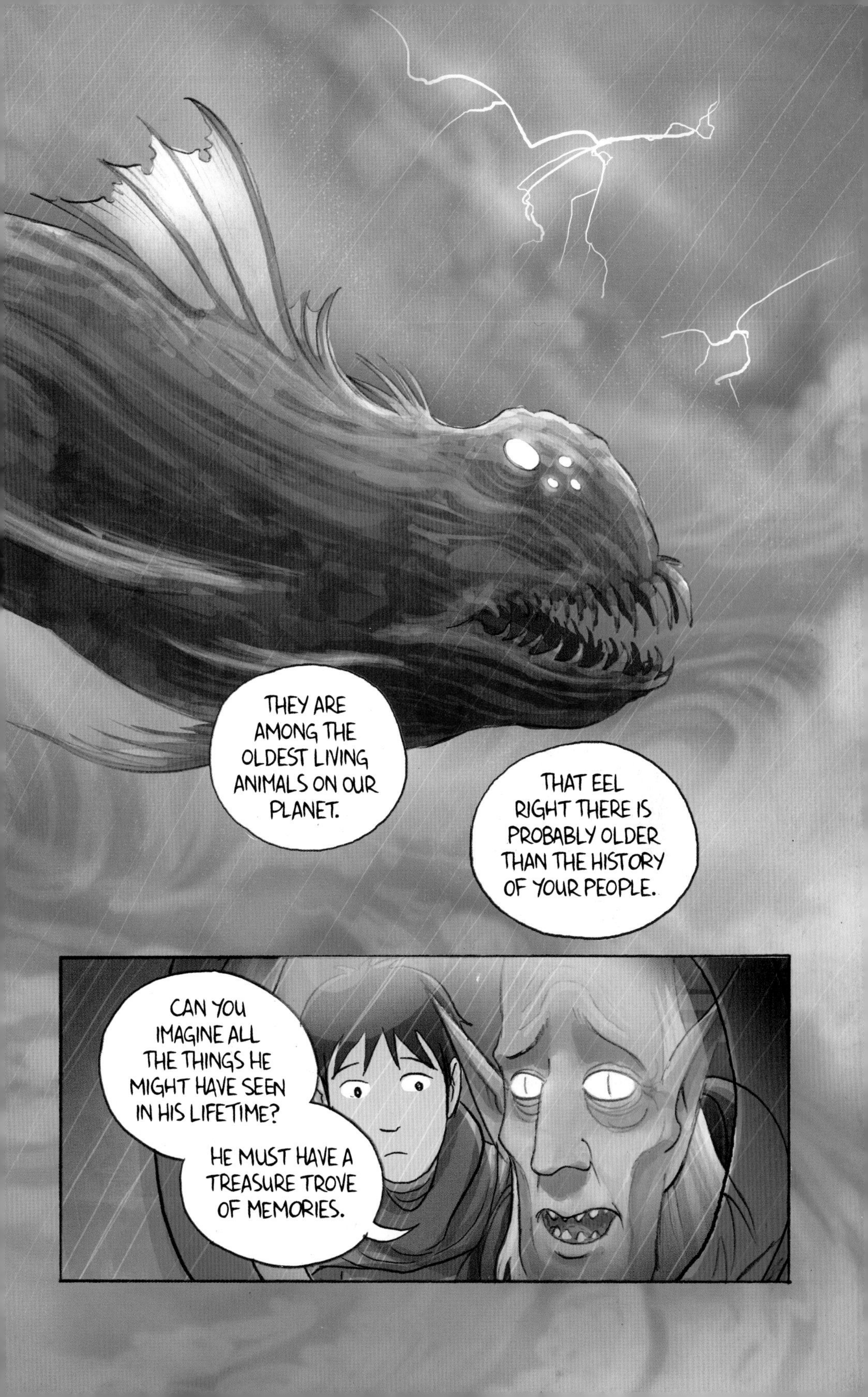
THEY ARE AMONG THE OLDEST LIVING ANIMALS ON OUR PLANET.
THAT EEL RIGHT THERE IS PROBABLY OLDER THAN THE HISTORY OF YOUR PEOPLE.
CAN YOU IMAGINE ALL THE THINGS HE MIGHT HAVE SEEN IN HIS LIFETIME?
HE MUST HAVE A TREASURE TROVE OF MEMORIES.

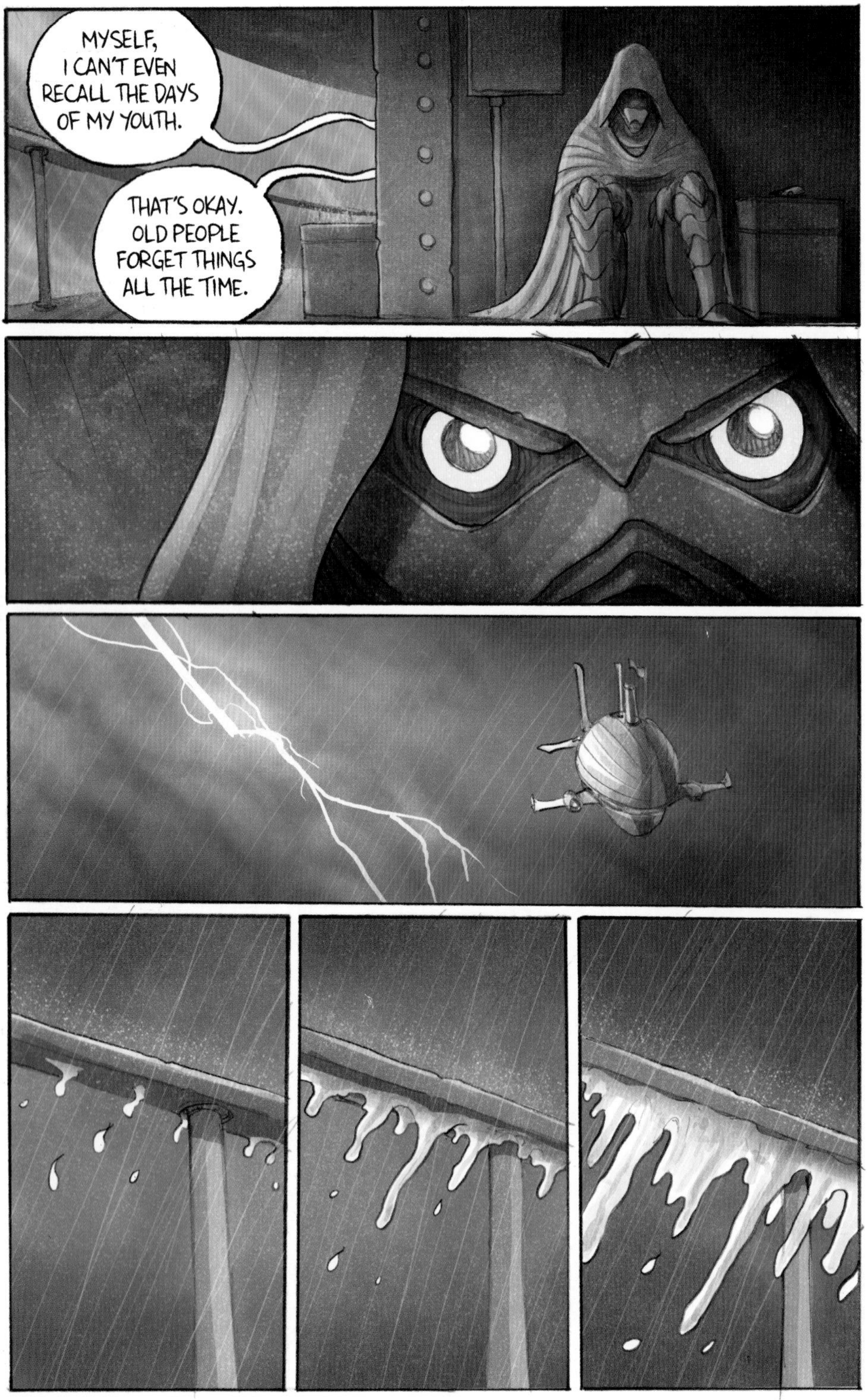
MYSELF, I CAN'T EVEN RECALL THE DAYS OF MY YOUTH.
THAT'S OKAY. OLD PEOPLE FORGET THINGS ALL THE TIME.

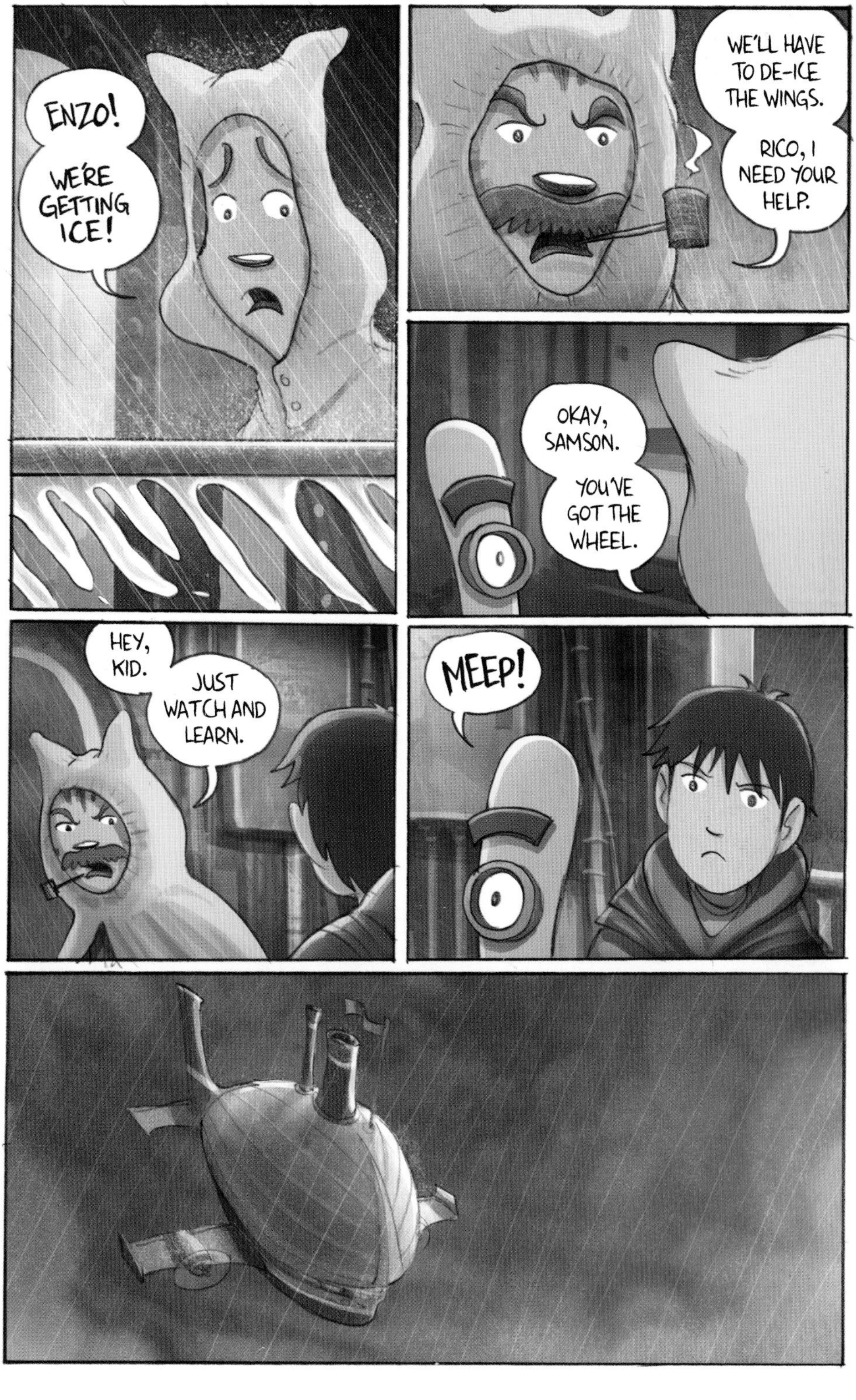
ENZO!
WE'RE GETTING ICE!
WE'LL HAVE TO DE-ICE THE WINGS.
RICO, I NEED YOUR HELP.
OKAY, SAMSON.
YOU'VE GOT THE WHEEL.
HEY, KID.
JUST WATCH AND LEARN.
MEEP!

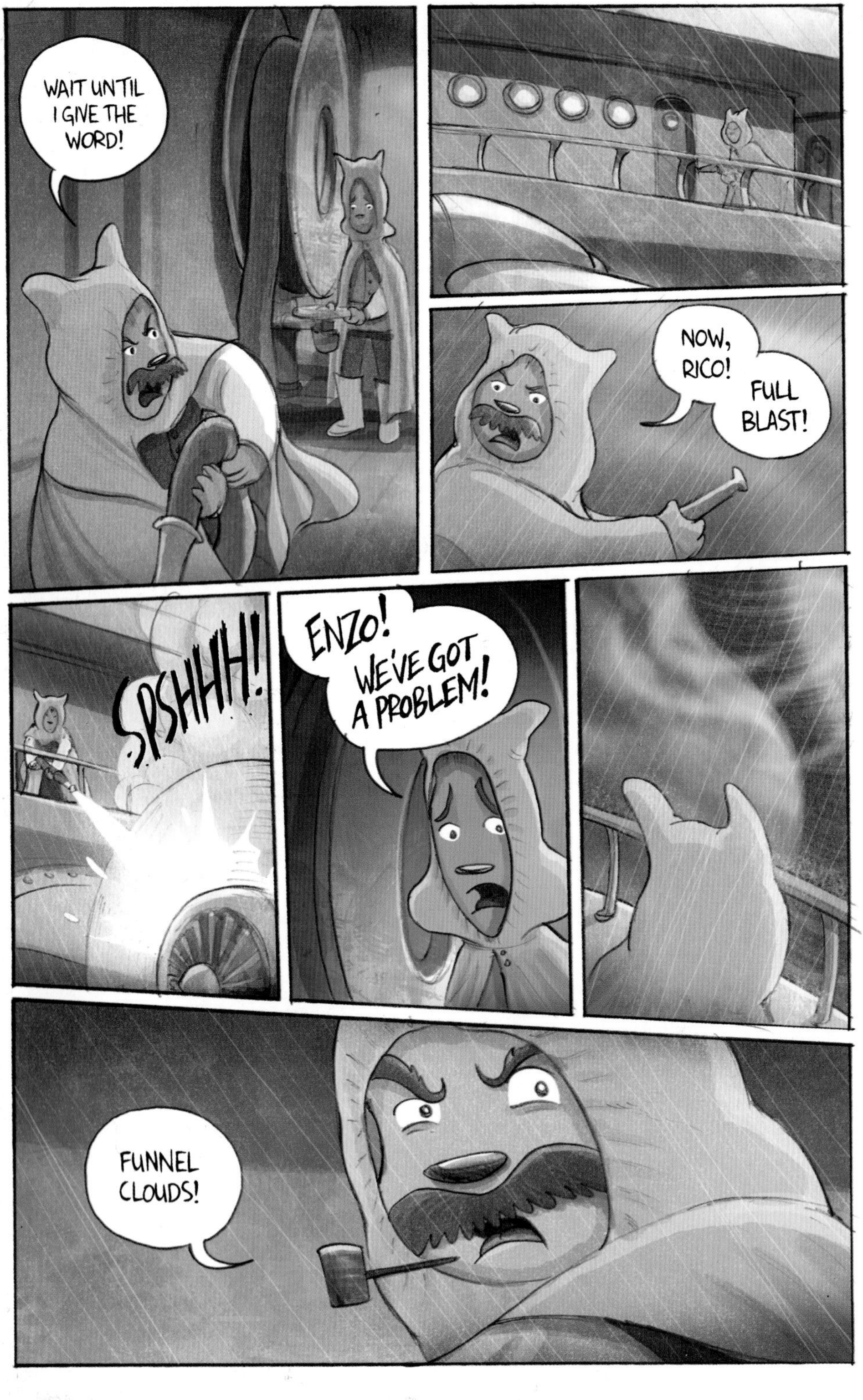
WAIT UNTIL I GIVE THE WORD!
NOW, RICO!
FULL BLAST!
SPSHHH!
ENZO! WE'VE GOT A PROBLEM!
FUNNEL CLOUDS!

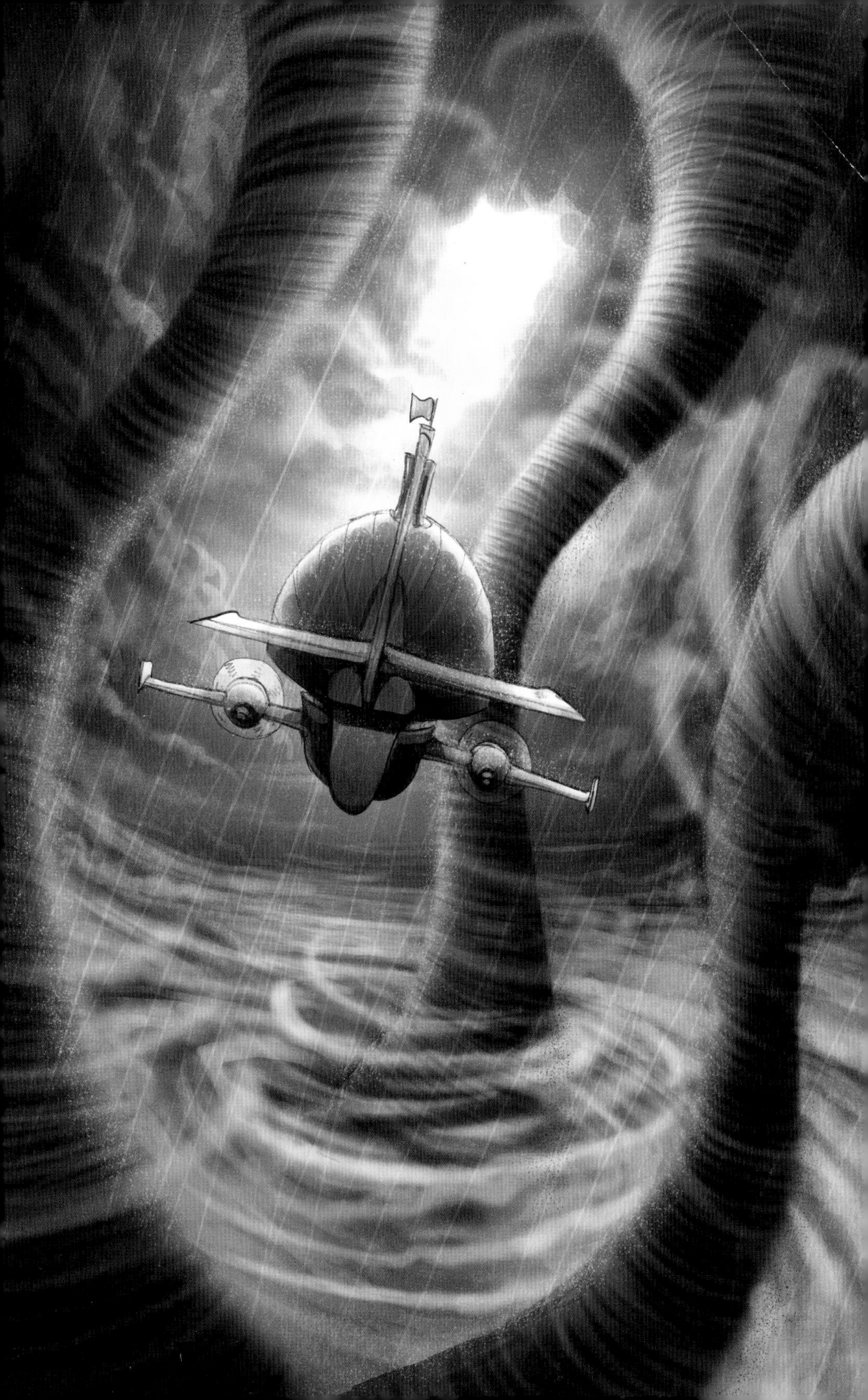

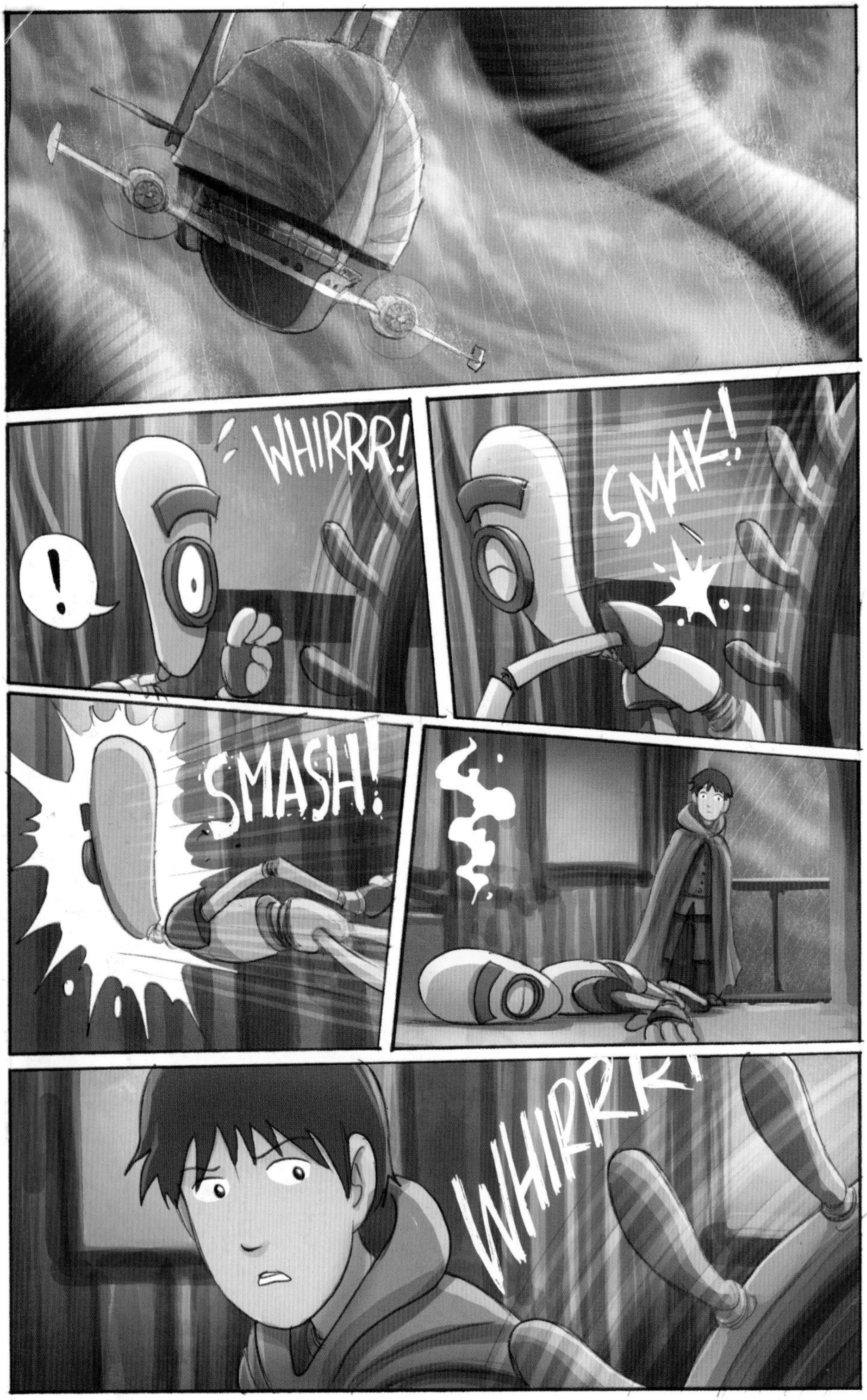
!
WHIRRR!
SMAK!
SMASH!
WHIRRR!

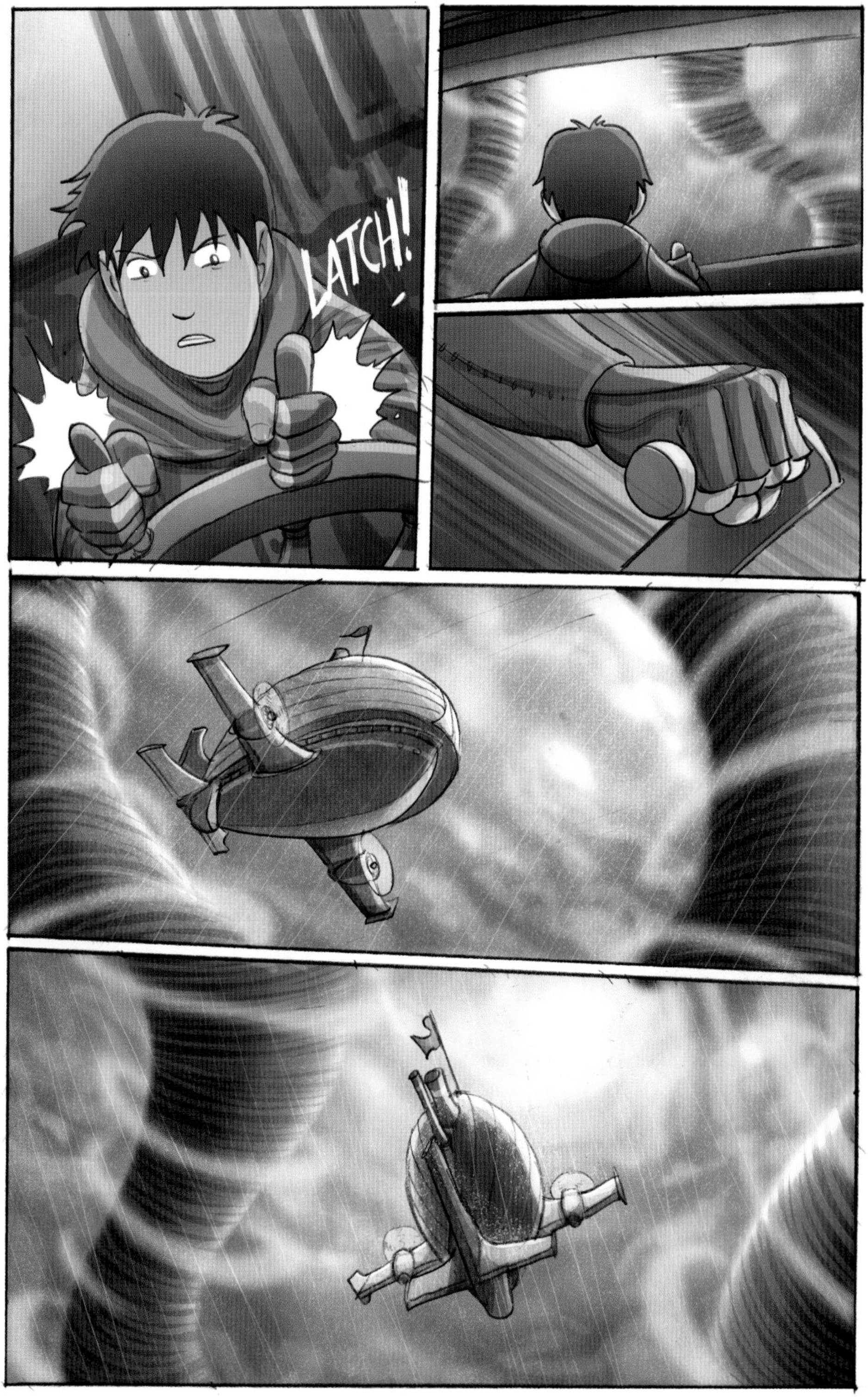
LATCH!

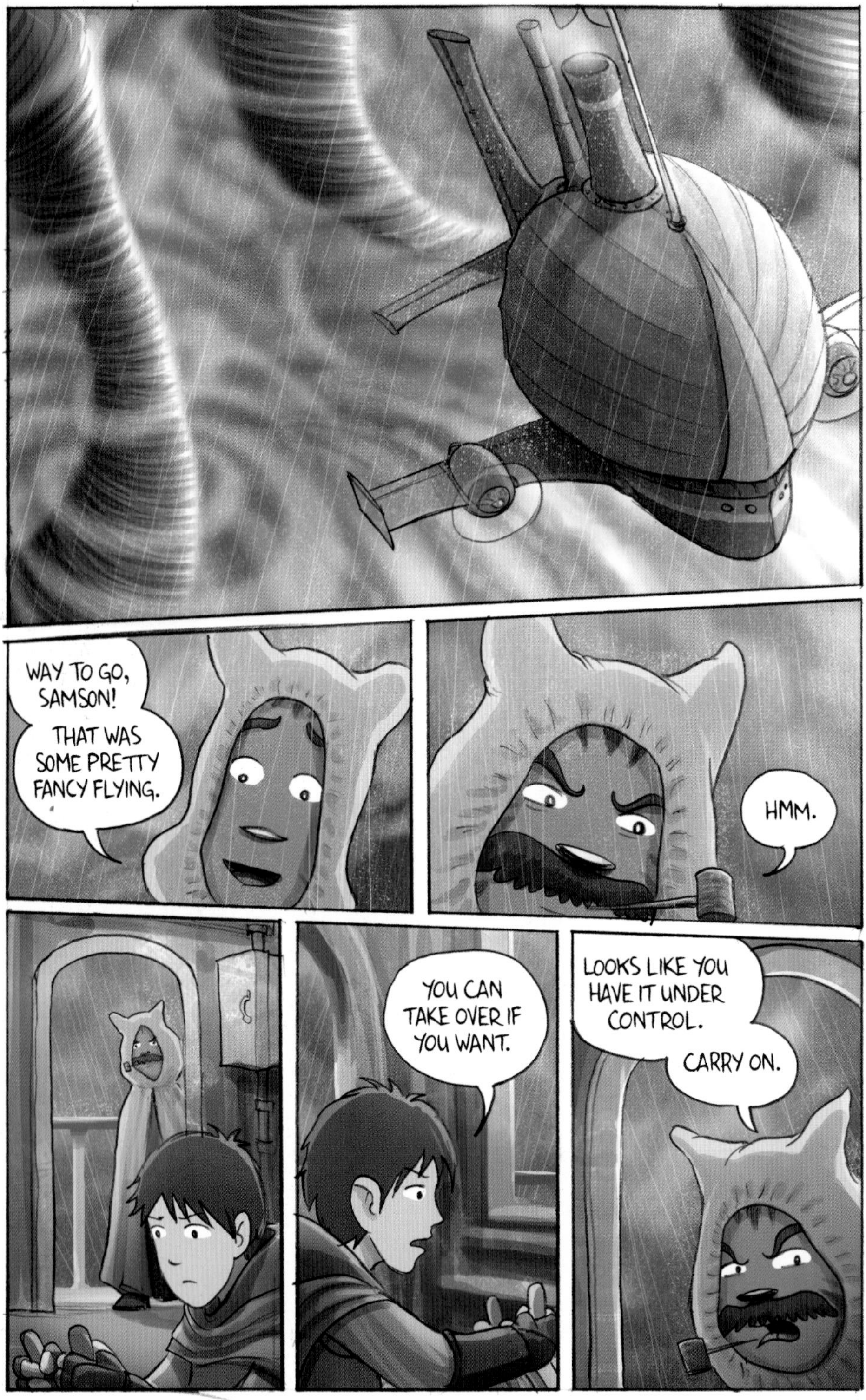
WAY TO GO, SAMSON!
THAT WAS SOME PRETTY FANCY FLYING.
HMM.
YOU CAN TAKE OVER IF YOU WANT.
LOOKS LIKE YOU HAVE IT UNDER CONTROL.
CARRY ON.

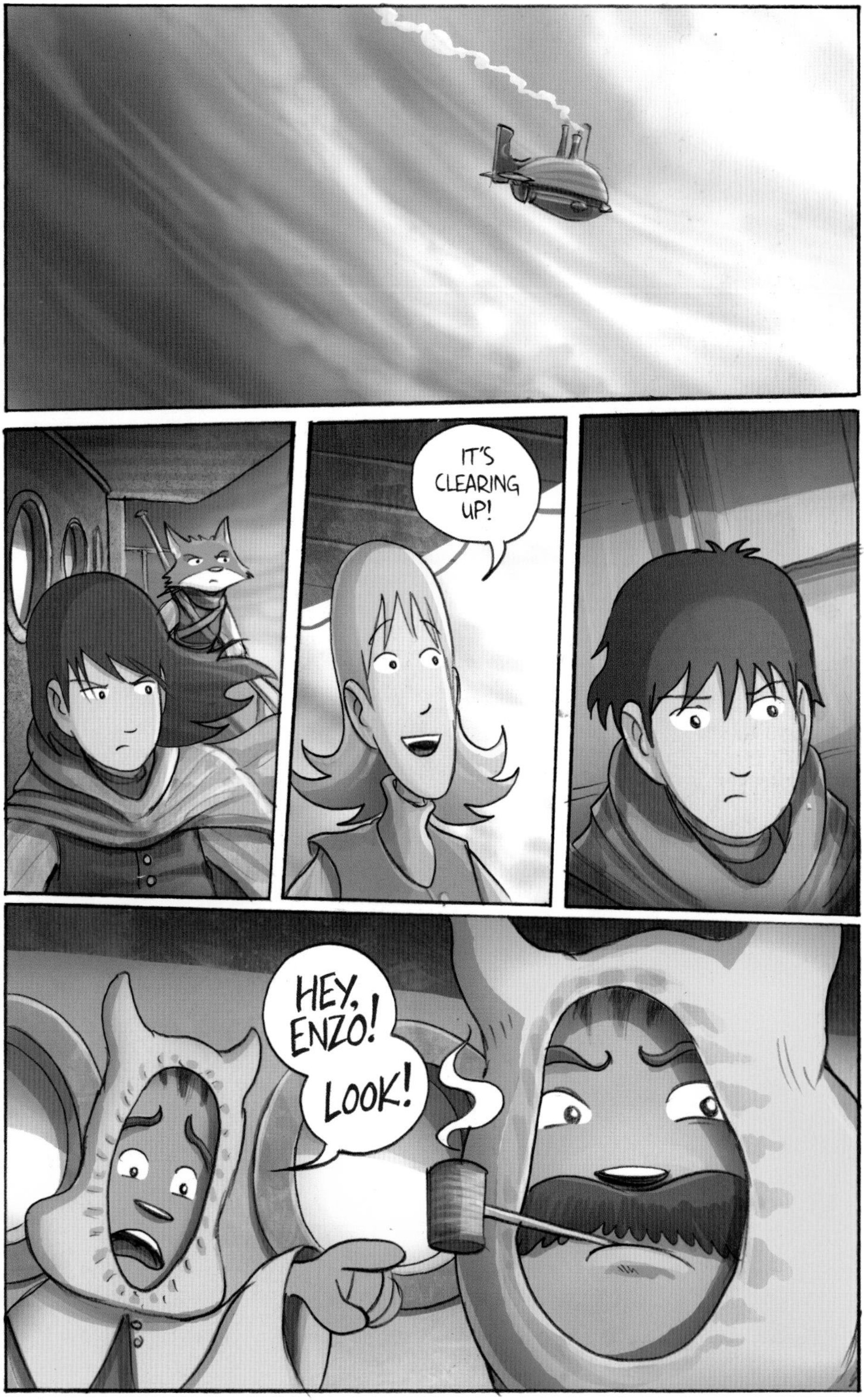
IT'S CLEARING UP!
HEY, ENZO!
LOOK!

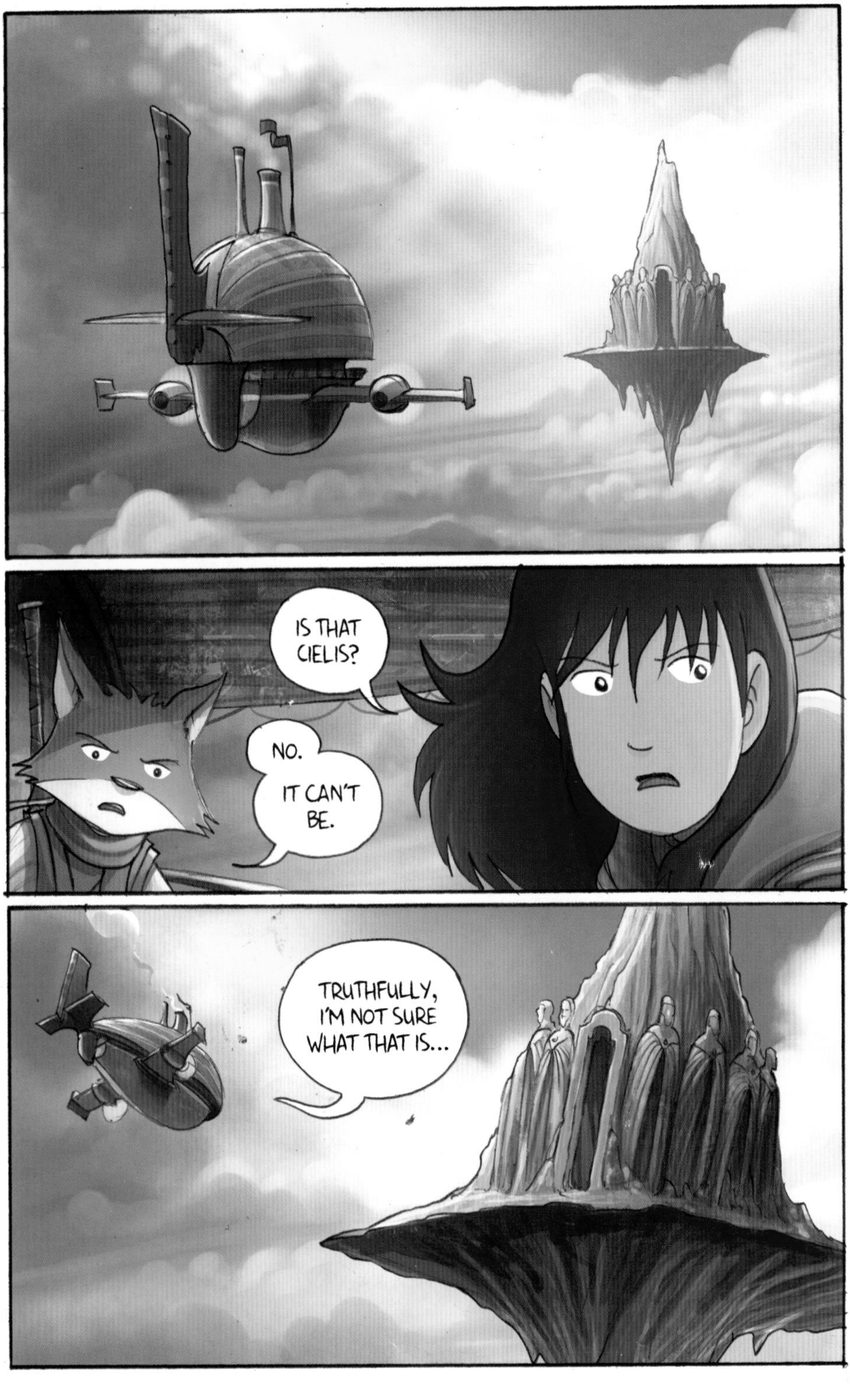
IS THAT CIELIS?
NO.
IT CAN'T BE.
TRUTHFULLY, I'M NOT SURE WHAT THAT IS...

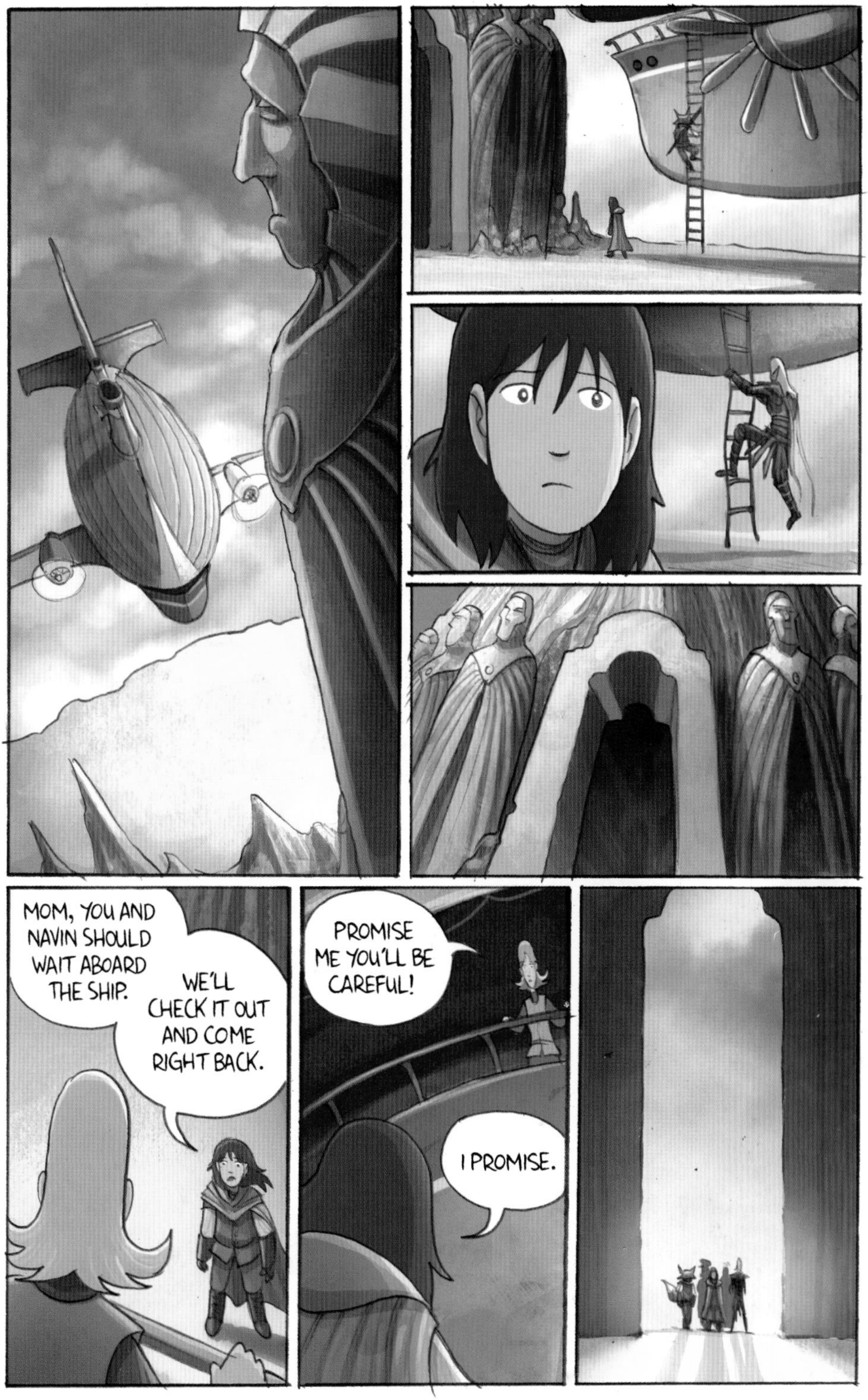
MOM, YOU AND NAVIN SHOULD WAIT ABOARD THE SHIP.
WE'LL CHECK IT OUT AND COME RIGHT BACK.
PROMISE ME YOU'LL BE CAREFUL!
I PROMISE.

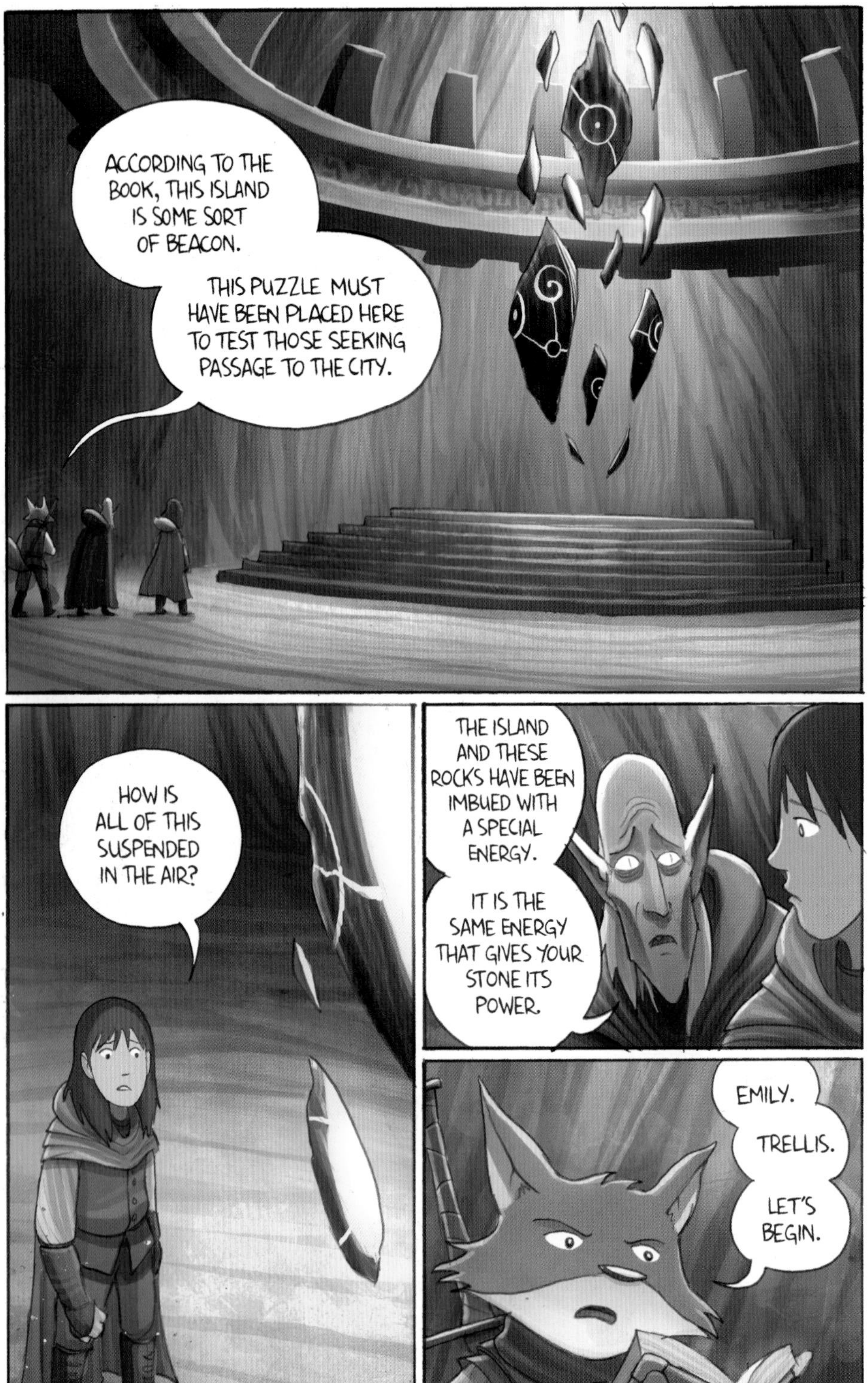
ACCORDING TO THE BOOK, THIS ISLAND IS SOME SORT OF BEACON.
THIS PUZZLE MUST HAVE BEEN PLACED HERE TO TEST THOSE SEEKING PASSAGE TO THE CITY.
HOW IS ALL OF THIS SUSPENDED IN THE AIR?
THE ISLAND AND THESE ROCKS HAVE BEEN IMBUED WITH A SPECIAL ENERGY.
IT IS THE SAME ENERGY THAT GIVES YOUR STONE ITS POWER.
EMILY.
TRELLIS.
LET'S BEGIN.

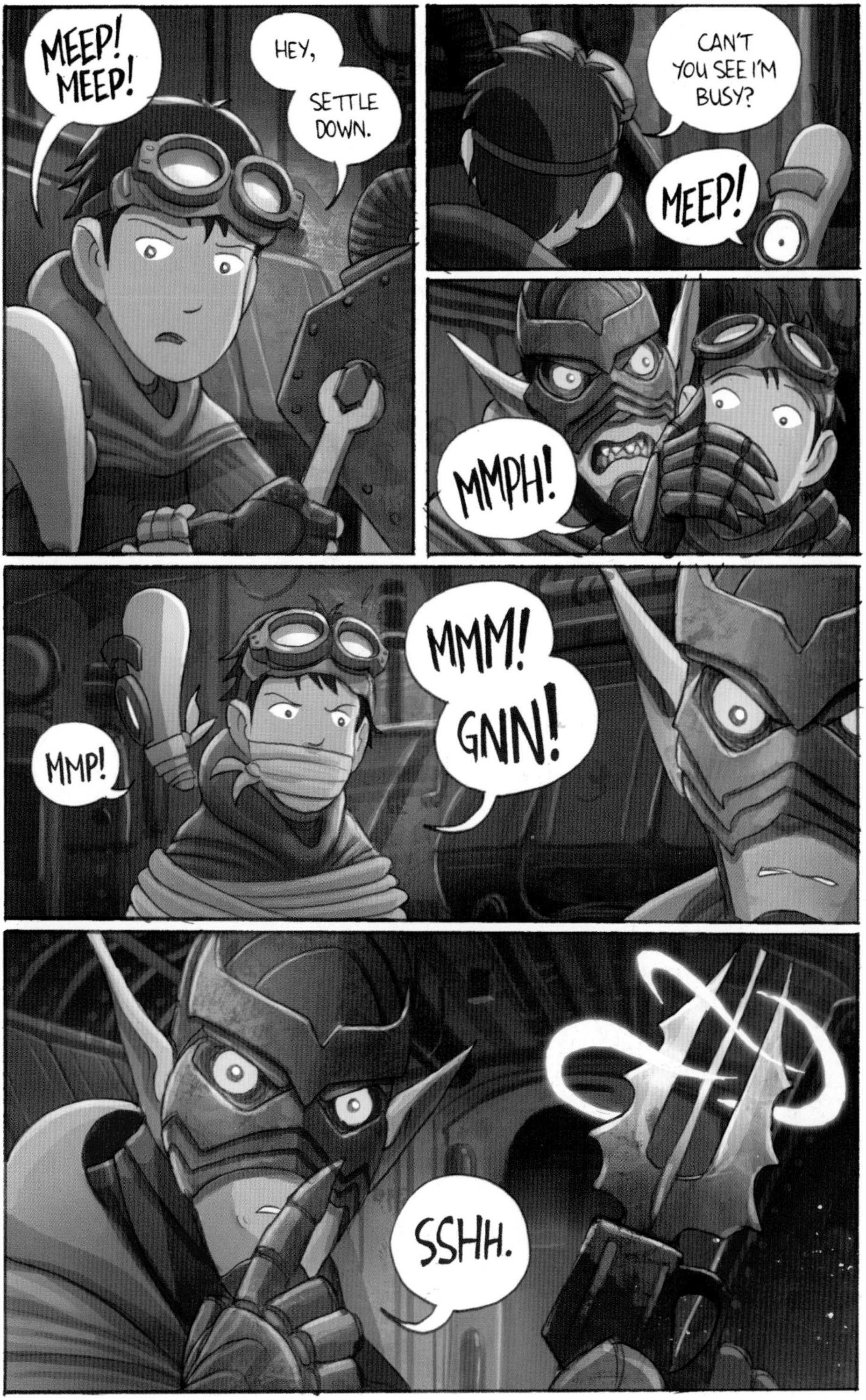

MEEP! MEEP!
HEY,
SETTLE DOWN.
CAN'T YOU SEE I'M BUSY?
MEEP!
MMPH!
MMP!
MMM!
GNN!
SSHH.

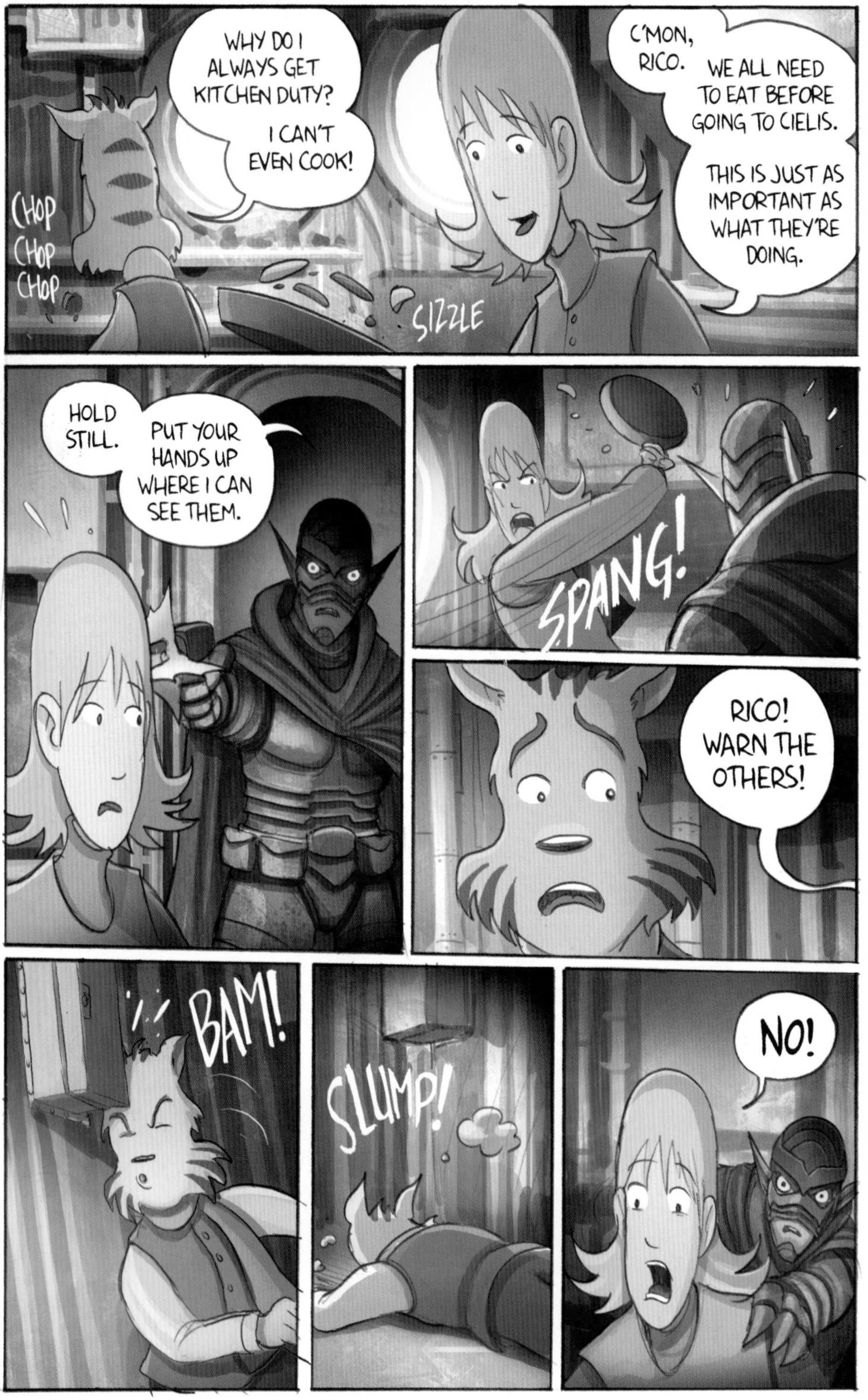
WHY DO I ALWAYS GET KITCHEN DUTY?
I CAN'T EVEN COOK!
C'MON, RICO.
WE ALL NEED TO EAT BEFORE GOING TO CIELIS.
THIS IS JUST AS IMPORTANT AS WHAT THEY'RE DOING.
CHOP CHOP CHOP
SIZZLE
HOLD STILL.
PUT YOUR HANDS UP WHERE I CAN SEE THEM.
SPANG!
RICO! WARN THE OTHERS!
BAM!
SLUMP!
NO!

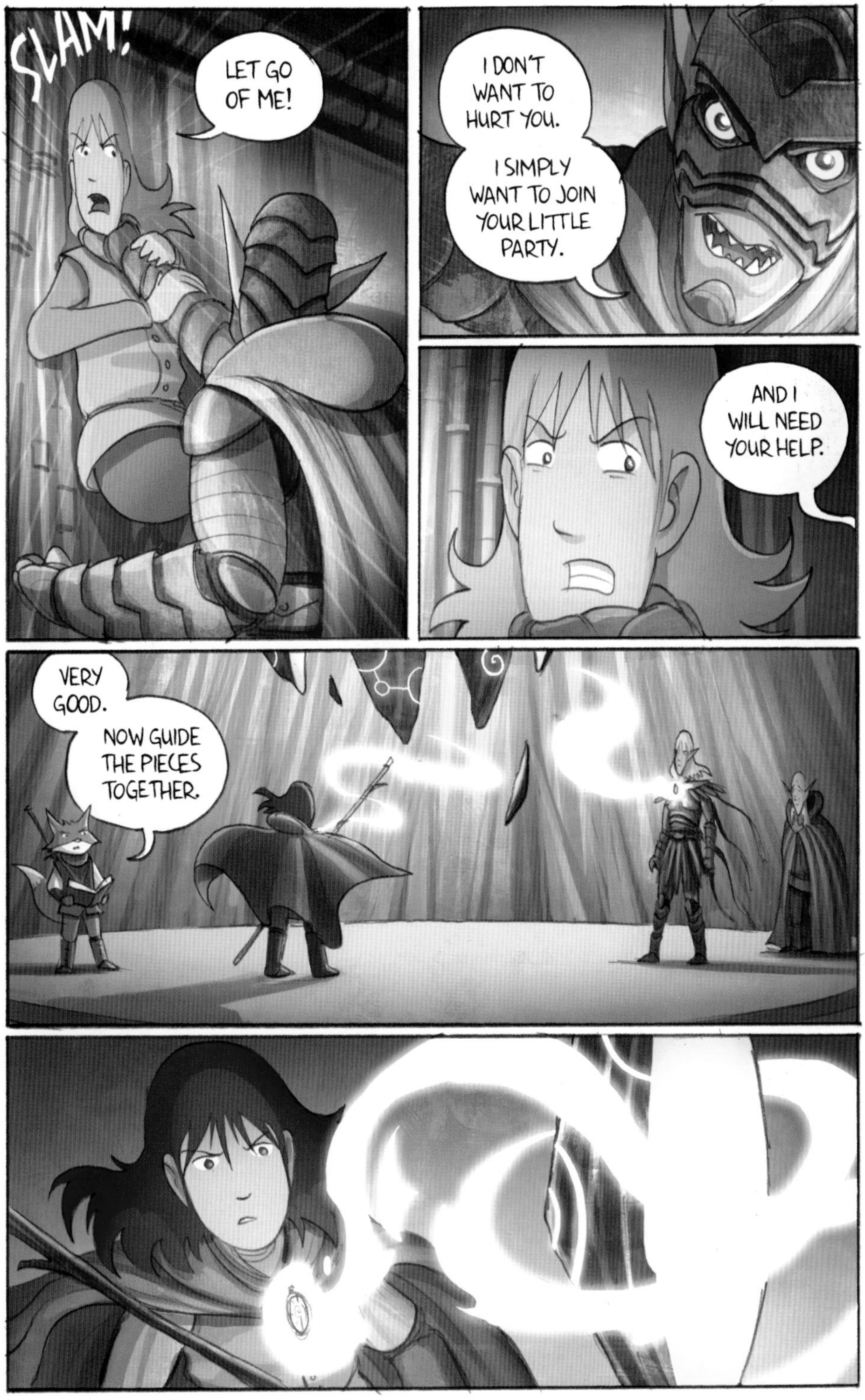
SLAM!
LET GO OF ME!
I DON'T WANT TO HURT YOU.
I SIMPLY WANT TO JOIN YOUR LITTLE PARTY.
AND I WILL NEED YOUR HELP.
VERY GOOD.
NOW GUIDE THE PIECES TOGETHER.

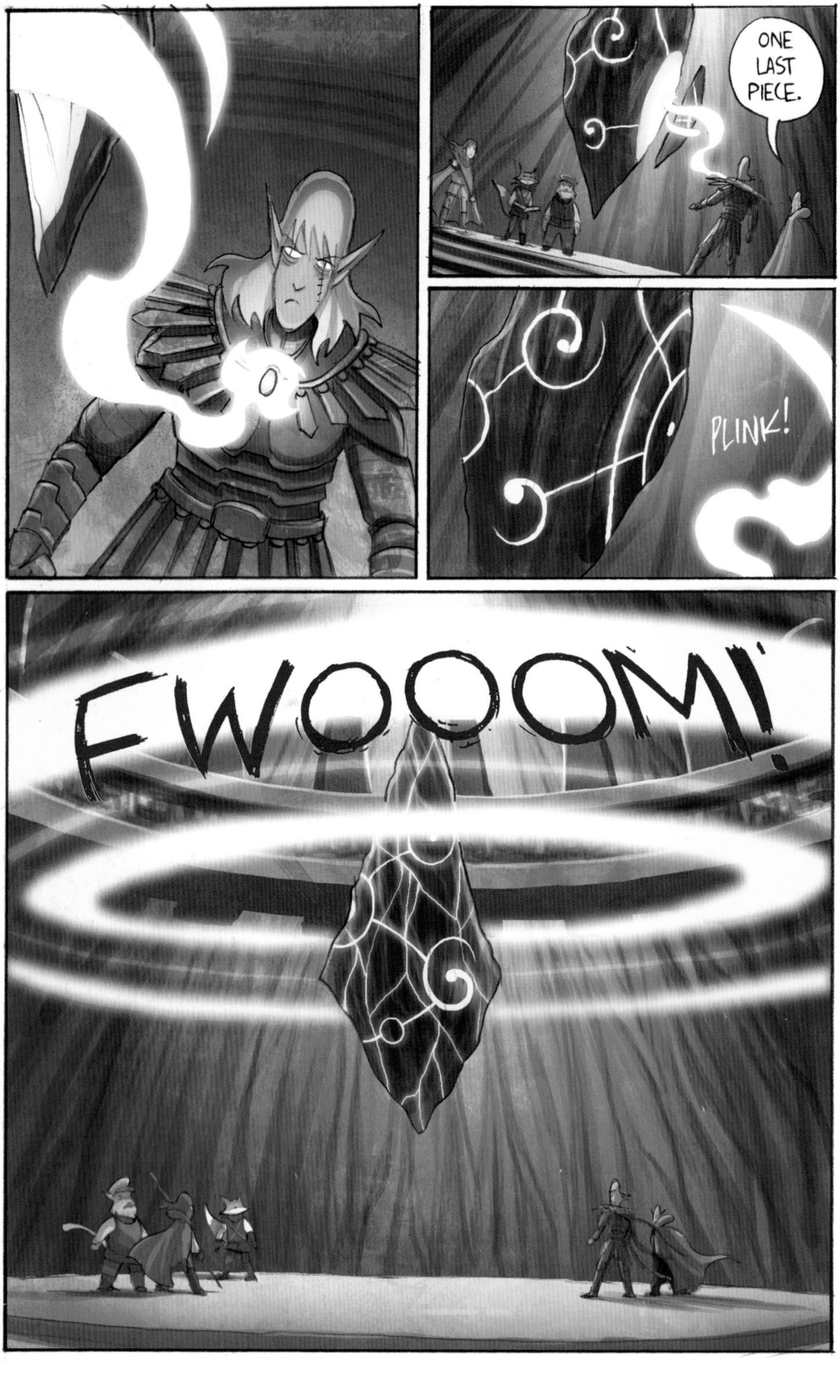
ONE LAST PIECE.
PLINK!
FWOOOM!

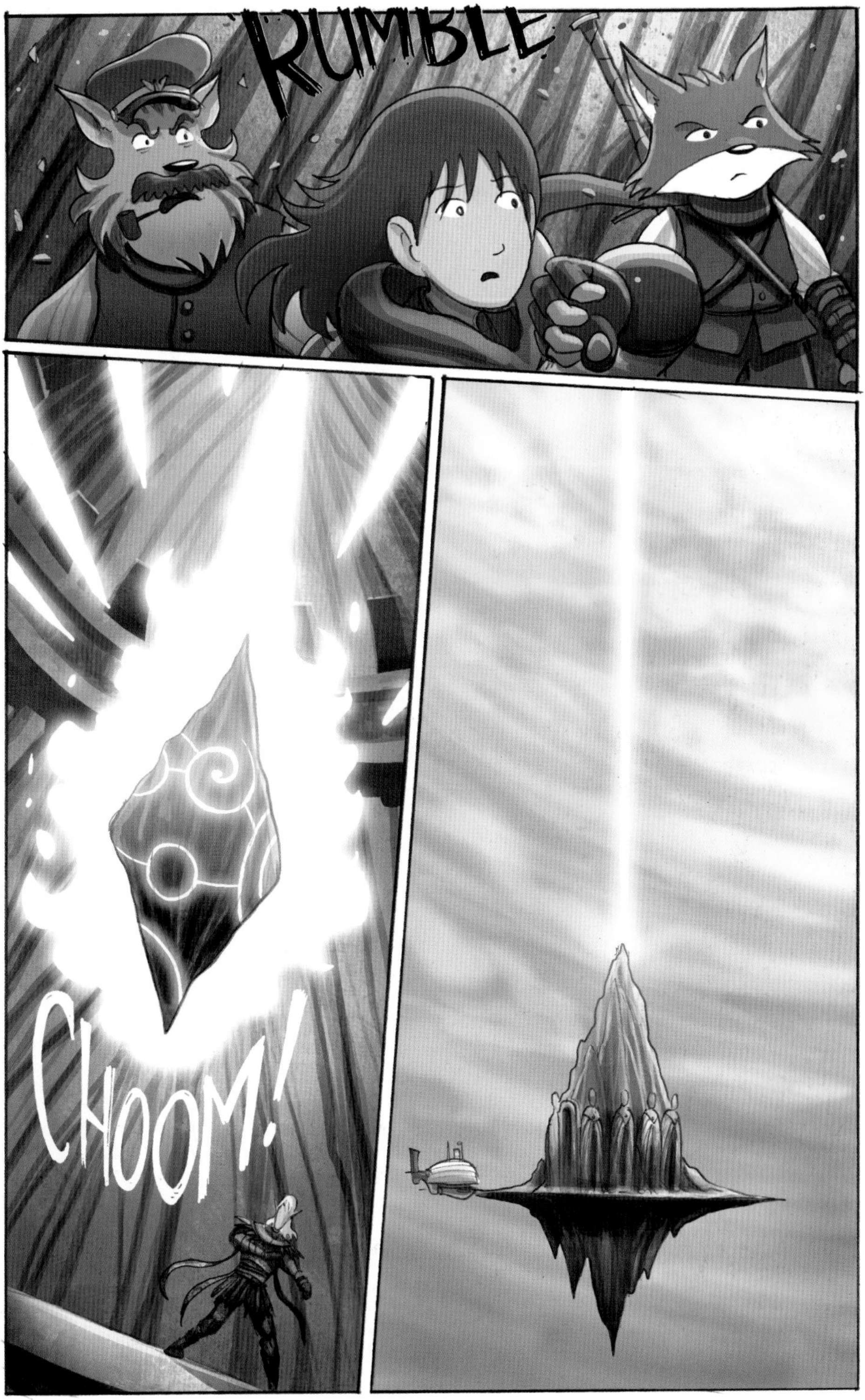
RUMBLE
CHOOM!

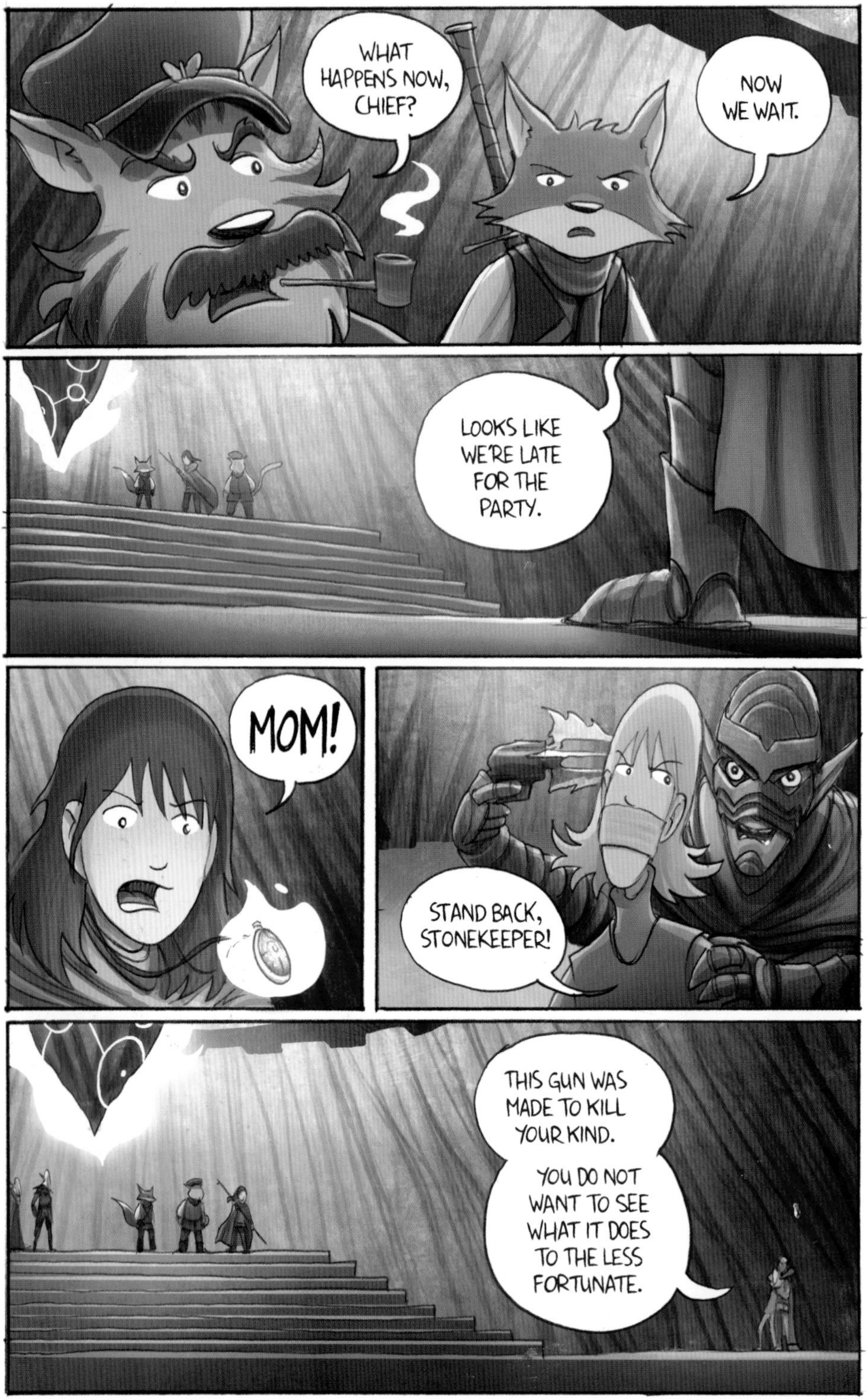
WHAT HAPPENS NOW, CHIEF?
NOW WE WAIT.
LOOKS LIKE WE'RE LATE FOR THE PARTY.
MOM!
STAND BACK, STONEKEEPER!
THIS GUN WAS MADE TO KILL YOUR KIND.
YOU DO NOT WANT TO SEE WHAT IT DOES TO THE LESS FORTUNATE.

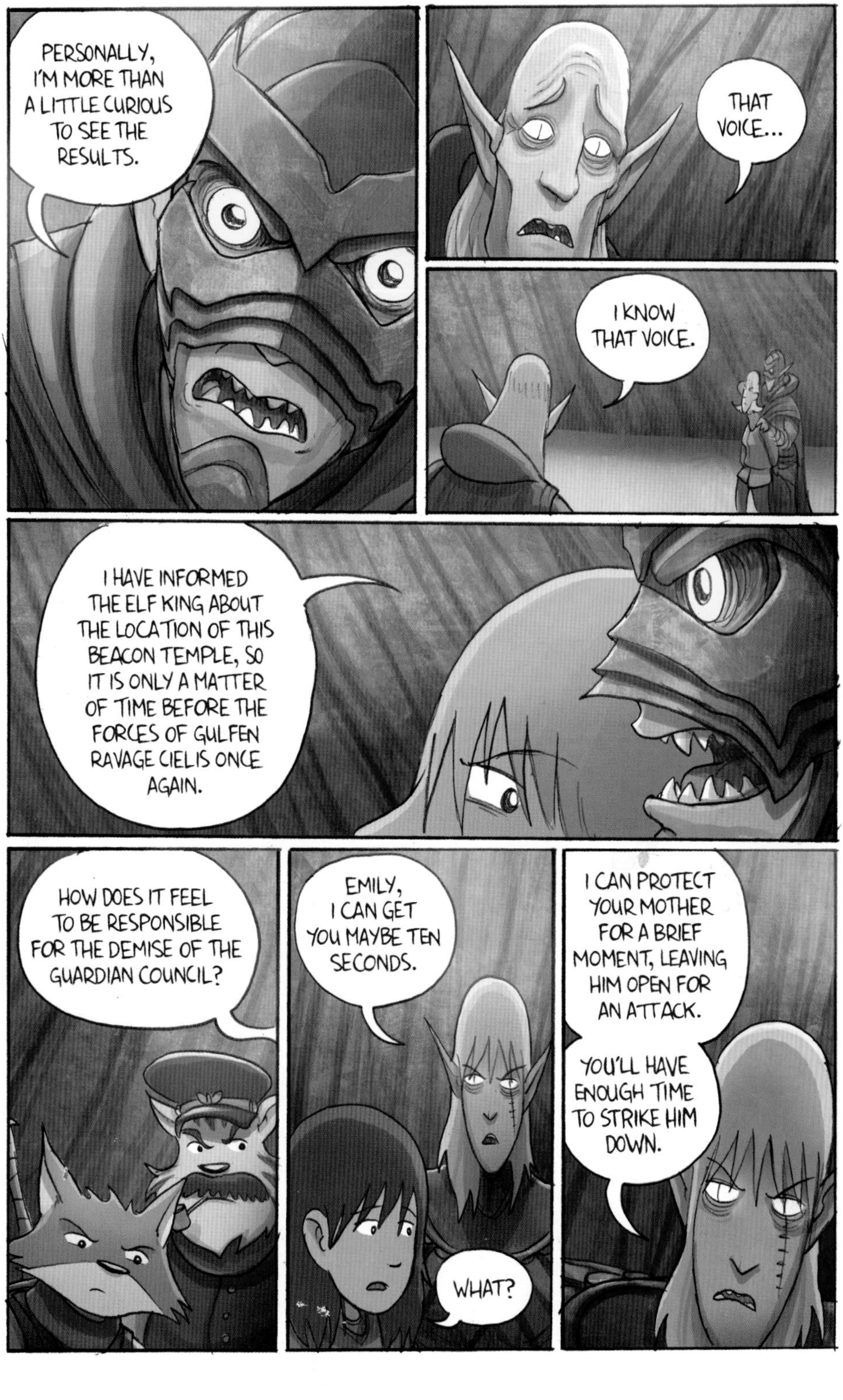
PERSONALLY, I'M MORE THAN A LITTLE CURIOUS TO SEE THE RESULTS.
THAT VOICE...
I KNOW THAT VOICE.
I HAVE INFORMED THE ELF KING ABOUT THE LOCATION OF THIS BEACON TEMPLE, SO IT IS ONLY A MATTER OF TIME BEFORE THE FORCES OF GULFEN RAVAGE CIELIS ONCE AGAIN.
HOW DOES IT FEEL TO BE RESPONSIBLE FOR THE DEMISE OF THE GUARDIAN COUNCIL?
EMILY, I CAN GET YOU MAYBE TEN SECONDS.
WHAT?
I CAN PROTECT YOUR MOTHER FOR A BRIEF MOMENT, LEAVING HIM OPEN FOR AN ATTACK.
YOU'LL HAVE ENOUGH TIME TO STRIKE HIM DOWN.

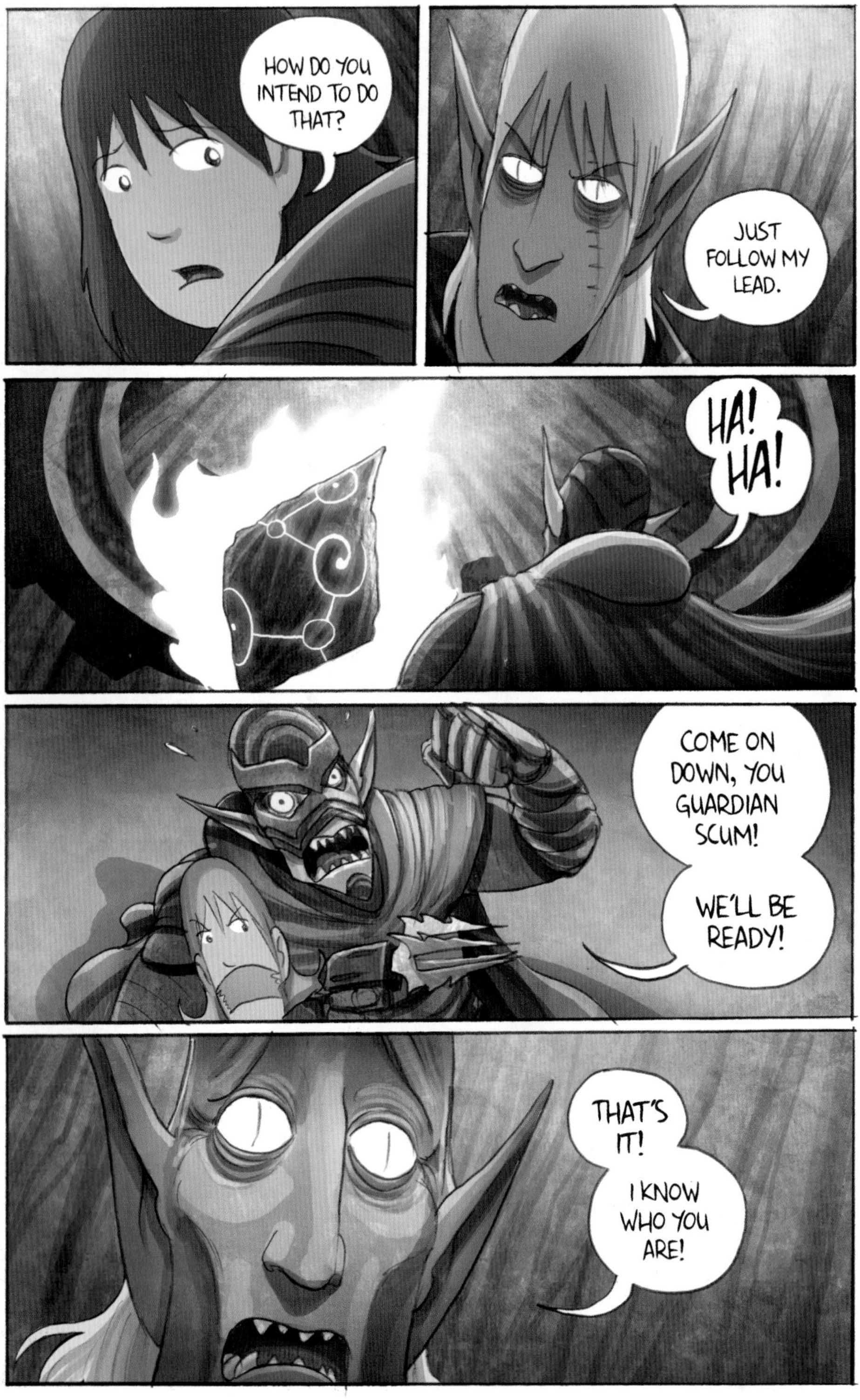
HOW DO YOU INTEND TO DO THAT?
JUST FOLLOW MY LEAD.
HA! HA!
COME ON DOWN, YOU GUARDIAN SCUM!
WE'LL BE READY!
THAT'S IT!
I KNOW WHO YOU ARE!

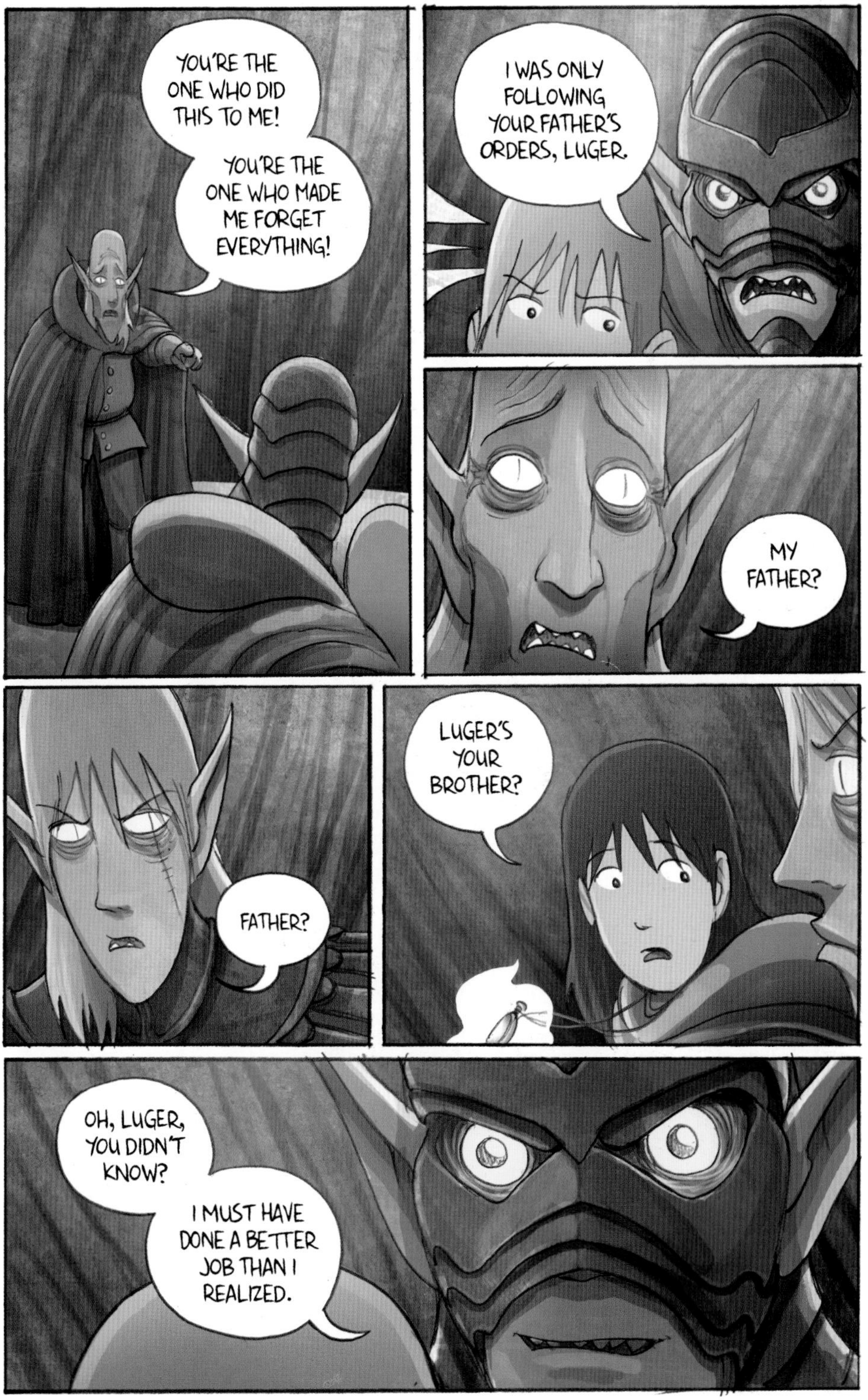
YOU'RE THE ONE WHO DID THIS TO ME!
YOU'RE THE ONE WHO MADE ME FORGET EVERYTHING!
I WAS ONLY FOLLOWING YOUR FATHER'S ORDERS, LUGER.
MY FATHER?
FATHER?
LUGER'S YOUR BROTHER?
OH, LUGER, YOU DIDN'T KNOW?
I MUST HAVE DONE A BETTER JOB THAN I REALIZED.

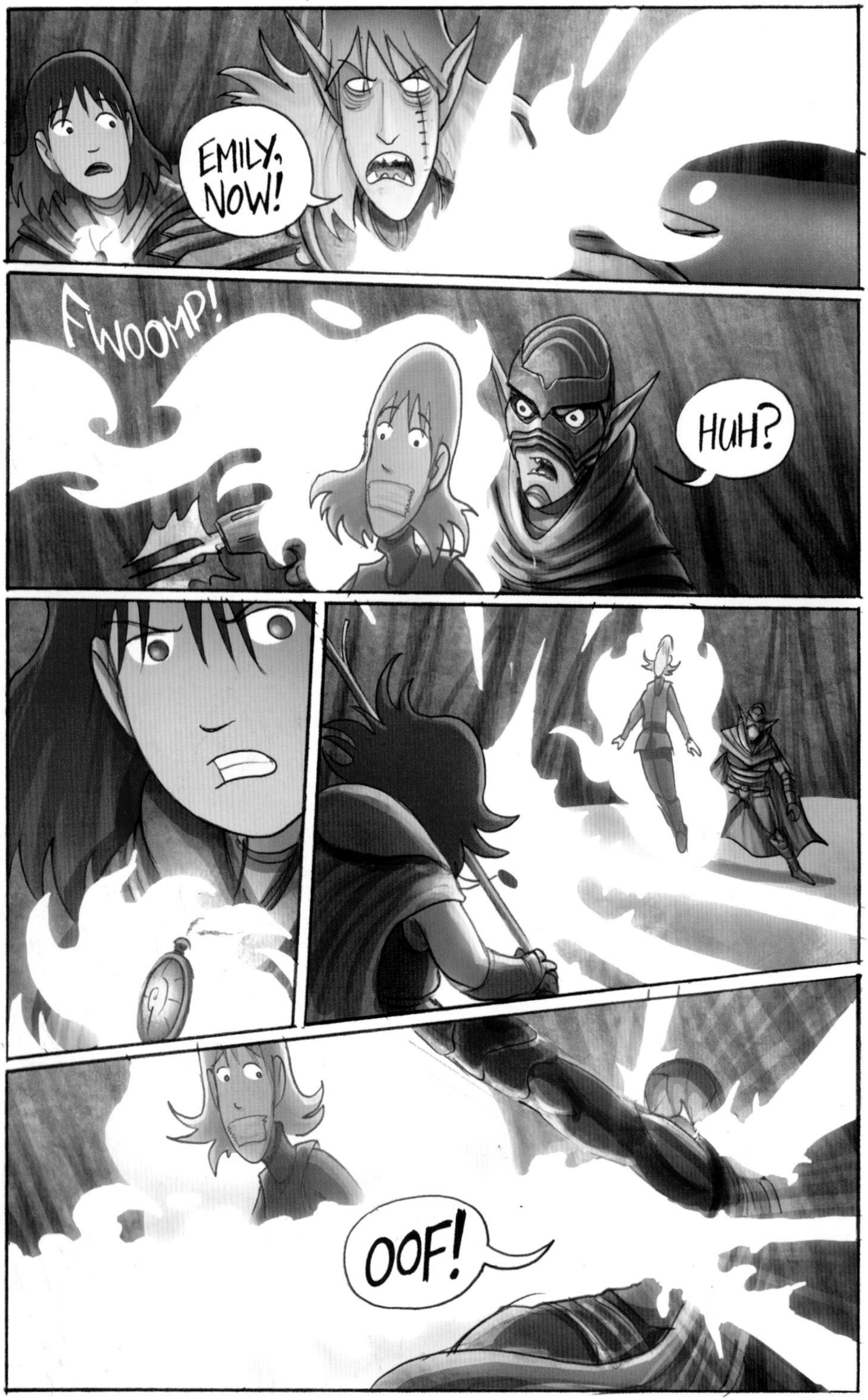
EMILY, NOW!
FWOOMP!
HUH?
OOF!

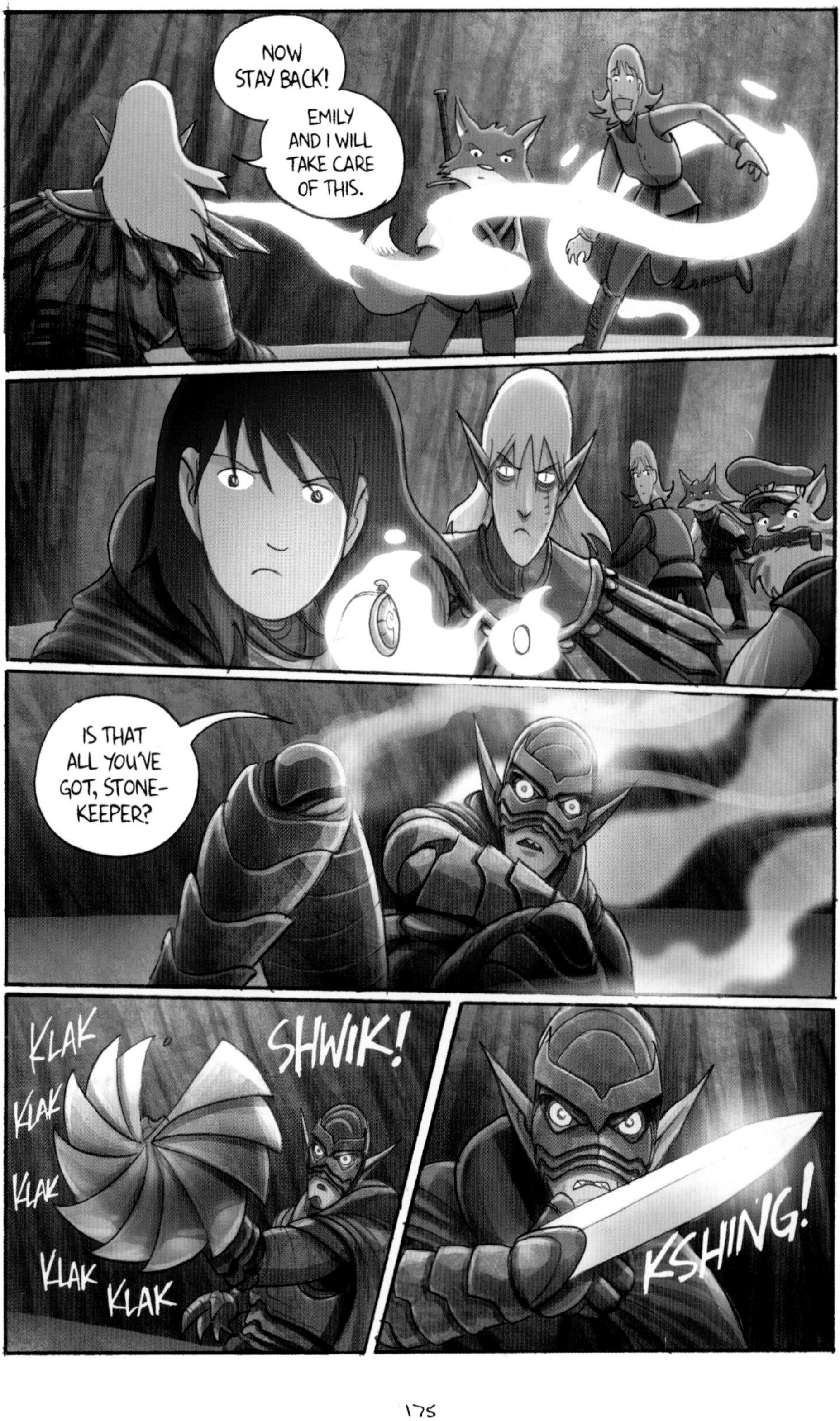
NOW STAY BACK!
EMILY AND I WILL TAKE CARE OF THIS.
IS THAT ALL YOU'VE GOT, STONE-KEEPER?
KLAK
KLAK
KLAK
KLAK KLAK
SHWIK!
KSHING!

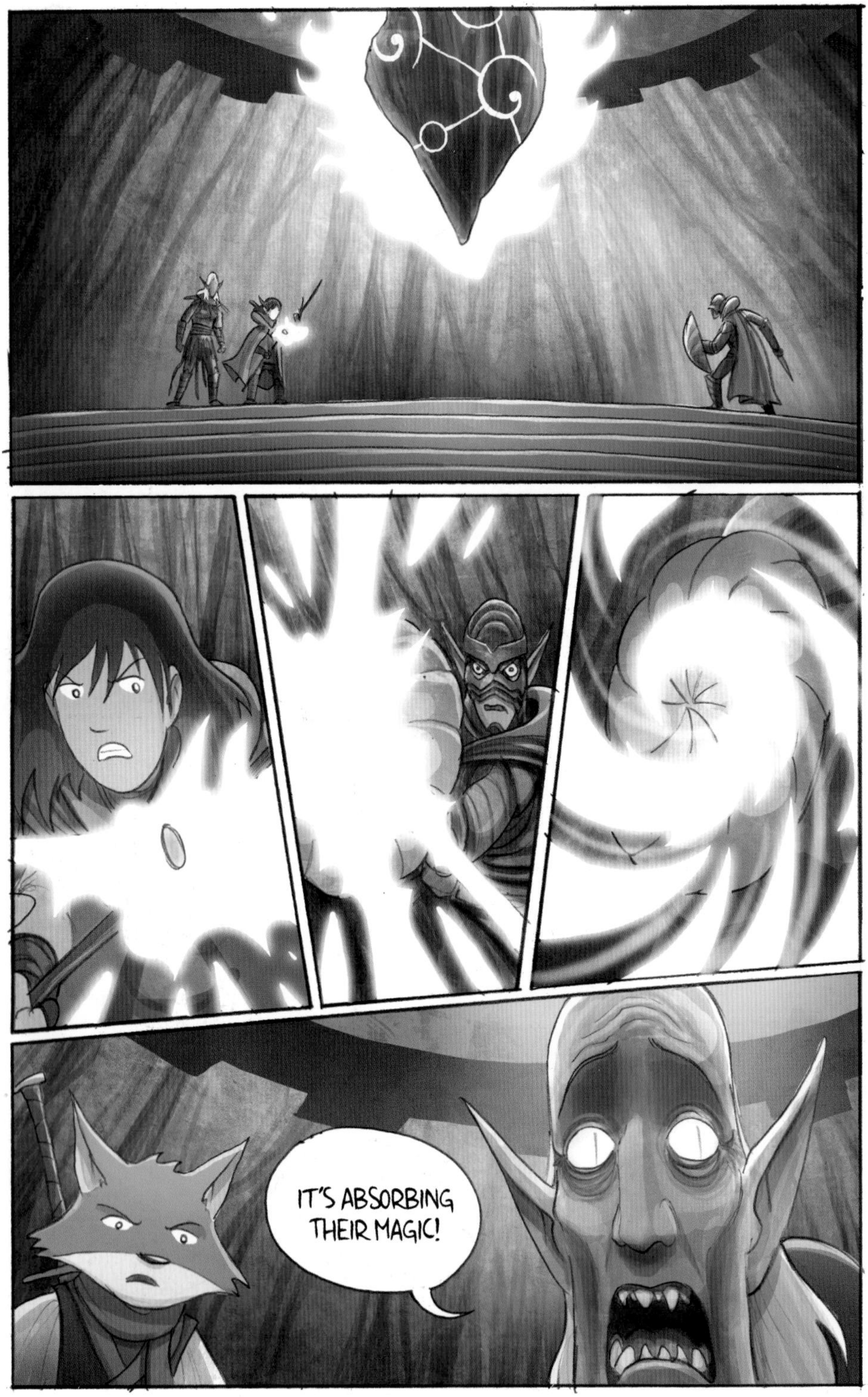
IT'S ABSORBING THEIR MAGIC!

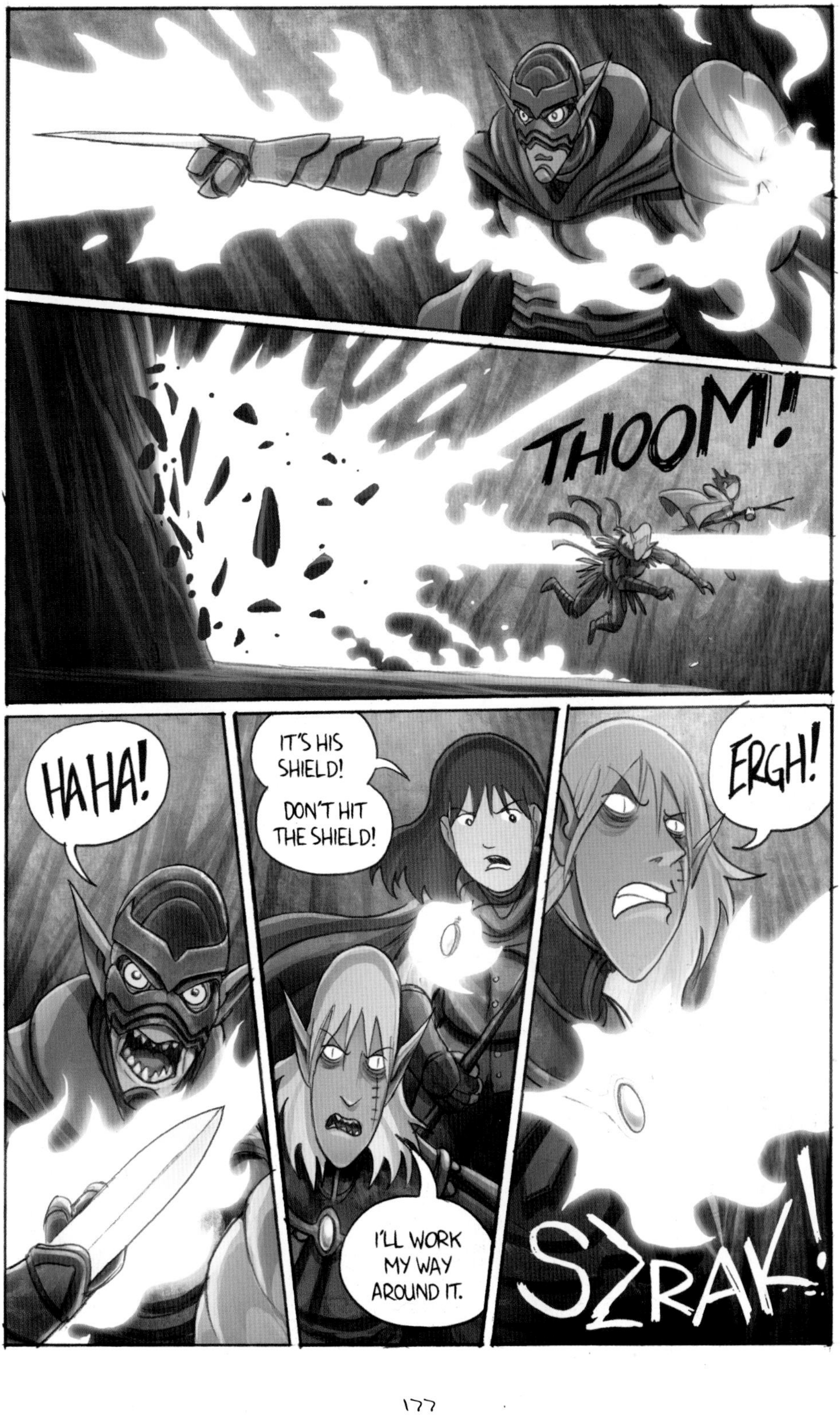
THOOM!
HAHA!
IT'S HIS SHIELD!
DON'T HIT THE SHIELD!
I'LL WORK MY WAY AROUND IT.
ERGH!
SZRAK!

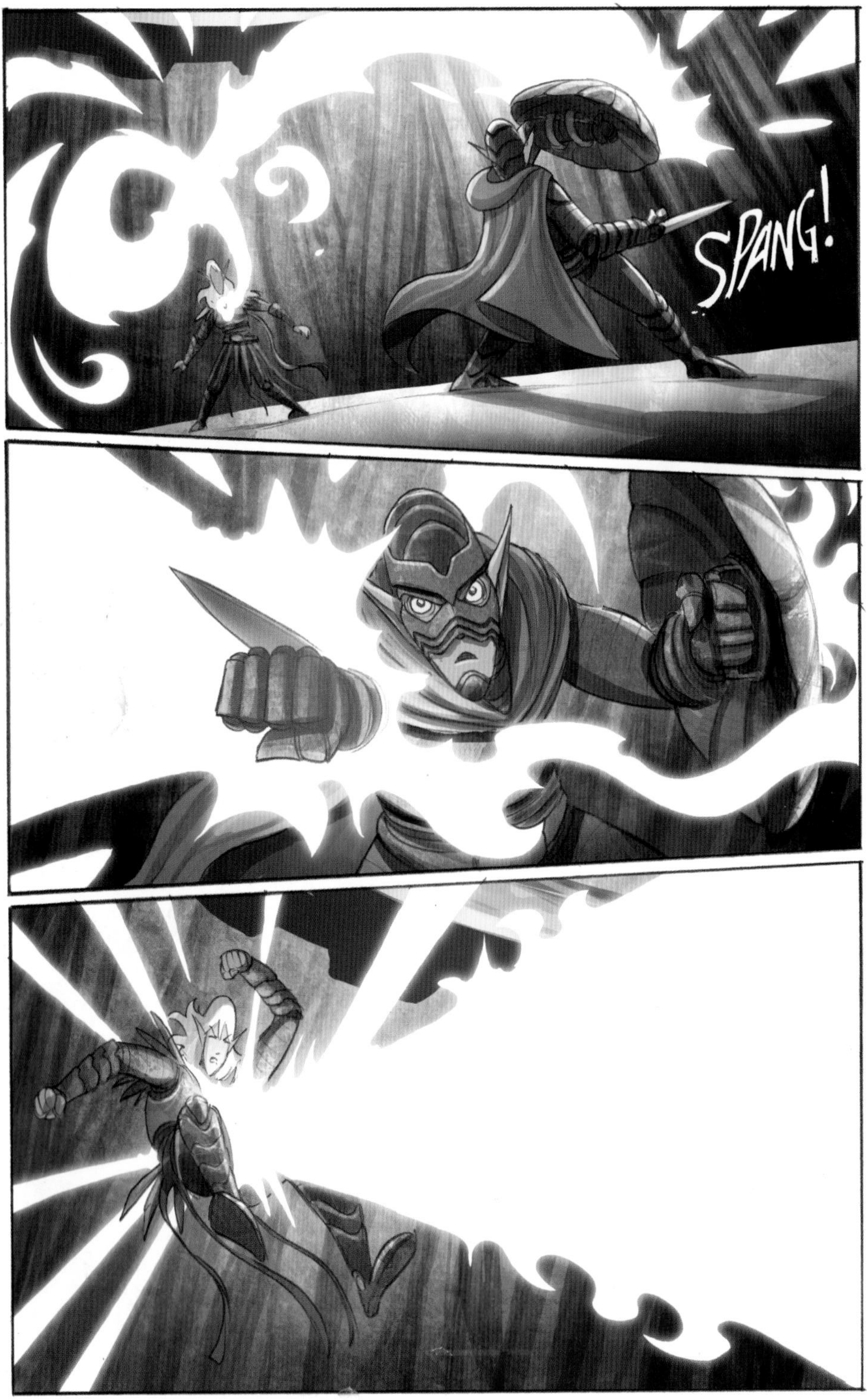
SPANG!

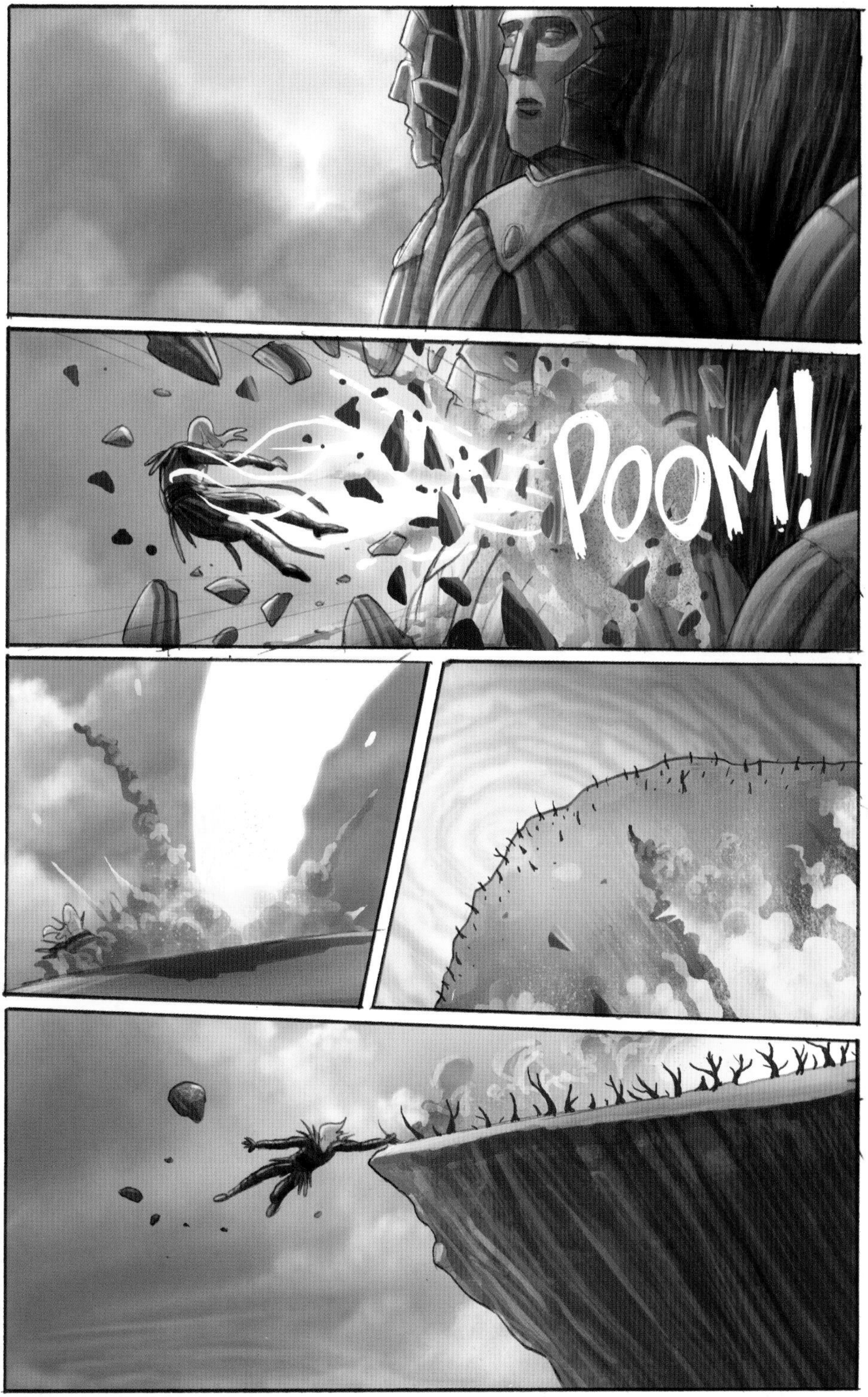
POOM!

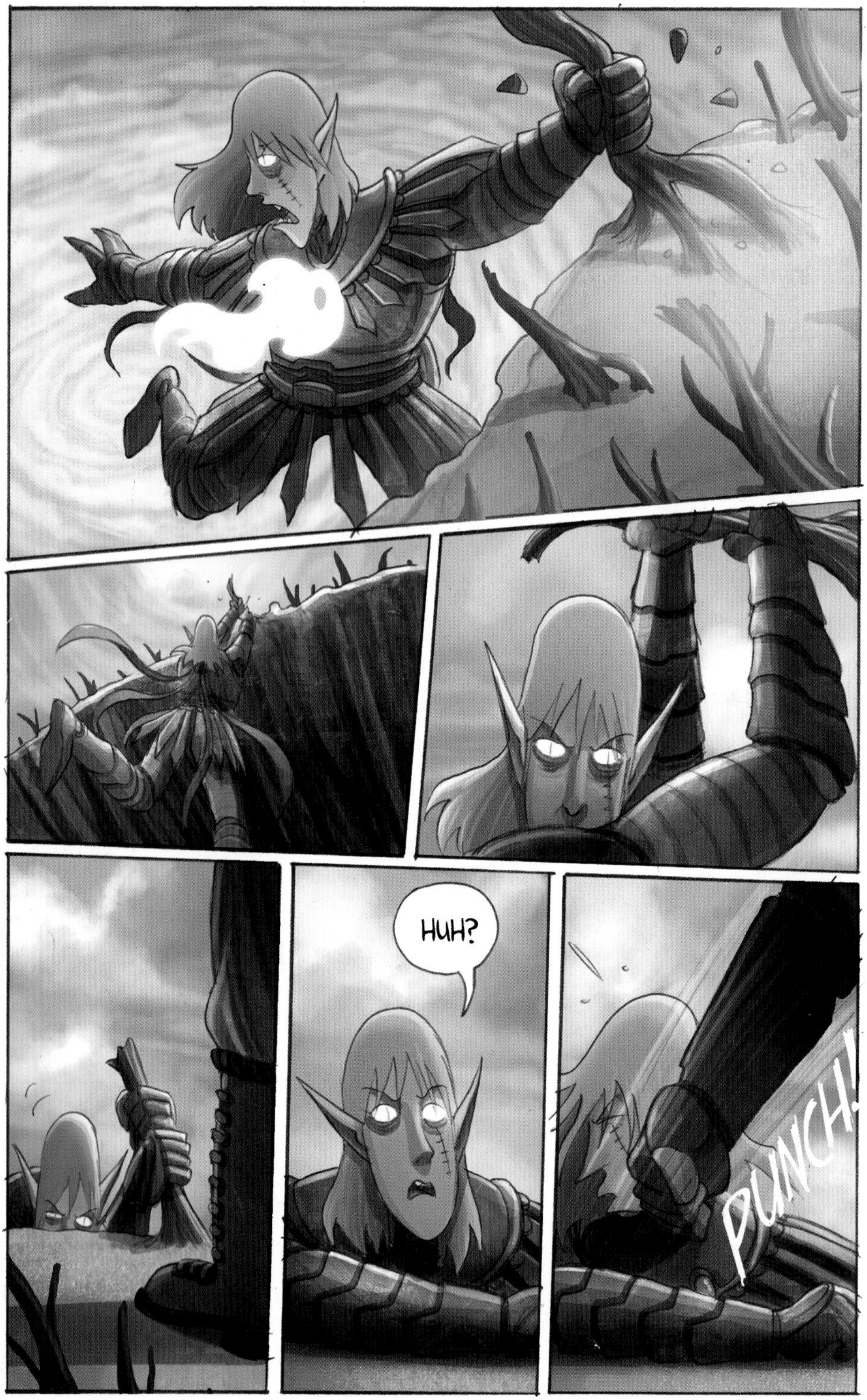
HUH?
PUNCH!

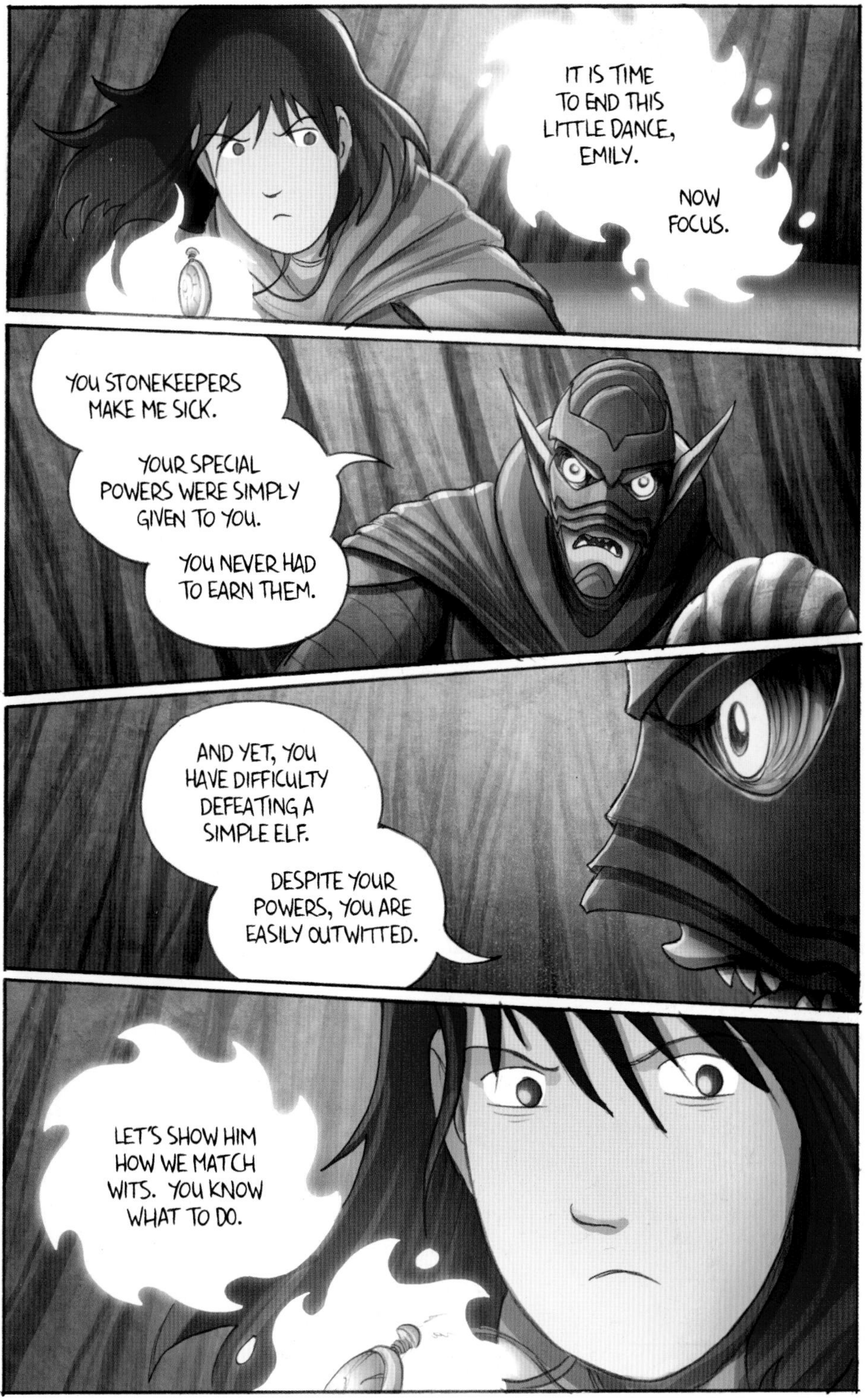
IT IS TIME TO END THIS LITTLE DANCE, EMILY.
NOW FOCUS.
YOU STONEKEEPERS MAKE ME SICK.
YOUR SPECIAL POWERS WERE SIMPLY GIVEN TO YOU.
YOU NEVER HAD TO EARN THEM.
AND YET, YOU HAVE DIFFICULTY DEFEATING A SIMPLE ELF.
DESPITE YOUR POWERS, YOU ARE EASILY OUTWITTED.
LET'S SHOW HIM HOW WE MATCH WITS. YOU KNOW WHAT TO DO.

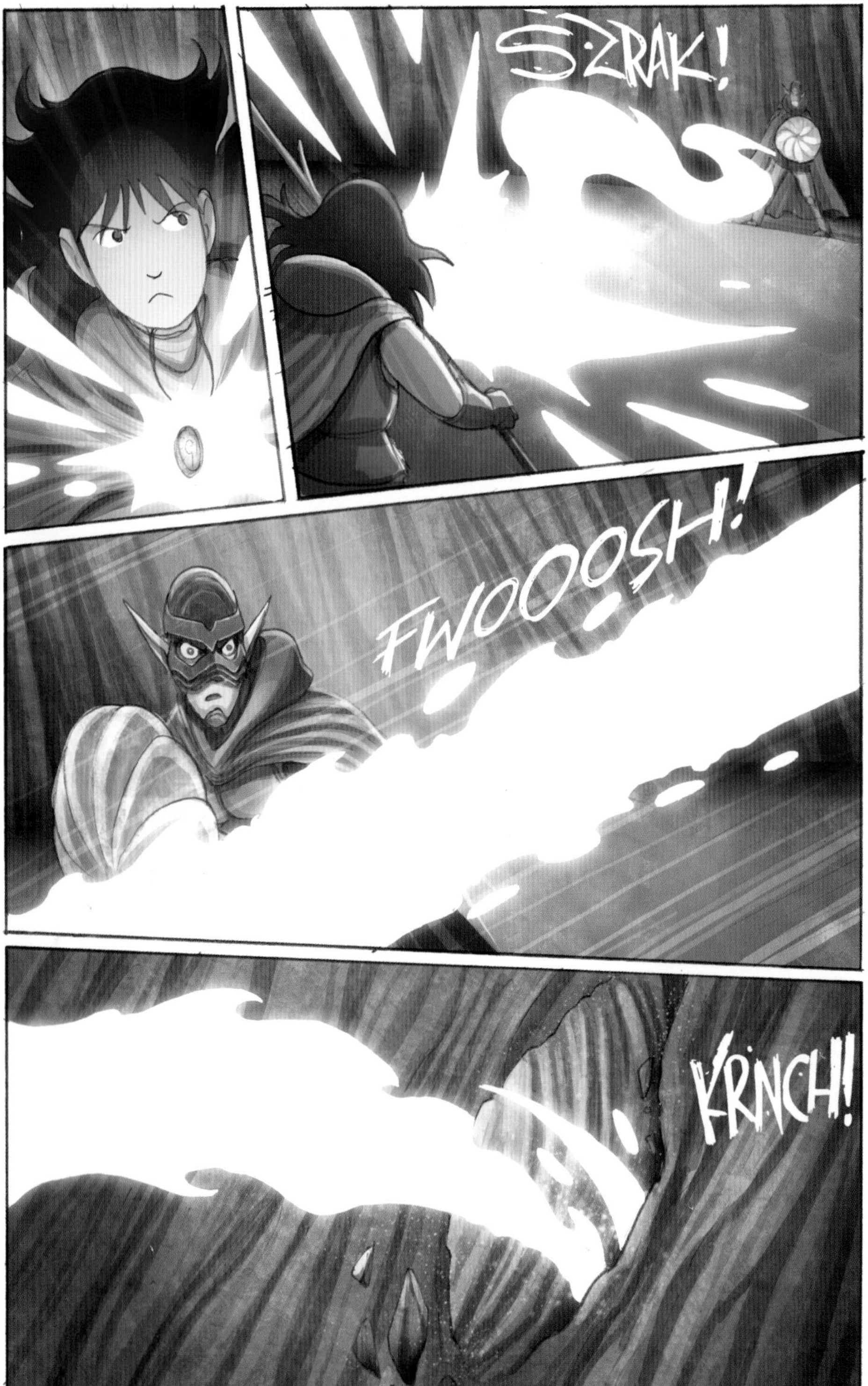
SZRAK!
FWOOOOSH!
KRNCH!

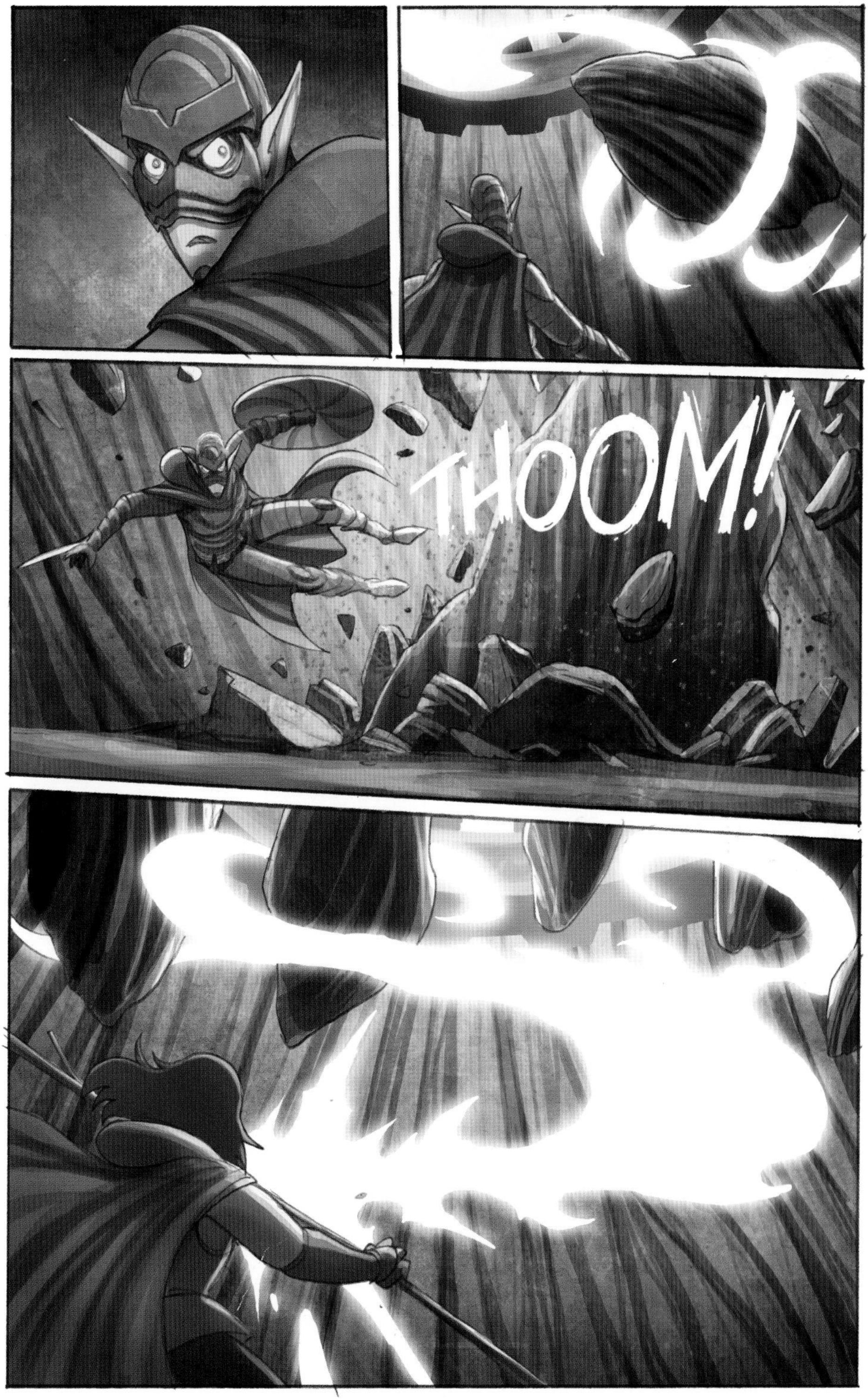
THOOM!

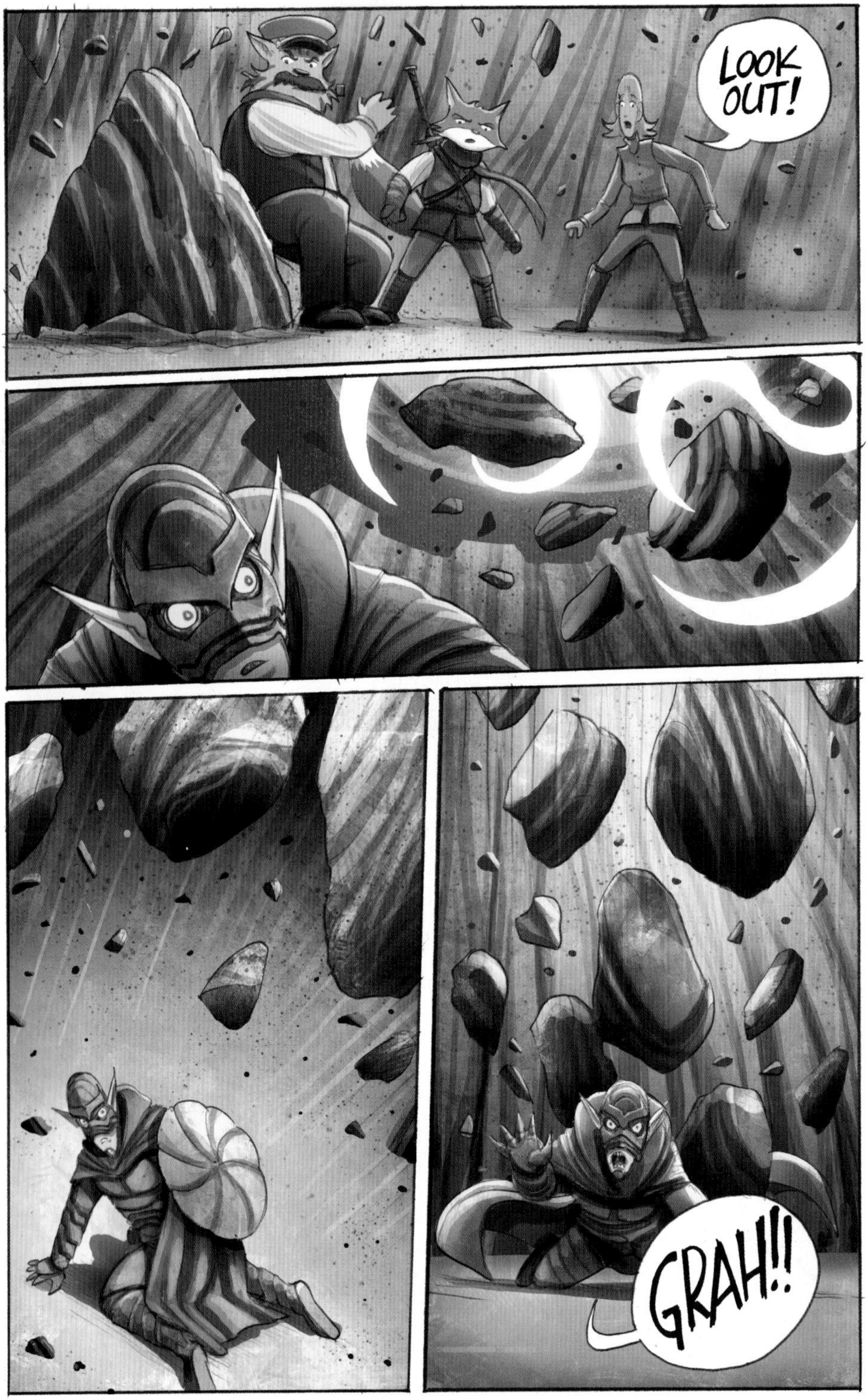
LOOK OUT!
GRAH!!

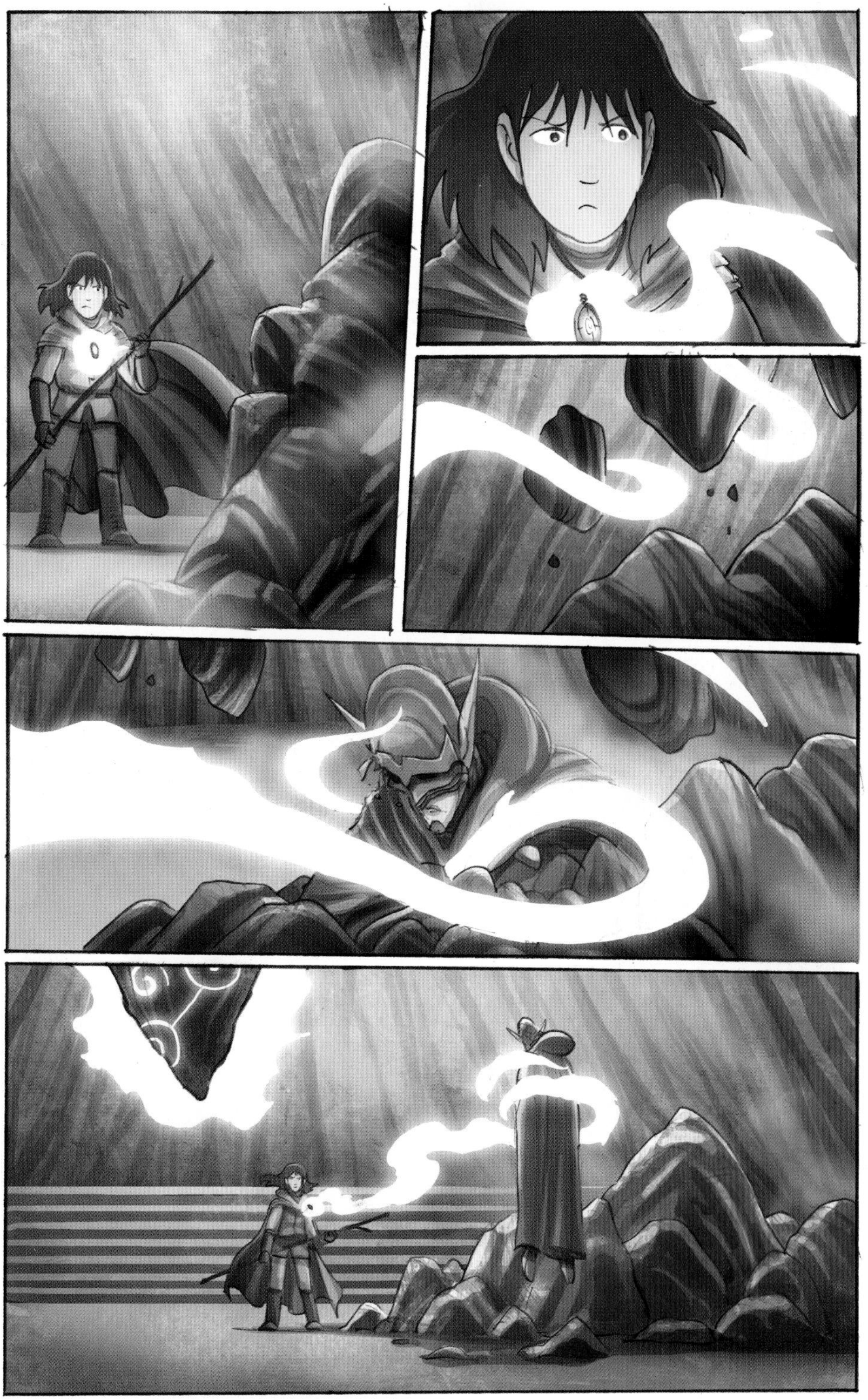

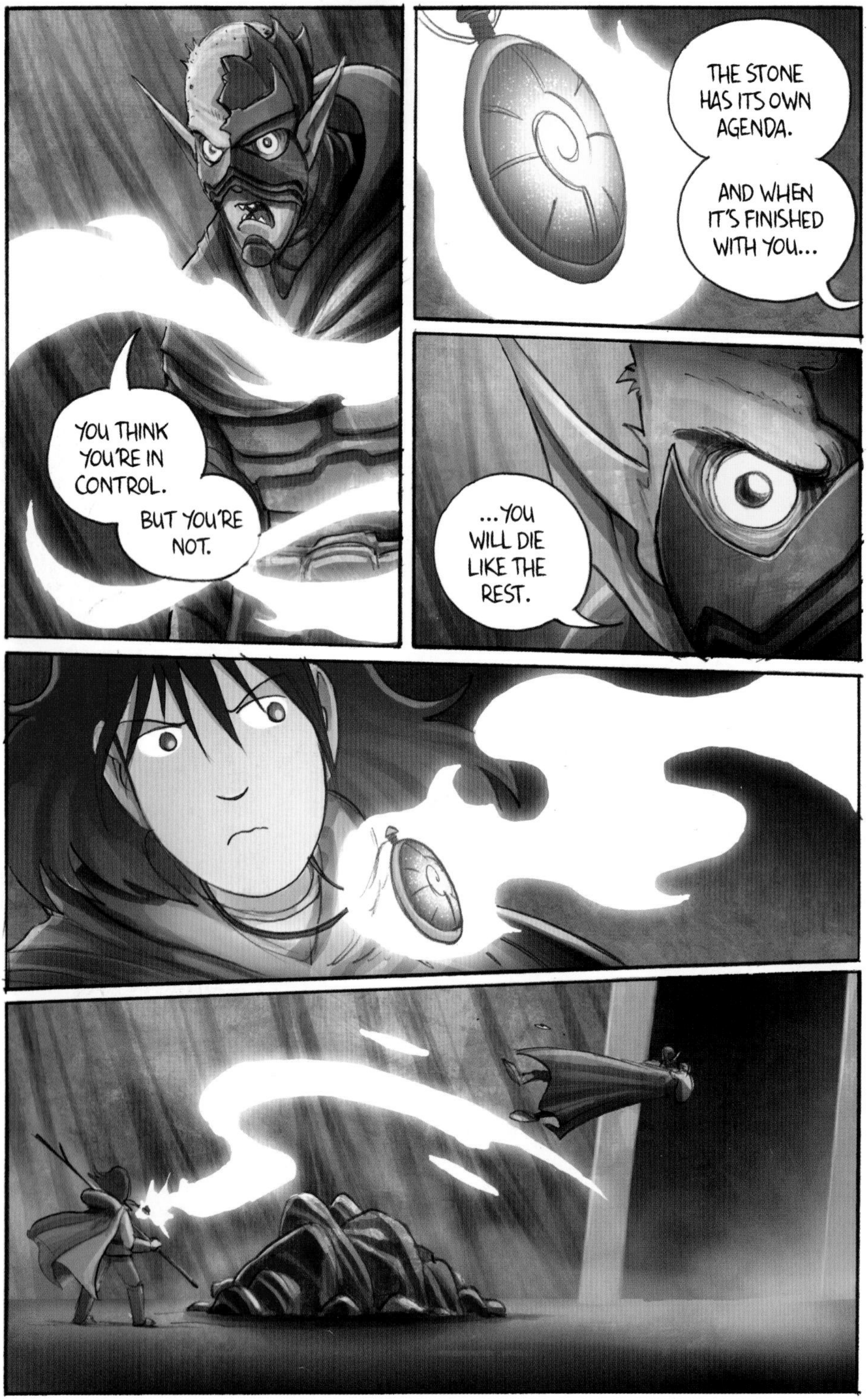
THE STONE HAS ITS OWN AGENDA.
AND WHEN IT'S FINISHED WITH YOU...
YOU THINK YOU'RE IN CONTROL.
BUT YOU'RE NOT.
...YOU WILL DIE LIKE THE REST.

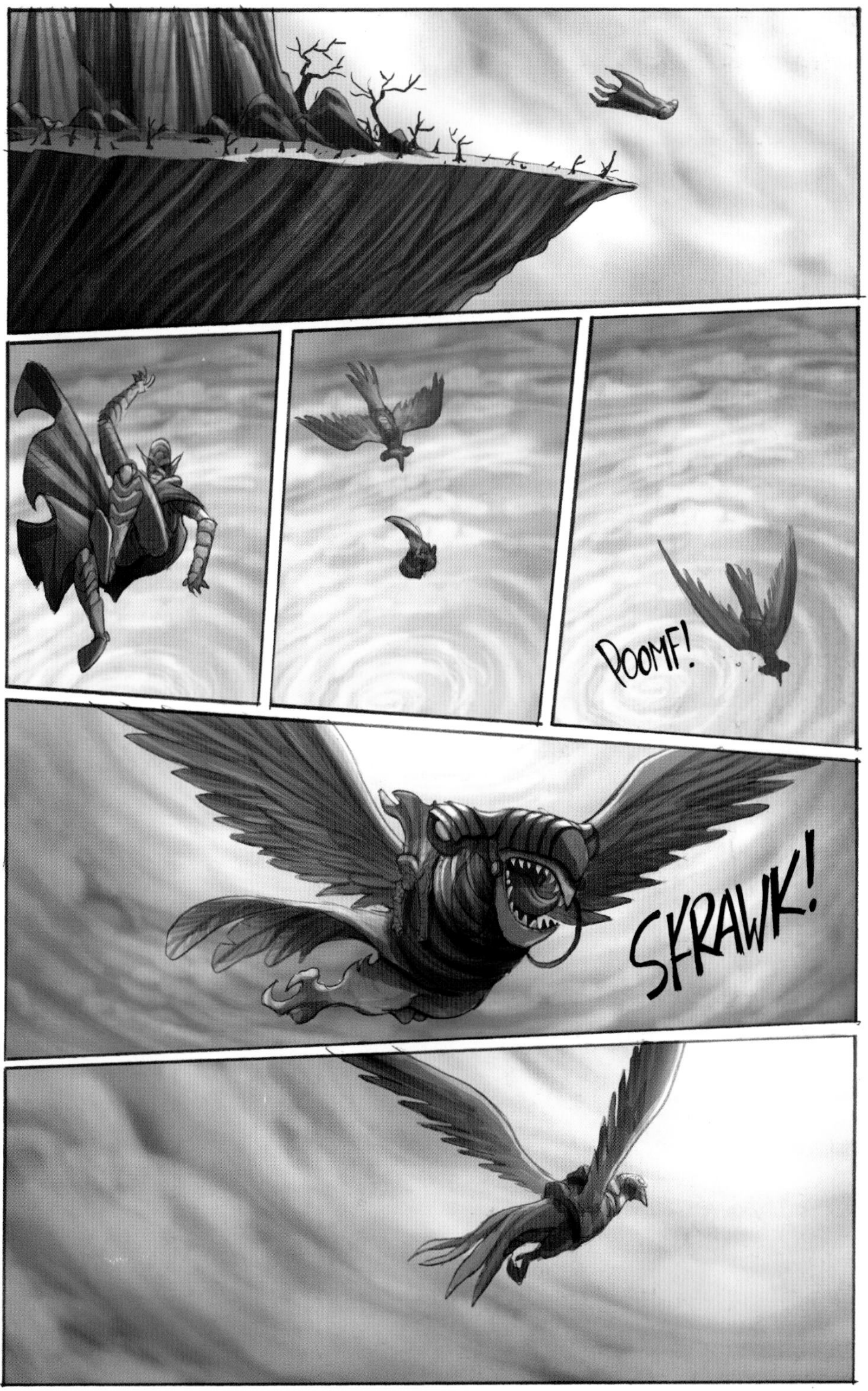
POOMF!
SKRAWK!

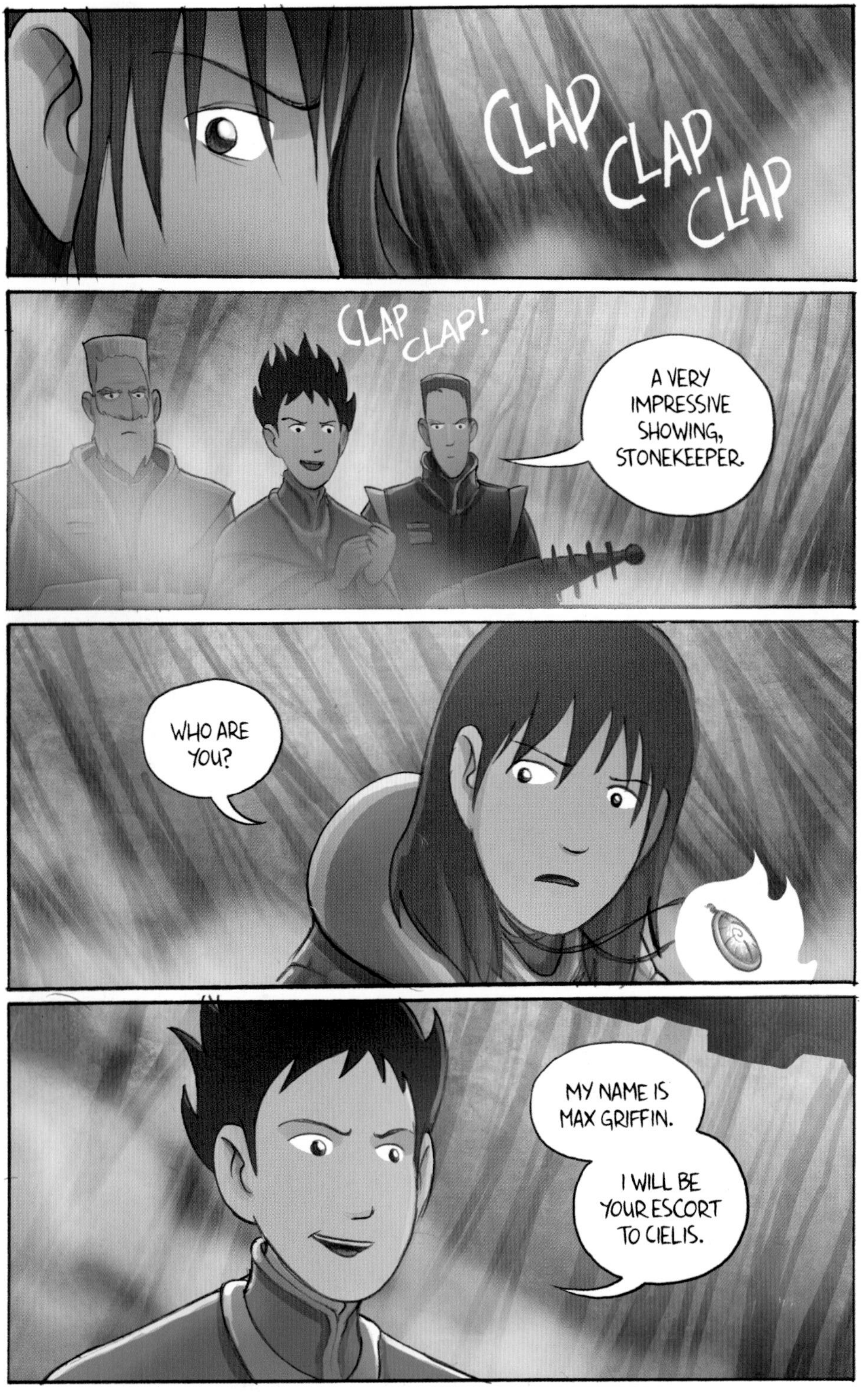
CLAP CLAP CLAP
CLAP CLAP!
A VERY IMPRESSIVE SHOWING, STONEKEEPER.
WHO ARE YOU?
MY NAME IS MAX GRIFFIN.
I WILL BE YOUR ESCORT TO CIELIS.

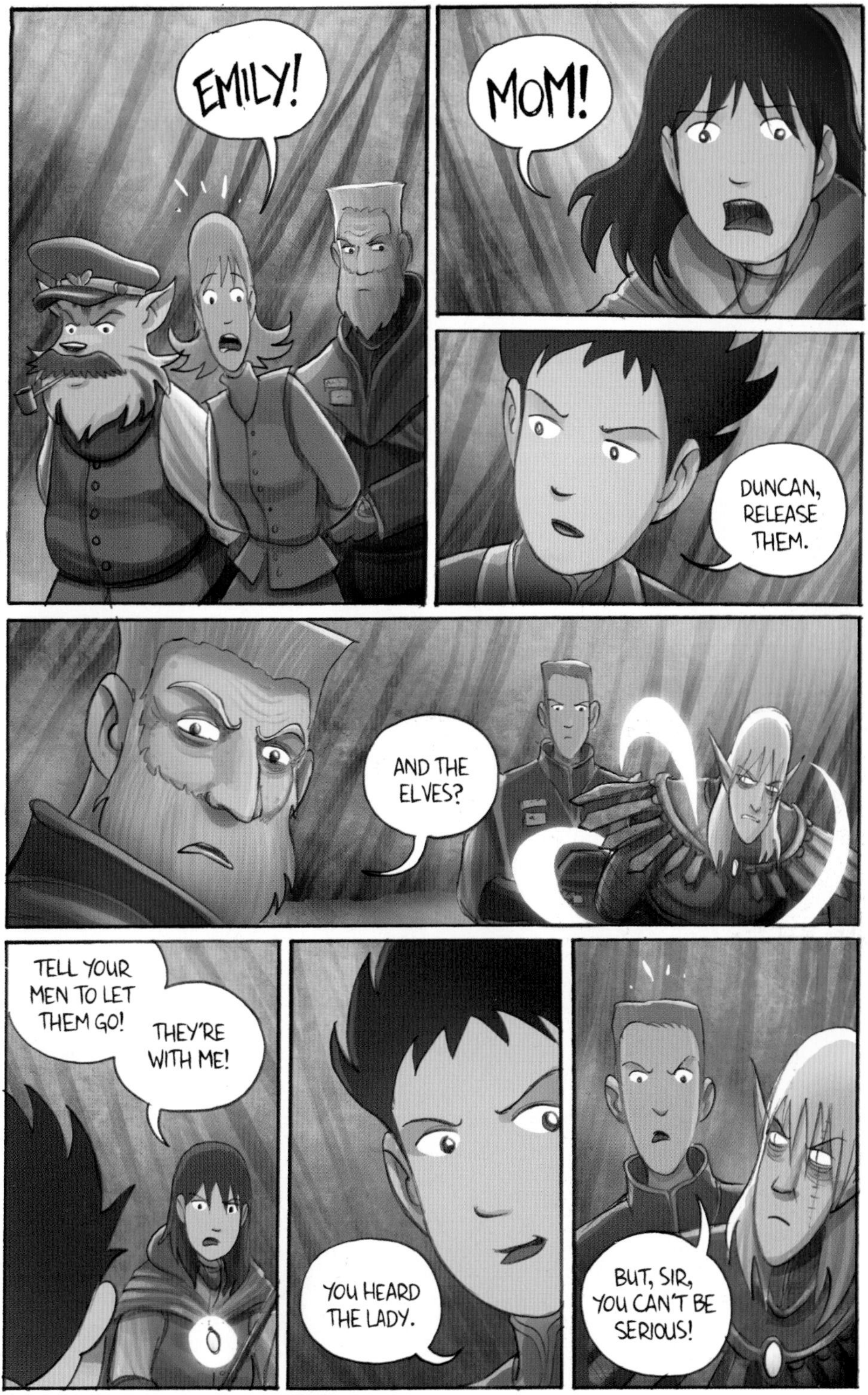
EMILY!
MOM!
DUNCAN, RELEASE THEM.
AND THE ELVES?
TELL YOUR MEN TO LET THEM GO!
THEY'RE WITH ME!
YOU HEARD THE LADY.
BUT, SIR, YOU CAN'T BE SERIOUS!

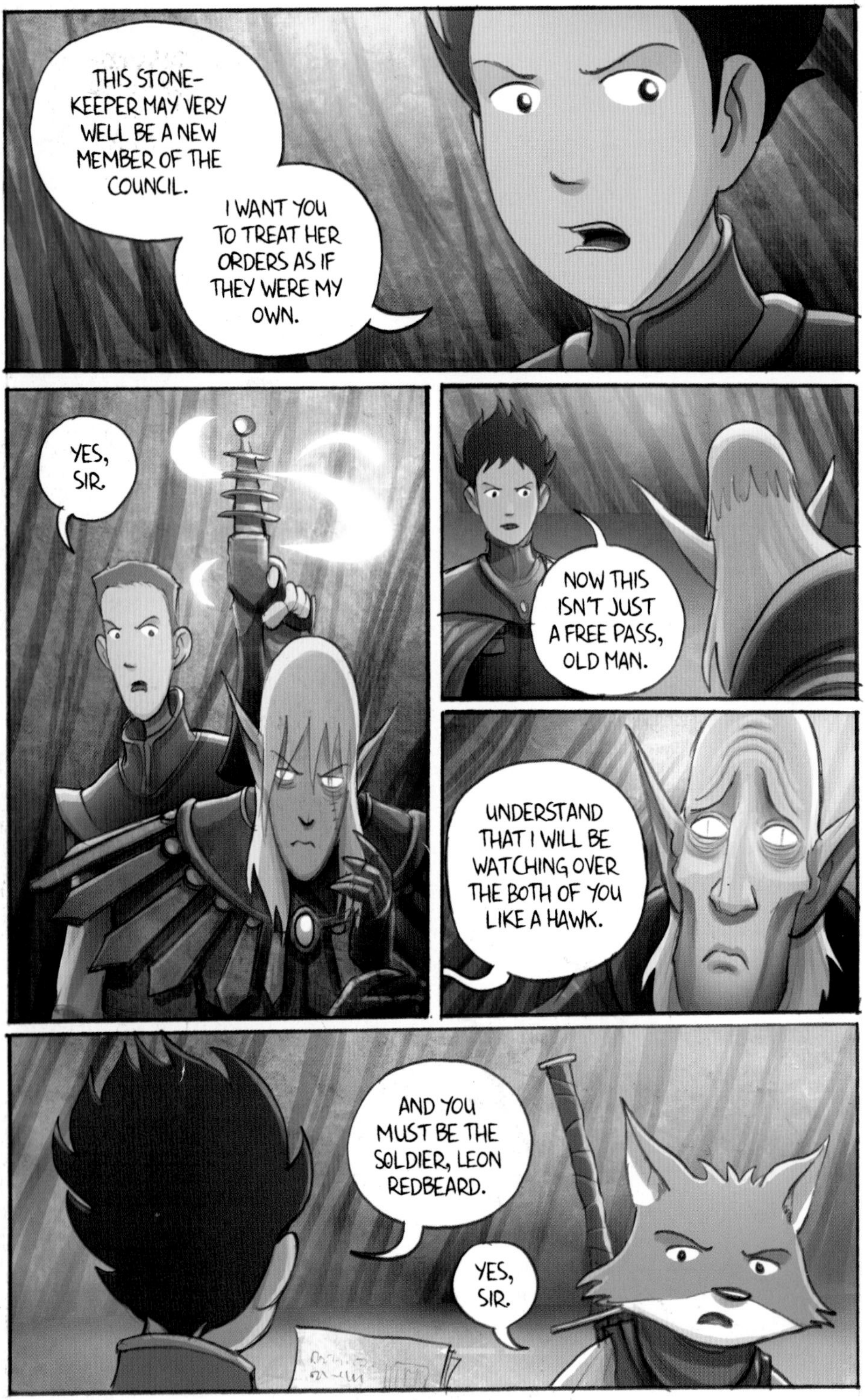
THIS STONE-KEEPER MAY VERY WELL BE A NEW MEMBER OF THE COUNCIL.
I WANT YOU TO TREAT HER ORDERS AS IF THEY WERE MY OWN.
YES, SIR.
NOW THIS ISN'T JUST A FREE PASS, OLD MAN.
UNDERSTAND THAT I WILL BE WATCHING OVER THE BOTH OF YOU LIKE A HAWK.
AND YOU MUST BE THE SOLDIER, LEON REDBEARD.
YES, SIR.

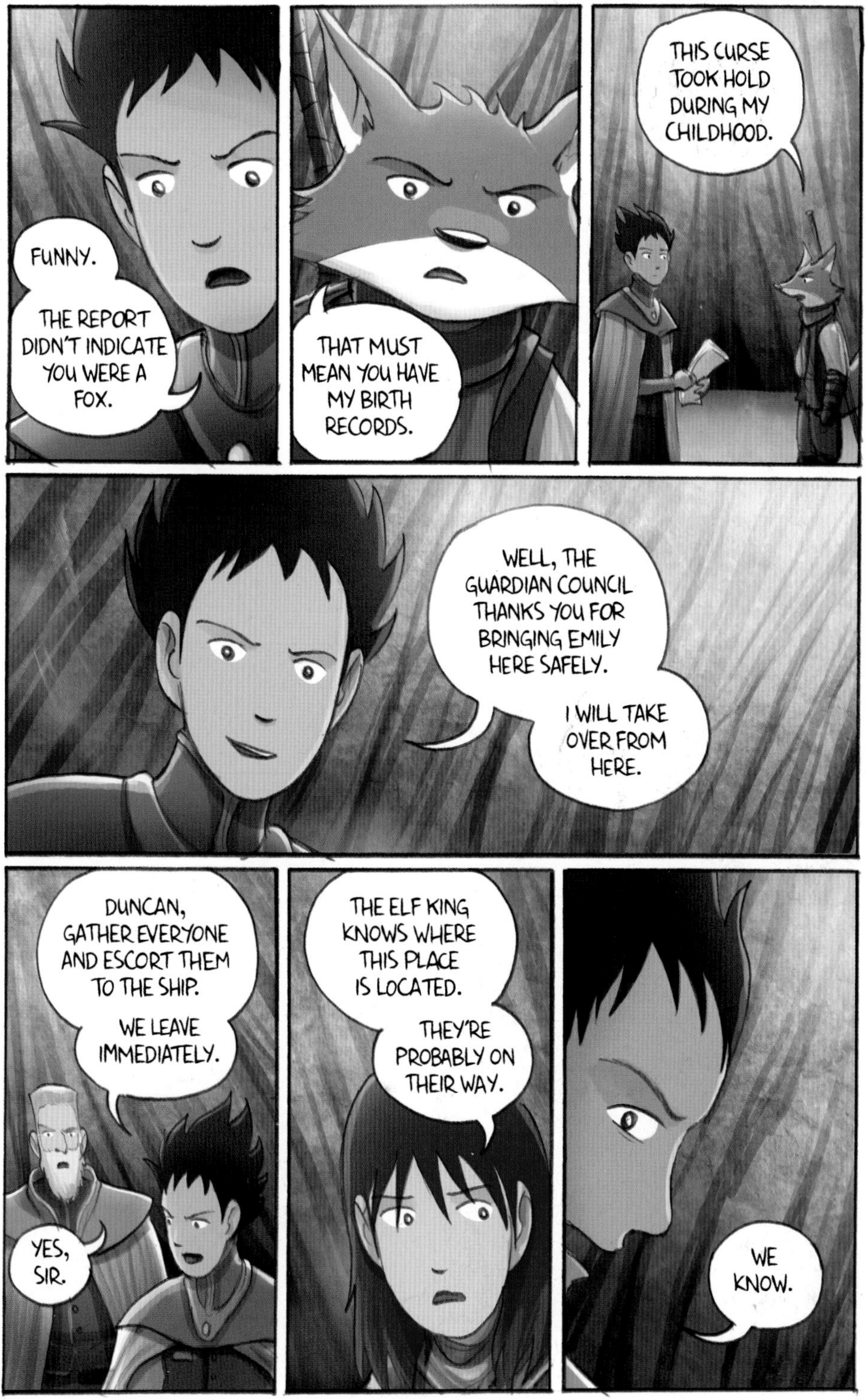
FUNNY.
THE REPORT DIDN'T INDICATE YOU WERE A FOX.
THAT MUST MEAN YOU HAVE MY BIRTH RECORDS.
THIS CURSE TOOK HOLD DURING MY CHILDHOOD.
WELL, THE GUARDIAN COUNCIL THANKS YOU FOR BRINGING EMILY HERE SAFELY.
I WILL TAKE OVER FROM HERE.
DUNCAN, GATHER EVERYONE AND ESCORT THEM TO THE SHIP.
WE LEAVE IMMEDIATELY.
YES, SIR.
THE ELF KING KNOWS WHERE THIS PLACE IS LOCATED.
THEY'RE PROBABLY ON THEIR WAY.
WE KNOW.

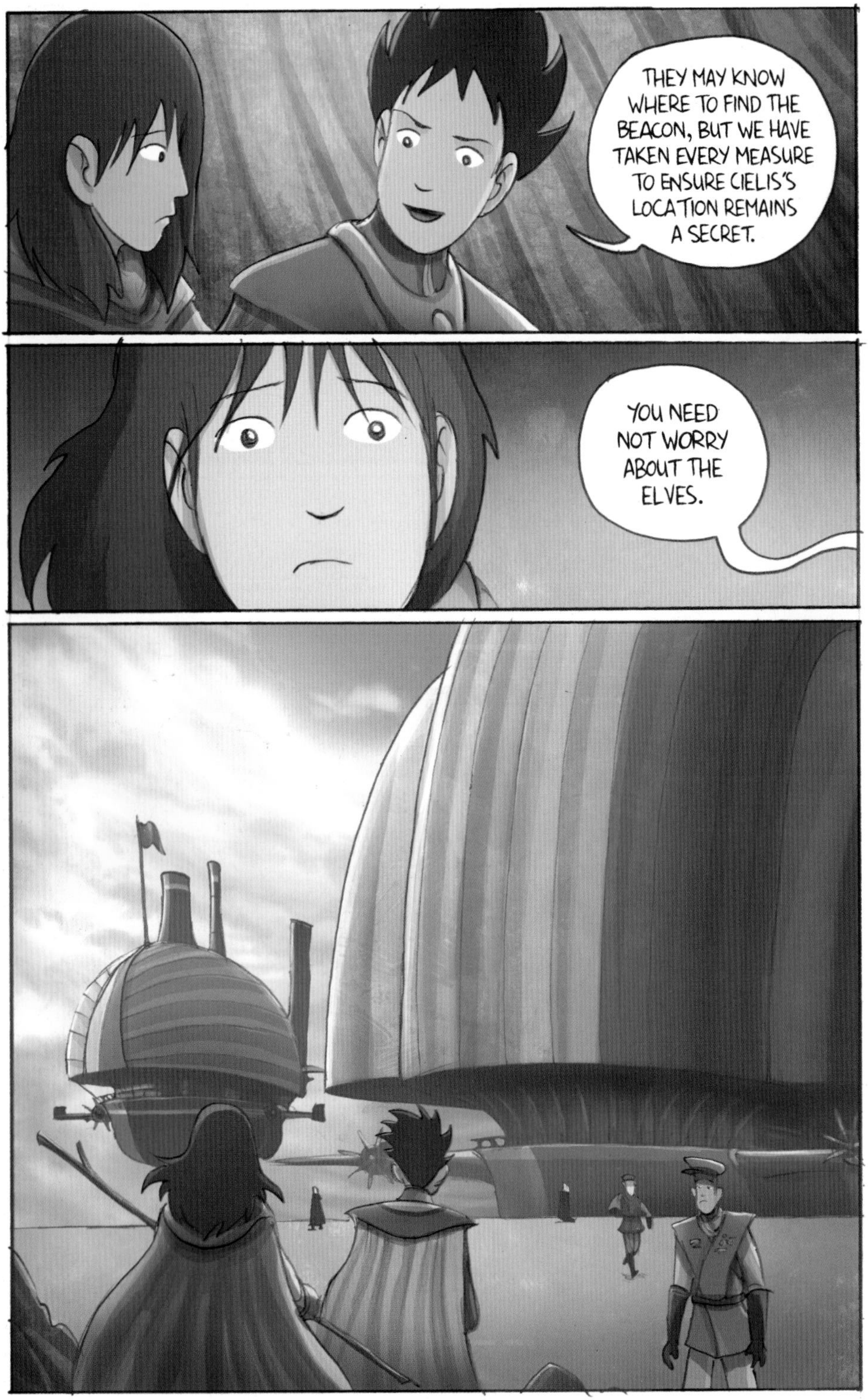
THEY MAY KNOW WHERE TO FIND THE BEACON, BUT WE HAVE TAKEN EVERY MEASURE TO ENSURE CIELIS'S LOCATION REMAINS A SECRET.
YOU NEED NOT WORRY ABOUT THE ELVES.

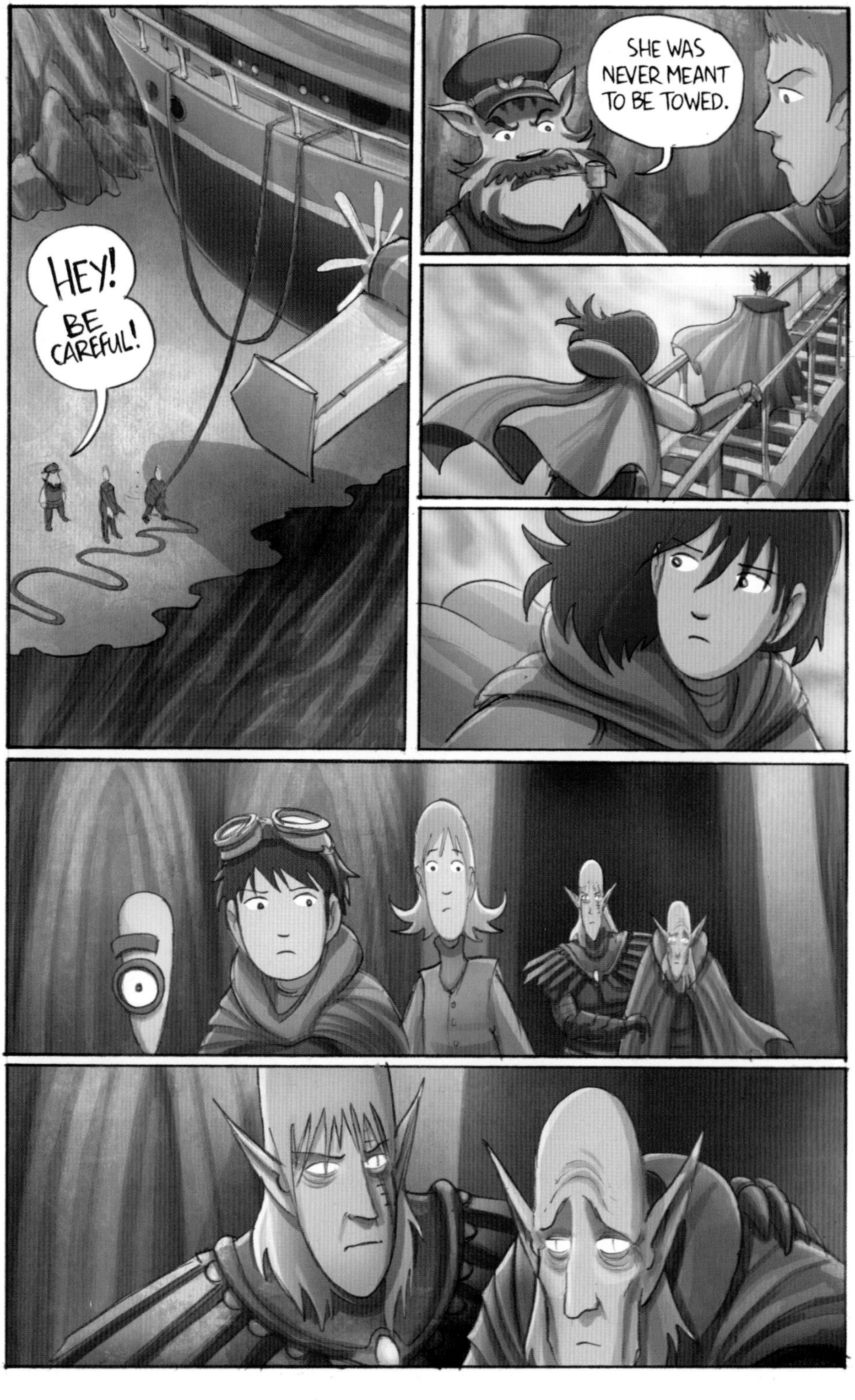
HEY! BE CAREFUL!
SHE WAS NEVER MEANT TO BE TOWED.

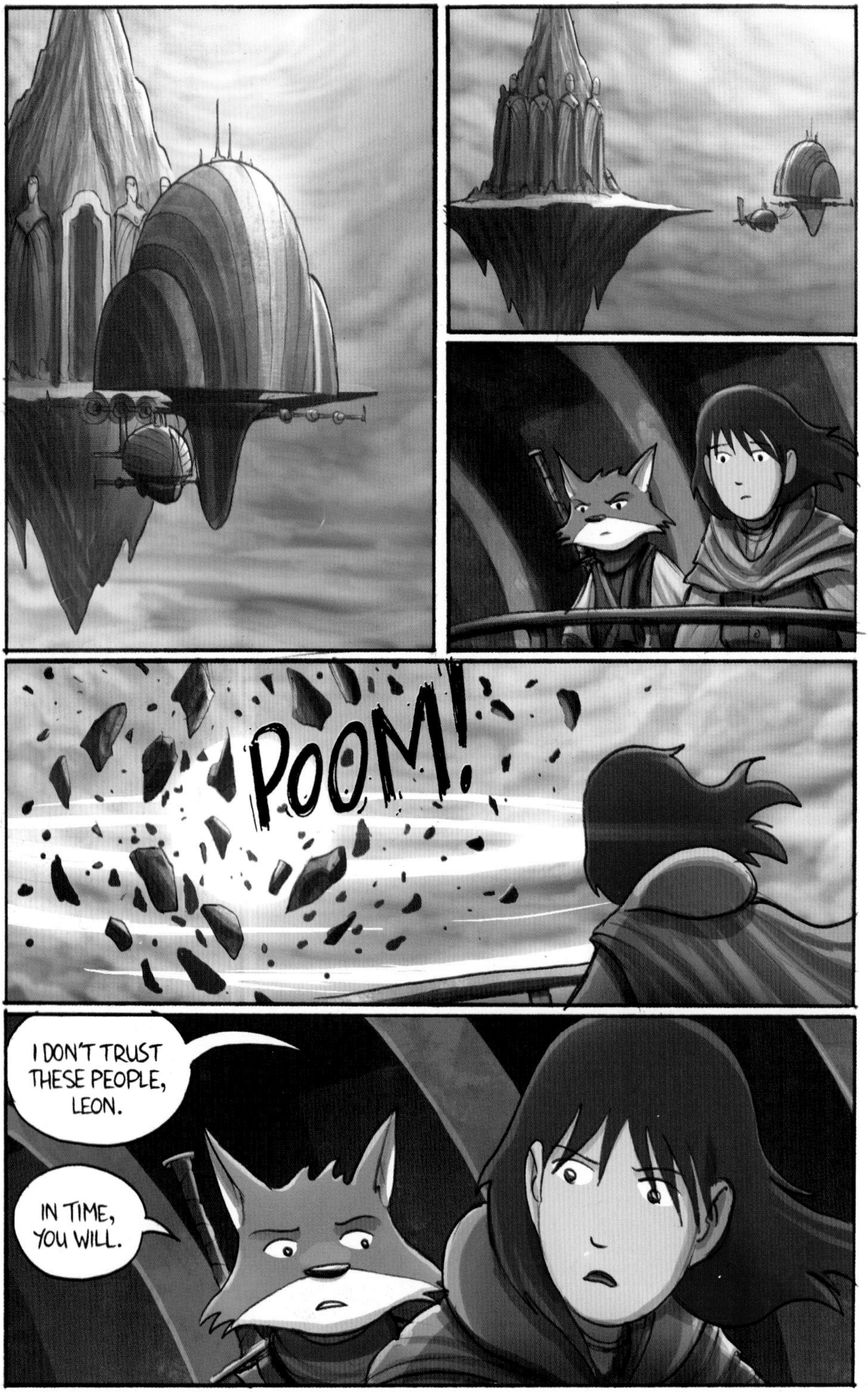
POOM!
I DON'T TRUST THESE PEOPLE, LEON.
IN TIME, YOU WILL.

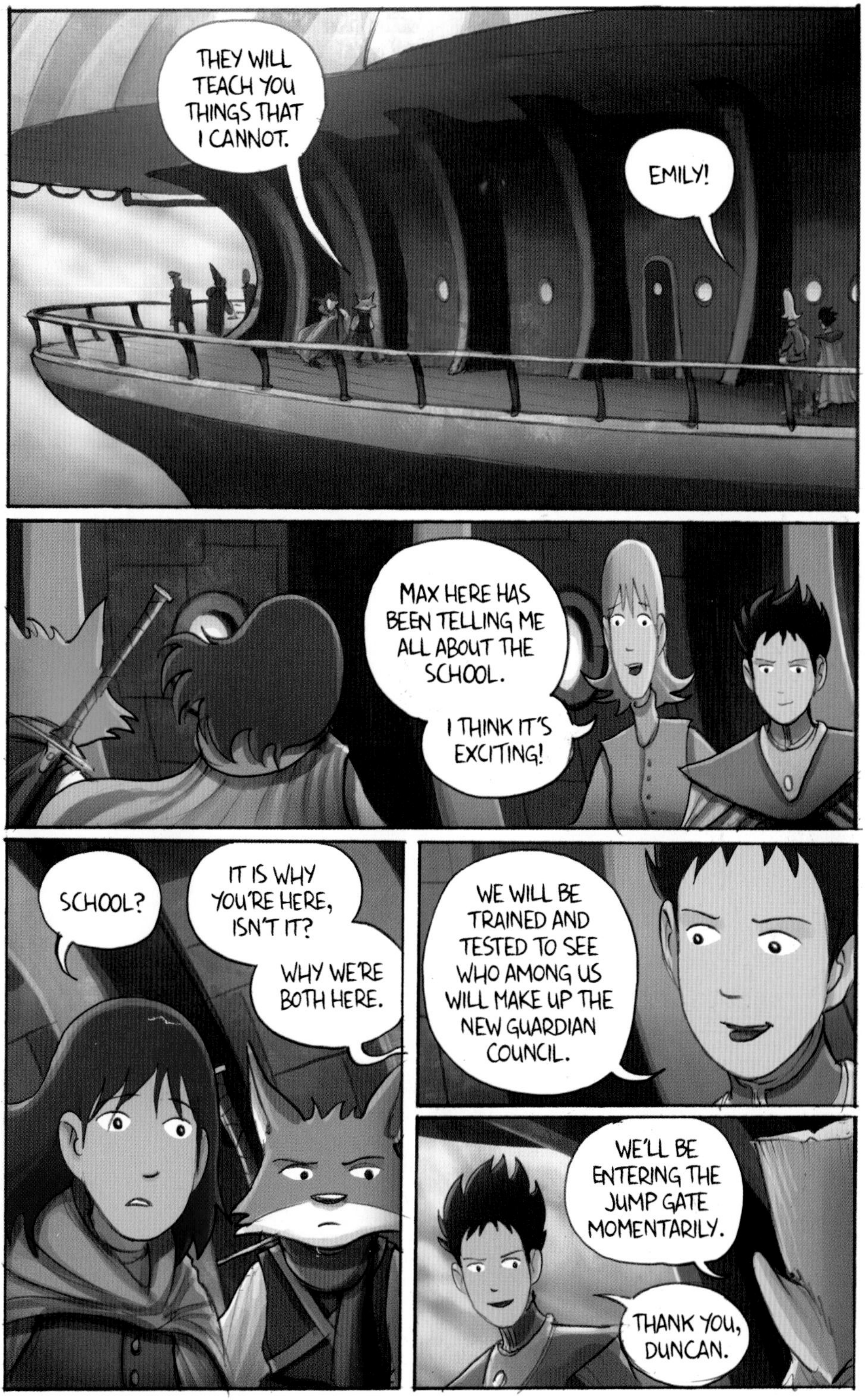
THEY WILL TEACH YOU THINGS THAT I CANNOT.
EMILY!
MAX HERE HAS BEEN TELLING ME ALL ABOUT THE SCHOOL.
I THINK IT'S EXCITING!
SCHOOL?
IT IS WHY YOU'RE HERE, ISN'T IT?
WHY WE'RE BOTH HERE.
WE WILL BE TRAINED AND TESTED TO SEE WHO AMONG US WILL MAKE UP THE NEW GUARDIAN COUNCIL.
WE'LL BE ENTERING THE JUMP GATE MOMENTARILY.
THANK YOU, DUNCAN.

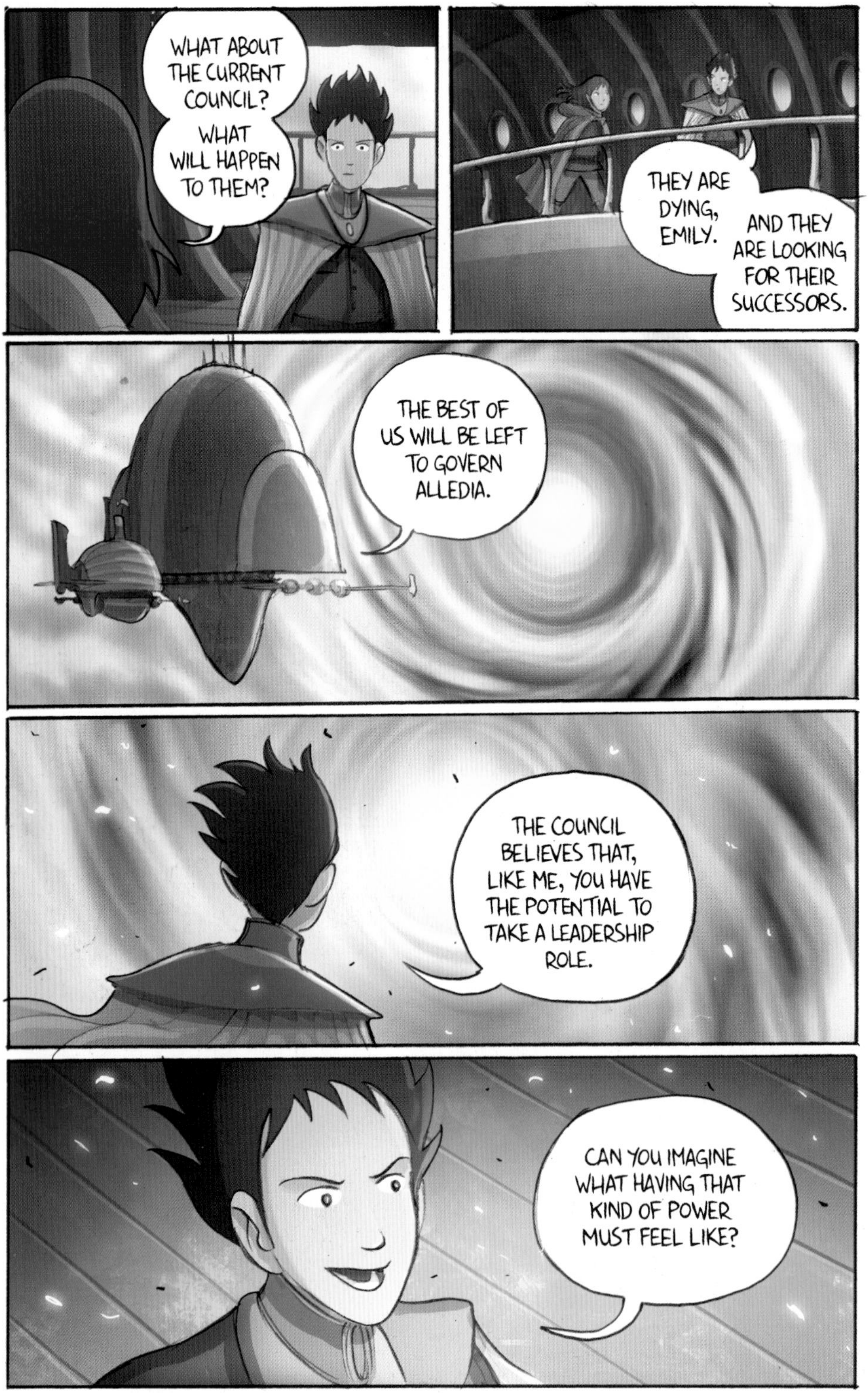
WHAT ABOUT THE CURRENT COUNCIL?
WHAT WILL HAPPEN TO THEM?
THEY ARE DYING, EMILY.
AND THEY ARE LOOKING FOR THEIR SUCCESSORS.
THE BEST OF US WILL BE LEFT TO GOVERN ALLEDIA.
THE COUNCIL BELIEVES THAT, LIKE ME, YOU HAVE THE POTENTIAL TO TAKE A LEADERSHIP ROLE.
CAN YOU IMAGINE WHAT HAVING THAT KIND OF POWER MUST FEEL LIKE?

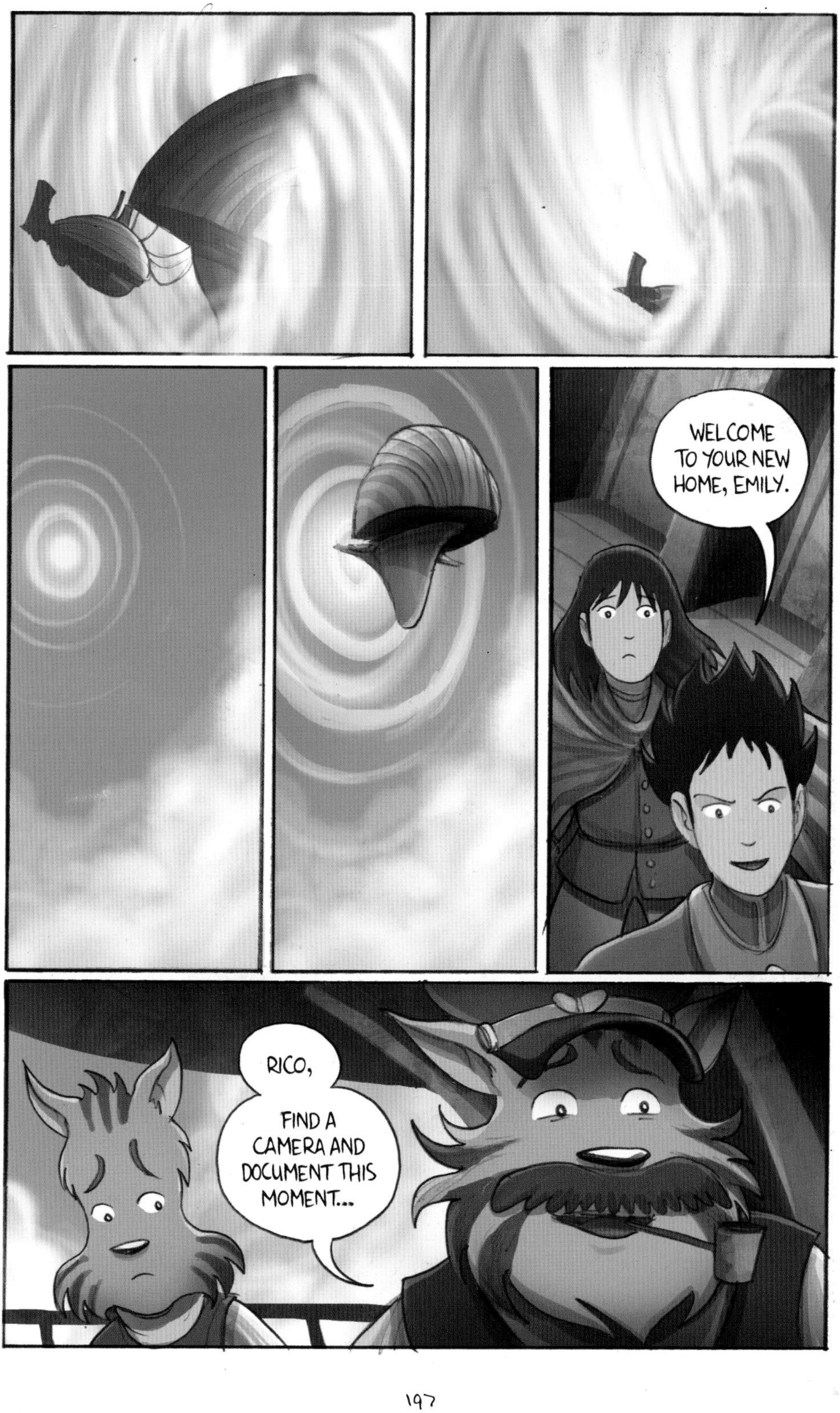
WELCOME TO YOUR NEW HOME, EMILY.
RICO,
FIND A CAMERA AND DOCUMENT THIS MOMENT...

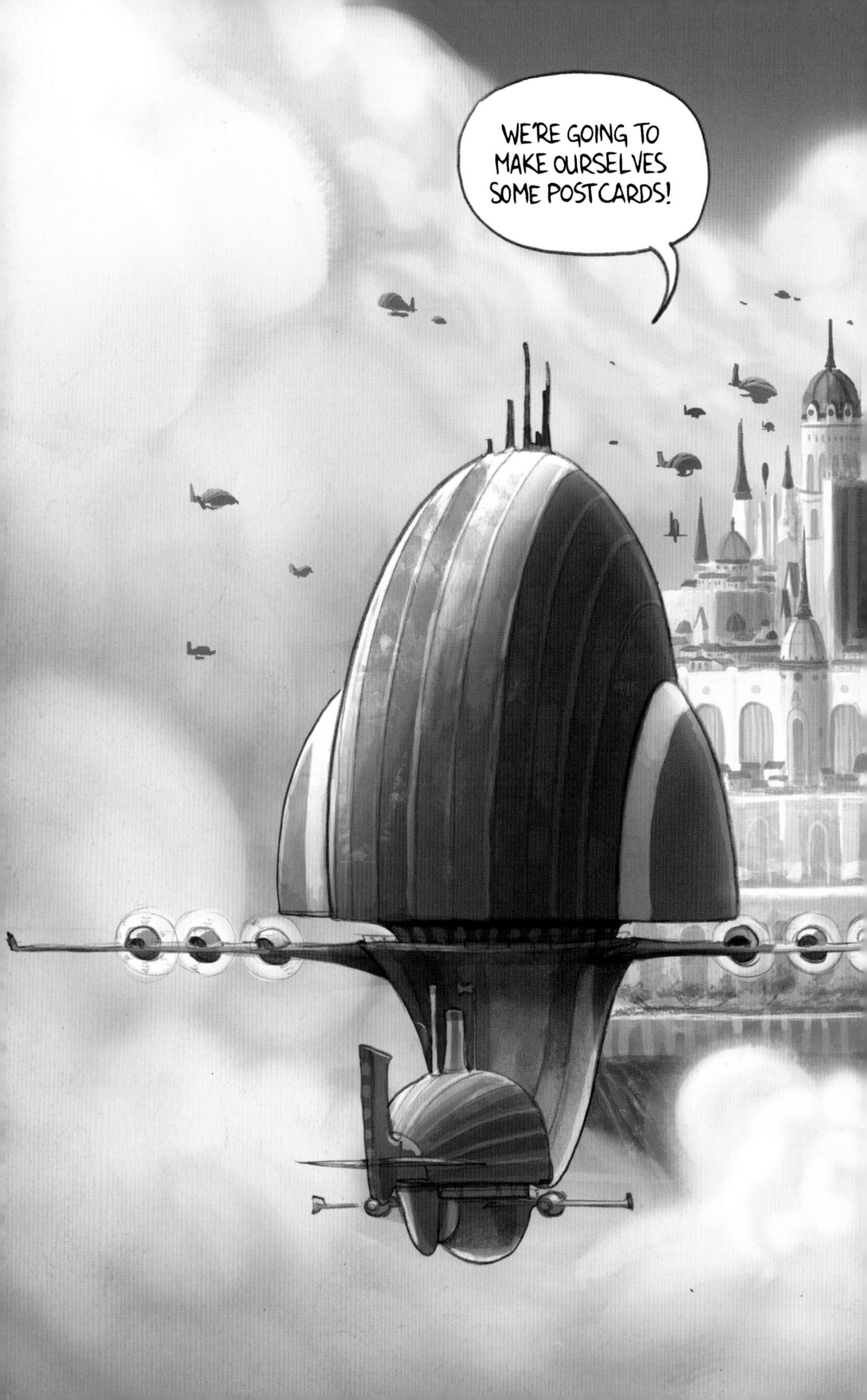
WE'RE GOING TO MAKE OURSELVES SOME POSTCARDS!

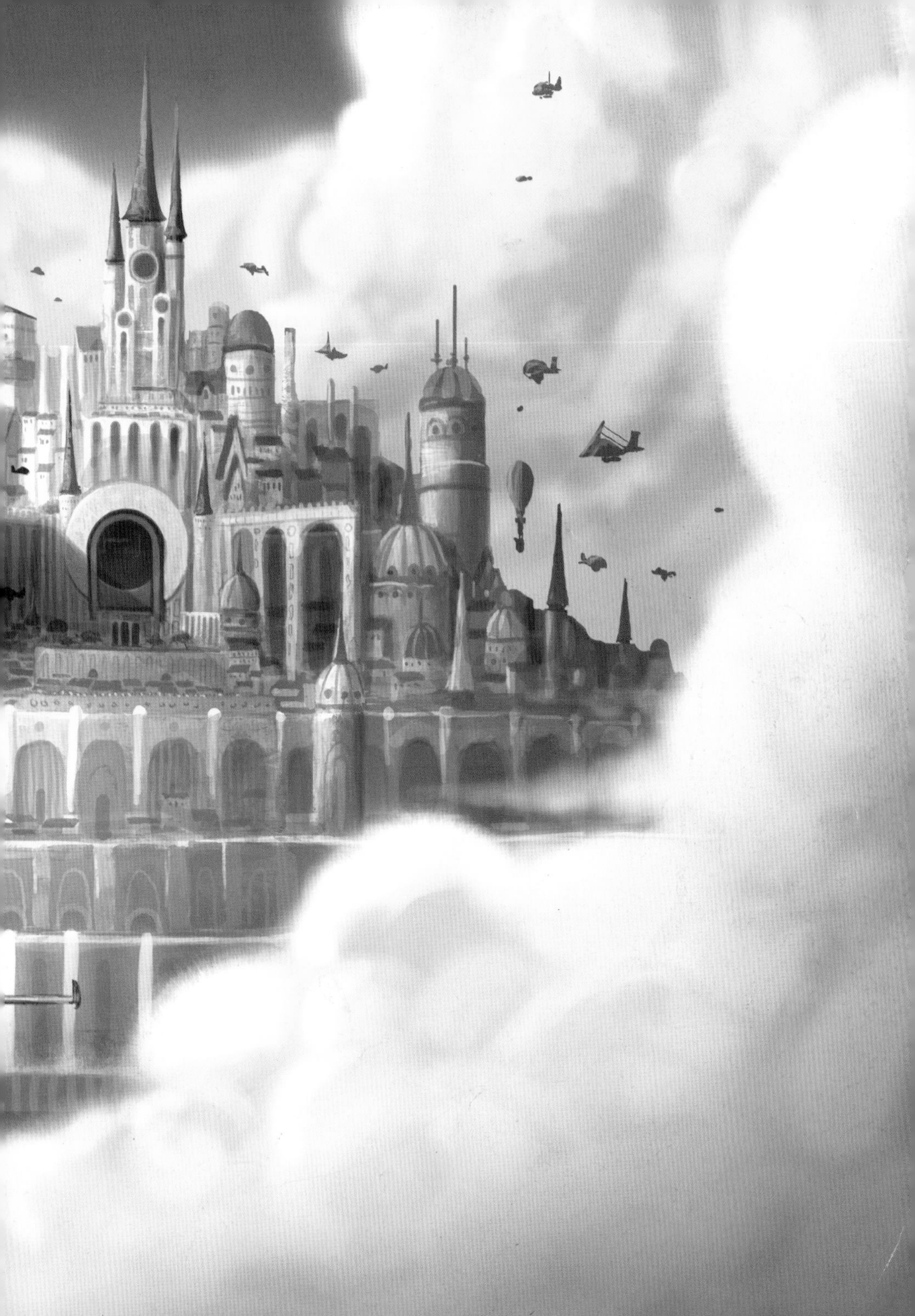

END OF BOOK THREE

Written and Illustrated by
Kazu Kibuishi

Lead Production Assistant
Jason Caffoe

Colors by
Jason Caffoe
Kazu Kibuishi

Color Assistance by
Anthony Wu
Michael Regina
Denver Jackson
Amy Kim Kibuishi

Color Flatting by
Denver Jackson
Jason Caffoe
Michael Regina
Stuart Livingston
Ryan Hoffman
Anthony Wu

Special Thanks

Judy Hansen, David Saylor, Cassandra Pelham, Phil Falco, Gordon Luk, Ben Zhu & the Gallery Nucleus crew, Nick & Melissa Harris, the Flight artists, JP Ahonen, Tony Cliff, Richard Pose, Rachel Ormiston, Tim Ganter, Taka Kibuishi, Nancy Caffoe, June Kibuishi & Sunni Kim

ABOUT THE AUTHOR

Kazu Kibuishi is the creator of the #1 *New York Times* bestselling Amulet series. *Amulet, Book One: The Stonekeeper* was an ALA Best Book for Young Adults and a Children's Choice Book Award finalist. He is also the creator of *Copper*, a collection of his popular webcomic that features an adventuresome boy-and-dog pair. Kazu also illustrated the covers of the 15th anniversary paperback editions of the Harry Potter series written by J. K. Rowling. He lives and works in Seattle, Washington, with his wife, Amy Kim Kibuishi, and their children.

Visit Kazu online at www.boltcity.com.

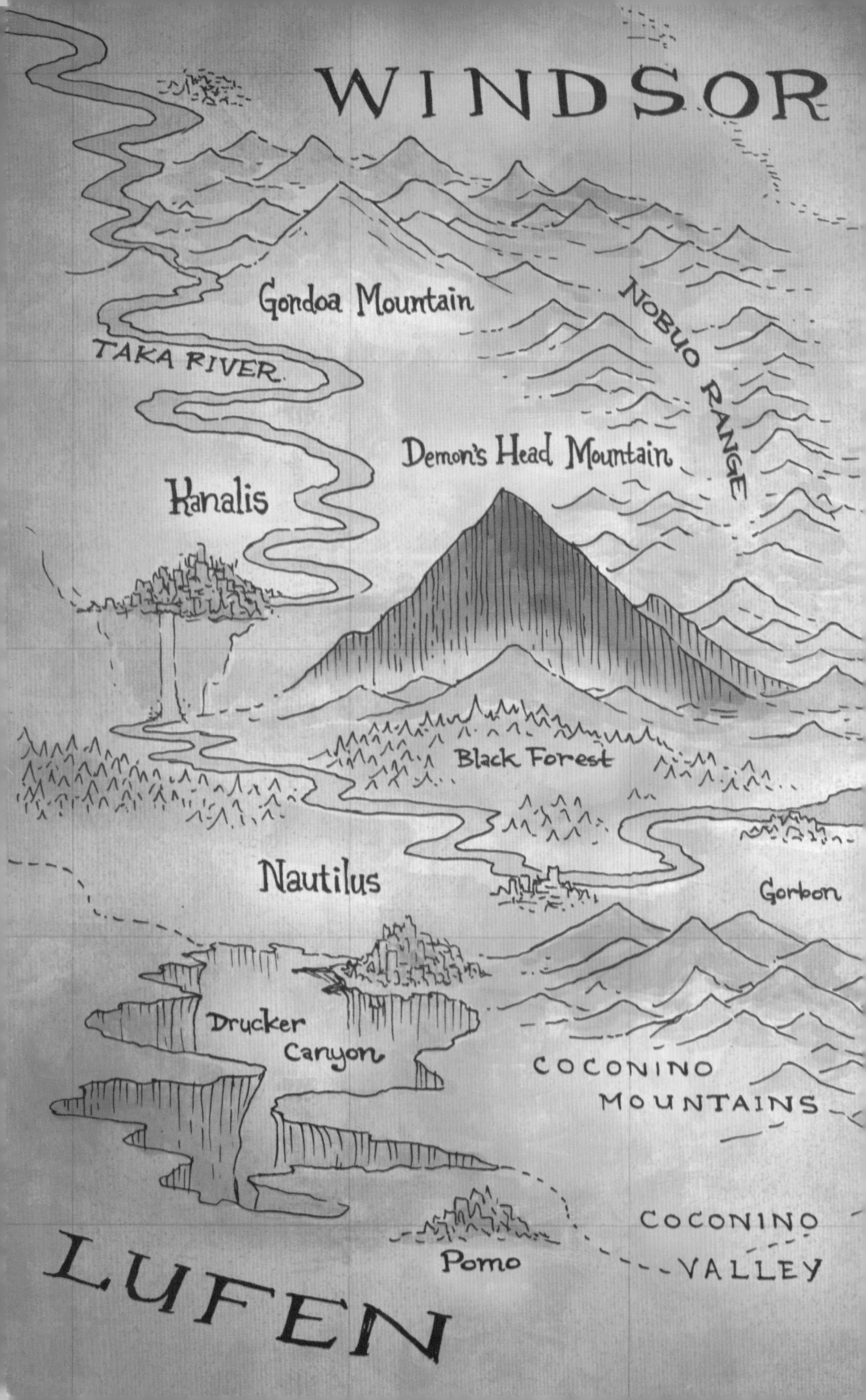

WINDSOR
Gondoa Mountain
NOBUO RANGE
TAKA RIVER
Demon's Head Mountain
Kanalis
Black Forest
Nautilus
Gorbon
Drucker Canyon
COCONINO MOUNTAINS
COCONINO VALLEY
Pomo
LUFEN

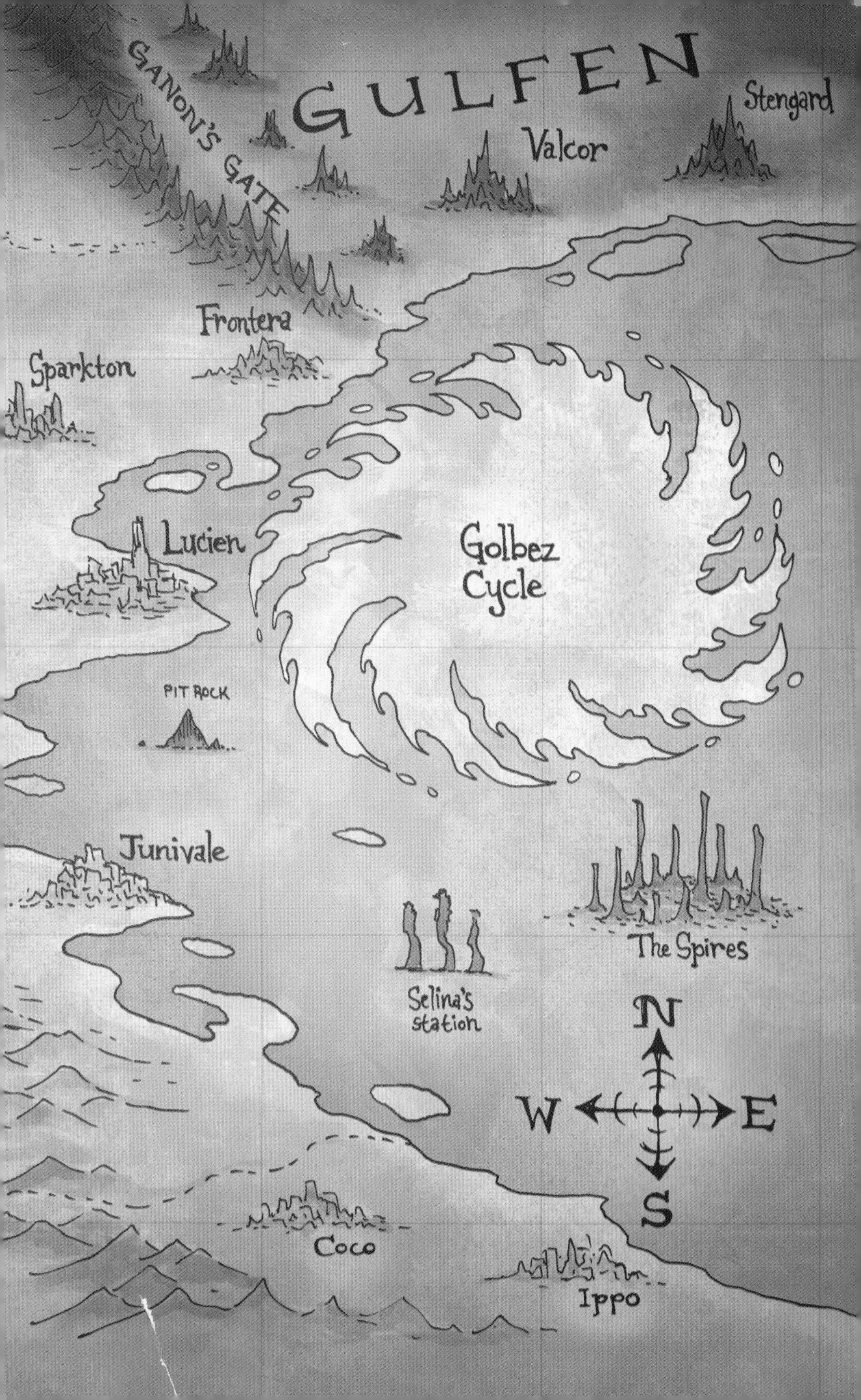
GULFEN
Ganon's Gate
Stengard
Valcor
Frontera
Sparkton
Lucien
Golbez Cycle
Pit Rock
Junivale
The Spires
Selina's station
N
W
E
S
Coco
Ippo

ALSO BY
KAZU KIBUISHI

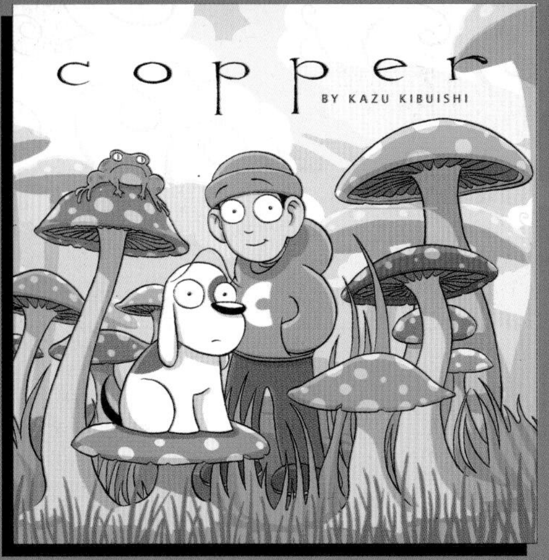
copper
BY KAZU KIBUISHI

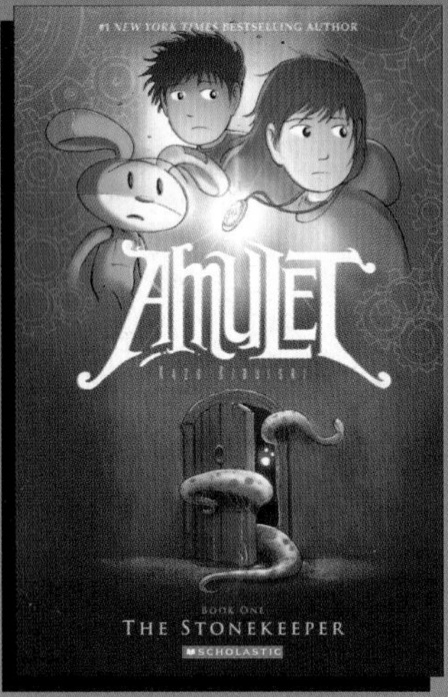
#1 NEW YORK TIMES BESTSELLING AUTHOR
AMULET
KAZU KIBUISHI
BOOK ONE
THE STONEKEEPER
SCHOLASTIC

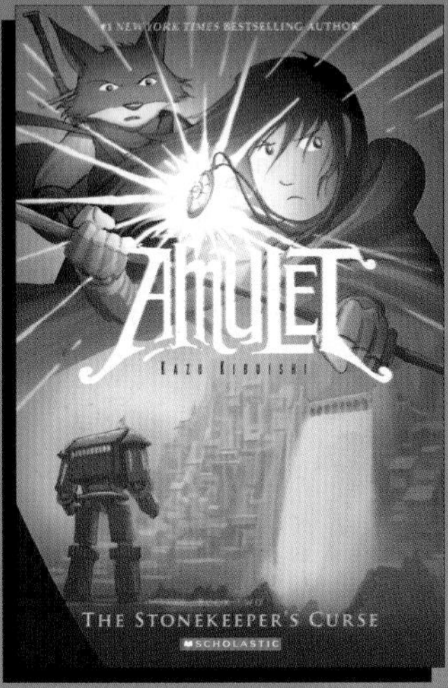
#1 NEW YORK TIMES BESTSELLING AUTHOR
AMULET
KAZU KIBUISHI
THE STONEKEEPER'S CURSE
SCHOLASTIC

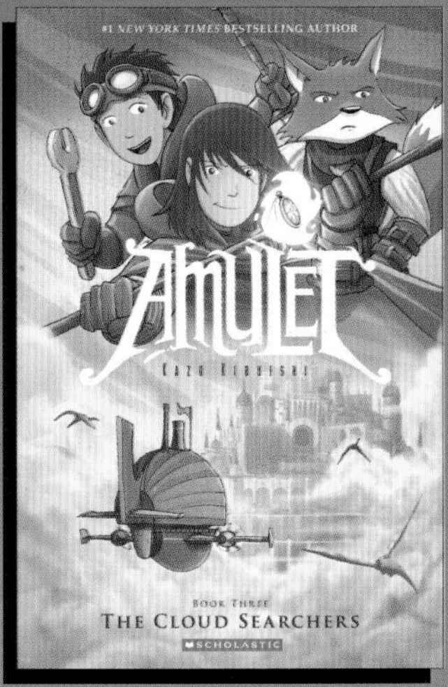
#1 NEW YORK TIMES BESTSELLING AUTHOR
AMULET
KAZU KIBUISHI
BOOK THREE
THE CLOUD SEARCHERS
SCHOLASTIC

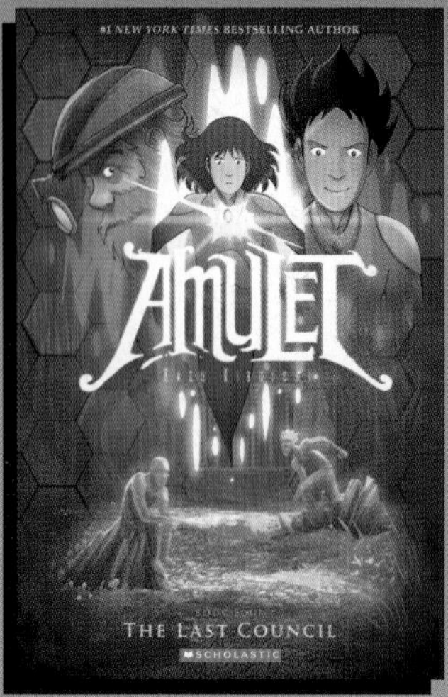
#1 NEW YORK TIMES BESTSELLING AUTHOR
AMULET
THE LAST COUNCIL
SCHOLASTIC

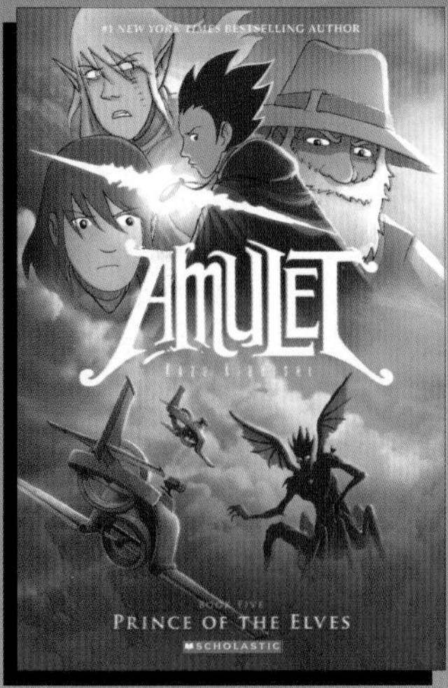
#1 NEW YORK TIMES BESTSELLING AUTHOR
AMULET
BOOK FIVE
PRINCE OF THE ELVES
SCHOLASTIC

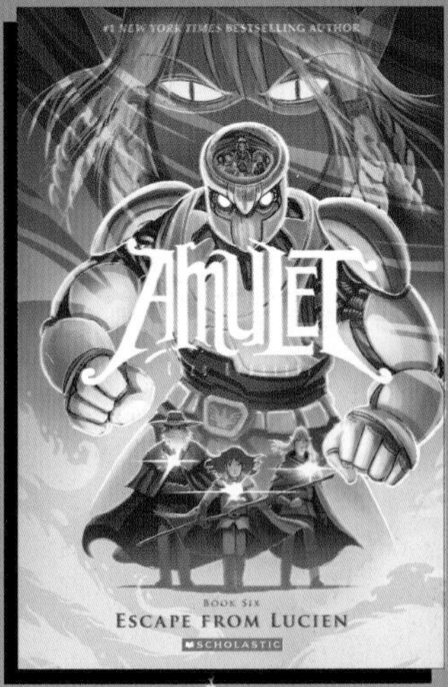
#1 NEW YORK TIMES BESTSELLING AUTHOR
AMULET
BOOK SIX
ESCAPE FROM LUCIEN
SCHOLASTIC